The Villain Edit

The Villain Edit

A NOVEL

Laurie Devore

AVON

An Imprint of HarperCollinsPublishers

THE VILLAIN EDIT. Copyright © 2024 by Laurie Devore. All rights reserved. Printed in the United States of America. No part of this book may be used or reproduced in any manner whatsoever without written permission except in the case of brief quotations embodied in critical articles and reviews. For information, address HarperCollins Publishers, 195 Broadway, New York, NY 10007.

HarperCollins books may be purchased for educational, business, or sales promotional use. For information, please email the Special Markets Department at SPsales@harpercollins.com.

FIRST EDITION

Designed by Diahann Sturge

Illustrations throughout © M. Dykstra; Piyapong89; Bibadash; Katerinova Pshycka; Christina Li/Shutterstock; Woman dancing emoji on page 218 © streptococcus/Adobe Stock

Library of Congress Cataloging-in-Publication Data has been applied for.

ISBN 978-0-06-333760-2

24 25 26 27 28 LBC 5 4 3 2 1

To Mama, who always took me dress shopping at Dillard's.
Thank you for everything.

The Villain Edit

Hello, my beautiful little one-ders! If you're spoiler-averse, stop reading now as I've got a big scoop on *the 1* season 32 coming up right after the break!

READ MORE

We all fell in love with Marcus Bellamy, the always smiling, quietly confident Chicago exec whose tragic (and quite controversial) breakup with Shailene Dowd on *the 1* last season left us all in tears. This season, he's out to find his own 1 and we can exclusively confirm he's met his match! Our sources tell us that Marcus has proposed to Southern belle Jacqueline Matthis during finale shooting of *the 1* in the Cévennes mountains of southern France. Thirty-two-year-old Charleston author Jacqueline was said to be a dark horse for the Chicago tech salesman's heart from the first episode and I'm told a late push ended with Miss Matthis scoring the ring. Stay tuned for more episode-by-episode spoilers coming in later posts this week.

LOS ANGELES

1

All Downhill from Here

My dress is red. Mom had scoffed at it when I grabbed it off the rack in Dillard's and showed it to her, my head tilted to the side as I looked at the way it fell over my body. It was a size we both knew would take some work.

"Lady in red?" she asked. "A little much, don't you think?"

"Just wear black and blend in?" I shot back.

"Black is slimming," she said with a smile.

I wore red anyway.

My producer keeps handing me fresh glasses of champagne, and I keep drinking them like the cheap date I am. My limo mates are Aliana, a stereotypically loud Italian-American girl from Jersey; Bonnie, a Texas beauty queen who, judging by the height of her hair, has achieved a closeness to God previously unknown to man; and Rikki, a twenty-two-year-old Santa Monica spin instructor whose calves keep catching my attention whenever she swishes them out from the split in her dress. I wonder if I was that hot ten years ago.

We speed up into the mountains outside of Malibu, a landscape I can't help but find desolate and brown. There's something beautiful and sad about it all, million-dollar homes in a dry wasteland that, if we kept going, would eventually descend into one of the world's most breathtaking views. The sun has set, the roads treacherous as the limo scales the mountain.

"You feel good about your intro?" Charlotte asks me. She's sprawled out on the floor of our limo in leggings, a tank top, and a zip-up hoodie, her back against the bottom of a seat, her legs spread

out in front of me as she rests her hands on her stomach; I'd estimate
she's seven months pregnant. What I want to tell her is that, honestly, I'd feel better if I were blacked out, but since I'm the mature
contestant, practically geriatric by *the 1* standards at thirty-two, and
Rikki is already well on her way to blacked out, I can't be the drunk
girl on night one. Marcus would send me home, and as embarrassing
as all this has been, the more embarrassing thing would be getting
sent home night one.

"Cool and casual," I tell Charlotte, trying not to wallow in the
rest of it. "Just like me." I give her a winning smile.

"And that's why you're my girl," Charlotte says, taking a sip of my
new champagne glass before handing it to me and turning to talk
to Bonnie.

"I'm just not sure," Bonnie is saying, "about the reveal." Subcon-
sciously, she tugs at the bathing suit under her dress. There's a sash
under there, too, that says Miss Texas—production had it made for
her as she did not, in fact, win Miss Texas. She was the runner-up.
Charlotte immediately launches into what a great idea it is *actually*.
I snort. *Sucker.*

"I like you," Rikki tells me, as if in response to the unladylike
sound that just came out of me. "You have that vibe. Real." She tilts
her head to the side, nodding slowly to herself. "Especially your tits,"
she says.

I blink, watching her across the limo, sizing her up. Then I reach
down and cup my own ample bosom, pushing it up for show. She
laughs, the sound like the wind chimes tinkling in front of my
mother's house. That's where I'd told my family goodbye, at my parents' tidy little ranch house outside of Charleston, South Carolina.

"Knew it." Rikki toasts me. "Realness is even better than the tits."
She slumps back against her seat, downing her drink.

"Rikki, you're out first," Charlotte calls. She's pushed up off the
floor to sit next to Aliana now, whispering in her ear. She points at
the 1 house as it comes into view. Aliana immediately starts screeching.

The 1 mansion, as it's called, is set up at the top of the hill. The
gates are open to let us into the private drive that secludes the house
from the public road. Lighting rigs dot the sky high above the house,

making the set brighter than daylight. Our limo takes the right up the private drive, and we get closer and closer to Marcus, the one.

This whole stupid journey had started last Friday, or maybe before that. "Journey"—I hate that word, but already Charlotte has me thinking that way, her words carefully rewiring my brain.

I'd flown in Friday to spend the weekend with my best friend, Sarah, in her new home in Santa Monica with her new husband, Josh, and her new baby, Esther. I'd whiled away the day at the beach while she'd worked, and then Saturday and Sunday, I'd wined and dined with them, and finally stayed with Esther Sunday night so they could have their first real date night since she'd been born.

And then, Monday, it had been off to quarantine, to the hotel where they'd taken away my phone and my laptop and every connection I'd had to the real world. Sometimes, Charlotte had come by and dropped off books for me: a couple of escapist fantasies, some lit fic, thrillers, the kind of shit I liked to read when I was pretending the world of romance publishing didn't exist. I'd had to leave the last one I was reading—a surrealist short story collection from Ling Ma—with Charlotte today, and she'd promised to give it back to me in no less than twelve weeks' time when this was over, with the page marked right where I left it.

Here I am now, pulling up. All this shit better have been worth it.

Aliana, Bonnie, and I watch in silence as Rikki gets out of the car and visibly stumbles. Charlotte chuckles as Rikki corrects herself and makes her way over to Marcus, the man we've all come to meet. I'm surprised by just *how many* other people there are to watch us exit the limo. Journalists and some producers I recognize and crew members everywhere, just offscreen. It was stupid of me to think anything about this might be private or normal or whatever, but I suddenly become conscious of my red dress, its plunging neckline, and how I will look and how I will sound and, still, right here in this moment, I don't know what the fuck I was thinking.

It's a few moments as us girls left behind in the limo watch Rikki and Marcus talk and laugh, and then I feel warm skin on mine.

"You're my pick, Jac," Charlotte whispers, her breath hot against my ear. "Give 'em hell," she says, and then she opens the door for me.

They'd tried to convince me to have a gimmick, to make a real ass of myself, but I'd eventually talked my way out of it, said I'd lean into playing the casual Southern girl. That was the whole plan.

"Hey!" I call to Marcus from too far away, letting my nerves get the better of me. I follow that up with "Hi," like more talking will make it better. He looks, frankly, better than he looked on television. Well over six feet tall, dirty blond hair with a slight wave, a jawline sharp enough to cut glass. His physique tells me he's been spending even more time in the gym than he had during his last season, broad-shouldered and sturdily built, in a light blue suit with a floral tie.

I didn't necessarily come here to find love, but I was certainly finding plenty to like in that first glance.

"Hello," Marcus calls back, and then I say, "Hola!" in response, and his smile warms to the level of the sun, his eyes crinkling charmingly.

"Would you like to come over here?" he asks me, because I'm still camped out by the limo.

"Actually," I say, "I know a couple more languages if you want to keep going?"

He holds out both hands, and I know that's the cue. I approach him, grabbing onto his outstretched hands. I can't believe how stupid this is, and how stupid I'm being, like I didn't know this was coming.

"I'm Jac," I say. "Jacqueline."

"Jac," he answers, savoring it in a way that makes me think he appreciates the taste. This is going well? "I'm Marcus," he tells me. I'm sure he feels my heart pounding, radiating out from my hands.

I point back at the limo. "I was supposed to say something cool back there," I tell him. "I had it all planned out."

He shrugs, a hint of mischief crossing his face. "What isn't cool about yelling every synonym of 'hey' you know across a driveway at someone?"

"It's really nice to meet you, Marcus," I say.

He glances down at our hands, the place where they're touching, and then back up into my eyes. "It's nice to meet you, Jac," he says at last, and I release a breath caught in my throat.

"I'll see you inside," I say, and he lets go of my hands.

"Actually!" Priya, one of the producers, calls, and the cameraman closest to me lowers his camera at her words. "Jac, that was great, but can you do it all again? Same way, you're really charming, but I think we weren't picking up your sound completely. Ari, can you check her?"

"Seriously?" I ask as a random crew member runs over to me. I have to reach into the back of my dress to pass over the mic pack before Ari gets too handsy.

"Yeah," Marcus says to me, an aside between just the two of us as Ari fiddles with the pack. "Beauty of show biz. Why be genuine when you can do it better?"

I like him, I think. I like him and I think I hate it.

"Just one more time, Jac. Do the whole thing with the yelling and saying you planned to be cool and all of that. Great stuff. You're a natural."

The journalists are staring at me, and I think of them going through the notes. *Failed author Jacqueline Matthis.* Failed author, failed love interest, failed person.

"You'll be perfect this time," Priya promises me.

"I thought you were perfect the first time," Marcus whispers, and winks. And with that to fuel me, I head back to the limo, Charlotte opening the door for me and giving me an encouraging squeeze of my arm as I get back in. "Happens all the time," she promises.

So I do it again, role-playing myself awkwardly. After the second run-through, with a thumbs-up from Priya, I continue up the driveway toward the house, where an assistant producer will meet me as per Charlotte's promise. But at the last minute, I chance a glance over my shoulder at Marcus.

He's looking back at me, too.

I had always been a casual watcher of *the 1*—back in New York, my Pilates instructor Margot used to host wine and cheese nights and we'd all watch *ironically*, we said, making fun of it all, of the bad outfits and the cheesy lines, and the brain-dead girls who thought they were in love with some stranger after one date.

But three months ago, after staring at a blank page of a supposed new book draft for five days straight, I was so deep into Instagram and a bottle of wine, I thought I might soon come out of the other end. That's when I saw an old contestant from *the 1*, sporting one million followers—an audience most authors only dreamed of.

This discovery led me down a rabbit hole deep into best of *the 1* videos, and the more I saw, the more I thought: What could be better publicity for my writing career than a romance author looking for her own happily-ever-after?

The show could be a huge sales boost to my backlist of failed titles. And then, maybe once I'd proved my worth, I'd have something to build on. Something new to sell. Either way, it was the best plan I'd had since leaving New York.

With the kind of reckless abandon one can have only when desperately avoiding a deadline, I clicked over to *the 1* website and applied to become a contestant on the biggest network reality dating show of the past twenty years. I wasn't sure if I would actually get picked—I knew I was of above average attractiveness, potentially intriguing, and most importantly, could create a great character, but there were no guarantees.

Until I got the call and passed through the casting rounds. I knew it was happening the first time Charlotte said to me during an interview, "We've never had an author on before."

So I'd spent all my time since obsessively researching and taking notes on previous seasons, reading blogs and advice, and doing what I was generally the best at—creating a perfect character. There was no money in this for me or the other contestants, so I had to make the one chance to build a fan base work for me.

To catch up on the most recent crop of contestants, I'd hopped on Zoom with Sarah, and we'd blasted through Shailene's season, watched Marcus and his mannerisms and his bad jokes, and halfway through, Sarah said, "This is your dream man. He's emotionally available, but not too needy. He's witty. He knows what he wants."

"You're delusional," I told her. "We're supposed to be making a game strategy to keep me on the show. That's it." There was a certain confidence, a straightforwardness to Marcus I admired. His bluntness on the show rubbed a lot of viewers the wrong way, but

I saw someone who knew what he wanted. It was tricky, balancing playing a love interest and being honest about your feelings—I admired the way he tried.

"Come on, Jac, be real! You didn't just randomly pick *the 1* of all venues to drum up publicity. Why are you going on *this* show," Sarah asked me, "if it's not to fall in love? This is *perfect*."

"*Sarah*." I sighed out her name. "I'm not trying to win the ring; I'm trying to win the audience."

She tutted. "Just make sure you're ready," Sarah told me at the time. "He's looking for the real thing."

And I have the ridiculous thought as Elodie, an assistant producer, shows me to the bar: Maybe Sarah was right. Maybe Marcus and I had enough in common that our chemistry would be easy. Maybe this would be fun.

I wasn't delusional, though. People didn't fall in love on reality television, especially this show. They gained social media followers and started shilling diet teas, no matter how often they claimed to be "here for the right reasons." They made money, made themselves into a brand. And *that* was going to be me in a couple of weeks if I played my cards right.

"Jac, do you have a minute for an ITM?" Elodie asks me as soon as the bartender has handed over my liquid courage. "In-the-moment interview," she explains.

"Sure," I say, and then a camera crew hurries over and gets me set up in a quiet room that has been blocked off for this purpose alone, walls painted deep red, decorative gold curtains as the backdrop.

"Seems like you and Marcus really had a moment back there," Elodie prompts me.

"I don't know about Marcus yet," I say, hedging. Playing a little hard-to-get, waiting for the real chemistry, was my move. "We just met. I want to make sure it's the right fit for both of us."

"You seem hesitant. Has it been a while since you've been in love?"

I frown at her, a little thrown by the question. I expected questions about past relationships—had already answered many—but I didn't spend a lot of time thinking about being in love on principle. "Uhm? I don't know?"

"Can you answer like I'm not here?" Elodie says with a smile. "We're going to cut everything I say out."

"I'm not hesitant about love," I tell the camera, amending the slip-up quickly. "I'm looking for something real," I say, because it seems like something they'll like. (In the episode, right after this statement, they cut to a shot of me throwing back a drink at the bar, and then another shot of me in the ITM room laughing.)

"Okay, fair enough. When's the last time you had something real?" Elodie asks me.

I bite into my lip, calculating my answer. Never one to share my feelings, this was going to take some finessing. "I'm not scared to open myself up," I tell her. Sounds genuine. "I've been hurt in the past, but who hasn't? I just want to make sure it's for the right person."

"That's perfect," Elodie tells me, nodding to the cameraperson, who kills the recording. "You're going to be so good onscreen, Jac." She hands my fresh drink back to me. "Why don't we head back to the party now? Some of the other girls should be here by now."

We walk back through a hall of the infamous *the 1* mansion, noticeably shabbier in person than it looks on TV, toward the sounds of the party kicking off, past another interview room.

I chug my drink—a bourbon this time, eat your heart out, Southern belles—and then head to the bar for another. I can feel Charlotte watching me now that she's made her way into the house, leaning into one of her assistants and asking how many drinks that is for me this hour. Just my second, if we're doing strict hour-to-hour counting. I watch the other interview room open up, and a man comes out first, likely another producer. And then I *really* see the man. Dark-haired, dark-browed, shirtsleeves rolled up, exposing ropy forearms, a tenseness to his body as if he's ready to spring.

He sees me.

I drop my drink, and it rolls off the bar, hits the tile floor, and shatters.

Five Days Earlier

I got in early on Friday morning on a red-eye from Charleston by way of Dallas. The Uber dropped me off at Sarah's Santa Monica house, beachy and modern, just off the always sunny Santa Monica Boulevard. Josh was at work—his job that had landed the two of them in California originally—and Sarah was in her home office with the baby, studying for the bar exam.

"Why don't you try and take a nap?" she suggested when I got there, and I had agreed. I slept fitfully, the way you do when your body knows it's not the right time to be asleep, and was up and showered by 2 p.m.

"Don't suppose you want to grab something for lunch?" I asked hopefully. She looked up at me from her sun-dappled desk covered in books and cases, bags under her eyes.

"Can't," she said. "I've got an online study group starting at three."

"You doing all right?" I asked her, stepping into the room as quietly as I could to not wake baby Esther.

"I'm doing," she said, and that was that. Sarah was pragmatic by nature, had made me her friend in college when she'd noticed how good I was in our English classes.

"Symbolism," she had told me wisely, "is bullshit. Most of these guys were drunk or high on opium or some shit when they wrote these books. They were probably seeing hallucinations on the wall. I refuse to engage."

I'd liked that about her, and she wasn't the judgmental type. We'd fallen into a best friendship the way desperate people fall into bed—an exhalation of *finally* after a grueling day to be around someone else who just couldn't be fucked with at all.

I'd never been very good at friendship before Sarah. I'd spent so much of my teenage years seeing everyone around me as competition—

for school rankings and scholarships and sports. It had been easy to let people in and then let them go. But I needed Sarah. I needed somewhere to land when reality hit.

Santa Monica was buzzing on Friday afternoon, people everywhere out walking, twentysomethings streaking by on electric scooters and bikes. On Santa Monica Boulevard, diners were sitting out on the patios, pints of beer, sparkling rosé and water and cider in glasses, shorts and tank tops and sunglasses, everything southern California was supposed to be in one shiny street.

I'd planned to go grab a salad somewhere, but I'd accidentally ended up inside a bar instead, the way I tended to do. I figured, worst came to worst, I'd eat whatever nachos they had thrown on their appetizer menu.

I scoffed at the menu when I looked down; the cocktails were obscenely overpriced, and my book sales certainly didn't support this kind of lifestyle. Prices like this had driven me out of New York. I nodded the bartender over and ordered a Bud Light. She smirked as she popped the top off the bottle and handed it over to me, but that didn't stop me. I drank almost half of it in the first gulp.

Calm, I had thought to myself then. *You're calm.*

Two weeks ago, Priya had shown up at my apartment in Charleston to film my package for the show. They'd filmed me playing with Yank, my boxer mix, doing my daily Pilates, typing away at a computer ("just try to look like you do when you write books") with my two book covers framed on the wall over my shoulder. Then Priya had slyly suggested we check out the brewery down the street, and they'd caught me sipping on a brew.

"I'm taking a break from writing to find love," I said to the camera when prompted. Priya was eating it up. "I'm tired of writing other people's love stories." It was a good line. I dreaded becoming another in their long assembly line of "girls next door" and knew I'd have to do something to break out of that box.

At a stool in this overpriced, too trendy Santa Monica bar, I clicked my phone screen to life to see that my mother had already texted the family chat three times to ask if I had arrived safely, with the texts growing progressively more hysterical.

> Did you land yet?

> Jackie, it's me, your mother!! Remember how you were supposed to check in?

> I'm sure you're not dead but I'm about 10 minutes from calling American Airlines to confirm.

I finally texted back, **Here. Fine.**

A text came through almost a minute later: **Well, you're there to try and find a husband on a reality TV show so are you technically "fine"?**

Austin, my younger brother. When he'd found out I was going on *the 1*, he'd started laughing hysterically, and presumably had not stopped since.

Shut up, Eileen, Austin's fiancée, texted back. **Jac, you're going to kill it! Good luck!**

And then my dad randomly responded: **I'm too drunk to taste this chicken**, and I set the phone down.

I finished off the rest of my Bud Light and gestured toward it as the bartender went by. She went to the cooler obligingly and brought me a fresh one.

"Are you drinking shitty beer at *Chalet*?"

I looked in the direction of the voice, toward a guy sitting two seats down from me, alone. He had black hair, golden skin, ratty jeans, and a USC crewneck sweatshirt, and was sipping on a dark cocktail. Whiskey at 3 p.m., and he was judging me? I took another long pull, holding my beer by the neck. "Does that line usually work?" I asked when I finished, tilting my head to the side as I watched him.

He smiled without showing any teeth. "You tell me," he answered.

I shrugged one shoulder. "Oh, I don't know. I'm an easy target."

A single dark eyebrow went up. "Don't do that," he said.

"What?"

"Sell yourself short."

"Then why don't you be nice?" I asked, shaking my just emptied bottle. He slid down a seat, taking the spot next to me.

"If I bought you another Bud Light here, that wouldn't be nice. That would be cruel, even. This isn't a place you drink Bud Light at."

"But I'm a girl you drink Bud Light with," I told him. "Not good enough for you?"

"No," he answered, keeping up easily. "This bar isn't good enough for Bud Light. I know a place that will treat you how you deserve to be treated."

I laughed; it was so bad. "Enlighten me?"

"Come on," he said, abandoning his drink and throwing a hundred on the bar, showing off. I didn't mind so much. I shouldn't do this, but I knew I would. I always did.

Together, we walked along the boardwalk to a dive bar in Venice Beach. It was the same kind of seedy I loved about Venice Beach, the mix of money and misery, the dirty and the beautiful, with pink sunsets behind the mountains every night. Knowingly, inside the dark bar with party lights strung up on the wall, he ordered a pitcher of beer and walked me out to a patio with the smell of the ocean in the distance, the homeless and tourists milling about the main road and golf blaring on the television.

He poured me a plastic cup of beer and then poured one of his own, sitting across from me at the picnic table on turf.

"A bar for a girl like me," I said, people-watching the crowd headed to and from the beach.

"Look at me," he said, and I did. He had dark brows and dark eyes. I learned later that his father was American and his mother was Malaysian and he'd grown up the most Californian you could, long sunny days and hot, happy nights, a boy who fit in instantly anywhere he went, whom people loved without question until he desperately wanted to crawl out of his skin.

I didn't see it then. Honestly, I just saw someone I thought it would be nice to fuck on my last night of freedom. "You look happy now," he said, and the smile tugged at my lips without my permission.

"Did I not before?"

He ruffled his hair, shook his head. "Not really."

"The Santa Monica welcome committee." I sipped my drink, enjoying his gaze on my mouth. "So what, you have like a catch-and-kill policy with tourists?"

"Meaning?"

I raised my voice over the music that was playing. "Do you fuck them?"

He grinned. "Just the ones who ask nicely."

"What's got a pretty boy like you drinking whiskey at 3 p.m.?"

"I don't know," he said, before considering it a moment longer. "Existential angst."

I set my elbows on the table in front of me, leaning my chin into my hands and staring over at him, open, almost interested. "Tell me about it."

He frowned. "I have these invasive thoughts about what it means to be a person," he said.

"Hmm," I answered. "Legally speaking, a person is anything that can be subject to legal proceedings. Or, metaphysically, you must be both conscious *and* self-conscious in order to be a person. A person must be a moral agent, making moral judgments if you want to be philosophical about it. Take your pick."

He gave me a flicker of a smile. "Fine," he said. "Let's focus on the moral one."

"A bad boy," I said, sipping my beer. "Got it."

"A person who questions a lot of the things they put into the world."

"Sure. No morals under capitalism."

He shrugged. "A bit more personal than that." He swallowed, thinking over his words. "You ever wake up in the morning in a sunny hellscape and wonder how you got stuck there?"

"Every day," I answered.

"I have this job," he started. Then he shook his head. "I have a work project starting tomorrow. I wonder if I wasn't involved in this work project if I would be a different kind of person. A better person."

"What are you, like, a politician or something?"

He snorted. "No."

I leaned forward to him, a moth to a flame. "A serial killer? Are you going to murder me?" I asked.

"Nah," he answered easily. "That's no fun. It's more interesting for me to make you think you'll get murdered and see if you want to live or not."

"Dark," I said approvingly.

"I watch a lot of horror movies," he answered. His phone buzzed on the table where his hand was resting next to it, and he didn't even let his eyes flick to it.

"Nietzsche," I said. "Nothing you do matters because nothing matters."

"Things are less complicated that way." He nodded, taking a long pull of his beer, and I laughed.

"It's bleak here, isn't it?" I looked around, slumped back in my seat, at the unassuming bar, the regulars and tourists alike, the passersby. "Los Angeles. Too sunny. I don't trust places where it doesn't rain."

He was studying me in his calculated way. I felt transparent in a way I never did, a wide-open window that I needed to pull the curtain on fast. "I get the feeling you don't trust much."

I hated it—being seen. So, I pushed myself forward again, balancing my face in my hands, my elbows pressed into the picnic table between us. "And you're a brooding single guy with too much money, some sort of weird masochism fetish, and, frankly, an uncalled-for bias against Bud Light." I couldn't stop watching him now, eyes flashing in the sun sinking down over the horizon.

"So just your type?" There was the promised fun.

"I don't know," I said, drawing the words out slowly, leaning down a hand and pressing my fingers against the picnic table, drawing nonsense shapes. "It doesn't really matter, does it?"

"No," he returned. "I guess not."

I reached out a hand. "I'm Jac," I told him.

"Henry," he replied.

"Henry," I said, taking the pitcher into my hands and downing it. "You want to get out of here?"

He smiled then, the first time it seemed the cloud had completely lifted from his face. "As a matter of fact, I do."

"Great," I said. "I've been starving myself for three months. I'll let you buy me pizza."

2

Curse of Curves

For a moment, everyone is staring at me—the other girls, the camera crew and lighting crew and sound crew and producers. Then Rikki screams, "Party foul!" and everyone laughs. An assistant hurries over to clean up the broken glass.

No one is looking at me anymore. No one except him.

My palms are sweaty and my hairline is sweaty and my armpits are sweaty, which shouldn't even be possible given the current amount of Botox in my glands. I leave the bar before I get into more trouble, and I lose sight of him, weaving through cameramen and tech and lighting crew, running headfirst into Aliana and Bonnie from my limo, who have apparently decided they are friends.

"Y'all having fun?" I ask them, and Aliana smiles wickedly.

"Not as much as you," she tells me.

Bonnie tilts her head to the side like a confused puppy. "'Y'all' sounds fake when you say it."

Great, now my Southern authenticity is being questioned. "That's because I enunciate," I tell her.

"Guess what Bonnie did?" Aliana says excitedly.

"I'm guessing she took off her dress and paraded around in a bikini and sash," I answer, only clocking that I sound like a sarcastic bitch after the words leave my mouth. They both blink at me. "How'd it go?" I try again with a smile.

Ali, almost reluctantly now, says, "She looked hot as hell. Marcus was eating it up."

"I was runner-up Miss Texas," Bonnie says proudly, grinning. My

returned smile is halfhearted, my eyes searching desperately for anyone else I can latch on to, but most of the crew is busy and the other
girls are sitting in separate rooms together, paired off by the limo
they arrived in. I've never been very good at making fast friends,
and here I am marooned as usual, with my choices of who to talk
to ranking from bad to worse. Then I see our last limo mate, Rikki,
sitting alone in a chair, guzzling her drink. I make an excuse to the
other girls and hurry over to her.

"Hey!" I say enthusiastically. I hear the hint of desperation in my
own voice, hoping no one else will notice.

"Jackieeee," Rikki says, drawing out a name I only allow my
mother to call me and leaning her head into my arm, where her hair
tickles my skin. It's dark but highlighted to a brassy blond with an
ombre fading down to the tips. She has on a loud sparkly pink dress
that she is almost spilling out of and a slit cut dangerously high on
her thigh. "None of the other girls are being nice to me." She pouts.

"Fuck 'em," I say, a line I know they won't be able to air on television (actually, they absolutely air that line on television, between
thirty and fifty times in previews for the season).

"Do you want to be my best friend?" she asks.

"Yes," I agree without hesitation. Whatever.

"Did you see the hot producer that came in with the second set
of girls?" she asks me, her voice like a whine.

I feel my face heat up. "Hot producer?"

"That girl over there," she says, pointing at a slender redhead who
is delicately holding a glass of champagne. "Shit, I can't remember
her name," she slurs. "Anyway, her, she told me his name is Henry.
That's totally a hot name, isn't it?"

"What about Marcus?" I ask her.

"I think I met him in casting," she says. "Henry. He asked if my
tits were real. Wait. Actually, maybe that was Charlotte."

"That's kind of a fixation for you, isn't it?" I ask, and she laughs
loudly.

"'Course my tits aren't real!" she yells into the room at large. My
eyes scan again, looking for the producer in question, but he's still
nowhere to be seen. I'd met all the producers, too, hadn't I? Charlotte

and Priya and Janelle? There were even more, and they'd all interviewed me on that final casting call.

Except the one producer who hadn't been there. The one who'd had a family emergency. The producer was *Henry*.

Shit. Fuck. Hell.

"Ladies, can we gather round?" Charlotte yells over all of us. "Brendan and Becca will be here shortly."

Brendan and Becca. The co-hosts of *the 1*, who had met and married after the fifteenth season—one of the few successful relationships to come from the show. Even if you didn't leave the show with a spouse (and few did), scoring a spot on *the 1* was different than other reality shows. It had a certain cachet, a certain level of perceived classiness that streaming reality shows could never hope to match. Sure, the antiquated idea of engagement or bust, of a man deciding which of twenty-five women met his exacting standards, were all the antithesis of me as a person. But when had being me ever gotten me anywhere? I was great at creating characters for books, and I could certainly create one for this show. I'd play their game, and I'd win it. Not win a man, but win an audience.

Becca and Brendan meant Marcus would follow shortly.

We all wait in anticipation and Rikki reaches down and laces our hands together, giving mine a squeeze that fills me with momentary warmth. Then the double doors to the mansion open and Becca and Brendan come inside, flanking Marcus.

On cue, we all scream and catcall accordingly. "Hello, ladies!" Becca calls to us with a smile, getting us going all over again. I'd like to say I play it cool, but I get caught up in the mob mentality of the moment.

"Marcus has come here tonight to meet his wife," Brendan tells us. "Just like I did, in this very same mansion, over ten years ago."

"Aw," Becca says, "he's such a softie." I hadn't watched Becca and Brendan's season of *the 1*, but I'd seen the pictures, and it was clear that both had made significant changes to their faces since airing, slowly becoming less wrinkled and more plastic over time.

"You ready to do this, Marcus?" Brendan says, pumping him up like the huddle before a football game.

"Well, I don't know." Marcus looks out at us, his smile dazzling. "Are *you* ready to do this, girls?" he asks. *Girls*. I bristle at that.

I haven't been a girl for a long time.

"I can't wait to meet as many of you as possible tonight," Marcus says. "And for us to start this journey together." He holds up his champagne glass, and we all do the same in unison. "A toast," he says, "to finding the one." He winks. "To season 32."

"Season 32," we all chant back, and Rikki hits her glass against mine so hard, champagne splashes onto the girl next to me, all over her ivory dress. She swears and then starts crying, immediately moving to cover herself with her hands. My eyes go wide.

"I'm so sorry," I apologize, but she's not listening.

I look up and he's there. He's looking at me. Henry. It wasn't an illusion.

"Fuck," I say.

I MEET THE other girls. Aaliyah, the beauty queen from New York, and Grace-Ann, the beauty queen from Louisiana. Andi, an extremely hot accountant (yes, really) from Seattle. Social influencer—though her eventual TV chyron will say "Professional Dog Walker"—Kady from Canada, and nurse Candy (yes, really) from Florida. They all seem nice enough until Rikki, so drunk I don't think she could possibly know what's going on, locks herself into the bathroom insisting that the other girls were being mean to her and that she is never going to be able to fall in love with Marcus.

"All the drama already with that one," Kady says. "I just told her I liked her dress."

"Rikki," I say, knocking on the door. "Rikki, why don't you come out?"

She sobs in response. I sigh.

"Jac!" someone calls from across the room. "There you are!" Then Charlotte is marching over to me, latching on to my arm. "Come with me," she says.

Charlotte had been the first producer I'd talked to from *the 1*. She'd reviewed my application and said she was very interested in me, in my background. She'd asked me all sorts of questions in that quiet, confident voice of hers, never having much response to the answers. Sharp as a tack and quick as a fox, she'd turn things around on me.

"I love a good story," I remember telling her on our first call. "That's what I love about *the 1*, how consistently, despite sometimes having so little to work with, you make the story happen."

"Because it's not real?" she prodded. During half our interview, she'd been taking notes, to the point I wasn't sure they were even about me or what I was saying, but at that moment, she was looking at me intently.

"No," I told her, shaking my head. I knew that was the wrong answer. "Because it's not always as interesting as it could be. Some people fall in love that first night, right? And nothing ever changes their mind, but there still has to be a story. I love *the 1* because it's not just about love. It's about everything else, too. Like when I was watching Shailene's season, I knew she would never pick Marcus, but that didn't make their dynamic any less interesting to watch, it didn't make it any less compelling to see his arc play out on television.

"I'd be happy to find love, Charlotte, and I'd be happy to be a part of your story."

She had smiled.

Back at the mansion, I allow Charlotte to lead me away from the bathroom door, out the glass double doors in the back and onto the patio, where the crew is abuzz.

"What have you been doing all this time?" Charlotte asks me, the chiding whisper of a girlfriend who you'd made plans with and subsequently ditched.

"Rescuing sad girls from the bathroom."

Charlotte shakes her head. "Wrong choice," she says. "You're one of my contenders, girl. You need to go talk to Marcus."

"Oh," I say. "I get it. This is when you need me to interrupt whoever he's currently talking with and cause some drama."

Charlotte rolls her eyes. "Jac, listen, I know your type. You've seen this show, you're not easily manipulated, but that doesn't mean you don't have to make any effort. The interruptions are expected. Just, very sweetly, grab his hand and ask to steal him for a minute."

"I assume you want me to do that while the current girl is dead in the middle of her sob-worthy backstory?"

Charlotte smiles sardonically. "That charm. That wit. That humor." Charlotte winks at me. "That's what we brought you on for. Now, go," she says, giving me a little push toward the tidy pagoda where Aliana is curled up with Marcus on a couch. I step forward, tilting my head to one side. Aliana is, predictably, tearing up.

"Oh," I say. "Hey, y'all."

Marcus looks up at me, relieved. I can tell I'm his life raft in this moment.

"You wanna get out of here?" I ask him, thinking I'm being funny. Aliana stares at me like she wishes I were dead.

But Marcus says, "Definitely," shoots up from where he's sitting with Aliana, and grabs my hand. I pull him in the direction of the pool in the mansion's backyard, fairy lights glowing all around us. If I was writing a romantic scene into a book, I might set it here.

"You look like you've been waiting for a knight in shining armor," I say to him.

"Mm-hmm," Marcus says easily. "And is that you?"

I remembered Sarah telling me he was the perfect guy for me less than three weeks ago. I remember the way she'd sighed sweetly over the webcam.

Just make sure you're ready.

I'm not. Because I know this is fake.

I'd known it from the first application and every interview since. I'd done what I needed to. I'd said things about falling in love and failed relationships and tragic backstory and whatever they wanted. I'd simpered and joked around and given my everything into getting on this show.

I am thirty-two and I've spent enough of my life running up this fucking hill.

Marcus stops at the edge of the mansion's pool. I look down at the water, then back up at him.

"Well?" I say. "Are we doing this?"

I slough off my heels and crouch down, sitting at the edge of the pool, hiking up my evening gown, and dipping my feet into the water.

With a laugh, Marcus gets down beside me, untying his shoes and then removing his socks.

"Don't get your pants wet," I warn him.

"Eh." He shrugs with an easy grin. "What's the worst that could happen?"

"I don't know, I guess you could just disappoint your future wife," I return.

"Maybe I'd disappoint my future wife if I didn't get into the pool with her," Marcus says, and despite myself, I feel my cheeks warm. I sit there with no answer until he finally saves me. "How's your night going so far?"

"I wasn't sure we'd get to talk again," I admit to Marcus.

"But you wanted to?" he asks.

"Yeah," I say, leaning my body toward his as much as I can while still sitting beside him. I think of kissing him, the bourbon I'd had taking a powerful hold of my bloodstream. "I might even move in, if you really want."

Out of the corner of my eye, I see Charlotte grinning.

Marcus is looking at me, and I see his eyes flick down to my lips. "I'm not supposed to give anything away," he says after a minute, then swallows, his Adam's apple bobbing up and down.

"Well, in that case, I'd hate to pressure you," I say. "Why don't you ask me some standard questions? Actually," I interrupt him when he goes to speak, "don't. Jac is a thirty-two-year-old writer from Charleston, South Carolina. She was born and raised in South Carolina, took a sojourn to New York City, and left when it got too expensive and too lonely. She has been in Charleston for almost a year with her dog, Yank, who is currently staying with her funnier and better-looking little brother and his fiancée. Both parents living, no life-shattering divorces or deaths or sad single-mom tales, and nothing but casual, failed relationships for—" I start jokingly count- ing on my fingers and then stop. "You know what, let's just not. It's been a while."

This. This was the part I was good at. Being untouchable, being easy and smart, never spending too much time wallowing in anything too intimate or sad. This was how men loved me, until they didn't.

"Is that all?" Marcus asks. It's a speech I had semi-planned out before I got here, and one I'm sure the producers will love. Marcus is playing his part so perfectly, I'm impressed at what a good love interest he is already.

"Well, I can't reveal my tragic backstory until after a few dates, Marcus; those are just the rules."

Then he leans down and kisses me.

It surprises me, how quickly it happens, but it's a pitch-perfect culmination of our meet-cute. I sink into it. He has firm lips, and the kiss lasts longer than expected, but I can't help but feel aware of all the cameras on the two of us, of the way this is playing out like a rom-com.

I'm really part of their story now.

Finally, he pulls back, and his eyes go to my lips again and then to my eyes, and we both laugh nervously.

"Marcus!" someone calls. We both look up and it's Andi the accountant. "Can I steal you for a second?" she asks, smiling saccharine sweet.

Marcus, carefully, so as to not get any water on my dress, gets up and out of the pool, grabbing his shoes. "But you didn't tell me any of your secrets," I whisper to him, grabbing on to his hand before he can leave.

"I will," he promises me, leaning back down closer—too close in front of another girl, I think. "Soon."

Then he goes; I stare at his backside as he does.

Charlotte rushes over to me with a towel, helping me up out of the pool. "That was good!" she gushes. "Jesus, you are sexy."

"Yeah . . ." I say slowly. "Yeah, I am, aren't I?"

"The sparks were flying," she assures me. "If you need any more towels, let Elodie know," she says, pointing to Elodie crouching nearby so the camera won't catch her as Andi and Marcus make their way to another part of the house. "I have to run, but call me if you need me."

"Sure," I say, wrapping the towel around myself. I slide back into my heels.

"You look great," Elodie assures me, hurrying over. "I know you're going to be a star on the season."

"Uhm—thanks."

"It's my first season as a producer," Elodie tells me conspiratorially. "I've been a production assistant the past few seasons."

"Congrats?" I venture.

"Thanks," she says, genuinely smiling. She pauses as noises come through from her headset. "Can you head back inside okay? I need to go set up something for one of the girl's one-on-one time. Priya will grab you as soon as you're back inside."

I nod, but Elodie has already taken off. Alone, save for the staff everywhere, I begin walking across the blindingly lit patio toward the house. I go in a side door where it's dark, and right as I do, Henry walks past me.

"Hey, wait, stop," I say, reaching out and grabbing his arm. He does; he was practically running in the other direction, but he stops, stands there across from me. "I need to talk to you," I say. He doesn't meet my eye.

"Later," he says, his gaze darting toward the door where his next assignment surely awaits. "We have to get through tonight first. I have to produce." He looks exhausted and alive, and my mind races at the sight of him, at the memory of his bachelor pad in Venice Beach, at what he'd told me that night. He'd been a person headed back to a place he didn't want to be. Of course he had.

He doesn't look like that now. He looks like he's thriving, a low energy thrumming from him like an engine.

"Fine," I say. "Later. But I'm serious, we need to talk. If I survive the night."

"You're on the list," Henry says, and his eyes finally meet mine, a current going through me like an electric spark. "So later it is." He begins to walk away, but then turns back around and says, "Red," eyes skimming my dress. Thusly fucking up my whole life, he hurries off after his pretty little contestant.

Well.

I guess I'm on the list.

The night drags on, endlessly on, and girls are drunk and crying and a couple are napping sitting up in overstuffed chairs. Priya asks if she can grab me for one more ITM before the elimination ceremony. I sit through it, dead-eyed, feeling as if I barely have anything left to give, the camera trained on me with Priya looking increasingly bored with my answers.

"Let's try one more," she tells me. "I just need one good answer from you, Jac, and then we'll be done." As she says this, Charlotte slides through the door, watching me from a corner, arms folded over her chest. She speaks over Priya. "Come on, Jac. You've met Marcus. You've met the other girls. What do you think of them?"

I stare at the camera, completely drained, yet confident at what I'd already managed in one night. I steel myself to give a good answer, take a sip of my champagne, and say it without thinking about it: "The other girls? I don't think about them at all."

Charlotte smiles. "Cut and print."

Another One Podcast, First Episode of Season 32

JULIA: On today's episode of *Another One*, we're talking to Monday Night Football host and former St. Louis Ram, Drew Clayton.

DREW: Thanks for having me, Julia.

JULIA: No problem, Drew! When our mutual friend Courtney Thomas told me you watched the show, I knew I had to get you on. How long have you been watching *the 1*?

DREW: Keonte Smith actually got me into it. *Claimed* he used to watch it with his mom. Became a big thing during the playoffs—the only non-game film I watched up to Super Bowl Sunday was usually episodes of *the 1*.

JULIA: [Laughing.] That's incredible. Who's your favorite former lead?

DREW: Call it recency bias if you will, but it's gotta be Shailene. And I think Keonte would agree.

JULIA: Shailene is a great pick. Her season was so juicy. I'll have to have Keonte on sometime.

DREW: He'd love that.

JULIA: So, I always like to get a man's perspective on this stuff. What are you thinking so far of Marcus's girls?

DREW: Seems like there's a lot of good girls to pick from. I was really digging Aliana and Andi the accountant.

JULIA: Ohmygod, Aliana was so great! I loved that little joke she told about the pineapple, and it was really sweet to see her with her daughter.

DREW: She's got a great story for sure.

JULIA: Right. So far, I'm *very* confused about Marcus's taste in women. And I want to circle back to Marcus in general and the controversy surrounding him after we talk about the girls. It really puts an interesting spin on the season.

DREW: I have to say, I was so shocked at him sending Bonnie home. They set her up as someone with an interesting backstory who might be around all season.

JULIA: Totally agree! Maybe they'll bring her back for *1 in the sun* and let her get messy drunk in Mexico. She's only right around the corner in Texas, so seems like a good fit.

DREW: She still might not get as messy drunk as Rikki. She spent at least half the night locked in the bathroom, didn't she?

JULIA: Yeah. I couldn't believe Marcus kept her! I thought she was toast after that. I actually ended up feeling a little warmer toward Jac than some of the people online did last night when she was trying to coax Rikki out of the bathroom. Seems like there might actually be some good there.

DREW: If it is, it's buried very deep down. She was so nasty about some of the girls throughout the night, wasn't she? And that comment about not thinking about them at all was brutal.

JULIA: Totally, it was a step too far. The season preview didn't exactly show her in a positive light either.

JULIA: And Drew, I don't know if you know this about me, but I go *deep* on *the 1* research, and Jac is suspiciously silent on social media. Nothing about the show so far. It makes me think there's some real shit to come for her.

DREW: It's cool that she's an author—had there ever been an actual published author on the show before?

JULIA: Not that I can remember.

DREW: Have you picked up any of her books?

JULIA: I have one in my Amazon cart right now. Just need to pull the trigger. I'm so curious as to what kind of writer she is based on her persona on the show.

DREW: What are they called again? *Fair Play*?

JULIA: And *End of the Line*. It looks like there was supposed to be a third that never came out.

DREW: Sounds kind of Hallmark-y. Not really Jac's thing.

JULIA: The reviews made it seem a little darker than that. Like maybe there's some edge. But still, romance, yeah.

DREW: Well, she has her eye on the ball when it comes to that, I guess. There's definitely chemistry between her and Marcus.

JULIA: One hundred percent. Maybe the mean girl act was just some first week jitters and she'll chill some as the season goes on? Though the previews didn't exactly look like it would play out that way.

DREW: [Sighs.] I sure hope so. Not sure I can stomach another winner like season 26.

JULIA: I guess only time will tell. In the meantime, maybe we'll get some insight into that calculating mind of hers from her oeuvre.

DREW: [Laughs.] You'll have to let me know.

JULIA: In Jac's defense, every season needs a good bitch.

DREW: That is so true. That's why the last male *1* was *so* boring. The guys just can't carry it themselves—no offense, Marcus.

3

Flavor of the Weak

Before the sun comes up, the elimination ceremony begins.

It's long and we're all wrung completely dry. I'm pretty sure I committed a cardinal sin earlier by joking to a drunk Rikki that I thought it was minorly embarrassing that Bonnie was bragging about being runner-up Miss Texas. I hope that part doesn't air (it does, and I still kind of think I was right). In a moment of weakness, standing on the risers waiting for Marcus to begin calling girls' names, I can't stop my eyes from traveling over to where he— *Henry*—is standing, referring back and forth to a clipboard he has his assistant holding to his phone, where he is either texting or typing notes. Nothing about him looks as tired as I feel.

He glances over at me, feeling me watching him, and I quickly look away, back to where Marcus is standing with Brendan and Becca, who only seem to appear when a camera is nearby.

"Ladies," Becca says, "Marcus will be inviting those of you he wants to spend more time with to move into the house. If you do not receive an invitation to next week, your journey ends here tonight."

"It was wonderful to meet you all tonight," Marcus says diplomatically. "I can't thank you enough for traveling all this way to try and find love with me, and if I can't offer you an invitation tonight, I hope we can still leave as friends."

I try to keep my face neutral.

Marcus hands out invitations to twenty girls, eliminating five. I count and end up getting mine fifth: "Jac, I'd love for you to stay another week." The invites are over the top, written in formal font that says "Marcus Bellamy invites you to move into *the 1* mansion." Then at the end of the ceremony, Marcus looks the unchosen few dead in the eye and says, "*Insert name here,* you are not the one."

I can't help it. I'm drunk. The first time he sends someone packing with that catchphrase, I start laughing. It's a quiet laugh but not so much that those nearest to me don't notice. The girls all shift uncomfortably, and I try to clear my face, burying it in my hands until I can get hold of myself. I should be embarrassed, but my brain can't bother to process that emotion, and I see Marcus is smiling at me like he noticed me laughing, and liked it. Only, recently eliminated Bonnie is crying, and I wish I could take it back. Laughing is my psychosomatic response to discomfort.

Unfortunately, the statement sounds even funnier the second time, and my giggles persist, but by the third time Marcus says the absolutely absurd words, I have it under my control. I finally can release a breath once the director calls, "Cut!"

Rikki, who has practically been sleeping standing up, curls into my side and lays her head on my shoulder. I don't know how this happened, this compulsory intimacy between us, but it pretty clearly has and now I feel oddly protective of her. I brush her hair back from her face softly. I'm pretty sure she threw up right before the ceremony started.

"Okay, folks," Charlotte announces to the group of girls lined up on the risers. "We're going to get you back to the hotel for a couple of hours of sleep and then we can all officially move into the house. The cars will be here shortly. You'll get your room assignments on the way back. Try and have your stuff packed and ready to go by five. Heard that, ladies? Five p.m.!"

"Are all pregnant women so grumpy?" Rikki mutters into my arm. I hadn't known she was taking in anything being said.

"Probably just the ones producing twenty-five women for twelve hours straight," I tell her. I glance at Charlotte, who has gathered the remaining producers around her and is muttering to them, her mouth moving nonstop. "Honestly, I doubt Charlotte needs sleep," I mutter as an aside to Rikki. When she doesn't answer, I wonder if she's fallen back asleep.

It takes an hour to get back to the hotel, to the point the sun is fully up. I want to collapse directly into bed, but I remember instead that I am trying to be a Real Girl and all that, the kind a guy on a reality TV show would fall in love with—or at least keep around long enough for her to sell a couple thousand books to curious fans.

I start wiping the layers of makeup off my face. It hasn't escaped my notice that most of the other girls are between five and ten years younger than me. Sure, Marcus himself is thirty-four, but what interest would he have in a thirty-two-year-old when there were so many bouncy girls in their mid-twenties around? It also didn't escape my notice that fillers and veneers were almost a prerequisite to come on the show these days, adding even more to everyone's youthful appearances. I knew plenty of women in New York who engaged in the ritual, but Botox was as far as I could go.

I sigh, moving in on the moisturizer my dermatologist recommended to me. Just as I finish up, there is a knock on my door.

I don't know why—probably lack of sleep—but I expect it to be Rikki, come back for more emotional support. But when I open the door, it's him. It's Henry.

Four Days Earlier

I woke up and I was pretty sure I was dying.

A beam of sunlight found me, creeping in from a big, open window to the east. It was early—too early for me when I lived in my real life on the East Coast, barely scraping myself out of bed before 10 a.m., but just right for me in this life, where the real had ceased to exist.

I was naked in an unfamiliar bed, the taste of alcohol and pizza coating my mouth, and I was dying. So things were going really well.

"Shit," I said out loud. "Shit."

"That's exactly what you said last night." The voice was a deep baritone and it was light. Easy. Last night.

I almost laughed. Last night.

"Shit," I said again and turned over to face him.

"Good morning," I said, keeping my voice breezy. Something about knowing a relationship was already over before it began made it easy. It always had.

"It's too early," he answered, burying his face back in his pillow, an arm draping over the sheets covering my body casually. Almost too casually.

"Running on East Coast time," I answered, and he laughed against the pillow.

"Don't I know it."

"I talk too much," I confessed, almost ashamed, "especially after a couple beers."

"I live in LA," he reminded me as if I could forget, turning back over to look at me. He blinked, and for a moment, I did forget. Why I was here. Instead, I thought about his long eyelashes, and how I didn't want him to disappear. "Your honesty is refreshing."

"Mm. Maybe you should try being less honest," I told him, and I thought he liked it from the way he laughed. I slid out of the bed and pulled my shirt over my head. "I need to go. Shower."

He sat up, his black sheets—dead giveaway for bachelor status—pooling at his stomach. "You're welcome to shower here," he told me. "I have the snob coffee."

"Of course you do." I pulled up my shorts, the last comfortable outfit I would wear for weeks. "But I'm a cheap date, I'll grab Starbucks." I started putting on my sandals that I had tossed off last night. We both sat in the awkward silence before I said, "Thanks for letting me crash. It was fun." I turned back to look at him, and he was looking at me with bright-eyed interest.

"So a no on breakfast then?" He was smiling though. "God, you look so good in red," he almost-moaned, eyeing my ratty old tank, the bottom skimming my belly button. "Did I mention that?"

"A couple thousand times last night," I answered. Then I leaned in closer, letting him in on a secret we both already knew. He smelled like stale alcohol and sex. "C'mon," I said. "I bet you're good at this."

"Like really good," he agreed. "But I figured I'd offer. You were 'like, so fucking hungry' last night."

He didn't know the half of it. I grinned and beared it. "Back on my diet as of today."

He didn't comment on it, didn't try to tell me what to do with my body or how he thought it might look best, which I liked. "Can I at least drive you somewhere?" he asked.

I tilted my head back and smiled. I'd remember him in that patch of sunlight, I thought. The way he looked. And then I'd forget all about last night, the way you were supposed to. "Wouldn't that just ruin all the mystery?"

He laughed. "Well, there's no mystery where I'm going."

"Ah," I said. "The job you hate."

He stared at me, lost for a moment, before he remembered himself. The game we were playing. "You have no idea."

"Don't get too lost in your nihilism, Henry," I called to him as I made my way toward the door, ordering a Lyft on the way.

When the car pulled up a couple minutes later, I watched him unguarded through the large windows into his house, brewing a coffee in sweats, no shirt on, as he faded away into the sunrise.

He never looked up.

4

Just the Girl

Well," Henry says, walking into my hotel room and closing the door behind him, "that explains why you looked so familiar at the bar. Casting photos."

He stops behind my door, his black T-shirt, black and blue Jordans, and dark jeans against the white walls of the hotel room, and we size each other up quietly. He's broad-shouldered, dark-haired, a few inches taller than me. Bronze-skinned, brown-eyed, and radiating a heat that most people don't, and I'm there, sans makeup, in a bathrobe, and more exhausted than I've ever been in my life.

Jesus.

"I met," I say, "with every producer on *the 1*. They put me through the wringer, and you"—I pointed my finger at him—"were not there."

"Family emergency," he says. "On one day of casting. Didn't they mention it?"

Yes, of course, I thought, *of course they had*. "Isn't that just so fucking convenient for you?"

He gave me a look, a look like who-the-fuck-implies-a-family-emergency-was-convenient? "Who has a one-night stand the night before they are joining a reality TV show to get married?" he asks me, like he has a right to be mad.

"Oh, fuck off," I say. "Everyone does. '*Get married*.' Spare me."

"Okay," Henry concedes. With a quiet kind of desperation, he runs his hands through his black hair. "Okay. This is going to be fine. This doesn't have to be a thing."

"You could have just *said* something," I tell him. "Mentioned you were a producer on the biggest reality show in the country."

His eyes meet mine. "There wasn't exactly a lot of talking going on, as I recall."

My face goes red. Here I am, thirty-two and single and still doing the same stupid shit I've been doing since college. I feel shame rising up in my body. "I asked you, though. I did ask you what you did and you hated it so much, you wouldn't tell me." When he doesn't answer that, I take a deep breath and say, "Maybe I should just go home."

"What are you talking about? The producers are obsessed with you."

"They are?"

"Yeah," Henry says, sighing. "Charlotte thinks you're hilarious. Keeps saying that you're going to make amazing television."

"What exactly does that mean?" I ask suspiciously.

He gives me an assessing look before he answers. "We like to have a stand-in for the viewers. Someone who says what we're all thinking— that's you."

I roll my eyes, secretly pleased. It's not far off from who I wanted to be when I game-planned with Sarah.

"See," he says, flashing me a winning grin, "the skeptic giving into love. Just what they like."

"And if someone finds out what happened between us?"

"Oh, you'll definitely get kicked off the show. And probably some on-air misogynistic slut shaming, but that's *the 1* in general, isn't it?" He shrugs. "I might get fired. Depends on how much they value me."

"What?" I ask, momentarily distracted from my own plight. "You don't know how much they value you?"

He leans back against the wall, hedging for a moment before he says, "I know how much they valued me a couple of seasons ago." He shrugs again. "I've been told I can get pretty old after a while."

I give him a cold look. "I can't imagine why."

When he doesn't answer, I groan, turning away from him and going to sit on the bed. "Fuck. This could only happen to me." I bury my face in my hands, and we both sit like that, in total silence. After a moment, he makes his way slowly across the room toward me.

"Do you . . . *want* to leave?" he asks, in a way that almost sounds like a test. I look up at him from where I'm sitting.

"I don't know," I say after a minute. "I only barely managed to drag myself out here in the first place."

"Yeah," he agrees. "I looked and you were on the 'might not show up' list. But you're here to sell books, right?"

I swallow. "I'm here to fall in love."

"Right, right," he says, holding up his hands. "We're all just here because we love love." He drops his hands. "Look, I know you need this show."

I blink a couple of times. "This is all starting to sound very threatening."

"I don't mean it that way," he says. "It's just in both of our best interests to pretend it never happened, right? That night."

I'm so exhausted, I feel like something is sitting on top of me, pressing me down against the bed, against the choices I make over and over again. "That's what we would've done," I say. "We'd have pretended it never happened." That's what I always do.

We both sit there, with that hanging between us. It is true, and maybe it isn't.

"I should've known," Henry says at last. "It's on me. It's literally my job to know who the contestants are."

I raise an eyebrow at the statement. "Maybe you did."

He looks up at me, startled. "That's a bold accusation."

"Yeah, well, seems to me you hold all the power here. Like you said, I confess, I get labeled a slut and sent packing. Maybe they'll even have Brendan and Becca throw me under the bus in a nice closing scene."

I see something flash in his eyes then, a darkness I've seen before. "Harder to buy books from a slut." He sees the story this would become, and so do I.

"Why do you want me to keep this quiet?" I ask, tilting my head to the side as I look up at him. "You hate this job."

He blinks slowly. "Yeah," he says after a minute. "No. I don't know. I don't hate it. I hate what it makes me. What it makes me feel."

"Which is?"

He doesn't say anything for a moment, thinks about it, swallows. "Good."

(The thing I would grow to love and hate the most about Henry was the way he was so easily, effortlessly handsome, and the way he wore that like punishment. Of course he could produce women with ease, the way he only handed out real smiles when you'd done more than enough to earn them, the way he'd tip back a shot of tequila and not even have to ask you to do the same. Everything about him screamed for you to give him what he wanted, just to earn that kindness in his eyes that he withheld from everyone, most of all himself. Henry Foster. Dark eyes and high cheekbones, broken promises and kept threats.)

"Listen," he goes, "producers have slept with contestants on this show before. Especially in those first few seasons, it was like the wild, wild West. It hasn't gotten out, but it has happened. We can keep this quiet. We didn't even know."

"*You* didn't know," I correct him. "I couldn't have known."

He's staring at me in a way that makes me feel like he's remembering what I look like without clothes. He'd dropped that intensity, just for a bit, that night, and now here we were and he was in charge of everything that happened to me and I was trying to date another man.

"Will you help me out?" I ask him. "With Marcus."

He smiles a little. "Of course I will."

I don't know why—a memory, an impulse—but my fingers go to my bare collarbone, caressing the skin there softly. His eyes dart to it and then back to mine.

"This needs to be worth it for me, you know?" I say.

"I do," he answers. He turns back to the door, and I watch him go. "Try to get some sleep, Jac," he says as he touches the door handle. "I'll see you later."

Writers' Room Private Slack Channel

AW | **Anika K. Wright**
Bestselling author of *In Your Arms* series
Am I on mushrooms or is Jacqueline Matthis on the new season of *the 1*?

BR | **Brynn Riley**
I write books and shit
girl lmao her *publicist* told me last month that she was on the new season

CD | **C. Duncan**
Catch My Love out next month
I KNEW that bitch would do anything for sales!!!

Y'all think it will work?

AK | **Annie Kate**
Texas Stars at Night, *Rhode Island Lights*, *Last Stop in Carolina*
Sorry, who is Jacqueline Matthis?

CD | **C. Duncan**
This author who got paid a million dollars for her series, which later tanked. One of the sales highlights from her publisher was all about how she was a beautiful twenty-six-year-old ingenue. I used to run into her at parties around nyc but I heard she bolted a few months ago. I am fucking dead that she's on *the 1*

BR | **Brynn Riley**
end of the line, right? I remember when that came out

CD | **C. Duncan**
It was about this all-female country music group or something? And in the first one, this lead falls for some

guy and they have lots of hot sex and then at the end SHE CHOOSES HER CAREER OVER HIM AND THEY BREAK UP

The internet fucking hated it. All that buzz, a film option, and then, just a massive tanking.

Anika K. Wright
tbh I heard it was completely mismarketed

C. Duncan
I guess the second one ended with an HEA but it was too late. Her pub bailed on her. Canceled the third book in her contract.

Brynn Riley
her amazon ranking is way up

Annie Kate
Oh! I liked her book. The chemistry was INSANE

Anika K. Wright
Annie, please lol

Annie Kate
It had good sex scenes ¯_(ツ)_/¯ I don't make the rules

C. Duncan
I am like 99% sure she was sleeping with a lit fic editor at one point. Desperate for validation, that one. I swear she thought she was too good for romance.

Brynn Riley
she always got drunk at events

she's hot as shit, so maybe it will work out for her

Anika K. Wright
Well . . .

They're sure hating her online

Annie Kate
Online hates everyone though

Brynn Riley
listen, I'm not going to lie, if it would help, I might shake my ass in front of some bland ass white guy too

C. Duncan
Honestly, just watched the season preview and it looks like a hot mess

I'm in

5

High School Never Ends

The sun rises in an unfamiliar room, white comforters against white walls, four girls piled into twin beds, flashbacks to the college years so many of my competitors had recently experienced dancing in my head.

"Rise and shine," Rikki says, giving me a bright, sober smile, fully recovered from the first night's antics. I remember those days myself, though I remember the dread I would so often wake up with, wondering what I had done now in my drunken stupor. Rikki rose with the confidence of a girl who never regretted her decisions.

Rikki had immediately sought me out to be her roommate when we'd arrived back at the mansion, and the two of us had ended up paired with Kendall, a software seller from San Diego, and Andi the accountant. Kendall is a dark-haired, dead-eyed aspiring Instagram influencer. She's got a look like she'd kill me and not think twice about it—she's thirty and, one would think, my natural ally, but so far everything coming my way from her had been frost on more frost. Andi, on the other hand, is friendly, if more than a little awkward, twenty-seven, bright-eyed and trying her hardest, which is just a little too much, with wrists so tiny, I could wrap a hand around them. I automatically dislike them both for different reasons, probably ones that aren't even real. "You want mimosas?" Rikki calls as we are all applying copious amounts of makeup. "I'm *dying* for mimosas."

"I want mimosas!" Andi answers, even though no one asked her.

(The alcohol was available 24/7 and while there were limitations in place, we were never discouraged from drinking. Every night on *the 1* set was like walking through a college downtown at two o'clock in the morning.)

"I can't start drinking at 9 a.m.," I tell them. "Old, remember?"

"*Old.*" Kendall cackles from her bed. I didn't think she was awake. "Would you all shut the hell up and get out of my room?" She shifts her body away from us, and Rikki quietly laughs in response.

I last about halfway through the group breakfast that Aliana and Kady made before I do in fact start drinking, simply to tune out the inane conversation about Marcus and makeup and sticky boobs going on around me. I go with a Bloody Mary in an attempt to pace myself. Charlotte isn't here today, but Henry is, and despite my best efforts to ignore his presence, I feel him there.

In the daylight, it is clear that there is a certain slapdash nature to everything around us. Chipped, hastily applied paint on the walls, never a color you'd really want in your house, but one that will pop on television. I'd heard that a family actually lived in the mansion when they weren't filming, kicked out for two full months a year for a full renovation to become the shooting spot for *the 1*. The house was open, a bar in the foyer, leading to a huge sitting room and spacious kitchen. What would presumably have been a dining room in better times was filled with couches, another staging area. The office and a bedroom toward the back were cleared for ITMs. The furniture was mostly overstuffed and overly bright, the hideous décor—curtains (over windows or not), paintings, mood lights—numerous. There were some cameras on the walls, but those were much easier to escape than the mics (we'd figured out all the dead spots by the time we were uprooted).

"So," Aaliyah says as Andi cleans up our plates, "what do we do now?"

"Whatever you want," Elodie the first-time assistant producer says. "You can work out or sit by the pool or—" She stops, almost like she's surprised.

"Or sit by a window and stare at the sun until your brain melts out of your ears," I supply. Some of the girls laugh while others just look confused, and this time, I know Henry is looking at me.

"You're bored already?" he asks, and there's something electric about him talking to me in front of all these people, where they can see the two of us.

"They took away my books and laptop," I return, not flinching from his challenge. "Of course I'm bored." The idea was to take away anything that might entertain us, might take our focus from Marcus. Charlotte had told me I could certainly bring a notebook and a pad of paper "in case I got the urge to write," but I couldn't imagine many things more creatively stifling than this bland mansion.

Henry smiles at me, obviously not finding it funny at all. "Well, let's change that then." He looks away, glances down at his phone. "We need everyone to gather around in the living room and get some film on who will get the first one-on-one date."

I sigh and comply.

Henry and the assistants get us set up on the couches in the living room and then prompt us to start speculating about who will get the first date with Marcus.

"Is there anyone you thought had a particularly strong connection with Marcus on night one?" he asks the surrounding crowd.

A couple of the girls raise their hands like they're in grade school, but then someone speaks up. "He liked Jac," Andi says, and Henry's eyes flit over to me.

"Yeah? Jac, how would it feel to get the first one-on-one date?"

I know it's absurd, but it feels like a test, one I am doomed to fail. Henry knows I'm a fraud. I know he knows I'm a fraud, but we're doing this dance in front of nineteen other girls. Still, no one jumps in to save me, and the camera is trained on me, so I have to say *something*.

"It feels like—" I start to say, then stop, grab my drink and take a sip to stall for time. My mind races, and I grasp for words, any words, that will get me through this. "I don't know," I finally say, "like it's not a big deal? Of course, it'd be great to get the first date, but it's not the end-all, be-all. It can only be one person, but Marcus wants to get to know all of us."

Ali crosses her arms, giving me a sour look. "Sounds like you're just trying to downplay it in case you don't get the first date."

I shrug. "Maybe. Maybe this is all just a defense mechanism, but I think it's an even playing field right now. If I don't get the first date, I'll make the best of the time I have." That's the right note to hit, I think. Play myself down.

I glance around at the other girls. Rikki and Andi at least look understanding, but I'm definitely getting some sour face. Henry moves on to another girl, asking about what Marcus said to her. As if from thin air, Kendall appears next to me, dressed in leggings and a crop top, her makeup perfectly applied.

"That was a good answer," she mutters. "They see you, don't they?"

I narrow my eyes, suspicious. "What does that mean?"

"We're only as powerful as the camera makes us," Kendall says. "And you are commanding quite a bit of power right now. Don't take offense," she says quickly, "it's a compliment. People are going to try and get in your orbit."

I take a slow sip of my drink. "Sounds like you're playing a game to me."

"Yeah," Kendall says. She grabs a glass of ice water with cucumber slices on the table in front of her and takes a long, measured sip, watching me. "We'd all be delusional if we weren't."

Kendall is prettier than me. Her short black hair brushes thin shoulders; she's ivory-skinned, and untouchable in a way anyone would find appealing. I'm not delusional about my own looks—I'm prettier than the average girl on the street, but I'm nothing compared to someone like Kendall. All I've got is my story, and that's what they wanted me for. Kendall—too sharp by half and looking for followers—is everything on late-stage seasons of *the 1*; she's my competition.

"What about you, Kendall?" Henry says, and his eyes go to the girl next to me. I feel my pulse quicken.

"Oh," Kendall says with a coy smile, "I think Marcus and I will find some way to spend time together."

The girls around her titter, and Henry looks at me, clearly awaiting my response.

The 1 Season 32 Trailer

Kendall, with a smile: Bitches get stitches.

Marcus, pacing with mountainous scenery behind him: What if I'm making the biggest mistake of my life?

[A montage of Marcus kissing women in different locations, ending with a long kiss with Jac.]

Jac, in a room in the mansion: I think I'm falling for Marcus.

Hannah, sitting poolside with a group of girls: She's evil.

The screen flashes to Jac, fingering a wedding dress: I'm not like other girls.

[Another montage of girls crying—Kendall, Aaliyah, and finally, Rikki.]

Shae and Marcus kissing in front of the Arc de Triomphe in Paris. Shae in voiceover: I'm in love with him.

[A shot of a closed door, splashing noises on the other side. Gasps from other girls and a woman's voice whispering, "Send her home."]

Eunice, sitting with a group of other girls around a pool: Oh, my Gooooood.

Someone yelling offscreen: You said he was talking about *proposing*.

Marcus, near tears in a dark room: I don't know if I can do this anymore.

A final shot of Jac laughing on a beach with dialog played over:
[*Bleep*] 'em.

Becca in voiceover as the logo flashes onscreen: Don't miss any of the
action on this season of *the 1.*

Brendan voiceover: This may be the most dramatic season *ever.* Stay
tuned on NBS, every Monday at 9 p.m., 8 central.

6

Cold Hard Bitch

I don't get the first one-on-one date, which, Charlotte explains to me, is because Marcus likes me too much. They can't start him off on a one-on-one with one of his favorites.

Instead, the date goes to Shae, who I am instantly jealous of. Shae has beautiful curly hair, dark brown skin, and an admirable job as a human rights lawyer in Portland. She's quick on her feet without being cutting, charming, and extremely popular with almost every girl in the house.

In other words, everything I'm not. I immediately know she will go far in the season.

The rest of us go to group date purgatory, split in half, with the first half going out that day, fighting over bathroom time to finish getting ready. I'm in the second group and left to wait for two days to see Marcus again.

The morning of our first group date, Priya pulls me into a room for another ITM. I've worn my navy romper with floral pink detailing, a sweetheart neckline hugging my chest, my legs looking a mile long if I do say so myself. "So," Priya says, adjusting her glasses as she looks at me, "tell us a little about the guys you've dated back home."

I blanch for a moment. I date as seldom as possible and the guys I meet—well, let's just say I don't know much about them. "Honestly," I start to say, "I haven't had much time to date recently, what with my writing and everything."

That's mostly true. I remember the last guy I was seeing in New York—casually, owing mostly to his excessive cocaine habit and

proclivity for sleeping with other women—sitting with me at a bar,
bleary-eyed as I scrolled through my phone, muttering to him.

"I can't believe she sold her book for that much. God, my books
are actually *good*, who wants to read this drivel?"

"Jac," he muttered.

"Oh, look, and of *course*, Carolina's publisher is sending her on
tour. Jesus, that's like ten stops. Wish my series had gotten that kind
of support."

"Jac, please *log off*," he said. "Come back to the land of the living.
I'm so sick of hearing about fucking publishing. I had a bad day
today, too, okay?"

I shrugged, chastised, putting my phone down. "At least you
make a living wage," I muttered under my breath.

"Speaking of," he said, turning to me in his barstool. He looked
haggard, the way the Wall Street guys who never sleep always did.
"I finished going through those tax documents you sent me, and
you definitely shouldn't re-sign your current lease. You're in okay
shape, but if you do another year at that place, your savings are going to be tapped out. You haven't even finished another book, right?
And with those sales?" He let out a sigh. Dan—that was his name. I
haven't really forgotten it, I just don't like to remember it. We were
friends before we started fucking and that had sort of ruined the
whole thing. Typical. "From everything you told me, even if you
sold another, it's not going to be for what you made on that first
trilogy. I'd get a roommate if I were you."

I hadn't said anything, staring down into my bourbon. I took the
hit. "This place is dead," I said. "Let's just go back to your apartment."

Priya is pursing her lips in the interview room, like she doesn't
believe me. "Sure," she answers. "Would you say your career has
made you not focus on dating?"

"I lived in New York," I say to the camera, already getting a hang
of what they want from me. "I got a huge book contract, and it was
really exciting. I thought my life would be, all, I don't know, single
and glamorous, real *Gatsby* vibes, drama and all, and then my book
didn't do well. I didn't like the idea of putting that much effort into

another aspect of my life like dating and not seeing it pan out either. I just . . . I needed a fresh start."

"Okay," Priya says, "a little depressing, but we can probably make that work." Priya isn't looking at me anymore, her eyes on her phone. "One thing," she goes on, glancing up at me then. "Charlotte says we're playing you as a successful author. The whole sad sack 'publishing fucked me over' thing doesn't really work for our audience. They don't understand."

"But, isn't that my whole thing? I'm rebounding in my career and love life."

"No," Priya says, "you're aspirational. You're a highly successful author."

"Oh . . . kay," I start. "But—"

But that was part of my persona. Successful author came off a little snobby. Failed author was relatable. Something about it didn't sit right with me, the producers stripping me of an important piece of my story.

"It's time to leave," Priya says, jumping up swiftly and shooing the camera guy out in front of her. I sit there, lost for a moment, unsure why, before I motivate myself to follow them.

I get into the last of the production vans before we take off, and when I look up, I see I've slid in right next to Henry.

"Oh," I say, "Jesus."

"I also accept God," he murmurs drily. A group of girls is tittering behind us so I take my opportunity.

"Why are you lying about my career?" I ask him, quick, to not give him time to think about my words too much.

"Because your book series getting canceled is depressing," he says as if he doesn't even know why we're discussing it. "And way too hard to explain to the audience."

"I know it's depressing," I say, pulling my sunglasses down over my eyes. We're not allowed to wear them on camera. "I lived it. But you have no idea how humiliating it will be when everyone up in New York thinks I'm touting myself as some bestselling novelist when the second book in my series sold two hundred copies and the third one got canceled."

"You think anyone is obsessed enough with you to know that?"

"It's publishing," I say. "Everyone's keeping score."

"Aren't you supposed to be the kind of person who doesn't care about what a bunch of smug New York assholes think of you?"

I look over at him, and there's something different in his expression than what I've seen since we got on set. He's sizing me up. I just can't tell if it's for manipulation or because he's seen me naked.

"I don't care what anyone watching this show thinks of me. I care deeply what people in New York think of me. I'd like to sell another book one day."

He smiles without showing his teeth. "It's funny you think people in New York City don't watch this show."

"Right, right. But they watch it for the laughs."

He shoots me a look that I don't miss. "Sure." Then he returns to his phone like anything I, a contestant, say is too inconsequential to give his full attention.

Irritated, I sit in silence for the rest of the drive.

About an hour later, we pull up to a big field. I take a look out at the vast emptiness, and then look back at Henry. "Not exactly California glamour."

"The budget's for later in the season, so try to be enticing."

I sigh. "Try not to humiliate me."

"No promises," he says, walking off to where the production team is gathering. I momentarily keep my eyes trained on his back until I spot Charlotte watching me. I wave at her and smile, going off with the other girls.

"What do you think's going on?" Rikki asks, catching up to me from the other van.

"Where's Marcus?" Candy says. She's unbelievably short and is bending her neck at a strange angle to try to see around Aaliyah.

Grace-Ann sighs. "I'm soooo fucking jealous of Shae getting the first one-on-one."

"Why?" I ask. "Did he give you some indication he was into you?"

She scoffs. "Didn't he give all of us that?"

I shrug. Kendall smiles her Cheshire-cat smile. "Not as much as

Jac," she says, nudging me. I'd think it was playful if I didn't know better.

"Don't you want to make sure this is real before you jump in headfirst, Kendall?" I answer with as much pleasantness as I can.

"I always jump in headfirst," she tells me. "It's my most charming quality." She winks, a game of one-upmanship.

"Ladies!" Charlotte yells, getting all of our attention. "Marcus will be here momentarily. Look alive. Smiles!" she says, pointing at me specifically.

I try.

"Great! And here comes our leading man!"

The girls go wild as Marcus gets out of a car, with a small blond woman in jeans on one side, and Brendan the host in an over-the-top patterned green sweater on the other side. Marcus is casual in jeans that hug his hips and a solid white T-shirt, accentuating the solidness of his body. The woman with him veers off to the producers, hugging Elodie and then putting an arm around Henry, grinning up at him.

She's Janelle, Marcus's producer, and she's fine. It doesn't matter. None of it really matters.

I turn away, focus all my attention on Marcus, who looks to be joking around with Brendan, laughing openly. For a moment, I think he looks right at me as he approaches our group with a charming smile.

"Hello, girls!" he says. *Girls*. That word again. We all smile up at him like he's the sun. "You all know I'm here to find my future wife and, well . . . I thought a little push might go a long way with that," he says, pointing at the white tent to our left. "Inside, I've picked out some wedding dresses for you all—but what I need now is to see which you'll pick out for yourselves."

The girls scream at this, going into a frenzy. So many of them have been dreaming of picking out their wedding dress from conception or whatever—maybe just since they got cast on the show. The producers encourage us to "act excited" as we head into the tent, which seems to be code for "try to kill each other so we can show women as animals desperate for marriage." In protest, I enter the tent last, which does not go unnoticed. One of the production assistants makes me have a staged conversation with Aaliyah about putting on wedding dresses and they get a clip of me saying the whole thing feels a little archaic to me. The things I shouldn't have said on camera are starting to pile up.

I go through the aisles, touching the fabric of each of the dresses. It feels too cliché for me to go with one that isn't white—I bet Kendall would get a kick out of that—so instead, I decide to go for an unexpected shade of white. What I said is true—I haven't spent much of my time thinking about wedding dresses. My entire life, I've lacked serious boyfriends and any desire to play into the blushing bride stereotype. It's a part of myself I don't much prefer to examine because it says something about my wanting so desperately not to conform that I turn into something I hate, which is a person who hates things just to hate them and won't let other people enjoy them.

Still, I hate these girls and their love for these wedding dresses, and I think it's wrong that they don't hate themselves, too.

"You should wear this one," Henry says, touching a dress as he walks over to me and pulling it off the rack. It's light gray, off-color and off-kilter but still elegant, an intricately laced top with a chiffon skirt tumbling down into an almost-black ombre. Henry is watching me thoughtfully as I run my fingers down the fabric of the front.

"Why?" I ask him.

One half of his mouth goes up. "Because I said so and I'm in charge?" he suggests, his eyes twinkling.

"So, that's what you think of me, I shouldn't wear white?"

"No," Henry says wisely. "That's what you think of yourself."

"I'm not like the other girls in that way, am I?" I do like the dress, I think as I look at it. It's a dress that doesn't give a fuck but it doesn't feel flagrantly anti-conformist either. "They look like they should be wearing white, but Jac—maybe we put her in something else.

"But then again," I say. "You being in charge? I need a better reason than that."

He looks down at the dress, really letting his eyes linger on it, and then back up at me. "Marcus will like it," he says. "And who knows, I might, too."

I'm taken aback by that, letting myself believe it's real. I'm struck by him all over again then, his soulful eyes, the way his forearms in T-shirts are almost obscene to me. "Are you allowed to flirt with me?" I ask him.

Simply, he says, "It's my job."

I can't help the way I feel my lips curl at the corners, my cheeks going up in protest to what I want to say. "Well, you suck at it," I tell him.

"Okay," he says simply, putting the dress back on the rack. "Bye, Jac." He turns easily and waves at me without a second glance, complimenting Rikki on the tastefulness of her ivory jumpsuit as he goes by her. She gives me a wry smile and winks.

"He's right," Priya says, from the other side of the rack, where it appears she was listening to our conversation. I jump at the sound of her voice, feeling like I was caught doing something wrong. "That's one of the nicer dresses we brought. Charlotte wanted you to have it."

"So she sent Henry to try and flirt me into it?"

"Yeah," Priya says, "and me to tell you what she wanted so you'd actually do it. We're about ready to get started, so get it on," she says, and then takes off, talking into her walkie-talkie.

I look up at Henry again. He's tousling one of Kendall's curls with a smile.

Fucking hell.

I put on the dress.

In front of the mirror, I take the time to admire myself for a moment. While the dress hasn't been tailored to fit me, it still hugs my body nicely with a dramatic effect I like the look of. I'm beautiful. Charlotte knew me well, something I have the foresight to find scary.

Ten minutes later, we all line up in our wedding dresses, the nine of us on this group date, varying heights in various shades of white. Marcus is looking at all of us with appreciation.

"Wow," Marcus says, "how crazy is it to know my wife could be out here dressed in one of these dresses."

The girls beam.

The stupid thing is, despite myself, since arriving here, I really want Marcus's attention. I came here with a plan, and the unwritten rules I'd signed up for were to be a clown in a wedding dress and laugh along with the audience at the ridiculousness of it all so they might be charmed by me. I'd flirt with Marcus and he'd kiss me in front of fireworks and then quietly send me home before the hometowns episode, wherein my hundreds of thousands of social media followers would feel awful for me and buy my books. But I wasn't supposed to be thinking about Marcus, about how much I liked his eyes lingering on me and how sure I was Charlotte had told him to let his eyes linger on me. I would allow myself to have fun but no more than that. I would not become another victim of *the 1*'s Stockholm syndrome.

"Marcus obviously wants someone who will look great in a dress. Think we've nailed that, don't you, Marcus?" Brendan asks him with a laugh. He returns the smile.

"Without a doubt." Marcus looks out at us again. "But my life isn't all glitz and glamour. I love to get back to basics and"—he shrugs—"I like to get dirty." One of the girls releases a quick groan. She'd probably already gotten too attached to that dress. "So," Marcus says, "I'm putting you all to the test."

Brendan points at the woods behind him. We follow as the entire crew moves in that direction until we see a ten-foot or so climbing wall headed into the woods.

Brendan, looking gleeful in an evil sort of way, announces, "Welcome to the first ever *the 1* wedding obstacle course."

I stare over at the producers as Brendan explains how the course will have us fighting off exes and mother-in-law obstacles and some other things that make me weep for humanity. The producers and their assistants aren't even listening, already they're plotting together.

I don't want to do this, but I'm going to do this. *That's* what I'm thinking.

After a lot of getting both us and the cameras in the places they want us to be, the assistants line us up, ready for Marcus to tell us to go. Just before, Charlotte saunters over, getting close to me.

"There's a bet going," Charlotte whispers to me, "and I have five hundred dollars on you."

"Bullshit," I say, turning to face her. "Are you just producing me to try and tear out another girl's throat?"

Charlotte laughs. "I mean, please do if you have the notion, but mostly I'm trying to take five hundred dollars off of Henry. He picked Kendall."

I narrow my eyes. Charlotte seems to take pleasure in this.

"You two get along well, don't you?" she says, without qualifying who.

I smirk. "I don't know what that means."

"Just get me the gold," she answers, stepping back.

And then Marcus tells us to go.

I take off, my competitive fire stupidly stoked. (I don't know if there was ever really a bet. There could've been; the producers loved to bet on everything.) And then there I was, in a wedding dress I'd been told to wear, climbing a wall I'd been told to climb, not letting myself think about it too much because that would cause me to finally off myself.

I've got a pretty good start on most of the other girls, but my feet are getting tangled up in my dress. I stop and tear off the bottom of it, and use the scrap to tie my hair up in a ponytail. The cameraman who catches it lets out a wolf whistle, and I give him a smile.

The next obstacle is one of those spiderweblike rope nets. Kendall catches up to me at the bottom of the net. I am fully aware in the moment that this is ridiculous and a joke, but I can't help it: I want to win now. I leap down on the other side of the net, my right ankle turns a little, and I keep going.

We have to crawl through the mud next because of course we do. Then it's up another wall with a hanging rope and the finish line. Kendall crawls a little faster than I do; we both take off toward the wall. My bad ankle gives out; I lunge toward the wall rope to beat her there and knock her down.

Fuck.

"Sorry!" I yell. "Sorry."

I get back to my feet and hold a hand out to her. She grabs it and uses her full weight to pull herself up, and my ankle goes again when I brace myself.

"Jac!" Priya calls out to me. "Are you okay?"

Kendall has taken off way ahead of me and wins—both the competition and the extra time with Marcus during the night portion of the date. I skirt the wall and limp in behind her.

Henry runs over to me as I limp over the finish line. "Did you hurt yourself?" he asks. His eyes are twinkling with the ghost of a laugh he doesn't give in to.

"I'm fine," I say. "Bad ankles, used to fall on them during softball. Probably just need to wrap it up tonight and wear flats."

"That was . . ." Henry starts. "That was something. I'll get medical."

Charlotte hurries over. "She says she's fine. Someone get Marcus over here. Jac, sit on the ground and grab your ankle."

"What? No!"

Charlotte gives me a light smile. "I will hold you down."

I sigh. I don't want to put the weight on my ankle anyway, so I go down, in my muddy wedding dress. Other girls are crossing the finish line now, but the crew doesn't have eyes for anyone but me.

"Jac!" I hear Marcus's voice as Elodie hurries him over to where Charlotte is sitting with me. She smoothly moves out of frame as Marcus crouches down next to me. "Are you okay?"

"No," I tell him, taking a deep breath. "I lost to Kendall."

He laughs. "Your ankle?"

I shrug. "I don't know," I say. "I probably couldn't run a marathon on it." I smile up at him and he returns it before he reaches down and helps me back to my feet.

"I gotta say," he tells me, "I think the dress looks better on you now than it did at the start."

I stick out my injured leg pointedly, flexing it. When I'd torn the dress, the slit had gone a little higher than I intended. (Honestly, at the time, I think I look pretty fucking hot, but when it aired on TV later, I look unhinged—my hair is matted and I'm sweaty, covered in mud and bug bites, but right then, I'm pretty sure I'm on top of the world.)

"Not bad, huh?"

"I wouldn't send you away from my room," he says. The words send my pulse racing. When I had watched Shailene's season, I had always liked how straightforwardly sexual Marcus was. ("At least if I'm going on this show, he'll make sure I have a good time," I told Sarah over Zoom.) "I have to go talk to the other girls," Marcus whispers to me.

"Aw," I answer. "Why?"

Even though we're close, he takes my hand and kisses it. "I'll see you for cocktails tonight, okay?"

Slightly dazed, I watch him go.

WE GO BACK to the mansion to clean up and get ready for the cocktail party later. Several of the girls are giving me looks of various coldness, and when I ask Rikki why, she whispers to me, "They thought you were faking your ankle injury for attention."

I show her my ankle tightly wrapped with ice, which medical had confirmed was sprained at the obstacle course. "Yeah, this is all for show."

Rikki shrugs. "I didn't say *I* thought that. You asked."

"You're right," I say, turning back to my reflection in the mirror. "But I'm not desperate like some of these girls."

Rikki laughs. "And you wonder why they aren't warming up to you."

I glance back at her. "No need to make good points when I'm injured."

"Just try to be nice tonight," she suggests. "If you want them to like you."

I think about it for a minute before I say, "I don't though," and we both giggle at that. "But I'll try," I say once we stop laughing. "To make nice."

"It worked on me," Rikki points out.

"Hon," I say. "You were just drunk."

"It's *the 1*," she tells me. "We're all a little bit drunk." Then she thinks about that for a minute. "I guess except that teetotaler from the season that was on when I was in high school."

"Rikki, if you're going to directly sniper me, could you at least wait until I'm standing over my grave so I make a clean fall?"

Even as she's still laughing, she says, "Don't say that to the other girls tonight."

"Why?"

"Because it will alarm them."

Cars come to get us at half past seven. My dress is one I'd thrifted beforehand, a long emerald green with the skirt flared slightly for maximum girl-next-door vibes, and my ankle taped, wearing the shortest kitten heels Rikki had brought along. We pull up to a hotel, a nondescript downtown LA spot, where we are ushered in and given champagne. We wait a bit for Marcus to arrive. There are *so many* of us still, a fact that Charlotte felt the need to bring up to me as we waited for drinks to arrive.

"I really think you should jump in there first," she tells me. "Priya agrees."

Priya is off talking to Aaliyah, but I doubt if there's ever been a time in Charlotte's life when she's sought advice from Priya.

"I don't know," I say. "Seems a little aggressive."

Charlotte laughs. "Aggressive is what Marcus wants. You watched last season, didn't you?"

Yes, I had, and her point was well taken. Marcus had no interest in shrinking violets, and I need to make sure Marcus continues to notice me.

"I don't know, Jac, it's just really easy to fade to the background at this point in the journey."

"You're right. I do want to make sure I'm not stealing the other girls' time, you know?" I say, thinking of Rikki's words earlier.

"Trust me, Marcus is much more interested in talking to you," she says. "I just want to give him that chance."

Listen, here's the fucked-up thing about this show. There are so many times when I straight up know what's happening—I *know* that I'm being told what to do, and at some point, I become convinced that I *do* in fact have to do that thing. And anyone watching me sees that and thinks, "Not only are you a terrible person, Jacqueline Matthis, but you're an idiot for getting tricked into that."

I put a whiskey into Marcus's hand as soon as he arrives. He hugs me first, and I wait as patiently as I can while he hugs the other girls. "Marcus," I say, after he has greeted us all and given the obligatory toast. "Can I actually steal you for a second?"

It's the thing they all say—everyone on *the 1* since time immemorial—and it just came out of my mouth.

And then I get exactly what I want: "I would love that," Marcus says.

We get settled on a couch, distancing ourselves from the other girls in another room, set up for this purpose. Priya is there with Marcus's producer, Janelle.

Immediately, Marcus's hand is on my leg. It's an odd thing, but I like it and I don't. The intimacy feels presumptuous but also good, like maybe it's the right presumption. I know deep down that it's a good thing for me because it means he likes me. He wants to touch me.

I hate how hard I think about it, but it makes me feel special.

"I've been looking forward to seeing you again," Marcus tells me.

I do my best to look coy (later read as disingenuous). "Was it worth the wait?"

"You better believe it." He leans in, his hand going to pull me in closer to facing him. "You were really something during that obstacle course today."

I look down, almost embarrassed. "I get a little competitive," I admit.

When I glance back up at him, he tilts his head to the side. "I did say I wanted a girl who was willing to fight for me. I haven't always gotten that."

We both laugh lightly at that, but what he says, it's a bit on the nose, and I immediately wonder if he's talking about Shailene, playing into some storyline. My eyes find the camera lens right over his shoulder. "Not at the camera," Priya quickly chides me. I look back at Marcus, his expectant eyes on me, a correctly trained puppy.

"My ankle is—uh—a little swollen," I tell him then, not sure what else to say. I show him my ankle through the slit in my dress and he grabs onto it, his bare skin against mine. His hands are big; that's one of the things I like most about him, physically. The way he takes up so much space, how his hand can hold on to so much of me at once.

In some ways, I'm a simpler girl than I wish I was.

"You're tough. I like that about you." He drops my ankle and leans his elbow into the back of the couch we're sitting on, his body turned fully into me. "I can tell the stress of the show won't get to you."

"Really?" I ask, mimicking his position. "Did it get to you?"

"Sometimes," he admits with a sheepish grin, as if remembering some past embarrassment. He leans in closer than me, like he can shield us from anything the mics we're wearing might catch. "It's the oddest thing about the producers. You know they're trying to manipulate you, but you'll still always be trying to please them. Eats away at your soul a bit."

"Yeah?" I say. "I'm still managing to hold on to my soul right now."

Marcus shrugs, but his smile falters a bit. "Just watch out for Henry. He was my producer last season."

My eyebrows go up. "But he's not now?"

Marcus doesn't answer for a moment, and then, "C'mon, Marcus," his producer, Janelle, calls. "You know we can't use any of this. Can you talk about something else?"

"Fine." Marcus smiles, aggressively pleasant, and I read it as us being in on an inside joke, that we are following the rules that we don't want to. "Who are you, Jacqueline Matthis?"

"Shit," I mutter. (To be clear, none of this conversation will ever air on television because *the 1* is only interested in the depth on the shallow side of the pool. Please list your job, interests, and trauma and proceed through the door to the left.) "I guess that's kind of the thing about me. I'm never quite sure who I am."

"Yeah," Marcus says. "I know what you mean. You don't go on this show if you have perfect clarity in where your life is headed, do you?"

I laugh, feeling that moment of kinship, one I feel like I've been looking for in the past five years, as friends have gotten married and had kids and progressed in their jobs. *Of course not.* "It doesn't scare you to be in your thirties and still lost?" I ask.

"Scares the shit out of me," he returns.

"Can I kiss you now?" I ask, biting into my lip. He leans forward without hesitation and captures my mouth with his own. The kiss lasts longer than our kisses before; it's slow and suspenseful and leaves off with the promise of another before Marcus walks me back over to the other girls and leaves with Grace-Ann.

Henry grabs me for an ITM and I say some bland, predictable things about Marcus, and he looks tempted to fall asleep.

"So, how do you feel after today?" he is asking, going for it at a different angle.

"I think this process could be working for us," I say.

"Journey," Henry says.

"What?"

"Say that again, but say, 'I think this journey might be working for us.'"

"Absolutely not," I return. "That's a nonsensical sentence and I'm a writer. I'm trying to use language in a precise way."

"Right," Henry says, "but on this show, we say 'journey,' not 'process.' Otherwise, it makes it sound like we're sticking you all in a big assembly line and spitting out a couple at the end for ratings."

"Yeah," I say slowly, "but to be clear, that *is* what's happening here." I cross my arms; something about him makes me feel particularly antagonistic. "I am still allowed to think my own thoughts."

"Journey," Henry repeats.

I flip him off with both hands (which eventually airs with my hands blurred during a fight I have with another girl later in the season), and then he looks at the cameraman next to him, making the kill gesture. "I think we're done here."

When I go back to the other girls, a dull conversation about manicures is going on. A few girls come and go with Marcus. When Aliana leaves for her time, Kady turns to us excitedly. Kady is a short, perky redhead with a gift for gossip and, in my opinion, short-term staying power on the show. There's just not much substance there. But she looks like she's itching for conversation when she launches into her news.

"Ali's not doing so hot," Kady says, twirling a piece of long, auburn hair around her finger.

I squint at Ali's disappearing form. "Why?" I ask.

"Because she misses her daughter," Kendall says, throwing her hands out at me like it's obvious.

Rikki jumps in politely and says, "I'm sure Jac didn't know she had a daughter." She takes a long gulp from the wine in her hand.

I don't answer because, honestly, I don't care, and neither Kady nor Aliana interest me in the slightest.

We wait and wait and wait. Time seems to have stopped moving as we talk to each other, and then the producers, and then each other, and it's so deadly dull, I'd kill for something interesting to do.

"I quit my job to be here," Grace-Ann says, pulling me out of my reverie.

I almost spit out my drink. "You quit your *job* to be here?" I demand. "*Why?*"

"Because Marcus is my person," Grace-Ann says, serious as a heart attack. I toss back my head and laugh.

"Are you insane?" I ask her. I've been drinking too much, again.

"Actually," Kendall cuts in. "Plenty of contestants have quit their jobs and ended up with the lead."

"Oh, come off it," I answer. "Join a dating app."

"*Jac*," Rikki whispers under her breath but actually loudly enough that we can all hear it because she also doesn't realize how drunk she is. "You're being rude again."

I sigh. "I'm sorry. You're right. I know not everyone can just leave their job behind for three months." I glance at Rikki. "I guess you just hope shit works out for the best. Because that's how life so often works, am I right?"

Kendall glares at me. "You know we're not all too stupid to understand sarcasm, right? Maybe you should come down off your high horse, Jacqueline."

"Why don't you tell the other girls what your job is, Jac?" Priya says, easily hopping into the convo. I glance at her, ready for a fight, but when I look back at the other girls, they're watching me with interest.

"I'm an author," I say after a beat too long.

"What, like, for real?" Grace-Ann asks.

Kendall's eyebrow raises delicately. "And would we have read any of your books?"

I glance up at the producers and camera crew who are watching us. I can role-play as someone successful. "Oh . . ." I draw out the word. "I don't know. Probably. If you're a person who reads books." I meet Kendall's eyes as I say this. "They're pretty big in book clubs." Lie. Lie, that I can only inevitably be caught in, but Henry smiles at me over Kendall's shoulder.

Suddenly, Aliana is back upon us and she is crying. "Stasia," she tells us through tears, "took my time with Marcus. We were talking about my daughter and she just . . . she said she needed him."

"Hey," Grace-Ann says, quickly jumping up and putting an arm around Aliana, "hey, it's fine. It's all going to be all right."

Aliana sits down next to Grace-Ann, still sobbing. Aliana is drunk; we're all drunk. I glance over at Rikki, who shrugs in response to the shit show currently happening.

"I just—" Aliana is still saying. "This is so hard, and we were really getting somewhere. She's been trying to get in between us since the obstacle course today."

"What do you mean?" I can't help but ask, a mixture of boredom and alcohol fueling me.

Ali looks up at me with tears in her eyes, and my cold heart melts for a moment. She really does look heartbroken. "She told Grace-Ann during the race that me having a baby as a teenager showed a lack of class and was why Marcus would never pick me."

Rikki's mouth drops, and I frown. "She said . . . *that* to you?"

Ali starts to say something, shakes her head, and falls into Grace-Ann's side again. Grace-Ann just nods.

"In what context did she manage to throw that in?" I ask, perplexed. And then for good measure, I say, "That's so fucked up."

"Surely you can find another way to say that," Elodie interjects into the conversation.

"If shit's fucked up," I tell Elodie, looking over at her, more belligerent than I have any business being, "I'm going to call it fucked up."

Kendall inclines her head toward me. "When she's right, she's right."

As the volume of the girls increases in line with their consumption and indignation over what to do about Stasia, I get up and sneak over to the bar. Elodie follows me in a deeply obvious way.

"Old-fashioned," I tell the bartender as Elodie sidles up and leans into the bar next to me. I lock eyes with her so she knows she has my attention.

"Maybe you should talk to Stasia about what she said to Aliana," Elodie suggests. "Clear the air?" She shrugs.

I haven't said a word to Stasia since I got here. I only vaguely know what she looks like. "I think not," I mutter back to Elodie.

Elodie's eyebrows knit together, confusion. "Aren't you trying to ingratiate yourself to the other girls? Stand up for women? It's kind of slut shame-y, what Stasia said, isn't it?"

I sigh deeply. "Elodie, I'm sorry, but I didn't discover feminism last year. Save your social media buzzwords and talk to me when you have a better pitch for me to do something incredibly stupid."

Someone chuckles from the corner, and I know who it is, his voice getting right under my skin. Henry is looking at me again, the way he did with that wedding dress earlier. "What do you want?" I ask, watching him over my shoulder and feeling Elodie walk away behind me. Without prompting, I scoop up my drink from the bar and go over to him, leaning back against the wall next to him, off-camera.

"You're not allowed to hide by standing next to me," he says.

I survey the scene from this distance, the girls all mostly too drunk to make intelligible conversation, comforting a crying Aliana. "So, send me on my way," I answer Henry, but when my eyes meet his, he's smirking. This is the closest we've been since my hotel room, and it's so surreal, the way we existed there in real life and now nothing is real, and everything is about Marcus and Marcus's favorite thing, and the date with Marcus. Henry's whole physical presence is like a lodestar, a reminder that my entire life is still real, and when all this is over I am still fuckup Jac, and that's good and it's bad.

I don't know. It's all still there.

"So, you put a teen mom on this season and then talked Stasia into saying some judgy shit."

"I don't know. Maybe," Henry concedes. "Some people stir the pot when they realize they have no chemistry with the lead and know it's the only way they'll get on television. Not a problem you have."

His face is neutral as he says it.

"Why me? Why should I defend Aliana?" I ask him. "She doesn't even like me."

"Have you given her any reason to?" Henry asks, a glance at me that gets under my skin.

I take a sip of my drink. We both already know the answer to his question.

"Look," Henry says, "you don't need the extra screen time, but if you're going to be here awhile, then what you do want, when push comes to shove, is for some of the other girls to have your back. Otherwise, you are not going to be in for a fun twelve weeks."

"What are you suggesting?" I ask, turning my body around fully to face him. "I lead some sort of mob in to dispatch Stasia in an attempt to make her public enemy number one instead of me?"

Henry laughs out loud. "Jesus, you have a dramatic imagination."

"It's what I get paid for," I answer, stone-faced.

"Just start the conversation. Reconcile them. You can do that, can't you?"

I study him, chewing my lip. Take another sip of my drink, survey the girls. "Just a conversation?" I ask.

"Isn't this what you asked for me to do for you?" he responds in a low voice.

It was. *Help me*. This was a chance he was offering me. A chance to be the person I'd planned to be on this show. To be the kind of person other people would like. *This* was my character.

I march back over to the group. "I'm going to go talk to Stasia," I announce to them. Everyone looks up at me in surprise.

"*You?*" Grace-Ann asks.

"I just think we should squash this," I tell them. "Peacefully."

Exactly, I think. *Exactly*.

"I'll walk you over," Elodie tells me before anyone else can respond. She leads me to a different room than the one where I met Marcus and opens up the door. There are Marcus and Stasia together on a white couch against an ornate backdrop, a room too big for the small amount of space they're taking up. My stomach drops when I see that Stasia is crying and Marcus is leaned in close, wiping away her tears.

"Jac?" Marcus asks.

"I just wanted," I start, walking into the room, "to talk . . . about Aliana . . ." and then I trail off.

Stasia devolves into loud, racking sobs, and Marcus quickly gets up, putting an arm around me and ushering me out of the room.

"We'll talk soon," he says, though his voice doesn't lack affection. Janelle appears at my side.

"Don't worry about it, Jac," she says. "It's not the right time."

"What's going on?" I ask. "Is she okay?"

Janelle gives me a pitying look. "Stasia was telling Marcus that her dad just died, and she's leaving the show to be with her family."

That hangs in the air between us like a dead body. I am fairly sure I can feel my soul floating away, humiliation ringing in my ears. I take a deep breath, and then I leave.

(Here's what I can tell you about how this episode aired. I whiningly complain to Marcus about my ankle, which the other girls have spent the last ten minutes reminding the audience is definitely a fake injury. I call Grace-Ann insane, which I actually did and which was a kind of fucked-up thing to say to her as she's really a lovely person. I cockily tell the other girls what a successful author I am. Then I storm into the room to demand more time with Marcus. I tell Stasia, who is in the middle of a tearful monologue about her father, that she's a selfish bitch as they show only her mortified face. I'm not even sure where that audio came from but my best guess is that it was me telling either Charlotte or Henry that I would not do something they were asking of me because I didn't want to look like a selfish bitch. The audio itself, by my estimation, was spliced in from at least three different ITMs or conversations I had while on the show. Stasia's teen mom comment never airs.)

What happens in real life is Janelle comes out ten minutes later and tells us the rest of the cocktail party is canceled. With some girls looking very sour indeed ("Maybe if Jac hadn't tried to get more time with Marcus," Kendall complains in the episode), we are filed back into vans in our evening wear.

Instagram DM from Amberly Morgan

Amberly Morgan

Freelance photographer by day, the 1 recapper by night.
Yes, I was on season 25 of the 1 and if you want to get into it,
I guess we can. Small-town girl in the big city. Podcast &
website—amberly will tell you anyway dot com.

Wednesday, 12:46 a.m. (after the airing of the first episode of *the 1*)

Hey Jac! I don't know if you know me, but I write a fairly popular the 1 weekly recap for Glow. I was *obsessed* with your first-night gown! If you don't mind dropping the link, I'd love to share the dress with my readers. Hope you are well!

Tuesday, 11:18 p.m. (after the airing of the second episode of *the 1*)

Jac—me again! I didn't hear back from you after last week, but I'm hoping you might see this message. The romper you had on before the (ridiculous) group date was fantastic! Any chance you could drop me the link?

Tuesday, 11:21 p.m.

Look, I also just wanted to say, I know people online can be brutal and I see what this season's edit is doing to you. I hope you're all right. I try not to get too involved with the contestants during their seasons to remain unbiased in my reviews but I'll keep pointing out the inconsistencies in editing where I can. I know Cat Butler from Amar's season would be willing to talk to you if you'd like to commiserate. If not, just wish you the best. I won't follow up on the outfits again if I don't hear from you. xo

7

Calm Before the Storm

The next day, Andi has the second one-on-one, and in the evening, I put on a pair of leggings and a tank top and busy myself with being alone. The producers have asked for volunteers for numerous girl chats, where a set of three to five girls must sit around and discuss a topic of the producers' choice. I can only imagine how many of those girl chats have been about me, which is likely the only way I've been able to avoid getting pulled into them. My ankle is still swollen and achy, but I try not to drag it too much, for fear of being called a faker. The assistants at least keep a steady supply of ice coming.

I go out to sit alone by the pool at first, but Shae, Aaliyah, and Hannah, a former Auburn sorority girl who won't let you forget her brother plays in the NFL, make their way out there with wine, and I scurry into the kitchen. I only last about twenty minutes before Priya shows up with a group of girls to shoot a chat. I decide to head up to the bedroom, even though the house is still too loud for me to sleep—not to mention that my brain is still buzzing too much. I've considered writing some of the thoughts swirling around in my head in the notebook Charlotte gave me at the start of filming, but it feels like the risk is too great that one of the other girls would find it and read it—or worse, one of the producers. At least reading could take my mind off things. My head feels so desperately loud, with nowhere else to turn my attention.

Upstairs, Kendall is alone in her bed, sitting up with her hair in a high pony.

"Oh, I can leave," I say as I come into the room and see her, but she waves her hand at me.

"It's fine," she tells me. "I won't bother you; I'm about to go to sleep."

"What are you doing?" I can't help but ask. She gives me a bored look.

"Meditating," she says. "I normally read before bed, but they can't have that, can they? Would give me less time to focus on Marcus."

"Yeah," I say, laughing. "It's hard to nicely say, 'Hey, Marcus is great but my brain actually needs more stimulation than that.'"

"They like to fuck with us actual women," Kendall tells me wisely. "The girls can find something to entertain themselves with but we actually know what we want. We're not going to fight like little kids to get it."

I raise an eyebrow at the clear dismissal of the other women, but nod anyway. It feels like an olive branch.

"You didn't do anything wrong last night," Kendall tells me. "So you shouldn't feel bad."

"And yet, I do."

Kendall shrugs. "The show is designed to make you feel that way."

"You seem to know a lot about it."

Kendall smirks at me. "I did my research. I'd never enter a situation like this not armed with as much information as possible. I like Marcus. I *want* Marcus, and I'm here for him, so I'll play along if they want, but I'm going to take precautions, too. Aren't you?"

"Trying," I say. "Sometimes—you probably won't be surprised to hear this—I do deeply want people to like me."

"Not that surprised," Kendall says. "Or otherwise you'd just own being a bitch. You're pretty good at it."

"Condescension is my love language."

"So you made a couple of mistakes. Kiss the producers' asses a little. I'm sure you can still get a good edit. What matters most is Marcus really likes you."

Briefly, I feel warmth in my traitorous stomach. But then I more fully assess the situation and come to the conclusion: Kendall is better at this than me. "Yeah," I say, "I guess that's true."

"Well, I'm out," Kendall says, flipping a sleep mask down over her eyes. "Some of us need eight hours a night to look hot in the morning."

She flips out the lamp next to her bed and crawls under the covers, turning away from me. I watch her, a mix of intrigue and trepidation. I don't know what to make of Kendall because some part of me actually thinks we're more alike than any other two girls in the house. But that might be what makes her most dangerous.

There's a knock on the door, and I get up to answer it. Henry is there. I step out into the hallway and close the door gently behind me.

"Here. Your ice," Henry says, handing over a frozen ice pack. "Elodie was busy and I told her I'd bring it to you."

"You're taking lowly assistant duties? Stop, I might start thinking you want to see me."

"Just doing my job," he says.

I smile. "Your job? Right. Kind of like when you told me to go call out a girl whose dad just died. That was cool."

He doesn't even deny it. He shrugs.

"What?" I say. "You're not going to pretend you didn't know?"

"Literally, just doing my job of talking to you; you make your own decisions. Well done, by the way."

"I thought you were going to try to make me look better," I say. "Not worse. You turned a request I made to you in private against me."

He sighs. "We just need some conflict, Jac. It's not personal." *Jac.* It rolls off his tongue so easily. "It's going to blow over. There'll be some new drama tomorrow, no doubt."

I lean back against the wall next to the door. "Is that the storyline?"

"You're a front-runner," he says. "Marcus loves you. We're not going to crucify you. That doesn't work for us."

I look at him for a moment too long, and I mostly believe him, but it sticks out in my mind, the way he weaves words together into half truths, and I still remember that first night. He didn't want to come back here, to this.

But we're both in it, and he's so good at it.

I could be good at it, too.

"But I do want to help. That's part of why I volunteered to bring up the ice."

Intrigued, I watch him. He leans in close to me—so close we could practically kiss—and says, "Kendall is coming for you."

I pull away, surprised. "What the fuck does that mean?"

He shrugs. "Just telling you what I hear."

I quickly look around again to make sure no one is listening to us. "But just now . . . I thought we were getting along."

Again, he shrugs. "Kendall's playing the game. You get girls like her sometimes, superfans who know what they're doing. Her cousin was on the show two years ago. I'd just watch out and see how it goes."

"You're just trying to play me against her, aren't you?" I ask, narrowing my eyes at him, and a corner of his mouth lifts as his eyes rove my loungewear.

"You want to do a shot?" he asks me.

"What?" I ask, pulling back from him. "Like, now?"

"Obviously," he answers.

Henry's eyes are like closed doors. Dark brown and stupidly infinite. I wonder so often if he even knows anymore what is authentic and what is absolute horseshit, because I don't.

"Yeah," I say. "I want to do a shot."

"Meet me out by the pool," he tells me. "I'm going to tell the girls we need to clear it out for something tonight."

"Why?" I ask.

"Because I want to hang out with you without everyone else around," he tells me easily. I didn't know that was something he was allowed to say to me.

"Fine."

"Ten minutes," he says. "Then come down."

I do as instructed, go back into the room, where Kendall has somehow managed to fall asleep despite all the noise in the house. I have no doubt many of the girls plan to stay up late drinking because the elimination ceremony is tomorrow night. For a couple of them, it will be the last chance.

After I grab a hair tie and go to the bathroom to check my

makeup, I make my way down the stairs, sneak past the party in the kitchen, and out the back door, walking to the far side of the pool. Henry is lying on a lounge chair, holding a bottle of whiskey. I blanch.

"You trying to get me drunk?" I ask wryly.

"Never," he says. "Two-drink maximum, remember?" We all got reminded of that pretty frequently; the rule was put in place five seasons ago to protect the contestants from themselves.

"Seriously?" I ask, plopping down on the chair next to him, facing him and keeping both my feet on the ground.

"Nah," he says, and we both laugh. "Fuck it. Let's have fun tonight. Consider this my apology for earlier."

"Here." He scoops up the shot glasses on the chair in front of him, pours me a shot and then one for himself. Our fingers brush as he hands mine over, and I try not to think about it even though I already have. We clink our glasses together and drink. Henry sets down his shot glass next to the whiskey bottle on the ground and then pulls the earpiece out of his ear and sets it down next to him, a move too unsubtle for me to think he doesn't want me to notice.

I sigh contentedly and shift to lean back in my own lounge chair, letting the mild LA night roll over me.

"I got my job on *the 1* because I was good at taking shots."

"I don't believe that," I say, looking over at him quickly.

He smiles. "I'm dead-ass serious."

"Okay, I'm intrigued. Why?"

"They needed an assistant who could go shot for shot with contestants until they got drunk enough to say whatever horrible and/ or hilarious thing we needed them to say."

"And that was you?"

"Try not to be too impressed," he says with false smugness. "The first time I met John, he said, 'Who is that blacked-out Asian kid?' And I stared back at him, fucked out of my mind, and said, 'I'm hapa, you dick.' Mind you, that was before two-drink minimums existed."

I giggle at that. "Who is John?"

"You haven't met John?" he asks. Then he thinks about it and says, "Well, I guess not that many of the contestants do. John Apperson, the creator of this little show you're on."

"Will I meet him?" I ask, intrigued.

"Probably," Henry says. "He'll love you."

I raise an eyebrow. "What does that mean?"

Henry almost looks like he'll laugh as he says, "He likes hot, mean women."

I think about that for a minute and then nod, agreeing with the assessment. "You don't even look like you could take that many shots down."

"Well," he says with a sad smile, "I was twenty-three then. And I *really* liked drinking."

"And now?"

"Thirty-five," he says slowly. "And I like drinking slightly less. Fuck. Twelve years of my life."

"What's your favorite season?" I ask. He thinks about it for a minute, and I hold my shot glass out to him. He splashes more whiskey into it.

"Maybe . . . uh, Lauren A.? That was my third season, right before I got promoted. It was obvious from the first day of filming she was going to pick Rhett, so the whole season was a bitch to produce, but I don't know, they're really happy together. I like when it feels like I've done something good, you know, led people to happiness."

"I wouldn't know anything about that," I say.

"Come on, don't you write romance novels?"

I shrug. "No one reads them."

"Well, either way, you're a romantic. Deep down in there somewhere."

"You too."

We sit with that for a minute, and then we both take our shots.

"So, what do the producers actually do all day? Just sit around thinking about how best to fuck us over?"

He chuckles at that. "Exactly."

"What then?"

"I don't know," he says. "Just what's going on with all of you. What your mental state is, what you're saying about Marcus and each other. We're just here to create opportunities for you to show-case who you are."

I lean forward toward him eagerly. "And who am I?" I ask.

He flashes me a sly grin. "A lit match on a very dark night."

I know the foray into poeticism was for me. "That's how wildfires get started."

I can tell he likes that when he answers, "Then sounds about right."

"What about Marcus?" I ask now that I've got him talking. "What does he say about me?"

Something passes over his face, though it happens so quickly, I'm not sure I didn't imagine it. "Come on, don't play dumb, Jac," he says, and then I'm definitely sure I imagined it, the way the words roll off his tongue. "You're number one on his list. He says he can't believe someone like you is even here."

"Hmm," I say. If that's true, it works for me. "Pour me another shot." I hold out my glass, and he obliges. I take the shot.

"Hmm? That's it?"

"Well, you have to tell me that so I'll be invested in this stupid show."

"Eh, if he wasn't really into you, I'd tell you to make some grand gesture to get his attention or you'll be going home tomorrow."

I look over at him as he throws back another shot. "I think you might be a bad person," I say, holding my glass out to him. He refills it.

"You think so, too?"

"Marcus said you were his producer," I say, looking for a telltale reaction.

He blinks, unaffected. "Yeah."

"Well, why aren't you his producer now?"

Henry shrugs. "Sometimes, it happens that way. Janelle is good with leads anyway, and we're all always kind of producing."

"Just seems weird if you were the one who knew him best."

"Marcus is a complicated guy" is all Henry says in response.

"How so?"

He takes a shot. "That's for you to find out for yourself."

We're both drunk now, I'm pretty sure. I doubt he hangs quite the same as he did when he was twenty-three. God knows I don't.

"I'm really different from Shailene," I tell Henry then. "How could Marcus like us both?"

"Aren't you sick of talking about Marcus?" Henry asks me, leaning his head back and staring up at the sky. "I thought you were above all of this?"

"Everyone has been begging me to talk about Marcus since I got here," I say. "It's conditioning at this point."

"Marcus probably likes you because you *are* different than Shailene. That's what happens when runners-up become leads. They're desperate for something new. I guess it's like breakups in real life. Shailene was a God-fearing sorority girl from a small town in the Midwest without much bigger aspirations. You're a hot intellectual who says rude things to be funny."

"You don't like Shailene?" I ask.

"You think I don't like her because she's not a mean intellectual?" he asks with a laugh. "What kind of New York stereotyping is that? I *love* Shailene."

I bristle slightly at the way he says "love," jealous a woman I don't even know is so easy to love. I wish I was easy to love, have wished that for a long time. But I am what I am, Henry's got me pegged there.

"I wasn't much of a New Yorker," I confess to him. "Maybe that's the romantic in me."

"Really?" he asks, and I see his dark eyebrows go up. "You have the vibe."

I chuckle darkly. "I thought so, too."

He sits up, suddenly more interested. "So, what's the story then?"

Our eyes meet, and I offer him my shot glass again; he refills without fanfare, and I down the whiskey. "I'll tell you mine if you tell me yours."

"Fair enough," he says, chasing down his shot.

"Why do you hate this job so much?" I ask him.

He glances at the door back to the inside of the house, whatever else is buried there. "Can't really talk about that here, and it's complicated. My past—" He shakes his head, batting the thought away. "Some things are better left buried so they don't eat you alive." He pours himself another shot without prompting. "I don't really hate it, though. The job. I don't know. I like the ending."

"Because you feel like everything you did to get there might suck, but you got there eventually. You helped two people fall in love."

He stares at me, blinking as if moving in slow motion. "Because when it's over, I get to sleep for three days straight."

I laugh, shifting my body around, leaning on my side to stare over at him, draped across the chair. "I moved to New York when I sold my book. I sold it for a lot of money. Like, a *lot* of money."

"So, it was literally a big deal."

I point finger guns at him. "Good one. I guess I had this image of myself as this, like, cosmopolitan artist, right? Like I was this creative, independent-thinking girl from the South, and I didn't belong there. Clearly my destiny was leading me to New York, to bigger things, where I'd be fucking bohemian but also maybe preppy and spend long summers in the Hamptons or *whatever*. I didn't just want to be rich and beautiful, I wanted to be important, too, like I was always promised, and I was, I would be, this book deal signaled that I was on my way, so I'd stop feeling so out of place."

"Careful what you wish for?" Henry guesses.

"Yes, and no." I think about it for a minute. "I've always had this *thing*, this desire to fit in while also standing out, and I've contorted myself into what I thought that would be. What a person other people wanted to be would look like. Shot," I say, holding my glass out to him. He obliges. "I thought it was, like, making a name for myself somewhere new, somewhere where making a name for yourself mattered. But once I got there, I had this realization. No matter how many times I reinvented myself to impress everyone else, I wasn't special, and I'd never been special."

"Been there," he says, a whisper, unexpected in its intimacy and vulnerability. I curl closer in my chair in his direction.

The truth is, even before New York, I drank too much and slept with too many guys, but it was different there, with the emptiness so much more pronounced. I spent all the money I made, trying to become the me I wanted to be—lived alone in a one-bedroom, went to all the best restaurants, took taxis three blocks. Lived like an idiot because I thought that's how I'd become a real New Yorker. My books tanked and then the void started to feed on my very soul, until I had to run home to escape it, to escape my empty bank account, to escape everything I had become and always was.

"I remember," I tell Henry, "I was leaving a bar alone one night—I think it was a Wednesday—and it was the most humid summer day, probably had been raining earlier. I was in heels because I wanted to be the type of woman who wears heels to get hammered on a Wednesday night in the city. I walked the whole way anyway with the skin of my ankle being ground away step by bloody step, and instead of going up to my apartment, I just folded up on the ground right outside of it, and I had a panic attack. I couldn't even make it inside because there was nothing left. I was lonely and depressed and I knew there was something wrong with me. That was months after my book series was canceled and I'd never even cried, never even let it show, but a single night in New York tore me to pieces."

"You don't need to tell me this," Henry says then, like he is protecting me from me, or maybe him.

My head lolls to the side. "Don't you want me to tell you things?" I ask. I like saying it to him. I never say it.

Our eyes lock for too long, and he speaks to me in that low voice again, an affirmation—an oath. "Yes," he says.

"So, I moved home," I tell him. "I moved home and I applied to be on *the 1* for what I only can assume are deeply psychotic reasons rooted around change and instability." I close my eyes for a minute, savoring the complete feeling of drunkenness, of nothing mattering. "Remember when we met, Henry?"

We teeter on the edge of a knife, both wondering if the other one will say it, but we don't, and it's our secret, forever and ever amen.

"Yes," he says, speaking in the cryptic language only the two of us know.

I don't say anything. Instead, I sit up in my chair again, both feet planted and facing toward Henry's chair, teeter close to him, reaching an arm out. I think I'll touch him, the way I've seen him so easily touch everyone else. He leans closer to me, puts a hand up, stopping me just short, and gets out of his own chair, rises to his feet. He offers a hand to pull me up, and we are so close. My skin aches for it, for someone to touch me, and up close, his eyes are like heat on me.

"Don't," he says, his lips barely moving. "There's a cameraman sitting directly in those bushes across the pool."

Face burning, I glance over and see the telltale red light glowing from the bush.

"Is that you?" I ask, trying to keep my voice as low as his, fighting to keep my anger under wraps.

"No, I swear," he tells me. "I just noticed him five minutes ago."

I let the thought roll through me like a wave. The hand he pulled me up with still hovers inches from my skin—he could just reach out and touch me if either of us was either stupid enough or drunk enough. (With the little footage they use from this moment, the sound is barely audible but the team helpfully added subtitles to make my words clear.)

I flip the cameraman off, take a big step away from Henry, and go inside.

Exclusive Interview with Guy Danson

Steveisthe1.com: We have with us today a very juicy interview with an ex of Jacqueline Matthis who reached out to me a couple of weeks ago. Thanks for agreeing to the interview, Guy.

Guy: No problem, Steve.

Steveisthe1.com: So, tell us a little bit about how you know Jac.

Guy: Jac and I went to high school together and we dated a couple of months. We sort of lost touch once we left for college.

Steveisthe1.com: Can you tell us a little about what she was like back then?

Guy: Sure. I don't think it will surprise anyone if I say Jac was kind of intense. She cared a lot about her grades and being number one in our class, and she didn't always fit in. She took everything so seriously. And you know, I've noticed a lot of contestants on *the 1* will talk about being bullied, and people absolutely mocked Jac, but she didn't care. That was the kind of person she was.

Steveisthe1.com: Interesting. You have to wonder if she internalized some of that, right? Like, when I watch her gaslighting some of the other contestants, it makes sense to me if she was someone who suffered in silence as a teenager and is now mirroring those behaviors toward other people as some sort of way to take power back. It gives me a different perspective. NOT that it excuses any of her behavior.

Guy: No, of course not. I'm just not sure it bothered her that much, though.

Steveisthe1.com: Hmm. Maybe because she's a narcissist? Not to diagnose people . . .

Guy: No, of course not. But that does ring truer to me.

Steveisthe1.com: Can you share any more about what dating Jac was like?

Guy: Honestly, Jac treated dating sort of like she does everything else. With efficiency. She scheduled it in and you got her when it worked for her.

Steveisthe1.com: Do you think she can even feel love?

Guy: She definitely didn't with me. I think she thought it would look good to date me and that was it. Her head was always some-where else.

Steveisthe1.com: Did you stay friends with her after you dated?

Guy: As much as anyone could be friends with her. She was just so focused on college, on leaving her hometown behind. I did hear she chilled out some after high school though. You see her social media now, she's much more a guy's girl.

Steveisthe1.com: She ran away from her hometown she now pur-ports to love? Sounds about right.

Guy: Yeah, we've all had a good laugh about it back home. She couldn't wait to leave, but she's really changed her tune now, hasn't she?

Steveisthe1.com: Thanks so much for your time, Guy. Anything else you want to add?

Guy: Yeah, sure. I'll drop my socials below so anyone who wants to watch more content about Jac can. I've also got exclusives for paid subscribers to my Twitch feed.

8

First Date

Jac—

**Our feelings are already growing
too hot.
Why don't we cool things down?**

Some of the other girls stare at me with barely controlled contempt when the date card arrives three days later. It's not just that they want the date themselves; it's that they don't think I deserve it.

Rikki screeches, though, and gives me a hug. It's sweet. Shae hugs me, too, though I suspect it's because she's running for Miss Congeniality of the mansion (down to fifteen competing girls after the most recent elimination). It feels odd to feel like I've won something to go on a date, but that's part of the game we play here, and this date is huge in crafting my story with Marcus.

"Congrats, Jac," Kendall says, her face carefully neutral. I look over at her, thinking about what Henry said to me. *Kendall is coming for you.* I don't know what that means or what I'm supposed to do about it. What *he* wants me to do about it, which is clearly something.

"Jac," Charlotte says. "Can we grab you for an ITM?"

I'm getting used to this, I think, as I follow her back into one of the rooms set aside for this very purpose. To being forced to talk about things I don't even spend that much time thinking about.

I know nothing about Marcus yet talk about him nonstop, to the point where I wonder if he's even a real person at all.

"How do you feel about getting the one-on-one?" Charlotte asks me. "Full sentences, remember." Like I could forget.

"I'm really excited to get my first one-on-one with Marcus," I say obediently and without much conviction.

Charlotte cocks her head to the side. "Let's talk about this for a second, okay? Like straight up, stop just repeating back whatever you think I want to hear."

I sigh. The truth is, I like Charlotte, a lot. Something I find particularly annoying because I know her job is to get me to like her. But she's refreshingly honest and down-to-earth, and she has more substantive conversations with me than most of the other girls in the house.

"Shoot," I say, playing at being game.

"Why are you here, Jac?"

"I'm here to find love."

"Oh, fuck off," she says with a laugh, looking at the cameraman and basically forcing him to laugh with her. "You took a look at your life and its current circumstances and you applied to be on this show. Why?"

"It felt like the right time to try something out," I say, scrolling through my mental catalogue of things that are acceptable to say. *Because I thought it would sell copies of my books* would probably be frowned upon.

"Why?"

I bite my lip. "I was sort of lost," I admit.

"The first relatable thing you've said. Okay."

I shrug. "I watched Shailene's season of *the 1*, and Marcus wasn't just kind, he was smart, too. How many men can you say that about?"

"Not many I dated before Alan," she agrees. "And then he went and knocked me up, so that's kind of rude."

I give her a half smile. "I've felt directionless, and I saw Marcus and thought, 'Why not?' When I've talked to him, it hasn't felt like work. I'm ready for something in my life to be easy. I think I'm, like, on this journey for some kind of stability in my life, and that's how being with him so far has made me feel? That's even what I felt watching him last season. He's like a rock-solid foundation to stand on. That sounds insane, doesn't it?"

"Not at all," Charlotte says to me encouragingly. I feel myself getting sucked in, forgetting the camera is there, forgetting I'm talking to a producer and not my friend over a glass of wine. It's fucked how fast that can happen, how fast you can suddenly think, *Shit, I really want this person to like me.*

I really want Charlotte to like me.

"Why do you want stability, do you think?"

I hadn't, really, because I didn't know that was what I wanted until I said it. That seems right. "Because you can't move forward until there's solid ground beneath your feet."

"You know," Charlotte says, sitting back, looking satisfied. "I don't think any of the other contestants have the depth you do. No, listen," she says as I roll my eyes, "I'm not trying to speak ill of them but I can't have these kinds of conversations with them. Like, bless her heart, but have you tried talking to Aliana?"

"Aliana is a sweetheart," I say. I think it might be a moment to play to the audience, the one who will watch. To try to have a tiny bit of fun. "We all have that one friend like her, right? Kind of dense but in a lovable way."

"Exactly," Charlotte affirms. "What do you think about Shae? Marcus is really into her."

"Nice." I shrug. "Almost too nice." Then I find myself growing suspicious. "Why are you asking about all the girls?"

Charlotte laughs. "This isn't a trap, Jac. I'm just trying to talk to you."

"I thought we were talking about Marcus?"

"Kendall thinks you're too old for Marcus," Charlotte says offhandedly.

"*What?*" I demand. "Marcus is older than me!" Then I collect myself. "I don't know why y'all are trying to start something with Kendall and me."

"Some people like to know what the other girls are saying about them."

"Well, I don't," I say. "Knowing what other people say about me is my worst nightmare." I stare imploringly at Charlotte. "Is it okay if I go get ready for my date now?"

Charlotte glances down at her phone, and then back up at me, as if debating it. Finally, she says, "I guess," and I race out of the room as quickly as I can.

AALIYAH, A LOYAL viewer of *the 1*, speculated to me before the date that we would obviously be doing something involving water based on my date card. Turns out she's right.

I pull up to a yacht club with Charlotte and Priya.

The club is in Marina del Rey, so close to Venice Beach, I feel it like a brand on my skin. The day is perfect in the way every southern California day insists on being. We walk down a long sidewalk over to where the boats are docked, and in the distance, I see the rest of the production staff standing on a large boat called *Seas the Day*.

Marcus is there with all the camera crews and lighting guys and Janelle. He's giving an interview, I can tell, and Charlotte reaches out and grabs my hand as we walk over to him.

"Don't sabotage yourself, Jac," she says to me, and squeezes. It feels personal and far too knowing of me when she says it, but I do feel this warm ball of sunshine in my chest at the sight of Marcus in a striped navy shirt and casual, preppy shorts, looking born for this day. I have on a sheer green cover-up, long sleeved and flowy, along with a hat that came in our complementary gift bag when we arrived on set (however, only my bathing suit, a black one-piece with so many cutouts, little is left to the imagination, ever airs on television—and it airs many, many times). Priya and Charlotte peel off away from me so only I will be in the shot as I walk toward him, smiling despite myself. The look Marcus gives me is like he is suddenly warming up from the inside out after a day in the cold, the smile spreading slowly across his face. I can't help but quicken my pace to reach him faster. He pulls me up into his arms and does a full turn while holding on to me. I'm a healthy five-foot-eight, but he has no problem lifting me, making me feel small enough to be tender with. He sets me down with a kiss on my forehead, our eyes locked on each other's. Weirdly, in that moment, I think Henry's not here today, and that makes this easier, somehow. I can always sense him when he's around.

"Hi," I say.

"Hello," he says. "Bonjour. Howzit. Konnichiwa."

"You trying to get all our greetings in now?" I ask, unable to suppress a smile. (None of this will be shown on television because it makes me look too normal. Can't have your average viewers relate to such a terrible person, and it won't be clear they're terrible if they do anything relatable, or, dare I say it, cute.)

"I learned, like, ten more if you want me to talk dirty to you later today."

I cackle in delight.

The day is easy and fun. All jumping off boats into Pacific water and kissing and touching. Marcus clearly finds my bathing suit as intoxicating as the cameras do, his hands pressing into my skin where the bathing suit reveals my ribs, his fingers in my wet hair, all of it combining to make my blood boil. The chemistry doesn't have to be faked.

It's hard to describe what a thrill it is just being out of the house, where it feels as if nothing and no one exists except *the 1*. While *the 1* might still be here with us out on the water, other things exist here, too. Other people on boats and sun and air that's not continuously recycled throughout the mansion, and real things happening.

Considering what a short time it's been, it concerns me how fast I'm feeling completely lost to reality.

After we get back to the yacht club, Marcus and I leave each other to begin preparing for the evening portion of our date. I film for over an hour, telling Charlotte my thoughts and feelings and whatever-the-hell-else about the date, and then she even follows me into the bathroom back at the mansion as I go to get ready for the date. She sits with me as I put my makeup on and eat the salad I secured from the kitchen.

"What do you want to talk about with Marcus tonight?" she asks me.

I don't look at her as I say, "Sex, drugs, and rock 'n' roll." I blot my lips.

"Don't tempt me," Charlotte says, leaning back in the chair she dragged in and closing her eyes, as if she might take a nap.

"I don't know, Charlotte, what do you *think* I should talk to him about?"

"It's a first date, right?" Charlotte asks, meeting my eye in the mirror. "What do you usually talk about on first dates?"

Nothing, I think. *I usually try to drink as many martinis as possible.*

"My family's a pretty safe topic."

"And your career?"

I raise an eyebrow at her. "You know as well as I do. Decidedly less safe."

"It's not just about the success or failure of your career, you know that, right? It's about why you write. What it means to you. Why you write about romance yet seem so opposed to experiencing it in an open and vulnerable way."

"Testing out storylines, are we?" I mutter darkly.

She shrugs. "Maybe we'll save that for the second one-on-one." She's not looking at me now; she's texting.

"You ready?" Charlotte asks me after she puts her phone away.

I take a deep breath. "Let's go."

THEY REALLY DID the damn thing for this date with a table set up far on a ledge overlooking the ocean. Andi had mentioned to me that the dinner portion of her one-on-one date was at a generic hotel, but the backdrop of our date is beautiful, perched up just above the blue water of the Pacific Ocean with the flashing lights on the Santa Monica pier stretched out below us, palm trees swaying next to a long bike path, and the mountains just over my shoulder.

It's easy to talk to Marcus, looking especially dashing in his perfectly tailored blue sports coat. He's open and smiles often, in on a joke with himself. He tells me about his life back in Chicago, the tech sales job he's still able to hold down, even with his extended time on the show, the restaurants he likes to visit, and the things we'd do together there.

I lean into my hand, staring at him across our untouched food, a plate of red Italian sausage pasta that looks mouthwatering, but fits in with neither my diet nor the sound design of the show. "I can't believe I'm saying this, but I can see it. Us together in Chicago." And then I laugh at myself because it's embarrassing.

"Why do you hate to say it?" he asks, interested. I'm surprised by the question. Marcus had never quite seemed at ease with this process on Shailene's season either, so I'd thought he'd picked up on my discomfort.

"This," I say, gesturing around at the menagerie of people watching us not eat and talk, "is insane. I just wasn't sure how I'd cope. I'm not sure I *am* coping, but something about this whole thing, about *you*, is sucking me in."

He likes that, leans in closer and grabs my hand. Truthfully, talking to men has never been particularly difficult for me because I do have some idea what they like. What they want to hear. I feel myself retracting into that role because it's one I know well. It's the most ideal time of any in my life to playact, but some part of me wants to stop it.

"Can I tell you something that might weird you out?" I ask, unable to meet his eye, trying to flex my hand he's holding. "It's—" But I feel myself being too real and want to stop it. "I don't know, maybe it's—"

"No," Marcus says, tilting my chin up so he can see me, a bounciness still in his voice, "now you have to tell me."

"Fine," I say, blushing deeply. I push my hair back from my face. There's a breeze on the air. "Meeting you has been so wonderful and being with you really has lived up to every expectation I could've imagined, but—and this is going to make me sound so ridiculous—a little part of me fell in love with you last season."

I notice then that Marcus has absolutely been whitening his teeth because his smile is so bright, it almost blinds me. He lets me go on.

"But not—not just what the edit showed of you. There was this moment, when you were talking about your dad's cancer diagnosis, and it was so vulnerable and so real, and you were so damn articulate." I almost choke on that, but I manage to keep it together. "I don't know, my grandmother had cancer, but it was different. I just—it was devastating, what you said, *you* were devastating, and something about it—it just clicked."

It really hadn't been a part of my game plan—it might have been the first time I really just let my narrative go with no thought—but I can see the effect it's had on Marcus, the way tenderness has crept into his eyes, his expression so open that even I momentarily buy into our love story. His hand caresses my face, his index finger feather-light as he rubs it against my skin. "Why are you so amazing?" he asks.

"I'm glad he's okay," I say. "Your dad." He kisses me softly.

I still remember it, his tears falling onto Shailene's shoulder—a purple sleeveless dress with a high neckline—as he told her about his father's cancer diagnosis. "Every day, I feel like I get closer to the reality of life without him," he said. "I go to sleep imagining living in that world, and it's worse than a nightmare, to imagine losing the one person who made you who you are. It's like losing an essential organ, but not all at once. You slowly watch them go, turn brittle, lose more of themselves, and you hang on for dear life. You hurt them with your wish for them to stay, and you hate yourself for that, too."

His dad had told him to go on the show; I don't think I could have left my dad under similar circumstances, but I don't know. I never had to make that choice. And then he'd gone into remission. Even Marcus's most virulent critics had been ecstatic.

"I feel like you know so much about me, but you're still a mystery to me. A good one," Marcus adds quickly. "You used to live in New York?"

Did I tell him that? I can't remember.

"Yeah," I say, wanting quickly to change the subject. Things had been going so well. "But I just moved back to South Carolina to be closer to my family. My brother is getting married next year."

"How long were you in New York?"

I swallow. "Five years."

"And . . . were you happy there?"

My skin is prickling dangerously. Everything in New York is over, but failing feels like it never stops being over.

"I guess not," I finally say, hearing the walls going up in my voice.

"A lot of people have told me New York wore them down. Is that what happened to you?"

It's nothing, I'll just brush over it, but my throat starts feeling like it's closing up. *New York. Failure. Empty bank accounts and shitty mattresses on the floors of shitty apartments and drinks and more drinks and publishers telling me my book is canceled.*

"It's a great city," I manage to say. "But I was homesick. Family is so important to me." That's what people watching the show always wanted to hear, how much you love your family.

Betrayed, I look at Charlotte, who's whispering to Janelle. I feel tears pricking my eyes. Angry tears. That story wasn't meant for the show.

"Jac," Marcus says quietly. "Are you okay?"

"I'm fine," I say, but then a tear escapes down my cheek, cementing me as a liar. "Sorry," I mutter, grabbing up a napkin and dabbing my face.

"I didn't mean—" he begins.

"It's nothing you did," I tell him, feeling more raw and exposed than I ever want to feel. "It's hard to explain."

"I'm listening," Marcus says, squeezing my hand tighter. I try to give him a closed-lip smile. His dad almost died and I'm crying over a fucking city.

"New York was hard," I finally settle on saying, since I know that's what they want from me. "Turning thirty and feeling lost was hard. It's just—" I take a deep breath. "I've spent a lot of my life searching out happiness. Which seems ridiculous. There's nothing wrong in my life, no reason I shouldn't be happy, but I keep looking for it like it's a hidden treasure everyone else understands and I don't."

"It may not seem like it," Marcus says to me quietly. "But I know what you mean. That's how I felt last season, like that happiness might be right there. Might be Shailene. And it broke my heart when it wasn't."

"But it's not just—it's not just love, Marcus. It's everything. It's all of it." I think I should be able to explain it to him, to this man who could be so straightforward and real with his father dying. A dating show didn't fix that.

But instead he says, "Do you think maybe you could find it here?"

And that's not what I meant, it's never what I meant, because the happiness I need is so much bigger than romance or fairy tales or beautiful dinners where I starve because starving is how everyone might like me best. That's not *real*. That's not what I want.

But that's what this show is. It's not about bone-deep sorrow or aching loss or anything that really matters. It's about a happy ending, however it has to come. And I'm here to play along. "I think maybe I am," I tell him.

Marcus kisses me tenderly, and when I pull away, Charlotte is smiling.

"TELL US ABOUT tonight's date," Elodie says. It's after three in the morning, and I'm stuffed in a small room with her, Priya, and a cameraman, still wearing my tight black minidress from our date.

"No," I say, emotionless. "I'm done. I want to go to bed."

After dinner, there had been fireworks, which had required more cuddling up and kissing. Then a long car ride back to the mansion where fourteen girls were sitting around in a circle, waiting for me to return. Everyone looked exhausted—Kendall looked murderous—and I could only imagine how long they'd been stuck sitting there, discussing my date with Marcus.

When they'd asked me how it was, I had simply said I wanted to go to bed.

It had taken about thirty minutes to squeeze a couple of platitudes out of me, mainly because Priya said they wouldn't let anyone else go to bed until I talked. Then they'd released the girls from the hostage situation and whisked me to an ITM room.

"You're not going to bed, Jac," Priya says, like an asshole.

"Or what?" I demand. "We'll all just die here?"

She stares back at me like it's not out of the question.

"We just need a little more from you," Elodie says placatingly, a good cop to the end. "How was your date with Marcus?"

"I'm done with this," I tell her. "You know *exactly* what you did. I didn't want to talk about—" I stop myself, swallowing around the words "New York." I hate having such a vulnerable underbelly, and even more, I hate having it exposed. "I want to talk to Charlotte," I say. "I want to talk to Henry."

"They're sleeping," Priya says, about three levels past over it.

I shrug. "Fuck off then." I lean back in the chair, closing my eyes. "I want to go to bed."

"What if we got Becca?" Elodie asks.

"Then you could have footage of me telling Becca to fuck off," I snap.

None of them says anything for a moment. I wonder if I've finally crossed some kind of unholy line. The irony of me getting kicked off *the 1* for being a bitch instead of for having sex with a producer is not lost on me.

"Okay," Elodie finally says. "How about a compromise? Just let us get a clip of you saying you're falling for Marcus, and we'll let you go to bed."

I imagine if I could've seen myself, I would've seen my eyes bulge out of my head. "Say 'I'm *falling* for Marcus'? I hardly know Marcus. We just had our first date."

Priya levels a deeply disgusted gaze at me. "So you don't like Marcus?"

Instead of looking at her, I lock eyes with Elodie. "Is the only way to become a producer on this show to be a massive dick?" Priya is seasoned enough to remain stoic, but Elodie snorts.

"Can I please have a little time to process things?" I plead to them both.

"Marcus is hoping to propose to someone ten weeks from now," Priya tells me, very seriously. "You don't seem like you're on the right path for that kind of commitment."

"Have you considered being on the path to suck my ass?" I slump down in my chair.

"So," Elodie says slowly, "you *can't* see yourself getting engaged to Marcus in ten weeks."

I'm not proud of it, but I actually scream. "I. Slept. Three. Hours. Last. Night. It is *4:30 a.m.*"

Priya leaves the room without saying anything, and I let out a sigh. Elodie, seeing the way my body relaxes, says to me, "She's just going to get coffee. Don't get too excited."

But I sense blood in the air. My chance. "Elodie," I say, coating my voice with desperation, "I am so tired. Please." And then, unbidden, because I really thought I was acting, tears come flowing down my cheeks. I am extremely aware of the camera pointed at me—at some point, you really do just get used to the fact that they're always there, and there's always a person behind them, running up closer to get a better shot as you make out with the man of their choice.

Elodie reaches out and grabs my hand. She's probably close to ten years younger than me, baby-faced and always supportive. "You're fine, Jac. I'll let you sleep in tomorrow."

"Can I go to bed?" I ask.

Elodie squeezes my hand, looks up at me with her doe eyes, and softly says, "Just say it."

I close my eyes; another tear runs down my cheek. I press my palm to my cheek, wipe it away, look directly into the camera.

And I say it.

Shailene Dowd's TikTok

150K
followers

[Video begins with Shailene running with her dog, Scout, entering her house, and kissing her boyfriend, Bentley.]

Bentley: Our FunFit boxes came in today. Check out my new socks.

[Bentley holds up a pair of blue socks with pizzas patterned on them.]

Shailene: You mean *my* new socks.

[Cut to Shailene and Bentley watching TV with Scout squeezed between the two of them, Shailene's pizza socks prominently displayed.]

Shailene: All right, y'all, use code SHAILENE at checkout for an extra 15 percent off your first month of FunFit box and get your own perfect workout socks.

Bentley: Maybe order two.

[Bentley props his feet up on the coffee table to show off his own pizza socks. Shailene shrugs.]

Shailene: Or three.

[She shows off Scout's pizza socks.]

[Click here link leading to FunFit box sign up.]

9

Ocean Avenue

The irony—if that's what you want to call it—is I don't sleep at all. I get up when Rikki does at 6 a.m. after tossing and turning for two hours. There's a cocktail party scheduled for that night, and some of the girls are trying to get a little extra sleep. I know it's a futile effort, but I especially admire Kendall for trying. Girl knows what she wants.

Rikki starts making me pancakes without prompting, and I immediately grow suspicious.

"So," I say, innocently grabbing an almost-bad banana up from the counter and peeling it back. "What did they say about me last night?"

Rikki doesn't look at me as she mixes the batter. "Everyone thinks Marcus likes you."

"Oh, so they were extra nice?" I ask, making my words syrupy sweet. "C'mon, Rikki, I'm a grown woman."

She cuts some butter off of a stick and throws it onto a griddle. It starts sizzling. "They asked if we thought you were unstable," Rikki finally says.

I take that in for a moment. "And what did everyone say?"

"I don't know. Some of the girls thought the whole thing with Aliana was weird, since you don't even appear to like her."

"Never going to live that one down, am I?"

"Kendall says you're just bad with people."

I bite my lip, tapping my nails against the counter. "What do you think she means by that?"

Rikki gives me a long look before she answers. "Do you think you're good with people?" She flips a pancake.

"Obviously not," I say, sighing and putting my face into my palm, leaning against the counter.

We both go silent as we hear someone coming through the house, whistling. Sounds like a cameraman is following, always following, always there.

"Good morning, ladies," Henry says with a cruelly devastating smile as he comes into the kitchen.

"Someone slept last night," Rikki answers, putting a pancake on a plate for me.

"Four whole hours," Henry answers triumphantly. "And there's an extra fifteen minutes of private time with Marcus for you if you make me a pancake."

Rikki says, "Deal," and goes back to cooking. Henry sits down and nudges my arm. I look over at him, not so subtly grinding my teeth. He knows.

"I heard you wanted to see me," Henry says. "I'm here."

"I'm going to finish my pancakes by the pool," I say, grabbing up my plate. Henry watches me go, his face carefully controlled.

As I close the door behind me, I don't miss his sigh. "Jac!" he calls, finally coming after me as I make my way over to the pool. I sit down, dipping my feet in. He stands there next to me in his black Nikes with gold detailing as I eat, staring straight ahead.

"What did you expect to happen?" he asks. "We were on camera." I chew.

"That's what this *is*, Jac. If we can't get through that rock-solid shell of yours, we have to make moments happen. We want the audience to *see* you."

"I don't want to be seen," I finally say.

He laughs. "Then you picked a really shitty midlife crisis to have."

"Midlife? You guys really are ready to ship me off in a coffin for daring to be over thirty, aren't you?"

"I'll make it up to you," he says, crouching down next to me. Up close, his dark eyes are on mine, and I wonder who he is. I wonder where he slept last night, back in his Venice bachelor pad or nearby.

I wonder who he slept with. "Marcus is coming to the house today. Pool party before he sends people home."

"*God*," I say, and he gives me a sympathetic smile. "I just needed a little time today."

"There's no time on *the 1*."

"Only Marcus," I answer him.

"I heard your date went really well last night." He waits a beat, and when I don't say anything, he says, "Pulling out the monologue about his dad. He basically cemented himself as the one with that."

"It wasn't a *move*," I answer, secretly pleased at how well it played. "I was being honest."

"Well, even if it wasn't a move, it was a pretty brilliant one," he tells me.

"You're sick," I say.

Henry stares at me, and it's too long. We both know it's too long.

Then he breaks eye contact and looks toward the house. "I should go do my job," he says.

"I'm pretty sick of you doing your job. I'm especially sick of you promising to make it up to me."

"Would you believe me if I told you I was, too, actually?" he asks. I don't answer, and silently, he gives up and turns away.

He's walking back toward the house, when I say, "Henry."

Mid-stride, he stops and turns back to look at me. It's cliché to say at this point, but he's picturesque, something about him unbelievably flawless—his skin and his eyes and his smile that looks like a lie.

"Was it real?" I ask him. "It felt real."

"Jac," he says, walking back over to me and crouching so we're eye-level again. We're both not saying what we really want to say, and that's what's so wrong. The code we speak in. The things we attempt to say with only the way we look.

"It can't be real," he says, his voice low. "That would be against the rules."

I swallow slowly and he backs away.

IT's 11 A.M. and I've been mentally preparing for a pool day for hours. Kendall and I are alone near the front of the house while a girl chat is happening in the den. I'm splayed out on a couch, and Kendall is staring out the window, holding a sparkling water, probably hoping something will happen. Even so, it still shocks me when she says, without a hint of surprise, "It's Shailene."

"What?" I ask, going to stand next to her at the window. She gives me a look, clearly seeing it as an invasion of space.

There she is. Shailene Dowd, the charming Midwestern lead of last season's *the 1*. She'd shown up to the first episode of the season, dressed as a fairy-tale princess, and left with practical, extremely sexual, and a touch possessive Bentley Routh, after romance had come crashing down for Shailene and Marcus.

Marcus had been steady and goofy, and more than a few people had found him irresistible, but something about Shailene had been so clear to me watching her season. Shailene was the picture of traditional values when she needed to be, but that wasn't really Shailene. She was as down-home Indiana as it came, but when you really got down to it, Shailene was a freak.

Dark brown hair, skinny as a rail, and fierce as fuck, I'd liked Shailene, even if she was so generic in her white, Christian beauty ideals, she'd practically been made for *the 1*. She'd sent more than a few guys packing for being absolute dickheads. There was one other guy in her final three, Alex, a hardcore Christian like her, and he'd played it against her, managing to hang on as a contender by constantly convincing Shailene it would be sinful to end up with Marcus or Bentley. In the end, after what was thankfully Alex's last temper tantrum—after Alex found out Shailene supposedly slept with Marcus during the overnight date—she sent Alex packing, flipping him off all the while. Shailene had her own code. When she told Alex to fuck off, she stuck to it, despite Alex insisting his code was the right one. It was oddly empowering to watch. I kind of admired Shailene, what a great character she was, and I admired that Marcus saw something in her.

She's here now, walking down the sidewalk in a white dress, legs like a dream. The producers appear to greet her—Charlotte and Henry and Janelle—and Shailene screams when she sees them, effusive as ever. She takes the rest of the sidewalk in a run and makes a leap into Henry's arms. He catches her with ease and spins her around, holding her into a hug before putting her down. It startles me, seeing him be so openly affectionate with someone, in contrast to the guarded way he's been treating me. He's not my producer, but he wasn't hers either. When I see it in that moment, I know: he's had a wall up with me since I've been here.

Elodie and Priya gather us around when Becca arrives with Shailene, and Becca tells us about the pool party on camera. We react with the obligatory excitement. Then she tells us Shailene is here to give us a real idea of what dating Marcus is like.

I change fast—I'd already done my makeup and mentally picked my bathing suit (a deep red bikini with an unbuttoned black cover-up that flowed down to my ankles) when Henry told me about the pool party. And, as I sit poolside, drinking a whiskey and waiting for something to happen, Charlotte grabs me.

"Shailene wants to talk to you," she says.

I pause, stare up at her. "Me?"

"Come on," she says. "Over by the cabana."

And there she is, in all of her bright, bubbly glory. I'm about six inches taller than her, and she hugs me like an old friend, grabbing my hand and pulling me to sit in the cabana with her.

"I see you," she says as I sit down, immediately picking up on my hesitation. Her smile could take out the whole of LA. "You don't have to be scared of me, Jac," she tells me in her soft, flat, Midwestern affect.

I smile, reserved. "I loved you," I say, "last season."

"Aw, you're sweet." She sips her own drink, a comically large margarita, to make me more comfortable. The producers and camera crew surround us. "So, tell me," she says. "Tell me all about Marcus."

Here's the thing about Shailene and Marcus—no one ever really knew what happened.

I maintain there was a zero percent chance she wasn't choosing Bentley; when they were together, they were practically insatiable for one another. But there was something with Marcus, too, a different kind of chemistry, a different kind of physicality.

Shailene was, famously, the virgin. All season had built toward an explosion—toward the deflowering. Like I said, *the 1* is predict- ably puritanical in its storytelling, always looking for the best sto- ryline. They'd tried virgins before, but none had resulted in quite the fireworks this one did. Marcus had been Shailene's first over- night date, the obligatory episode when you are finally allowed to spend time together alone, without cameras, with three suitors left. When Marcus's producer asked him the next morning what had happened, he'd been coy at first. But then the producer asked him, directly, "Did you sleep with Shailene?"—a question so important that they'd left the producer's audio in, Marcus famously said one word that launched a thousand TikTok ships, started a million Red- dit wars: "Yes."

The confrontation had led to epic, gripping television. Shailene had cried, asked him over and over again why he'd told them. Mar- cus had said it was because he needed to have an honest relationship. Even after everything, she'd begged him not to leave her there. But he did anyway.

It started an online firestorm that hadn't died down since.

That's what I see when I see Shailene asking me to tell her about Marcus—a girl broken down and humiliated. Instead, here, she's fresh-faced and breezy, talking about him with ease. I glance down awkwardly for a moment, the scene playing in my head, and then meet her eyes. "This seems like a trick. I was hoping *you* could tell me about Marcus."

"Oh, I got it. More of a giver than a taker." She leans in closer, her eyes bright and clear. "Yes, I totally see it. You're definitely his type."

I swallow, glance around at the producers. No Henry. "I thought usually when they bring exes on, it's to give the leads a big scare? Make them wonder if they can truly get over their past heartbreak?"

Shailene leans her elbow into the top of the seat behind her and her face into her palm, staring at me, a slight smile playing at her lips. "Marcus and I made our peace. I just want him to be happy," she says to me. She never breaks character; that's one of the things I grew to admire the most about her. There's no way she wants to be within ten feet of Marcus, much less talk with all of the girls he's dating. But you would never know from watching her.

"So," I say tentatively, "what kind of girl do you think would be right for him?"

Shailene tilts her head to the side, giving me an assessing look as if deciding how honest to be. "Marcus is an easy person to love," she tells me finally. "Bentley will be jealous to hear me say that, but there's something that's just giving about him. He wants people around him to be happy; he pours himself into them." She studies me closely. "Our breakup was hard, you know?"

"Sure." I nod. Shailene had been on the floor, begging Marcus to stay when he decided to leave. Some had said he was cold and calculating; others had thought that Shailene simply hadn't emotionally given him what he really needed.

"But that's because we're both the kind of people who feel things all the way, even if they're the wrong things," Shailene says. "What are you thinking?"

I swallow. "Scared that sometimes I half-ass feel the wrong things."

"Nah," she says. "Not you, I can tell. After the show, the thing I really realized I had learned about Marcus is, he wants you to want him. He's always excited about that."

"That's not a problem," I say. "I want him."

"I feel that," she says with a nod, but in a way that makes me sure she stopped herself from saying something else. "Hey!" Shailene suddenly shouts, looking from me to the producers. "I'm starving. Can I get some food?"

Charlotte sighs, crossing her arms over her protruding stomach. "Fine," she says, "but we've got to do a couple more of these."

"Of course," Shailene agrees, looking to me conspiratorially. "Jac, walk with me?"

They've brought in catering for Shailene—a stipulation, she tells me, she made production agree to before she would come to the mansion. Together, we walk, blessedly, out of view of the cameras.

"They wouldn't have let you come if I hadn't asked so pointedly," Shailene tells me, piling her plate up with sandwich quarters and chips in the front dining room. "The crew is going to love me though," she says, piling several pickles on top of her haul.

I grab a pickle myself and follow her to a corner, where she sets her plate down on an end table and grabs up one of the sandwiches, eating and standing there with me. "Why did you ask me to come?" I ask her.

She shrugs. "It's what I would've wanted if it were me. A break from the monotony." Her eyes travel around the room. "God, I do not miss this place."

I give her a feeble laugh.

"Do you like Marcus?" she asks me.

Curiously, I answer, "What I know of him, I like."

"Sure," she agrees, slurping down a pickle. "Marcus is plenty likable. Very plausible. What about the other girls?"

I shrug noncommittally and she laughs. "*Girl*. Watch out for the producers if you're digging that hole."

"Which ones?" I ask her.

She smirks at me. "All of them." She eats a chip and offers her plate to me. I take one. "Which ones are you worried about?"

"Jac!" Henry calls my name in the hallway, and our eyes meet as he hurries by. "We need you back on set in five!" he yells and then disappears. Shailene doesn't miss it.

"What was it like for you?" I ask her. "Not on your season, but when you were a contestant? How did you deal with it?"

Shailene shrugs. "I had my fights, but I was lucky enough that they wanted to set me up as a lead. Though to be honest, they made me look *so* good that my season was kind of a relief—some people turned on me after it aired, but at least the girl I saw onscreen felt like she had some relation to who I truly was, flaws and all."

"I liked you better after," I say, even though I hadn't seen much of her season as a contestant.

"See, I knew I liked you." She eats another sandwich quarter. "Some girls weren't as lucky with their edits. You've got to suck up a little, and if you have to resort to being a villain, you should cut a deal with your producer before you do anything too bad to get on *1 in the sun*. Work with them, not against them."

"Play into the storyline they want," I say.

"Sure. It's all about the followers you pick up, the deals you can cut after the show. I quit my job recently. Just didn't make any sense with the amount of money I have coming in from sponsored content." She eyes where Henry just disappeared. "You want to know about Henry?" she asks me, tilting her head to the side as she watches me.

It was something I noticed about Shailene on her season. She was perceptive. The only time she wasn't was when it came to Marcus abandoning her.

"Henry's good at getting me to say things I didn't mean to say," I admit to her.

She grins. "I bet he is." She takes another bite of one of her sandwiches. "Do you know how many girls on my season wanted to fuck Henry? On all the seasons?" She dabs mustard from her face, and I watch with jealousy at the gusto with which she eats the food. "One of the girls on a different season—she told me this at some event we were doing together after she got a little too drunk—she made a pass at him. Actually went for it, right after the season was over."

"And he was into it?" I prompt.

Shailene laughs. "*Henry?* Nah, I don't think he'd ever touch a contestant. But what I'm telling you is that's how he operates, Jac. You spilled too much to Henry? We all did. Who wouldn't spill their souls to a man who looks like *that* who you know you can absolutely never have?"

My cheeks burn, and I feel strangely called out. I slept with him before I knew, but he's been consistently manipulating me since well after we both knew, and that's how he did it.

You want to give Henry whatever he wants.

"Besides," Shailene says, "when Rachel tried it with him, he was engaged."

I stumble over that, momentarily forgetting my role. "Henry was engaged?"

Shailene taps her manicured fingernails against the table. "Yeah. His ex looked like a supermodel. Actually, you know what? She might have *been* a supermodel. I think they broke up while we were filming last spring." She glances up at me. "But we're here to talk about Marcus, right?" She gives me a knowing smile, and I wilt at the sight of it. Right.

Right.

"I better get back to filming before I get in trouble," I say.

"Godspeed, Jac," she says, taking another bite from her sandwich.

"CAN I TALK to you, Jac?"

I glance up. I'm in a corner of the back patio, drinking my whiskey and lounging alone.

"Come *on*," Charlotte said to me earlier when she found me in this same place. "You look like a real bitch right now. Loosen up. Have some fun."

"I am fun," I returned to her. "This is me having fun."

"Jump in the pool. Skinny-dip. Anything," Charlotte begged me.

"Charlotte," I said, meeting her eyes. "Come on. At least let me be me. That's all I've got in this godforsaken place."

She sighed and left me alone.

But I guess she'd sent Marcus after me now.

"Of course you can talk to me," I tell him easily. Before I've even finished, he reaches his hand down to me and pulls me up, interlacing our fingers as we walk over to the designated filming area under the cabana. When I go to sit next to him on a wicker loveseat, he instead pulls me gently into his lap.

"Hello," he says.

"Hi," I whisper, leaning forward and pressing my lips to his. As I pull away, he grabs my head and pulls me back more aggressively, his grip on me somehow soft but commanding. I take the hint, our mouths devouring each other in a way, to be sure, that radiates nothing but sexual chemistry.

As soon as it's happening and I'm thinking about it, I know Henry is there. I find myself wondering again and again what he's thinking.

He doesn't think about me. Not unless it means good TV. He never thinks about me.

"I needed that," Marcus says, smoothing my hair back as he pulls away.

"So, you missed me," I say, leaning my forehead into his. I want this. I can want this.

I want this.

"I missed everything about you," he whispers back to me, and in the way I sometimes can't help, I start to wonder about that. What it means. Me—the real me. My body. My face. Who I pretend to be when I'm with him?

Who could miss everything about me?

"How's the pool party?" I ask him, scooting back into my own seat. His arm stays tightly wrapped around me.

"Well, I just kept asking the producers where you were, which I think annoyed the other girls."

I laugh, even though the producers know as well as I do that this will only rile the other girls up.

"You do stuff like this back in Chicago?" I ask him.

He shrugs. "Sure, sometimes. Summertime in Chicago is the best three months of your life."

"What do you think we'd do together?" I ask.

"We'd take a boat on the water," he says. "Then go out to Au Cheval, this cheeseburger spot that doesn't take reservations."

"So we'd get drunk at the bar next door while we waited for our table?"

"Exactly," he says with a laugh. "You'd fit in perfectly." He kisses me again. Easy. "What would we do down in Charleston?"

I don't answer for a minute, see myself there. Alone. Stuck. Wondering where to go to get out. Wondering where to go to fit in.

"Pretty much the same," I say. "Just for eight months of the year instead of three."

He laughs. "Ouch and also touché."

"Your family's in Chicago?" I ask, turning him away from me and my life as quickly as possible. He tells me all about it—about his nieces and nephews and his mom's Thanksgiving dinner, and Marcus is so sublimely simple and loving and all the things I should be.

All the things I want to be.

Rikki comes to steal him, giving me a wink when she does, which the producers then make her film again.

I head back over to my corner I'd been sitting in before and stop when I see the scene before me. My chair is gone. I give the nearest production assistant the nastiest look I can manage, and reluctantly make my way back to where a group of the other girls are sitting in another cabana.

"Mind if I join y'all?" I ask sweetly.

I don't miss two of the girls, Kady and Hannah, exchange glances with each other when Aaliyah says, "Yeah, of course."

"Where have you been?" Kady asks me, twisting around to look at me.

(Once we get further into the season, some of the girls start realizing that just being in my orbit, picking fights, will guarantee them screen time as the producers push them toward me.)

"Just." I shift for a moment, already knowing my answer is wrong. "I needed a little time to myself, you know?"

Aaliyah laughs out loud. "No, we don't know! We're all trying to get time with Marcus, but I guess you've already gotten it locked up."

"Of course she does," Kendall says. She's sipping her cucumber water again. Kendall is always careful how much she imbibes; I almost never see her with a drink in her hand and certainly not if it's before 5 p.m. I suspect it's part of her strategy, and also suspect it should be part of mine, too.

But, old habits, as they say.

"C'mon, Kendall," I return, halfheartedly, a plea I hope she sees through. I need some room to breathe.

"What do you want me to do?" she asks with a giggle, taking a sip of her drink.

It's all clear to me then. The way she's been nice to my face, but gathering up support behind my back. Encouraging the theories about me. Turning the other girls against me one by one.

I've been a threat. One she can't afford.

"We don't want you to sit with us," Hannah then says, the clear voice to stand up against me.

I turn to look at her, square in the eye, more aware of the camera there than I had been in days, even while making out with Marcus. I'm sure she's aware the camera is there, too, and this might be her only moment to shine. "Why?" I ask her. I'll make it difficult. I won't let them get away with shunning me without a fight.

"Because you're a stuck-up bitch," Hannah says.

I absorb that blow. The other girls laugh behind their hands. I know their game, but I don't want to play it.

"We know you sit around talking shit about the rest of us, up on your high horse where all the producers love you," Hannah goes on. "You get all the special treatment, and you can barely be bothered to even speak to us. News flash, you're not the only one Marcus likes."

I blink, mostly in shock at all of these accusations. Somehow, that works against me, too.

"Come *on*!" Hannah demands. "Say something. We are so tired of all these eye rolls and looks from you."

It breaks me, for some reason. I'm so exhausted, so tired of pretending to be someone. Every time I've let my guard down, every time I've trusted someone to give them a second of my truth—Marcus excluded—it has backfired. I forget the character for a moment, forget anything but me and my failure and inability to relate to anyone else.

I turn calmly toward her. She doesn't get to decide who I am. "I don't even really have to say anything," I tell her. "Because this isn't a competition. Me and you?" I tilt my head, surveying her, taking in everything about her, from her terrible contour to her ratty blond extensions. "There's nothing about you that Marcus would ever find more attractive than anything about me. But what I do want you to understand is that it's not just the way I look. It's about the way you carry yourself, the way you could never have a complex conversation in your life. I don't respond to you because you have nothing on me. I can barely be bothered to listen to you speak."

"Oh, my God," Aaliyah whispers under her breath.

"Bitch" is all Hannah says as the tears well up in her eyes.
Bitch.

I hate that moment I gave in to it. Into who I am. Played into exactly what Hannah accused me of.

Bitch.

I get up from the cabana and walk away.

I go back to my corner, trying to avoid the camera following me, hoping, praying no one else will notice. I stand there alone until the cameraman finally gives up, and I sit down, curling up into myself, sitting on the cement with my legs pulled into my chest.

Giving in to my worst self is so easy and so hard. It's always there, right when I need to call on it. The thing is, I know what I can do to those girls. I know what I can do with my words and my looks and my *everything*. Not every girl here—some of them truly have something I covet, that lovability, that *likability*, but Hannah, she has nothing.

It's so obvious.

I'm still not supposed to say it. I'm not supposed to make them all hate me, the way I'm so good at.

The way the boy I loved in college simply disappeared and when I asked why, said I was exhausting and he was tired.

The way nowhere loved me, not even the city I dreamed about for twenty-five years.

I stay collapsed in on myself, the moment never not replaying. I always lived there when it came down to it. It would play like shit on TV.

And I know him before I see him, existing in the periphery, put on Jac-watch to capture just what I might do next.

Henry crouches down next to me. "What are you doing?" he asks me, arm on my shoulder.

I look up at him, over at the camera that has followed him. I signal writing and he hands me a pen and pad he carries with him. I cradle the pen to me, writing a single word where the camera can't get it. *Panicking.*

Henry's brow furrows as he reads what I wrote. He writes a reply. *Do you need a doctor?*

I shake my head. I'd be fucked if they were getting me in front of that on-set psychiatrist.

Finally, he scribbles again and shows the pad to me. *I can't keep them from catching you like this.*

I meet his eyes and he gives me a little frown, an almost private moment between the two of us.

"ITM, Jac?" he says, stuffing the pad of paper and pen into his back pocket.

I take a deep breath, nod. He doesn't reach out, doesn't pull me up like Marcus would have, just waits as I get to my feet; then he leads me across the patio, back into the house. We go into one of the ITM rooms, the bigger of them, me, him, and the cameraman. Henry hands me a water bottle and I drink it down greedily, grateful. I'm alone. No one here hates me.

But still, the words race through my mind: *What does this mean? What's happening now?*

"So," Henry finally says after he's given me a moment to collect myself. "What's going on, Jac?"

I swear I could kill him then, kill them all. The camera is on me, the panic is rolling through me, I am frayed nerves and sleeplessness and worthlessness. And still he is doing this to me, finding and deconstructing me. I hate him so much.

I drink my water again. I swirl it around in my mouth, tilt my head back, and just focus. Focus on that rage. Let it consume me. I swallow and resettle my gaze on him. "Were you engaged?" I ask.

He flinches. For the first time ever, since we've been on set together, he flinches. It makes me see past all the rest of it, the way it's all been fake, all been faked to make me comfortable. He's uncomfortable for that brief moment of time, and I see who he was, see who he is not *here*, without this power.

He saw me see it.

The camera guy briefly glances at Henry, sensing the dynamic shift. It's quiet in the room for a moment, the kind of quiet I crave, where we all want to die.

Then Henry asks, "Shailene tell you that?" his mask carefully sliding back into place.

"What's it like?" I fling back at him. "To be doing all you can to help two people fall in love when your own relationship is falling apart?"

"Cliché," he answers, and I see him. I see him, I see him, I see him.

It shouldn't give me such a thrill.

I lean forward, putting my elbows on my knees. "What was her name?"

The moment he thinks about whether he will answer or not flashes across his face. He says, "Evanna."

I smile. "Of course." I glance over at the cameraman, still watching me for *something*, back to Henry. "You wouldn't propose to a woman not named something like Evanna, would you? That would just be beneath you."

"I'm not sure what that's supposed to mean." He fidgets with his phone. It buzzes and buzzes, the way it always does.

"Sure you do. Evanna sounds like someone special, and you feel like someone special, don't you?"

"Who's interviewing who here?"

"Come on, Henry." I lean forward even farther. "Turnabout is fair play. If you're producing my love story, I want to know what you know about love."

Henry swallows, his Adam's apple bobbing up and down. "We met at an industry party. Dated for two years and then I proposed."

"She was a model?"

He chews on that for a minute before he says, "Yes."

I smile at him. "What happened?"

"We weren't right for each other."

"Why?"

"Because sometimes people aren't." He sighs. "Is there a point to this, Jac? Why did your last relationship end?"

I sit back up and glance toward the camera. "Because I've got a bad habit of breaking everything I touch."

"Hmm," he mumbles.

"What did you like most about Evanna?"

His eyes are narrowed at me. "She didn't ask many questions."

I laugh softly at that. "No fun."

"You seem okay now," he says, going to stand up.

"I'm not," I tell him. "Wait," I say, grabbing for his arm. He stares at the spot where I touched him, shakes me off.

"What do you want, Jac?" he asks through gritted teeth.

"We get along because we both fuck things up, right? Charlotte's told you to attach yourself to me because she sees it. I'm giving you what I won't give her."

"Yes," Henry tells me point-blank. "Obviously. Congratulations to you, you've figured me out." He looks at the cameraman again, and I can practically see him sweating.

"And you hate it," I say. "You hate that. You hate looking at me and knowing I know."

"I don't know what that means," he says.

"You don't want to know."

"Are you getting off on speaking in riddles?"

I stand up. "Evanna saw the you you wanted her to see until that you got to be so much, it weighed you down. And then you hated everything Evanna did and everything you did. You had to break it somehow or you might've ended up with Evanna for the rest of your life. You might've ended up being that Henry for the rest of your life and *fuck*, you hated that guy."

We stand there, squared off at each other, both tensed up to the point of breaking, two arrows notched in unsteady bows.

"How'd I do?" I ask quietly.

"I'd give you a seven and a half out of ten," he mutters.

"Fine," I say. "Let's go."

"Yes," he says. "Let's."

We go back out to the pool where the party is never-ending, here where every day is never-ending.

I slide off my cover-up and go to the edge of the pool, eyes on the water.

"What are you doing, Jac?" one of the other girls calls, and I dive in, fuck all of it. My hair and my makeup and this bathing suit that's uncomfortable as fuck anyway.

I swim to the side of the pool and rest both arms in front of me, on the cement. I set my chin into my crossed arms, watching Henry, water dripping off me.

He catches me and stares back. I don't blink or turn away.

Neither does he.

the 1 personality test—Jacqueline Matthis

1. What was your last relationship like?
Short.

4. I have out-of-body experiences.
_ True
X False

17. How much do your drink on an average night out?
_ a. 1 drink
X b. 2 drinks
_ c. 3–4 drinks
_ d. 5+ drinks

54. I can control things with my mind.
_ True
X False

77. Have you ever wanted to kill someone?
Not that I can remember.

103. I sometimes have suicidal thoughts.
_ True
X False

124. What is your average weekly alcohol intake?
_ a. none
X b. casual
_ c. moderate
_ d. extreme

137. Describe your ideal man.
Smart, funny, and hot, if that's not too much
work.

150. Who is your celebrity crush?

Michael Strahan.

You have finished *the 1* personality test. Please submit the test. On the next page, you will find a list of accepted local labs that offer *the 1*-mandated STD testing.

10

Head On Collision

The pool party ends later that afternoon, and we are all sent back inside to change into our dresses for the elimination ceremony. Charlotte gives me a head start on the other girls, and I'm one of the first ready. No doubt the whispers of favoritism will increase.

I go down into the kitchen and find Henry sitting there alone on a barstool, AirPods in his ears instead of the usual earpiece. I sit next to him at the kitchen bar, bunching up the skirt of my lacy off-white maxi dress awkwardly.

"What are you listening to?" I ask.

He pops an earbud out and offers it up to me. I put it in my ear. A Future song is playing. It swaps over to Blink-182 and then Yellowcard. Taking Back Sunday, Dashboard Confessional, a completely out-of-place Japanese Breakfast song, and then back to Future.

"Emo much?" I finally mutter with a smile.

"I grew up in the aughts. What do you want from me?" he says, his gaze still straight ahead. I think we might still be in a fight from earlier.

"Oh, man, I know we're both old, but to hear you speak of the early 2000s? Might as well give it up, Foster."

I see the anger ebbing away from him, the way he sinks into the conversation. "You know the one thing that really makes me feel old lately? Apparently, men don't wear socks with tuxes anymore. All the contestants show up with these cropped pants and no socks. Like, what is that about?"

I laugh so loudly, it startles me, and then he does, too, an easy silence following while another verse plays.

"God," I say, at the end of it. "I love music so much."

He glances over at me, smirking. "It's just a playlist, Jacqueline."

"No, it's not. I miss . . ." I search for a word, one big enough for what I'm feeling. "Art," I say, "and having things that aren't this. I miss being alone in my bed with my dog and reading a new book. I miss spending an entire weekend on the couch watching HBO, and maybe that makes me pretentious as all fuck, but hot damn, is it good to hear New Found Glory again."

Apparently, he can't help but say more. "I used to be in a band back then. The 2000s? We mostly played covers."

"Are you kidding me?" I ask, delighted at this new fact I've uncovered.

He shakes his head, and the smile on his lips is so genuine, I want to keep it forever, like that is exactly how I'll remember him, withholding nothing.

"What instrument did you play?"

He frowns. "I'm not telling you that. You have to guess."

"Oh, come on," I say, sizing him up as Fall Out Boy bangs on in my right ear. "Lead singer?"

"How dare you," he says.

"You were a drummer," I decide then.

He agrees. "Of course I was a drummer."

"God," I say. "I bet you were so hot."

Our eyes meet, and it's joking and it's not, and we both know it. He almost says something else, but stops himself. "You want to hear anything else?" he asks me.

I shake my head and just start listening again. I like the silence. I like him hearing half the song and me hearing the other half, both of us humming along badly, mouthing the words in the most intense parts. I like sitting next to him, easily, feeling like I'm seeing through a lens that is only Henry.

The content way he sits makes me think he likes it, too.

Hannah goes home that night, all the girls standing around her, hugging her and crying as she says goodbye. She deliberately walks past me, meets my eyes, and I know enough to know that moment will be featured on televisions in approximately three months. None of the other eliminated girls get their dramatic moment, destined to disappear into the annals of "was that girl even on the show?" history.

We see Marcus for the time it takes to film the elimination ceremony and then he's gone again, leaving us all with metaphorical blue balls. Afterward, the producers gather us around Becca and Brendan.

"So," Becca says to the ten of us left. She's wearing an over-the-top sequined quarter-length black dress with the midriff cut out and a slit up most of her leg for this elimination ceremony, almost too obvious in her attempt to overshadow the less dazzling contestants. "What do you say we take this show on the road?"

The girls scream and carry on. That is not deemed an appropriate level of enthusiasm, so we are all forced to amp it up tenfold on the next take.

"Marcus is dying to take you all to his hometown of Chicago!" Brendan announces and we must blow our loads all over again. "So go pack your bags—we're leaving right now!"

We are not in fact, leaving right then, the producers quickly inform us. We are forced to pose for a few more shots, then are told we're allowed to go to bed to get three hours of sleep before being up to leave for Chicago at the crack of dawn.

Henry keeps shooting me looks. Something changed between us and he knows it and I know it, and we can keep dancing or we can stop. I don't know what either option will mean.

"What?" I ask him, when he's been looking at me too long.

The other girls are dispersing. A couple have decided to stay up all night and drink until it's time to go to the airport, while Kendall and a smaller posse are racing upstairs to try and claim the bathroom first so they can go to bed.

"Are you excited?" he asks me, trying to do his old thing. But that's over now. I know him now, and his power is gone. "For Chicago?"

I stare out the window; it's dark, but still in my mind's eye, I can see the brown mountains all around us. "It'll be nice getting a break from all this depressing scenery."

He laughs, despite himself. "Only you would find the LA scenery depressing."

I don't laugh. Instead, I gaze at him for a second. "Not only me," I say quietly, and we both see it. A hundred years ago and a thousand lifetimes before sitting across from a stranger at a bright bar on a bright day and looking for something else.

Statement made, I leave him there alone and walk back through one of the hallways that leads toward the back of the house. It's quiet; I'm the only one back here, looking for solitude, in the chaos of packing up for Chicago. Until—the sound of footsteps, quiet behind me. I turn.

He twists the knob on the bathroom door right in front of me and quickly puts a finger up to his mouth, the universal signal for quiet. His hand encircles my left wrist as he tugs me into the bathroom behind him. Almost methodically, he takes off his headset and sets it aside on the bathroom counter and then, still in total silence, reaches around me. His cool fingers run over my bare back, finding my mic pack. Catching on, I help him pull it the rest of the way off, handing it over to him, my heart racing. He tosses the whole mic pack out of the bathroom and into the hallway then slams the door, going through the motions surgically, swift and easy, natural, like he's done it a million times before, and then he pushes me back against the bathroom wall, his mouth going to mine. Instinctively, I grab onto the front of his shirt, some shitty T-shirt of the millions he wears, and pull him close into me. My hands first find the taut skin on his stomach, then snake around to his back as the space between us disappears. His mouth devours me, on my mouth, on my collarbone, my neck, all the places I want it to be. Our teeth tearing at each other as we kiss, one of his hands resting on the wall next to my face, the other tangled up in my hair. I am hot and his mouth is hot, and it is so fucking hot, all I want right then is everything.

It's two minutes, maybe three. He pulls away from me panting hard, and looks down into my eyes. I stare back at him, only the sound of our heavy breathing filling the room.

He turns away from me and walks out of the bathroom, putting his headset back on.

Bingham Reviews: *End of the Line* by Jacqueline Matthis

There's a certain elegance in Jacqueline Matthis's debut, *End of the Line*. The romance, centered around the lead singer of a country music trio as she finds love on the road, features characters that leap off the page and chemistry that sizzles.

Unfortunately, what it is not, is a romance.

Matthis plays around with the idea of love and art and the pain both can bring, but ultimately, despite a good showing, the whole thing comes down too far on the side of nihilism, something sure to drive readers away. This novel will leave readers longing for a happy ending that never comes. It's hard to wonder why not.

CHICAGO

11

Complicated

Flying to Chicago is, in short, hell.

We lose two hours on a night when we didn't sleep. The producers advise us strongly to try and get some sleep on the four-hour flight, but it's impossible for me. Everyone else is knocked out asleep, but they don't have the memory of Henry kissing them playing over and over every time they close their eyes.

I'd sat on the floor of the bathroom for at least two full minutes before someone had come looking for me.

"Jac!" Charlotte at the door.

I stood, straightened myself, and opened the door.

"What the hell are you doing?" she demanded, holding my mic pack out to me. Reluctantly, I took it out of her hand and stuffed it into the back of my dress.

"Using the bathroom," I said.

"Why did you take your mic pack off?"

I frowned at her, throwing my hands up. "Can a girl not take a shit in peace around here?"

"Don't be ridiculous, Jac." She turned away from me. "No one shits on this show unless they've taken a laxative or contracted dysentery. The code word is 'salami' if you need private time in the bathroom." She turned away and tossed one last thing behind her: "Don't take your mic off. Those things are fucking expensive!"

When we get to Chicago, we are driven directly to the Chicago Athletic Association, a swanky sixteen-story high-rise on Michigan Ave, with a rooftop bar cherry-on-top. Upon arrival, we are given only two hours to get checked into our rooms, film our amazement at our rooms (part of the agreement the show has made with the hotel), change and do our makeup, and be stuffed into the hotel elevators up to the top floor to share drinks and stare out over the city.

I vaguely remember what it was like to enjoy things before I joined this show.

At Cindy's, the rooftop bar, we are—God bless it all—allowed to order a drink. I grab a Goose Island beer, a favorite of mine from a summer visit a couple of years ago for a book conference ("Jesus, the *calories*," Kendall says when she sees my drink), and take it back to our designated table with me.

I keep looking for Henry and not finding him, until it drives me so crazy, I think I will combust. Instead, we are made to drink our drinks and chat like we're having a good time, me wearing a structured oversized red blazer Rikki had loaned me with a pair of black shorts, Rikki in leather leggings and a very cropped hot pink body-hugging tank top.

"Is this what it feels like to die?" Rikki asks, smiling at me all the while.

"I wish I was on drugs," I say.

She takes a long drink from her wine. "Don't say that," she finally says, and then gives me a reassuring smile to break the tension.

Taken aback, I simply answer, "Sorry," and clink my glass into hers.

And then the producers make the entire group toast. We do it time after time—first when we get our drinks, then again after we've had a sip or two, and then again before our drinks are gone. By the time they ask for a last toast, I just turn my pint glass over and sit it upright on the table.

"Very cheeky," Charlotte comments, and I give her a goofy grin. The beer and lack of sleep has me feeling looser than I have in a couple of days, and I tilt back my chair, balancing on its hind legs.

"Where's Henry?" I ask her.

She narrows her eyes at me.

"He had some scouting work to take care of today." She crosses her arms. "He gets cranky once the travel starts."

"Versus normally?"

"He's having a good season," Charlotte tells me. "He really fucked things up for us last year, and I wasn't sure he could turn it around, but he's earned his spot back."

"Were you going to fire him?" I ask Charlotte, turning fully to face her.

"Would you?" she asks, and goose bumps prickle down my back.

"I would," I say, "because I know when you mention the 'great season' he's having, you're talking about him getting to me."

"Oh, gold star, Jac," Charlotte says with a laugh. "You've known Henry was on you since he told you on the third day of filming. You asked if he was flirting you into wearing a dress."

"He was," I say. I'd known then and of course I know now, but I can't help but wonder how far would they go to get what they want. Would they let him kiss me?

Shit.

This show is really fucking with my head. I keep questioning everything I say and think and do, and it's not that I didn't do that before, but it's that at least I'd been confident there was a version of myself I could like. I keep questioning what's real and what's not and who I even am or thought I was.

"Darling," she says, "he's doing well because you're his girl and you're going to get engaged at the end of this season."

His girl. Like she knows something. *His girl.*

Right on cue, Marcus and his film crew make their way to our table. We all sit around stupidly and stare at him with the required awe; noticeably, in addition to the crew and producers, a few similarly tall, square-jawed men of multi-ethnic backgrounds to assure us Marcus is totally cool, converge behind him.

"Who is *that*?" Rikki whispers in my ear, eyeing one of the men.

"Down, girl," I mutter back.

Production gives us the whole song and dance: Marcus has brought some of his closest friends to meet the group of us, to give their approval. "Can't wait for you to meet the girls," Marcus says to his friend Grant.

It's all a show, but it makes me want to talk to my own friends. As fast as Rikki and I have trauma-bonded, she doesn't know me like

Sarah does, can't give me that knowing look that Sarah would every time Henry walks into the room.

And at that thought, I already want Sarah to shut up in my head again.

Priya sets me up on the balcony overlooking the city and Lake Michigan beyond, to pretend to casually talk to Rikki and Shae when Marcus and Grant approach us.

"Jac," Marcus says on cue, "I've been so excited for you to meet Grant. Grant, Jac is my Southern firecracker."

"Oh, am I?" I answer gamely. I don't really like it, though; sounds like something Janelle has said.

"Marcus has told me so much about you," Grant says, extending a hand, which I take. "You're an author."

"Guilty."

"Oh, and this is Shae." Marcus points to her. Rikki has disappeared into the background.

"I think we've met?" Grant says, extending his hand. Shae is blushing deeply.

"Oh, my," she says. "Yeah, how are you?"

"Good," Grant says, but I notice Shae's hand shaking as she takes his proffered handshake.

"Well, if you two have met before, no introduction needed. Grant, you must already know what a wonderful person Shae is."

"I do," Grant says, though his eyes dart away as he says it.

"Great to see you," she says through gritted teeth. "If you'll just excuse me."

Marcus and I watch her almost sprint back inside the bar to where the crew is, confused. Priya grabs Grant and pulls him away with her, talking quickly. I look back at Marcus, just slightly behind my right shoulder. "What was that about?" I ask.

"Producer hijinks, no doubt," Marcus says with confidence. It surprises me, how quickly he's cottoned on. "You think she's okay?"

I turn fully to face him, taking a drink of my beer. "Shae seems like pretty much anything would roll off her shoulders."

"True," Marcus says easily. "Can I try that?" He points at my beer and I hand it to him. He takes a sip and smiles. "You have good taste," he tells me as he hands it back to me. There's a certain intimacy to the moment, doing something a couple might.

"I agree."

"I found one of your books," Marcus tells me. "At a bookstore near here. Janelle wouldn't let me buy it. Said it might taint things or some shit."

"That's really thoughtful," I say, almost surprised.

His eyebrows go up. "I just want to get an inside look into the way your mind works," he says, like that's nothing. "There are so many cogs I can tell are always turning in there. I'm desperate to see it."

I laugh, flattered. "Nothing good happening, I promise."

"Don't I know it. Obviously, I don't read romance books or anything. Mostly nonfiction."

"Yeah," I answer, slightly deflated. "Like what? I try to read a little bit of everything. I've found ideas from everywhere."

"Well," he stalls. "You know . . . it's always hard when someone asks, isn't it?" He scratches his neck and laughs, so I attempt to give him a halfhearted one in reply. I know it's what he wants, my reassurance. "Oh, here we go," Marcus continues, reaching out for a lifeline as Grant comes back over to the two of us. "Marcus, can I talk to you for a second? Jac, lovely to meet you."

"Jac, I want you to meet Grant's wife," Marcus says quickly.

"Yeah. In a minute, if you don't mind," says Grant, and then I'm ushered off by Priya so they can have a talk.

(It turns out, when the episode plays, Shae dated Grant briefly in college. He and Marcus were friends but certainly not to the extent the show had made it seem—Grant worked in the Dallas office of Marcus's company, and the show seemed dead-set on breaking through Shae's unshakable exterior. She cried quite a bit; she was embarrassed. It was all sort of morbidly fascinating and sick. I can't believe they didn't try to pull that trick on me.)

Finally, after a couple hours of filming, Marcus asks Kendall if she'll go on a date with him. Of course she will. Oh, my God, she can barely believe it.

I barely suppress an eye roll (or don't, if the footage that later airs is to be believed). We are forced into filming a couple of ITMs, and then, gloriously, we are finally allowed to go to sleep.

Charlotte walks Rikki and me down to our shared room, but just before she lets us in, she calls, "Jac, can I talk to you for a minute?"

I stop with her outside the door, crossing my arms defensively over my chest. "Am I in trouble?" I ask her.

Charlotte shrugs. "Should you be?"

The thing that drives me the craziest about Charlotte is that I never actually know how much she knows. I always know it's more than she lets on, but I don't know how much more.

She's an enigma, a mystery, and sure of herself in a way I desperately long to be. Charlotte is there with her life together and her family together and her job together, and she sees right through me.

The oddest thing about this whole experience is how deeply paranoid I have become, how much I have begun to question things I formerly trusted about myself.

"Jac, I don't have much longer," Charlotte tells me.

I frown down at her. "Condolences."

She rolls her eyes at me. "I can't travel abroad. Chicago is the end of the line for me and this baby," she says. "That means you're stuck with Priya and Elodie."

She doesn't say Henry, and it bugs me. I don't want to ask, but now I'm suspicious; he kisses me and now he's disappeared.

"Aren't you supposed to destabilize me by just disappearing without warning when I least expect it?"

"Don't take this personally, babe, but you're the last person I want to destabilize. Especially not when things are going so well between you and Marcus."

I want to ask, *Are they?* but I know they are, feel the proof every time he looks at me. *Why* am I trying to fuck this up? Everything I planned is working, if not exactly how I imagined it playing out.

"You guys are really pushing this crazy thing, huh?" I say, feeling it always there in my periphery. Like I might snap at any moment, collapse into a puddle on the floor, give up, and they'd need to get the cameras over quick to capture that.

"No one thinks you're crazy, Jac," Charlotte says. Then: "Well." She tilts her head to the side. "Maybe Priya."

"Priya can't take a joke," I mutter, and she laughs.

"Look, we get a lot of contestants who don't do well in this environment. It's a *lot*. The cameras and the other women and just the general idea of spilling your guts when you don't want to. I get it; I would never do it."

Yet, she had talked *me* into it. Was the devil on my shoulder every minute of my waking life.

"I see it from contestants all the time, but rarely do I relate to these girls the way I do to you."

"Bullshit," I say immediately, spotting this for exactly what it is.

"I knew you'd say that," she says. "It's what I would say."

"Cut the shit, Charlotte. Make your point."

She smiles sardonically at me. "You can't keep half-assing the game," she says. "You've been skating by on chemistry with Marcus and your ass, to put it kindly, but if you don't start trying, you will go home."

"Maybe I should," I say, and her eyes spark with curiosity.

"Do you want to be here or not, Jac?"

"I want Marcus," I say, a lie that almost sounds true at this point. "I don't want the rest of it."

"That's what Marcus used to say last season," she tells me. "You two are perfect for each other, and you don't even know it."

"I do," I say. I bite my lip. I want to tell her how I've been feeling; maybe it will help me understand it. "When I watched last season, my best friend saw it, and she saw it because she saw me see it. Marcus didn't trust what any of this meant, and neither do I. Marcus protected himself, and I saw myself in him.

"I wasn't sure what all this was when I started, but I think I am now. I'm *here* for Marcus," I say, the first time I've verbalized it and meant it.

"Okay," she says. "Then I think we're getting somewhere." Then she reaches out and tucks a piece of my hair behind my ear. Charlotte is tiny, a waif of a woman, but some part of me wants to collapse into her, the way I would Sarah.

I want *someone* here to see the real me.

"Who am I, Charlotte?" I ask her.

"What do you mean?"

"On this show. To you. Who am I? What's my part in this story?"

"Jac." She shakes her head. "Most of that sort of stuff doesn't happen until we edit. I don't know what's going to happen. I don't know *who* you are."

I still want her to tell me though. "Sure you don't," I say.

"Get some sleep," Charlotte says, her hand warm pressure on my arm. "Okay?"

"Will Henry be there, too?" I ask, cursing myself the moment the words leave my lips. "After you leave? You said Priya and Elodie. Will Henry not be going overseas?"

She reaches out, gives my arm a reassuring squeeze. "Of course, how could I forget Henry?" She gives me a different smile than the others, one I see something else behind. Recognition, or something like it.

(Not then, I don't see it then. I see it later. I look back and I see it clearly.)

"Henry won't leave your side the rest of the way through this journey."

Reddit thread: Marcus Bellamy: Most Toxic Lead Ever?

 CrotchRocket75
Shailene's sluts

does anyone else think t1 will see a huge drop off in ratings
this season after casting the epitome of toxic masculinity and
gaslighting, Marcus? Vom can't wait to not watch this train wreck

 EvanisFoine
you are not the 1

People will watch it this season just like they do every season.
Y'all are delusional if you don't think the controversy of me
me me marc is going to bring the viewers in

 xxxtinabxxx
bellamy's bitches

Oh here we go again. Why don't you leave this sub if you hate
Marcus so much?

 CrotchRocket75
Shailene's sluts

u are so desperate for any average looking white man, you're
just fine with this abusive piece of shit

 xxxtinabxxx
bellamy's bitches

 Bbbeehappy

Marcus reminds me of every toxic relationship I've ever been
in. This season's girls need to beware.

Tho if he ends up with jac, those two deserve each other
sorry not sorry

xxxlinabxxx
bellamy's bitches

Jac doesn't deserve Marcus

She doesn't deserve someone to piss on her if she's on fire

 lalalalana89
Shailene's sluts

Finally, something we can agree on.

 CrotchRocket75
Shailene's sluts

Here we go again—trashing another girl to make up for
Marcus's inadequacies

 BrendannBecca4eva
team true love true stars
mod

Ok shutting this down, it's getting too nasty in here

12

I Miss You

Filming starts at 7 a.m. the next morning.

The fewer girls there are, the more brutal the schedule gets, the demands for us to be on camera at all times—if not on dates or with Marcus or in ITMs, in girl chats, talking about Marcus and who's trying to take Marcus away from us and how much we'd like for Marcus to meet our families and all of our insecurities as they relate to Marcus.

Even Marcus must be exhausted of himself at this point.

Henry meets me outside of the hotel first thing in the morning, and he's right *there* like nothing happened and now we're here and everything is *fine*, he hardly shoved his tongue down my throat at all. I only had to spend ten minutes in the shower masturbating and that's just *great*.

"How'd you sleep?" he asks me.

"Better than Kendall," I say, because she looks ghastly. I see now why she's attempting to sleep so much.

"You might want to stop feeding the beast," he says, and I glance at him out of the corner of my eyes. I'm miked, of course. I'm always miked.

"Isn't this great for you? Heard you're cleaning up this season."

"C'mon, Jac," Henry says as we get in a car with Rikki, who is listening to the two of us intently. "We're friends today, right?" He gives me a smile that we both know isn't a real smile as he slams the car door.

I hate it, the way I wonder what it means. I'm used to a certain ease when it comes to men, not necessarily understanding them, but knowing what they'll do and when they'll do it and how. That's how Henry had been that first night, but *this* is still happening and he is still here and he kissed me, but now there is nothing.

So, I try. "I told Charlotte I'd start playing the game."

That finally gets his attention. He looks fully away from his phone and over at me. I have on one of my favorite outfits, high-waisted, wide-legged white pants with a purple crushed velvet cami top, my hair in a ponytail like that first night, and I can't help but wonder if he notices. "Why?" he asks.

"Because I want to be a good girl," I say, and he blinks at me, slowly at that. I don't know what I'm trying to do; get a rise out of him? Piss him off? Please him?

"I can work with that," he says, turning back to his phone.

We drive through the city streets of Chicago to the Gold Coast neighborhood. It's an area of nice bars and million-dollar Greystones that I'd heard called Viagra Circle due to the common occurrence of rich older men with high net worths looking to pick up much younger women. We finally get out in front of one of the classic Chicago pizza spots, Lou Malnati's. I've practically burned a hole in Henry's hands, staring at them as he typed away on his phone throughout the car ride, his nails immaculately clean. He'd touched me with those hands two days ago. But I had to let that go.

I had to let it go.

"Are you okay?" Rikki asks me as we sit in the car together, waiting to be told what to do next.

"I don't know," I say. "Maybe? It's probably just the travel."

"I know what you mean," she says. "The jet lag is killing me."

"Mm-hmm," I answer, distracted.

After an absurdly long hour of waiting (always waiting), we are ushered inside the deep-dish pizza joint and informed the eight of us on our group date (Eunice and Aaliyah had one-on-ones that week) will be making a pizza, and—guess what—Marcus will be there to help us out.

I spot Marcus watching me and wave at him. He waves back, and I hate how much I want that little moment of affection. I don't look at Henry, but I do think about how he's the kind of person who would never give me that, who would always have me begging for the scraps of his attention because that's the kind of man he is, I can see it so clearly.

Marcus and the random guy from the pizza place tell us that each of us will be making our own pizza with the help of the Lou Malnati's experts and with some assistance from him.

"I need to see which of you can be the most authentic Chicagoan," he says with a shit-eating grin. I almost feel in on the joke with him, at how ridiculously we must contort ourselves to explain these dates.

Each of us is given our own workstations and instructions. I am trying to play along with it, but I can't concentrate. I go over to Rikki's station and am absolutely amazed by the catastrophe she is creating. It gives me an idea.

I go back to working on my own pizza and, making a big show of it, spill marinara sauce all over my prized top. It's minorly hilarious and they make me film an ITM with Elodie, making fun of myself.

"Would you say," Elodie asks me, "that making a pizza together shows a lot about how you would make a life together?"

I blink, stunned for a moment. Production loves to feed us lines that fit their narrative, but that was an all-time bad one. "Really, Elodie? You want me to say that?"

She laughs at my clear disdain. (When the episode airs, Andi says it word-for-word. Then they show my marinara spill in slow motion three times in a row, highlighting exactly how fake it looked.)

"We got you a T-shirt to put on," Henry tells me when I finish my interview, offering it out to me. "One of the production assistants can take you to the back to change."

I hate the new production assistants, not because they've done anything, but because I'd just gotten used to the ones in LA and now they're gone. Now there's even more people I don't know, even more instability.

"Let's not wait," I say. "I'm tired of waiting. Just go with me."

He knows what I'm saying, and he acquiesces, even though I can tell he desperately doesn't want to.

We make our way into the back of the building, into the kitchen with the giant industrial sink and dishwasher. I pull up the back of my shirt so Henry can take my mic off, his fingers caressing my bare skin as he hands it to me.

"Is it off?" I ask.

He steps away from me, giving me a long look. "Yes."

I pull off my stained shirt, tossing it on the ground, and Henry pointedly scoffs, turning away from me. "You've seen more," I say.

"Don't, Jac" is all he answers. I make my way to the sink, running water and combing it through my hair, where clumps of sauce have taken up residence.

"What the fuck, Henry," I say as I turn back from the sink. "What the fuck."

"Can you keep your voice down?" he asks me, his gaze still trained on the wall behind him.

"Why are you doing this? Why did you . . ." But I trail off because it feels too dangerous to even say.

"Are you dressed?" he asks as I slide on the Lou Malnati's T-shirt.

"Yes," I say, and he turns back around. "This shirt is stupid tight."

"This show is still the show," he answers, like we're all just stuck in a misogyny loop with no idea how to free ourselves. He ruffles his hair, distracted, running through the lines in his head; I can see him doing it. "About LA. I shouldn't have."

"Then why did you?"

He steps close to me, our faces inches from each other. "Don't you already know?"

"So is this it?" I ask him. "It's over?"

"Nothing is over," he says. "Because nothing ever started."

"If I recall correctly," I reply, "it started three times."

His face goes red, and he averts his eyes from mine. "Didn't the boundaries we established preclude you from bringing up any pre-show activities?"

"Boundaries?" I demand. "What fucking boundaries?"

"We're not teenagers; we can't just do whatever we want," he says.

"But you did."

"I'm sorry," he says, a note of finality in his voice. He's just decided to end it and it's over.

I don't know what makes me say it. It's ridiculous. "I don't think you're sorry."

"Jac." He puts his hands on either side of me, gripping my arms, his skin warm and bronze against my pale arms. "I'm sorry."

He turns away from me, and I fume. I don't know what I wanted him to say. I don't know what I hoped to get out of this conversation.

"Why did you break up with your fiancée?" I ask him.

He stops, his back to me, sighs deeply, ruffles his hair, then turns to face me. "Why are you doing this?"

"Just tell me."

He shrugs. "You were right. Is that what you want to hear? She got sick of my misery. Good enough?"

I pick up my mic and walk past him without saying anything.

I'm here for Marcus.

I head back into the filming room in high dudgeon. Marcus is kneading a pizza with Andi, and I make my way over to Charlotte.

"What was that about?" she asks me, glancing at Henry.

"Strategizing," I tell Charlotte without missing a beat. "Like we talked about." I hold my mic out to her. "Can you fix this?"

She does. "What are you going to do?" she asks me.

"I want to talk to Marcus," I say, still staring at him flirting with Andi. She's looking away from the eye contact Marcus is making with her. *I wouldn't do that*, I think. *I'd hold his gaze because I think he'd like that. He'd know what I wanted just like I know what he wants.*

Fuck, I was horny.

"Okay," Charlotte says. "So go talk to him."

"I have your permission?" I ask her, quirking my eyebrow.

"In fact, you have my blessing," Charlotte answers, typing out a text as she does so. *Red alert*, I imagine it saying, *bitch on the move.*

I approach Andi and Marcus and feel a camera immediately train on me. "Marcus," I say with a shy smile, "I think I missed some of the instructions when I splattered marinara all over myself. Maybe you could come help me?" I imbue my voice with as much innocence as I can, and I watch it work on him like a charm.

One thing I had noticed in Shailene's season was how much Marcus loved to be needed, to be reassured. He never seemed confident in her affection, constantly in his head about what things meant, but opening up and blooming like a flower when she focused solely on him. It may seem obvious in the structure of *the 1* how that would work, but Marcus seemed especially attuned to it.

When we get to my already rolled out pizza, Marcus looks down at it with a smirk. "You seem to be doing pretty well on your own."

I look up into his eyes with a grin. "I excel at most things I try," I tell him, trying that on for size. That's what I'd thought about myself at twenty-two, precocious and narcissistic and fresh-out-of-college, confident I was more than any of the other girls I'd gone to school with. Sure I was heading somewhere because every teacher and professor and adult I'd run across in my previous twenty-two years had assured me I was.

I wasn't shit, but it is fun to pretend to be that girl again.

"Somehow, that doesn't surprise me," he says.

"Why don't you taste this for me?" I ask, running my finger through the marinara sauce I'd made earlier, holding it up to him.

His gaze angles down at me, and then he dips his head, taking his time licking and sucking my finger. I smile. "Well?"

"That's actually," he says, covering his mouth as he laughs, "really amazing."

"Told you," I answer. And without my even needing to prompt it, he says, "I think I might know one other thing you're good at." Then he dips his head again and kisses me, like he could barely have waited another moment. I return it with glee, lifting up on my toes, making a shot of it for the other girls.

"I especially like you in that shirt," Marcus whispers into my ear, his voice so breathy, I shiver.

"All right, all, we need to get these pizzas in the oven in ten minutes to stay on schedule. Wrap it up!" the line producer calls. Marcus meets my eyes guiltily.

"I guess I should let you get back to that," he continues in a low voice. He's always speaking quietly, intimately, to me, a secret just for the two of us.

"I'll see you later," I tell him with a kiss on the nose. (When this airs, I look like such an insane bitch with Marcus wrapped around my finger at this point, it barely musters notice that anything I do can ever be considered cute.)

It's hours later, pizzas are cooked and not eaten (I win the tasting contest but it never airs because no one gives a shit), and we are all zipped up into our cocktail wear now. We are filming in a Cuban-themed bar connected to another top-dollar hotel in River North, another swanky neighborhood just north of the Loop with renovated warehouses and themed drinking establishments galore. The bar has kitschy little armchairs in outrageous colors and bright wallpaper in each of the connecting rooms.

"You're going to go second," Charlotte tells me. She and Henry are standing, talking to me in a corner of the bar. The bar is typically extraordinarily dark, Henry tells me, but the production team has lit it up brighter than the sun tonight.

"Second?" I ask. "Why?"

Henry locks eyes with me and smirks, raising his eyebrows. I hate when he does that. "Because we have your back," he tells me. "And we wanted to get you the alone time you so craved."

"Henry's idea," Charlotte confirms. "So you two play nice today."

Henry is looking so goddamn pleased with the whole thing, and I hate it deep down into my very bones. I'm saving his ass with our connection, and he's exploiting me. I have to do something to take back control of the situation.

"Get me a whiskey," I tell Henry, straight-faced, hoping to knock the knowing smile off his face.

"Fuck off," he says with a laugh. "Have one of the assistants get you a drink."

"Get her a drink, Henry," Charlotte says without humor, and he gets up without another word, rolling his eyes as he goes.

"Okay, listen," Charlotte says, leaning as far forward to me as her stomach will allow, "don't feel rushed tonight, okay? We've set aside time for you and Marcus specifically so just take advantage of it."

"Seriously?" I ask, used to time with Marcus being deliberately withheld.

"Yeah," she says, "and relax." She leans back, pointing as Henry brings my drink over to me. Our hands do not accidentally brush as he hands it over to me, nor do we make uncomfortably long eye contact. The fact that we haven't is then all I can think about.

Even with the pep talk, it's still an hour before I get to see Marcus. There's an easy-to-spot twinkle in his eye as he makes his way over to me and reaches his hand down to mine.

"May I?" he asks, and I take his hand easily, pulling it into my side as we walk away from the group.

"I have something special planned for you tonight," he says as the two of us make our way into the hotel lobby. "Just this way, right, Elodie?"

Elodie, who has basically appeared from thin air, says, "Yeah, we have a room for you two on the second floor."

I turn to look at her, shocked. "A room?" Then I look up at Marcus, his gaze slightly trepidatious. I smile.

"Is there a hot tub?"

Elodie answers, "This is *the 1. Of course* there's a hot tub."

We take an elevator up to a suite, where a wall of windows gives us a breathtaking view overlooking the river, with the city lights glinting in the background. The floors are polished wood, the furniture leather. Nothing like the spackled paint holding the mansion together; this was real opulence.

The camera crew is already set up in the room, filming as Marcus and I take in the view, his arms wrapped around me, chin perched on my shoulder. I look back over at him. "Just for me?" I ask him, both of us in on the joke.

He spins me around, hand going to my cheek. "I asked if it could be you," he says, and the fairy tale gets to me just then, the romance, all of it. I kiss him, and the lights twinkle in the background.

Elodie had asked me to pack a bathing suit a few days ago for safekeeping; now, one of the assistants hands it to me and I change into it. It's simple and effective, a hot pink bikini, the bottoms especially high cut to leave little to the imagination. Marcus can't help but grin as he sees it, and we get into the marble hot tub in the bathroom, clinking our champagne glasses together.

The romance is officially gone with the boom mic and camera and Janelle standing over the two of us like the Grim Reaper. Marcus puts his arm around my shoulder, skin-on-skin contact making my toes curl. He plays with the frizzy hair at the base of my neck that won't stay up in the ponytail I pulled the rest of it into.

"What are you thinking about?" he asks me.

I look up into his face, his green eyes and chiseled jaw. "Time," I say. "The way they're teaching us to covet it. To steal it." I shrug. "You?"

He chuckles. "Would you believe I was thinking the exact same thing?"

I grin smugly, my face inches from his. "No."

"Good," he says, "because I wasn't."

Then he closes the distance between us, his mouth on mine, confident, wanting. He shifts, turns his body more fully toward me, setting down his glass of champagne and then taking mine out of my hand to set it down, too. His hands go to my hips, lifting me in the water. I gasp in surprise as he pulls me around toward him, my legs straddling his lap, forgetting about the cameras, something else ignited as our bodies are pressed together. I lose myself in it, closing my eyes, forgetting everyone else is there.

Who is Marcus? I think, an annoyingly invasive thought. *Who am I? And who the fuck is Henry Foster?*

I hate the way I'm overthinking, especially when I'm dry humping Marcus and I *like* dry humping Marcus. Henry isn't even here. He's somewhere else, somewhere in this building, and I am *here*.

I pull back, and Marcus's eyes go to mine. "You good?" he asks, and that's another thing to like about him, to want about him. That he asks.

"Yeah," I say. I lean back, sitting next to him on the hot tub's bench seat, and he puts a comfortable arm around me, in the casual way you would someone you care about.

"How's it going with the other girls?" Marcus asks me. We'd had to shed our mic packs for this little jaunt in the hot tub, and now a man is standing in front of us, holding a boom mic. If I hadn't gotten so used to it by now, it would be weird, but my life has ceased being my own and I've been a willing participant.

"Well," I say, taking a long minute to measure my words, "I'm glad to be out of the house."

Marcus nods and swallows. "Andi says you've been having some trouble with some of the other girls."

I turn to face him, resting my cheek in my palm. "Trouble?" I echo.

"Sure." He shrugs. "She made it sound like you were mocking Hannah when she got sent home. Like, implying you made it happen."

"I—what?" I ask, genuinely confused.

"I don't know," he admits. "It sounded like she maybe heard it from . . ." His eyes flick to Elodie, his face saying everything he can't manage to get out of his mouth. "Maybe she heard it secondhand."

"So, Andi wants me gone?" I shrug. "What the fuck," I say, exhausted of it all at last. "I've never done *anything* to her. Jesus *Christ*, what does this show do to people?"

"Hey," Marcus says, holding up his hands. "Remember I'm the villain of last season. People can really push you into shit on this show."

I glance at the cameras, and then decide, *Fuck it*. "Henry?"

"You too?" he asks with a conspiratorial grin. "Yeah, avoid that prick like you avoid the plague."

Janelle interjects: "Can we please get back to the date?"

"No," I say stubbornly, "I'd like to have a conversation with the man I'm dating," I say, making eye contact with Janelle.

Janelle gives me a sour look, but I turn back to Marcus, who seems even more pleased with me. "Please elaborate."

Marcus just shakes his head. "You know how he does. I thought we were friends. Thought he had my back. Idiot. Then he started sabotaging me with Shailene. Getting in my head, telling me I needed to tell her things I had no business telling her. Convincing me I had to talk to her on camera about us having sex. Making me think I had to do things I didn't want to do. He's good at that."

I lean in closer. "He plays so easy. You want him to like you."

"Yeah." Marcus tilts his head down, smiling at me, nodding. "And then he does whatever it takes to make you blow it up. I told them not to let him near me this season."

"You know what?" I ask, so close to Marcus now I could tear into him. "All I've heard is how much he fucked up last season. What is that about?"

"*Enough*," Janelle cuts over us. "We need to wrap this up."

"We're in trouble now," Marcus says, leaning down until our foreheads are touching, our eyes aligned, and something about acknowledging Henry so openly has given him less power here.

Marcus hates Henry, and now it doesn't seem quite so hard.

I lean back into Marcus's mouth, my hand sliding up his cheek, and he hitches me back up to straddle him. "Okayyy," Janelle says. "We get it."

But we ignore her, Marcus's hand sliding up my thigh, teasing at the line where my bikini hits my skin, his thumb sliding under it. It is almost physically painful to feel his erection right there below me and not be able to do anything about it. I devour him, press against him as much as they will let me.

"So, like," I say, freeing my mouth for a moment and glancing over at Janelle, "can we get five minutes alone?"

She stares back at me, her gaze hard. "No," she says.

Marcus's mouth presses into my neck, and then he lays his head on my shoulder so he, too, can stare over at Janelle.

"Please?" he asks. She gives him a fond look.

"Two minutes," she finally says.

Then, miraculously, they clear out. They fucking leave.

It goes off like a rocket. I grab on to Marcus's hand and push my bikini bottom to the side, letting his warm palm dig into the skin there. "Fast," I whisper to him, and his eyes dilate with the realization of what's happening, him touching me and me biting into my lip to stay quiet.

I grab his hips, hurriedly guiding him to sit up from his bench seat, pushing his swimsuit bottom down to expose his body to me, hard and sculpted and so gloriously beautiful, and we awkwardly maneuver over so my knees are pressed into the bench, and he pushes himself into me then for one-two-three glorious seconds, and then we both startle apart with a knock on the door.

Just the fucking tip indeed.

Briefly, I think of the recklessness of the decision. But we were all STD tested before we were allowed on the show (Charlotte told me about once having to tell a contestant they had been removed from the cast list because they did in fact have syphilis), and I'd had an IUD put in a few years before. I'd done worse.

Burying my face into Marcus's chest, right where his heart is pounding, I laugh lightly against his skin as he pulls his swim trunks back up and I straighten my bikini. That was almost worse than nothing, and by the way he swears under his breath, I suspect Marcus feels the same way. My lust only grows.

"It's you, Jac," he suddenly whispers then, his voice in my ear again, making me shiver. "It's you."

I look at him, our eyes lined up straight across, and I think, *It's over.* I finally did it.

I did something gloriously stupid and joined this show, uprooted my life following the worst failure I could imagine. I met this man, and I just fucked him for fifteen seconds in this cheesy hotel room in a hot tub on a show that will air on national television, and he told me it was me.

What the fuck?

Also, why the fuck not?

"Send Andi home," I whisper back, caught up in my victory and in my desperate vengeance all at once. "Tonight."

He kisses the side of my neck in response.

Marcus's Breakup with Andi [as aired]

[Andi and Marcus sit together in front of a draped wall at a Cuban bar in the River North neighborhood of Chicago. Andi is clearly confused as she'd already had her one-on-one time with Marcus that night and the other girls—much to their chagrin—had been told the night was over after Jac finally returned from her two-hour-long one-on-one time with Marcus.]

Marcus: How are you liking Chicago so far?

Andi: Oh, I love it. I've been dying to visit. Is it too much to say I could see myself moving here?

Marcus, with a smile: You think you could handle the winters?

Andi, taking his hand: With the right person.

Marcus, not betraying any hint of nerves: Andi, I've been doing a lot of thinking this week. Things are really starting to get serious.

[Andi nods. The shot zooms in on Marcus running his thumb across Andi's knuckles, massaging her hand.]

Marcus: We've had fun together, but I'm just not so sure I see a future with everyone here. And I have to have that, you know? If I don't see it . . . that's what this journey is all about.

[Andi nods, clearly confused.]

Andi: I see that with you, Marcus. I wanted to wait, but with the time we've spent together today, I don't think I can. *[Andi takes a deep breath.]* I love you, Marcus.

[Marcus's hand stills.]

Marcus: I . . . I just think some relationships have progressed faster than others. We're running out of time and I think—Andi, I'm sorry, but I don't think I can get there with you. Do you understand?

[Andi jerks her hand back.]

Andi: But when we talked earlier, you said . . .

[Marcus heaves a heavy sigh].

Marcus: I'm sorry.

[Andi has started crying.]

Andi: I don't understand. You said you really felt something. What changed? What did I do?

Marcus, still unmoved: I've got to follow my heart.

[Andi is openly sobbing now.]

Andi: Wh-what did I d-d-do?

Marcus: Can I walk you out?

13

Say Anything (Else)

"Can you believe it about Andi?" Rikki asks me, her pretty face perched on the pillow on the bed across from mine. The remaining nine girls had just spent an hour by the hotel pool discussing Andi's fate, Kendall staring daggers at me the whole time.

Everyone was pissed I had taken all the time with Marcus on the group date tonight, which obviously hadn't been *my* plan. However, the shock of Andi's surprise exit had driven the conversation when we got back, with the producers asking the remaining girls probing questions about what had happened between Marcus and Andi.

"But," Elodie asked us, like she was genuinely confused, "hadn't things seemed so solid between Andi and Marcus all day?"

Elodie was baiting me, and I was smart enough to know it. It wasn't my fault Andi had talked shit and Marcus had gotten rid of her. Besides, I was still floating on the high of winning.

"It just goes to show you that we can never really know what's going on in Marcus's head," Rikki said gamely.

"What do you think, Jac?" Elodie asked pointedly.

"Marcus is here to find a wife," I answered, aware of stoking Kendall's fire. "Andi wasn't it. He thinks one of the rest of us is. Case closed."

"What did you do with Marcus for all that time?" Kendall asked me then. "So much time that none of the rest of us got to see him at all."

Normally, I would've bristled. I would've pointed out that Charlotte and Henry planned it, not me. I would've at least attempted to be the bigger person.

Instead, I winked at her. "Wouldn't you like to know?" (In the episode, sinister music played in the background as I said it, but honestly, I thought it was one of my most likable moments of the season. One TikTok user agreed at least, telling her followers, "I don't care what any of y'all say, I'd die for Jacqueline Matthis. A bitch who truly does not care. A Lady Macbeth with the Lord as her servant. QUEEN. Good for her, destroy them all.")

Kendall rolled her eyes and turned away from me. (In her confessional, she said she knew I somehow caused it; Elodie probably straight up told her that.)

After we'd finally been dismissed from the girl chat, I'd smiled secretly to myself the whole way back to our hotel room. It hadn't escaped Rikki's notice.

"Andi fucked around and found out," I explain. "She told Marcus I gloated about Hannah going home, which he saw straight through." Something about him knowing it was bullshit made me so much more confident in my feelings toward him. "He didn't want someone who spread lies." I shrug.

Rikki sighs, looking over at me longingly. "He really cares about you, doesn't he?"

I laugh, suddenly self-conscious of my own victory. "He cares about you, too. Otherwise, you wouldn't still be here."

"It's not the same. We all know it's between you and Kendall. But it's fine." Rikki gives me a shy smile. "Henry's already mentioned *1 in the sun* to me."

"Rikki Ly finding love on my television this summer?" I say, feigning being overcome. "As I live and die."

She tilts her head back, laughing in the way Rikki does everything, fully open, kind, and sharp-witted.

"Rikki," I say, once our likely-sleep-deprived laughter dies out. "What do you even like me for anyway? No one else here can stand me."

"I don't know," Rikki says, leaning back on her bed and putting her hands behind her head, stretching her body out. Then she admits, "You kind of remind me of my older sister."

I smile, despite myself. Sometimes, taking in something that could even be read as kindness is hard for me. "What's her name?" I ask.

"Sophie," Rikki says then.

"How old is she?"

"She's—uh." Rikki swallows. "She's dead. She died last year. She was twenty-eight."

Normally I fret over hugging other people and I don't know what to do when someone cries, but there's something easy about immediately climbing into bed with Rikki and pulling her into me, us cuddling there with her crying and me holding on to her.

I never would've met Rikki if not for this stupid show, and I never would've been so close to her if this wasn't such an absurd situation, and I find myself oddly grateful for that.

"Yeah," Rikki says once she can talk again, the soft hair of her bun tickling my arm, "I don't know. I felt sort of listless after she died. Like, I left school after her first stint in rehab and I never went back. I moved out to Santa Monica to be with her, and then I just never left. I teach spin and party, you know? I needed *something* so bad and here it was, and the show needed their token Asian girl, right?"

"That's not what you are," I say.

"Yeah, well." She sniffs. "Sophie didn't give a shit what anyone thought of her, like you, but I think maybe it did actually get under her skin. Sometimes, I wonder if she was so embarrassed about her addiction that she couldn't face it. Not Sophie. Not perfect, straight-A, beautiful, Sophie Ly."

"I'm so sorry, Rik," I say. And I want to say I get it, but I don't. What have my problems been in comparison with losing the person you love most in the world?

"I just see her in you, you know? The tough exterior. The marshmallow center."

"Hey," I answer, kissing the top of her black hair, "don't put that evil on me."

"You ever think you'll write about this in one of your books?" Rikki asks me.

I snort, a sound so unladylike, we start giggling all over again. "God, you know, I thought maybe this would be inspiration or something, but instead, I think it would feel like picking a scab. There's so much about this experience I never want to reexamine."

"But it's about love," she says with a watery smile and the kind of hope you only have in your early twenties. "Just like your books."

"Maybe," I hedge. I prop myself up on my elbow, facing her. "I don't even know why I started writing romance to begin with. I was never a romantic." When she doesn't say anything, my thoughts spill out. "You know, I think when people talk about romances, they think of them as simple: two people meet, fall in love, have a misunderstanding, and get back together at the end, right? But I think of them as so much more. Romances are about the complexities of human beings, about the way we all have a best and worst self, and they both live in the same body, and the most generous person you know can have the most toxic ideas of what a relationship is or how you can so desperately want the worst person to end up with someone perfect for them, can peel back all of their layers. I like how raw it is."

"Is that what you told the producers?" Rikki asks.

"Nah," I say. "I told them what they wanted to hear."

"I'm going to buy your book when I get home," Rikki says. "I tried to buy it at the last airport . . ." she starts, but trails off.

"Yeah, they didn't have it. No shelf space for failures."

"You're not a failure," she chides.

I am, though. I always have been. "She chooses her career," I tell Rikki. "The main character in my first book. She chooses art instead of love. It was stupid. Everyone hated it, and I don't know what I was thinking."

Rikki swallows.

"I always get it wrong. Romance." I bite my lip. "Even in fiction. Then I tried to fix it in book two and no one cared anymore."

"You and Marcus are going to get married," she says. "I can see it when he looks at you. You *are* romance."

I give her an affectionate smile. "I wouldn't have survived this far without you," I tell her.

"I know," she mutters into my skin, and I laugh.

We fall asleep like that, twined together, the way I imagine sisters do. I keep thinking about how I'd built up my life to be this great tragedy of millennial ennui and thought of the other girls as simple influencers, desperate failed models, and actresses on the prowl, but here was Rikki, a person with so much more to run from than me, and she was doing it without leaving utter destruction in her wake.

I'd kill to be magnetic like Rikki without hurting everyone around me.

I don't know exactly what time it is when I hear the knock on the door (all clocks have been removed from the room for the sake of driving us utterly insane), but it's still dark outside. I nearly fall out of the bed and onto the floor, I'm so surprised by the sound, but Rikki barely stirs, probably too tired and too cried out to bother.

"If there's a camera at that door," I say out loud to myself, "I may be forced to jump out of the window."

But I open the door, and it's Henry. Just Henry, looking sort of small and lost without the usual cadre of cameramen and assistants and producers behind him.

"Five more minutes," Rikki mumbles as she rolls over.

"What?" I ask, leaning against the door.

Henry swallows, his eyes traveling to Rikki and then back to me. "I need to talk to you," he says.

"Now?"

"Yes, right now." I lean my head out of the door and glance around the hall. Empty.

"Am I going on a date or something?" I ask him.

"No. Just throw on something. No one else is going to see you," he says. He's wearing jeans, a sweatshirt, and a coat. "Could you make it quick?"

"Yeah," I say. "Okay, just a second. No camera is going to pop out, is it?"

Henry shakes his head. "Take the elevator up to Cindy's."

"What about getting back in my room?" I ask. I had been informed when we arrived here, much to my absolute horror, that Rikki and I would not be getting cards to our hotel rooms while we were traveling. We were simply not allowed to leave unless it was for filming, unless we had a producer's permission.

"I'll take care of it," he says.

I turn away from him and close the door, already annoyed at his demands.

"Do we have to get up?" Rikki asks me as I pull a sweater out of my bag. Clothes packed for all weather, all occasions in only two bags, as was demanded.

"Not yet," I say. "I guess they need me for something." I hear myself lying to her and wince.

"I'm not even jealous," she says, yawning, her breathing almost immediately slowing back down.

Feeling oddly naked with nothing to take with me from the room but my clothes and myself, and with no mic on me or cameras trailing, I head to the elevator and press the up button.

When I get to the top, I have to walk out through the interior bar onto the edge of the rooftop to see Henry standing there, framed against the Chicago skyline at night, twinkling lights and water stretching out forever, his back to me. I make my way closer to stand next to him, leaning against the glass wall, and he doesn't turn to look at me.

"It was kind of hard to enjoy with all the cameras around," I say. The lights are still bright in the skyline, the lake sitting peacefully in the quiet of the night. An ambulance siren blares in the distance and a train rumbles by, and I remember the sound of a city like a lullaby putting you to sleep every night.

Henry chuckles, the vibrations reaching out to me from where his arm is touching mine. "Isn't everything?"

I don't answer, and he doesn't say anything more. We stand like that, side by side.

"What are we doing here?" I finally ask.

Henry keeps his gaze trained on the lake. "Did you have sex with Marcus in the two minutes you were left alone in the hot tub today?"

I wait a beat before I say, "Only a little bit."

His gaze shifts to me, and we make eye contact. I start to laugh, and then he does, too. Then we are both laughing here on the edge of the world in the middle of the night in Chicago, nothing but two fuckups seeing each other clearly.

"You are going to get *destroyed*, Jac," he says to me, still slightly gleeful as we quiet down.

"Ah, yes. Didn't wait to have sex until the producer-sanctioned overnights. It barely even counted."

"You're smart enough to know they kept filming when they left you alone in there, right?" (Strictly speaking, they were only filming a crack through the door—you couldn't see Marcus or me and you could only hear some splashing noise and whispers—helpfully subtitled—but the implication was enough.)

"Shit," I say, putting my head down. "I mean, I guess deep down, I knew, but my hormones . . ."

"Yeah," Henry says, openly smirking now. "I know."

I bite into my lip, aware of the ease the two of us have so quickly fallen back into. I find something almost distasteful about it, the easy way he slides into my side. The way I want him there.

"I don't want you to do this to me," I say, looking over at him as I push a piece of hair out of my face. "Keep manipulating me. Even using these small moments you carve out for us to manipulate me."

"It's called producing," he quickly corrects me. "And you knew what it was when you signed up for it."

"You kissed me," I tell him. "Was that part of producing me?"

He looks away from me, out over the city. "I thought we agreed to pretend that never happened?"

"We didn't agree to anything because you barely spoke to me." I throw my hands out in front of me. "*Everything* you do is all part of some scheme of yours, and I keep falling for it. Do you know how much I hate that?"

"I've read your file," Henry answers. "So yes, I know exactly how much you hate it."

"Fuck you," I return. "Marcus hates you. You forgot to mention that. That you're not producing him because he hates you. Because you did the exact same shit to him that you're doing to me."

His expression changes, becomes almost urgent, and he moves a little bit closer to me as he says, "It's not the same, I promise you."

"So you did fuck him over? Did you tell him to say he had sex with Shailene on camera?"

"Oh, come off it," he says, both of our voices rising. We can finally go at each other now, in a way we never could with the cameras rolling all around us. "Marcus fucked over Shailene all on his own. Not everything I do is a fucking strategy, I'm a real person."

"I've seen little evidence that everything between us hasn't just been so you can get more good TV out of me."

"You're right," Henry says, pushing away from the railing overlooking the rooftop. "I pre-banged you as part of my production strategy."

"Who *are you*?" I demand. "Are you some slick-as-fuck producer who hoards compliments and only gives them out when a girl has done exactly what you want, or are you some fucking California sad boy who hates himself and his job and the world? Like, what the fuck is this, Henry, and why are you doing it *to me*?"

"Don't," he says, "fall for Marcus."

"Jesus, you are trying to sabotage us both!"

"I don't actually care about sabotaging Marcus fucking Bellamy, thank you very much," Henry hisses. "Did I do everything in my power to keep him from becoming the lead this season? Yes. Is it personal? Also yes."

"So what is it?" I ask him, crossing my arms over my chest. "Are you jealous of him? Did he sleep with your fiancée or something?"

Henry openly rolls his eyes at me. "Please. You watch too many soap operas."

"Maybe . . ." I lick my lip, letting myself warm up to the idea. Even just to saying it to get a rise out of him. "Maybe you're jealous of him and . . . me."

A slow smile spreads across Henry's face after I say it, as we let it settle between the both of us. He's looking at me like he's just realized it. "You want me to be jealous over you, don't you?"

"What?" I answer quickly. Then I say, "Henry, why did you come to my room in the middle of the night when there were no cameras around?"

He turns away from me and walks back into the bar without saying anything. Prick.

I follow him back inside. That bar itself is designed to let light in with a sloping glass rooftop coming down on all four walls into brick accents, Chicago-style. Everything else is polished wood, slick, with fairy lights strung up in rows next to the windows, spherical light fixtures hanging down, turned off. The light from the night is enough to make Henry clear to me.

He is leaned over the huge bar back against the wall we came in from, fishing a bottle of Woodford Reserve out from behind it and pouring us both a generous amount into water glasses. He slides one over to me.

"We're too old to drink this much," I say to him as I take a sip from the glass.

"I think the reason I like the Southern girls the best is I get to drink a lot more bourbon when they're around," he says, glancing sideways over at me. I boost myself up onto the bar next to where he's standing, swinging my legs.

"So, you like the Southern girls?"

He taps his glass against mine. The air is electric, and we both know it. Everything Henry said to me at the pizza place about this not happening is bullshit and we both know it. I ease into it. "Since you know all the bad things I've done, it's only fair if you tell me something really fucked up you've done."

Henry thinks about it for a minute, leaning back against the bar, his lips pressed together. I see the way his posture changes when he arrives at the right story. "Okay, so one time," he tells me, "I was on the 405 for three hours waiting on this girl to cry after she got eliminated. John told me literally not to come back to set if she didn't cry."

"Fuck off," I say.

"Dead serious," he says, but he's laughing. "She wasn't a crier— she just wasn't. I don't even think she liked the lead. So I had to use this old trick one of the other producers taught me of rubbing

jalapeño under my eyes to make myself cry. That's how upset I tried
to convince her *I* was about the disillusionment of her relationship.
We took four shots together, and I eventually got her to cry by talking
about her grandpa." His voice fades as he continues. "Her grandpa
who died by suicide," he finishes, setting down his whiskey. "By the
end, I really was crying because—" He looks up at me and shakes his
head. "Because, I don't know, that's what's happened to my brain."

"Every day, you have to be both the least human and most human
version of yourself," I say.

He thinks about it for a moment and nods. "So," he says, hopping
up on the bar to sit next to me, "why'd you fuck Marcus?"

"I don't know," I say, taking a sip of bourbon and staring straight
ahead. "It's usually what I do when I want something."

"The Andi thing?" he asks.

"No," I say. "That was just spontaneous." Fuck, he knew about
that, too.

Which meant he probably knew the other thing.

It's you, Jac.

But he wasn't asking me about that.

"Why do *you* want me?" I ask him. "Do you think?"

He finishes his drink, which is actually quite a bit of work as it was
still over half full.

"Ah, well," he says, setting his glass back on the bar with a clink.
"I figure it's probably a mix of things. The fact that I'm the only
person in production right now with keys to this bar and that I
drank three bourbons already tonight is a contributing factor."

"Sure," I agree.

"Then there's the slick-as-fuck producer thing you so astutely
pointed out where I've had opportunities with contestants for years
and haven't taken them because I wanted to see myself as a good guy,
but you obviously know that nothing about doing this job would
ever even slightly allow you to be a good person, so what have I been
waiting for?"

I nod. "Right."

"And then there's the—what did you say again?" he asks, tilting
his head to the side as he looks at me.

"Fucking California sad boy," I supply.

"Right. That. That's kind of the main one, right? So, that makes me darkly, caustically desperate for you in a way that feeds even more into my self-loathing."

"Uh-huh," I say, nodding as I look over at him. "All that tracks."

We both sit in silence following that, absorbing it. Our shoulders are touching, and I can hear us both breathing in a way that I hate. A way that might drive me crazy.

"So," he finally says, "are we going to do this?"

I toss back the rest of my drink. "I thought you'd never ask."

As if on cue, we both go to our knees on the bar, our bodies turning to face one another as we collide. My hands immediately go to the front of his coat, pushing it off as his mouth presses into mine.

I feel my heartbeat all over my body, in my stomach and my fingers and head. It's like a wake-up call, an espresso, a cold shower to ward off a hangover. It's like seeing a girl you haven't seen in months and recognizing her, realizing that's *you*.

Henry's hands creep up my rib cage, his fingers sliding up my skin tantalizingly slowly as he pushes my sweater as far up as he can, his mouth going to my stomach, then my exposed breasts, the heat fire against my cold skin.

I grab the sweater and pull it all the way off, and then his lips trail up to my neck, his teeth against my skin there before he's back at my mouth, my chest pressed against his sweatshirt.

The first time, it had been like there wasn't enough time, there would never be enough time, but we've both thrown out how we're supposed to act, and now we're just letting ourselves have it, two brats who have decided to stop sharing at last.

His hands are back on my midsection, sinking lower until they push down the leggings I was wearing. Awkward, I maneuver back onto my ass on the bar, re-leveraging myself so he can get the leggings the rest of the way off, and he leans down forward over me, his mouth nipping my skin again before he's on top of me, a hand curling around my neck.

"Henry," I say between his kisses.

"Mm."

Before I can answer, his hand slips between my legs, one finger, then another. I gasp out, shivering, taking in short breaths.

"What?" he says again, pushing in farther. He pushes far enough that I let out a gasp before I respond.

I bite into my lip, trying to form words. "Take," I manage to get out as his fingers move faster, "off your clothes."

"Oh, fuck. Right."

He hops off the bar, pulling his sweatshirt and T-shirt off in one go before he even fully hits the ground, unbuttoning his jeans. I push myself up onto my elbows, watching him with a laugh. I love the sight of his chest, the flat plane of his stomach—someone who goes to the gym but isn't married to it.

I'm sensitive about so many things about myself, but being naked? Being naked is something I'm not worried about.

He kicks off his pants, his hands grabbing on to his boxers before I say, "Wait."

He stops, his hands not moving from his waistband. I can tell exactly how much he doesn't want me to finish this thought. "What?"

I feel my eyebrow go up as I say, "You could barely even look at me this afternoon." He keeps staring at me, waiting for me to make my point. "Do you just want me now because Marcus had me?"

"I had you way before Marcus did," he answers too quickly and spitefully, like he's sure it's true. Like he knows he has me even now.

I laugh. "So, this is just another way to control me?"

"Jac." He blows out a long breath. "I am not *producing* you. This is not part of the fucking show."

"It can't be real," I throw back at him. "That would be against the rules."

He gives me this helpless look. "Do I look like I give a fuck?" He gestures back to himself. "How do you see this ending well for me?"

I push forward, shove myself off the bar and onto the floor, grabbing up my leggings and pulling them back on.

He swallows. "You don't get it. I don't *do this*, Jac. This never would've happened if it hadn't happened before. You saw me outside and then you saw me inside, and that's the difference between you and every other contestant who's made fuck-me eyes at me before."

"So, you would've wanted any of them?" I demand. "You would be fucking Kendall right now if she had been the person you ran into at Chalet?"

"That's *not* what I said," he says as I pull my sweater back on. "Just . . . I don't know how to do this. I'm not even sure I should."

"Then I'll make the choice for both of us." I cross my arms, finally fully dressed, my anger at war with my raging libido, my disappointment that I'd rather not examine too deeply. Two beginnings, two disappointing endings. "I think it's time for you to take me back to my room," I say.

He re-dresses in silence.

the 1 season 32 contestants—producer notes

Kendall Dyer

30 and sensitive about it. Too hot for her own good but also surprisingly funny. WILL STIR SHIT UP WITH THE SLIGHTEST PROVOCATION. The desperate one? The narrator?

Rikki Ly

Tragic backstory—older sister's overdose. Instant tears. Loves drinks and spinning and talking about her fake tits. She is going to annoy the shit out of some people in the house.
The drunk one! (Viewers will be dying to see her on TTS).

Andi Brockovich

Accountant—don't let her talk about her job, it's an absolute SNOOZE. Will cry a lot and believes almost anything she hears (she is one wrong Facebook post away from joining QAnon at any time). Not smart enough to purposely create drama but definitely dumb enough to accidentally create it. Very sensitive. Might want to get Charlotte on her.

Shae Brady

Big lead potential. Smart, savvy. Relatable to middle America. Major diversity points here.

14

Up & Go

I'm awake too early the next morning, dressed and in makeup, and talking about Marcus again with the girls.

Girl chats have become a part of my daily life like flossing or eating carrot sticks. Things I don't see the point in but am obligated to do anyway. I try not to say too much unless there's only two of us. The more girls get eliminated, the harder it gets to disappear into the background.

The hour-long chat seems to be winding down when Elodie drops the bomb: "What would you all think if someone acted outside of the journey to get something they wanted?"

"Like what?" Kendall asks, suddenly intrigued. My blood runs cold; I see the hit job coming from a mile away.

Elodie shrugs innocently. "I don't know, like if someone got physical with Marcus in a way other girls hadn't or couldn't."

Kendall sips her beloved cucumber water, smacking her lips before she leans back in her chair and crosses her legs. "What do you know, Elodie?"

"You mean, like," Kady starts, "if someone slept with Marcus?"

I almost resist saying it but instead: "Since no one has revealed a heartwarming story about their virginity, I'm guessing we're all interested in sleeping with Marcus. I don't really see how other people's physical relationships are our business."

Kendall laughs. "Jac, did you sleep with Marcus?"

I sip the white wine I'd only grabbed to nurse. I smirk because it's all I've got. "Well, I guess we all know you didn't," I say.

Shae actually snorts. Kendall takes another sip of her water with an eyebrow raised. She knows. They all know.

"We saw Marcus on Shailene's season," Kady interjects. "He's sexually driven for sure."

"You think he could be manipulated with sex?" Elodie asks.

"Marcus is an adult," I say. "I think he can make his own decisions."

"What did you do, Jac?" Kendall asks curiously.

"Is this for real?" I ask, posing the question to Elodie, who is giving me a picture-of-innocence look.

Elodie answers, "Jac can choose to share whatever she wants about her relationship with Marcus. We all know the relationships with Marcus are going to the next level. Anyone here worried they haven't made enough progress yet? Grace-Ann?" And the conversation moves on.

When Elodie releases us, I follow some of the other girls out for their smoke breaks, lingering behind to catch a separate elevator. Kendall gives me a look when I come down into the lobby, where she's just handed off a list of essentials to one of the production assistants.

"What are you doing down here?" she asks. "You don't smoke."

"Air," I answer simply.

She gives me a once-over. "You think Marcus really slept with Shailene?"

The question takes me aback, not just for its abruptness but for the fact it's pointed at me. I had never really thought about it, except for briefly while watching the season. Shailene was ashamed of what she had done, sure, but I had been positive she was claiming she hadn't to preserve her relationship with Bentley, who was insanely jealous. "Yes," I say.

"Hmm" is all she says in response.

"Do you know something?" I ask her.

She sighs heavily. "Go smoke your cigarette."

More irritated than I was before, I make my way out of the hotel and to the side of the building where everyone is standing in groups, puffing on cigarettes with various smoke smells. I approach the first people I get to, Kady and Aaliyah.

"Bum?" I ask Kady.

She gives me a scathing look, but holds a cigarette out to me anyway. She's whispering with Aaliyah, which I assume means she's spilling the whole story to her. To the side of them, Priya and Brendan appear to be in conversation. There's an interesting duo.

And then I spot Janelle, smoking alone. I go stand with her.

"Jac," she says as we stand there, staring over a gray Chicago street, dirty water puddled around from a storm in the early morning.

"Janelle," I answer. I don't know much about her, aside from some of the other crew members calling her the lead whisperer.

"I didn't know you smoked," she says, sucking in on her cigarette.

"I don't," I admit, holding my cigarette out. Methodically, Janelle holds up a lighter, and I take a puff, igniting the end. I suck it in and then blow out, never really swallowing the smoke. "Just wish I did sometimes."

"Terrible habit," she answers, pocketing the lighter, giving me a sly smile. "Stress getting to you?"

"Something like that," I agree.

"You're tough," she says.

I chew on that for a minute, still surface-level smoking my cigarette. "You don't really know anything about me," I say.

She barks out a laugh. "No," she says, eyeing me. "Just that you don't know how to smoke."

My eyebrow goes up and I half smile. "How'd you get into this?" I ask her.

"I wanted," she says, tilting her head over as she looks at me with a hint of irony, "to be a writer. It's what I went to school for."

"Ah," I say, not really knowing what to say.

"What did you go to school for?" she asks me.

"Advertising," I say with a self-deprecating grin. "Didn't think I'd ever make enough money to be a writer, full-time. In some ways, I was right." I ash my wasted cigarette against the concrete behind me. "Did you ever write anything?"

"Half a screenplay," Janelle says, "before I got hired to work on this high school reunion reality show. It was all up from there."

"Do you like it?" I ask.

"Like it?" She smiles. "I love it."

"Plenty of stories to tell now, I guess."

"Something like that," she agrees, tossing her cigarette down. "I'll see you later, okay, Jac?"

She leaves me standing alone, staring off at the girls who hate me, staring back at me.

RIKKI IS GONE the next night, on a two-on-one with Grace-Ann, where one of them will be asked to stay and the other will be told she's not the one, joining Andi and another waif of a girl—Miley or Missy or something like that—who was eliminated last night. I'd be lying if I said I wasn't sweating that my best friend, my *only* friend, could be gone after tonight. It didn't take a relationship expert to see that her connection with Marcus was thin at best, her life at twenty-two in California vastly different from his at thirty-four in Chicago.

Her saving grace is likely that Grace-Ann is dull as dishwater. (Proven by the fact that, at dinner, Rikki had too much wine and briefly fell asleep while Grace-Ann was talking, which Marcus purported to find endearing instead of absurd. Though I'll always think him keeping Rikki was a favor to me.) I doubt, once the show airs, Grace-Ann will merit more than fifteen minutes of screen time getting whittled down to the final seven. The camera loves Rikki, and the producers do, too.

Or at least, that's what Charlotte told me.

She'd been in earlier, just to check in. Something about the check-in made me bristle, like I'd known there was an ulterior motive (I always suspected there was) but been unable to ferret it out.

"There's a certain inevitability," I told her, "to all the relationships here, isn't there?"

She was sitting on Rikki's bed opposite me and tilted her head to the side, not skeptically but genuinely curious. "What do you mean?"

"Well, obviously you, me, and everyone else know Marcus and Rikki won't be getting married. And, like, come on, I *knew* Shailene was picking Bentley last season. I know you guys knew. And yet, you have to convince each of us that Marcus is in love with us, and we know deep down he's not, right? It's all about the story we're telling ourselves, what we want to believe. You're just enablers."

Charlotte smiled gently. "And what do you want to believe, Jac?"

That I'm not a piece of shit, I don't say. Instead, "I want to believe in the fairy tale. That's why I write romance books. There's a missing chip in my head that's supposed to make me want to be the heroine in romance books, but I can't so I write them instead, looking for myself."

"I guess so," Charlotte said after a minute.

Charlotte noticed I had bought five books (one each by Mhairi McFarlane, Bora Chung, Robinne Lee, Kiley Reid, and Adrienne Brodeur) at the last airport we were at but didn't try to confiscate them, for which I was grateful. Maybe her pregnancy was making her soft.

I am reading one of those books right now—one, per the back cover, enthusiastically recommended by an author I used to run into in New York publishing circles, who could never be bothered with remembering my name, no matter how many times we met. I had the fatal flaw of not being successful or likable enough.

I'd seen Henry pulling Aaliyah and Kendall into a girl chat earlier, so I knew he wasn't on the two-on-one date. I'd started to realize that the whole setup of the producers this season seemed to aim to keep Henry and Marcus out of each other's eyesight, which made a certain kind of sense. I wondered if Marcus had been the real reason Henry didn't want to come back to *the 1* this year, as he clearly had no problem with any of the other heinous shit he did on a daily basis.

What had Marcus done that so offended Henry's delicate sensibilities?

I have a glass of wine and a lot of time to kill. I go to the bathroom, put on a face mask, and as I'm making my way back to my bed, I notice a binder shoved in the side of the entertainment center where a television would be had it not been removed before we arrived. It's pushed way into the back, almost suspiciously far into the back.

I remember the binder. Charlotte had been carrying it when she came into the room. Suspicious, I pull it out and look at the cover.

the 1 Season 32

The thing is, I know I will hate whatever this is. Know I will hate it deep down in my bones, the way you send an angry email and dread seeing the reply. I open it up anyway.

First, there is a shooting schedule, some notes written on it. Cancun. Paris. Saint-Étienne-Vallée-Française. Hotels scratched out, hometown locations jotted down, rental companies listed. It is both unsettling and an inevitability that I see my parents' address written in what I assume is Charlotte's sloppy handwriting.

The next section is room numbers for all the contestants and producers, plus the crew members, who mostly appear to be staying in a nearby, not-quite-as-nice hotel.

Then I reach the real meat of the binder. Pages on each of the contestants. Charlotte has meticulously combed through and put giant red X's on anyone who has been eliminated. Her notes are scattered though, scribbled around the margins of the papers, which have our basic bio info laid out next to a small picture of each of us in the upper left-hand corner.

Someone—the handwriting doesn't match Charlotte's on the other pages, so I'm not sure who—has gone through and given each girl a nickname in green marker that sits prominently on top of each page, even above our names. I ascertain that the words have been on these pages from the very beginning because each girl has one, even the girls who were eliminated on night one (one aptly named CANNON FODDER). Some girls have gone through transformations with their original name written and then scratched out. Kady exchanged from THE MANIPULATIVE INFLUENCER to THE HEART—based on what I assumed I'd find out when the show aired in a couple of months. Rikki has undergone several changes from THE DRUNK ONE to THE WEEPY ONE back to THE DRUNK ONE.

And then, there is me. My title hasn't changed since the first night apparently.

THE CUNT

I sit with that for a long time, skimming down the page to see what other notes have been included. *Drinks too much.* That seems a bit unfair since everyone drinks too much on the production, but I'll take it. *Petty.* Probably. Whatever. *Superiority complex.* Fuck, goddammit. Fuck. I spent so much of my life trying not to know what people thought about me and yet here it is. Here's what everyone thinks about me.

And it's exactly what I've always suspected about myself.

But, somehow, it's the last comment that really stuns me, hits me where I don't expect it. It says: *Jac Matthis thinks she's special, so make her feel special.*

And I know that handwriting. The way the *o* is a perfect circle and the *k* never actually touches. Just like the note he wrote me by the pool.

Henry wrote it.

Hatefully, I feel tears welling in my eyes as I snap the binder shut and throw it across the room, tearing my face mask off. I feel fury possessing me. I am so angry and so stupidly hurt. I'm still the same old me I've always been, a bitch who is bad at people, and now a million people across a million households are going to hate me, and the worst thing is, *I didn't even see it coming.*

Some chance to start over.

I was supposed to be the down-to-earth girl—the one guys wanted to fuck and girls wanted to hang out with—but I never actually was, no matter how hard I tried. I was always the one trying too hard and pissing everyone else off.

I leave the room, let the door close behind me and take off. The room numbers are burned behind my eyes just like every word about me. I'm at his door, and I'm banging on it, and if he doesn't answer, I don't know what I'll do, I don't know who I'll become.

Henry answers the door. I burst into tears.

"Jac?" he asks, then he grabs on to me and pulls me through the door, closing and locking it behind him. "What's wrong?" he asks, and I wonder if he is barely resisting the urge to go get a camera crew right now.

What do you think of me? I might ask him if I could get the words out. *Am I someone worth loving?*

Of course not. I never had been.

I shove away from Henry, a late-arriving instinct, and he holds both hands up in surrender. "Dare I ask how you found my room?"

"The cunt," I say, hiccupping around my stupid tears. "*The cunt!* From the very first day, that's who I was to all of you."

Henry's eyes go wide. "How do you—"

"You're not even going to deny it!" I scream. "What the fuck did I sign up for? *Who* did I sign up to be?"

"Jac," he says. "Listen."

"I'm *done* fucking listening to anything you say. I know what you think of me. God." I bury my face in my hands. This is what *they want*. This me. I'm a bad person and an unstable person and an unlovable person. "*What* is the point of all this? Why?" I beg him.

"Jac," he says again, and he moves forward, his hands wrapping around my forearms. I try to pull away from him, but he holds on to me until I'm looking up at him, his dark brown eyes on me. "Look at me. Talk to me. *Fuck* this show."

I blink, a tear creeping down my cheek. "Why should I believe you? 'Jac Matthis thinks she's special, so make her feel special.' You think I don't know who wrote that? How did you *see* that? *How?*"

"I wrote it because I wanted it to be true. I wanted to treat you like any other contestant," he admits sheepishly.

"I've been trying to hide for so long and you expose me in one fucking sentence, Henry."

His fingers are still wrapped around my wrists. "It's just a piece of paper. It's not you."

"It's what you think of me," I say. I'm crying again or I never stopped crying. "What they all think of me. That's my story. The cunt. That's all it's ever been."

"Hey," he whispers, his hand going to cup my cheek, where I'd opened up everything, spilled it out for him. The thought keeps racing through my mind like a high-speed train: *It worked. Everything he did worked.* "Remember when we met?"

I did. Two seats down from me at an overpriced bar in Santa Monica. I'd thought almost nothing about him, even though everything about him was appealing, a man perfectly designed to hit all of my weak spots.

"You wanted to fuck me," I say. "Just like Marcus." I avert my gaze, and his hands don't leave my face. "Shit," I mumble.

"I thought, *I've never wanted a person so much. I've never wanted to stare at a woman so long.*"

"You were engaged to a model, Henry."

"I thought this woman sees straight through me, and I was so sick of me."

"I didn't see through you," I say. "I just said whatever I thought would get us in bed fastest." My skin is still warm where we're touching.

"I'd torch this whole building to be back there, to forget all of this bullshit," he says. "You're so smart and so scared of yourself and everyone else when you don't have to be. You still haven't figured that out yet."

I look back up at him, through my eyelashes, stuck together with tears. "You've been wanting to burn everything down since the first time I set eyes on you."

"Finally caught up," he says, flicking a tear away with his nail, "have you?"

"Are you producing me?" I whisper to him then.

We're so close. We could crawl into each other, and we should, I would. He says, "Depends on if it's working."

I push myself onto my tiptoes and kiss him, frenzied and fast. *Love me*, I beg with my mouth and my body. *Love me. Please love me.*

"Okay," he says, and I know I've said it out loud, desperate and disturbed, and he's agreed to it, so I'm not sure which one of us is worse.

We both stop, and we stare at each other, like the absolute fuckups we are. This time, we know we're completely crossing the line in a way neither of us can take back, professionally or emotionally. We decide at the same time we're okay with that.

I push Henry back against the wall of his room, next to the entertainment console (where he does in fact have a television), my fingers going to the buttons of his jeans, pulling them down, my hands finding him hard, and he sucks in a breath at the cool touch of my skin.

His hands go under my dress to my bare thighs, and he pushes against me, swinging me around with ease so my back is against the wall, his fingers wrapping around the material of my underwear, pulling them down, and his fingers immediately going into me, so I gasp out, my head leaned up against the wall, tilted up to the blank white ceiling of the hotel room. I let myself go for the first time in weeks. I'm me in the worst ways and the best.

"Come on," I say into Henry's eyes, between gasping. "You can do better than that, right?"

He groans, his hands catching up in my underwear abandoned around my thighs and he pulls them off onto the ground until he can hitch me up against the wall, his arms looping around my legs as our skin slides against each other, him so close and then fully inside of me.

The tension doesn't release but it's almost like a sigh, like relief, like two bodies that have been so desperate to feel this again since the first time, and we'd been denying it, the way he braces his arms on either side of me and the wall bruises my ass in a way that feels more like reward than regret. We're drug addicts who've given up the sober life, and I can't believe I ever considered not getting high again.

Henry bites into my shoulder as he comes, lightly, but I still feel the pain, as real as being alive. He drops me, and I slide my feet down onto the floor, exhausted, but his fingers are back, and he works at me until I come, too, finally releasing a shuddering sigh, eyes closed.

When I open my eyes, the ceiling is still blank and white.

I'm panting, and I point in the direction of the bathroom. "I have to—" I start, and when Henry nods, still silent, I pick my underwear up off the floor and go to the restroom and pee.

I stare at myself for a moment in the big, bright, clean restroom as I wash my hands. I touch the dark spot on my shoulder, which will surely bruise. Something to think about when I select my clothes for the next few days.

And I'm already back at it, thinking about the show. Considering winning. Considering winning Marcus.

I shouldn't be this skinny, I think as I stare at my body. I'm hungry. I'm hungry and I look gaunt, and I'm still a cunt.

Maybe it's better we all know it.

Back in the hotel room, Henry is sitting on the edge of the bed, scrolling through his phone. I sit down next to him, our sides touching.

"Hey," he says, setting his phone aside.

"So," I say, "this is pretty fucked up."

"Sure," he agrees. We both sit there, staring straight ahead, until Henry finally says, "Do you want to talk about it?"

"Not really."

"Right."

"I could . . ." I say, gesturing with my hands awkwardly for a moment. I finally give up and drop them. "Again."

"So, the thing is," Henry begins, scratching the back of his neck, "I'm kind of sharing this room with another crew member and if he comes back to the room, and—"

"Yeah," I say, spotting the issue. So much for torching the place. "Okay," I say, slapping my hands against my bare thighs and standing up. "I guess I should go then."

"And by go, you mean—"

"You have to take me back to my room because you basically control every aspect of my life? Yes," I confirm. He grins to himself and grabs a key card from the mess of papers on his bedside table. We are both walking to the door when I stop. "Henry," I say. He's behind me, but I don't turn around. "I don't want all of America to hate my guts. I already hate myself too much, okay?"

"It's just a stupid thing we do," he says. "We slot people into the roles we think they'll play. It's a moving target, storylines change."

"Mine hasn't," I answer him.

Like a chill, I feel him behind me, his lips pressed into my shoulder, into the forming bruise, his hands light on my hips. I close my eyes for a moment, breathe in it.

"You don't have to keep playing," he says. His grip on my hips tightens. "It's not real. Marcus—" But he cuts himself off.

I twist around to look at him, his fingertips still resting lightly on my hips. "What about Marcus?"

Henry drops his hands and looks down at the hardwood floor

we're both standing on, the five-hundred-dollar sneakers he wore while he fucked me, steels himself, then looks back up at me. "He was never going to propose to Shailene."

"What?"

"He sabotaged their relationship, played it to make himself the victim so he'd get this role. He was never going to propose."

"That's because he's smart. He knew Shailene wasn't going to pick him, and that kept him from making a fool of himself."

"Why do you think that?" Henry asks me. "She begged him to stay. She was basically in pieces."

"Did she sleep with him?" I ask then. "Why would she lie about that if she was going to pick Marcus?"

"Because she was embarrassed. It was none of our business if she slept with him. And for the record, I still have no idea if she did or not. Only the two of them ever really knew."

"That's really rich, coming from you," I say. "When you had Marcus talk about it. And the show sure as shit wanted us to think she slept with him."

"The fuck I told Marcus to do that. Shailene only agreed to do the show if we promised not to mention anything that happened in the overnight dates. It was private for her. Marcus went rogue. I never trusted him, I *made* him who he was that whole season, made Shailene fall in love with him, and he used it to do that to her."

"Listen to you," I say. "Marcus is who he always was." But as I say it, I do wonder if he ever has been. I scroll through my Rolodex of conversations with Marcus, my fixation on his physicality.

Maybe Marcus had only existed in my head. I had always thought of him as straightforward, but that was only true about certain things. There was a certain aloofness to him that made me want him to see me, but maybe he had been playing a character just as much as I had.

"I don't think you believe that," Henry says, watching me coming to the conclusion he has just laid out.

"Marcus went through a lot." I can't help but defend him, can't help but want to. Until half an hour ago, he had taken up a good portion of my daily thoughts. "His dad had cancer. It was really fucking him up."

"Believe what you want to believe," Henry says, and something goes dead behind his eyes, jealousy or spite, I don't know.

"I do," I say. "I will. Marcus had no power; none of us do."

I drop back for a moment, lean against the door, surveying him. I'd always loved the way Henry looked, from the first day I'd met him. There'd never been a lead on *the 1* who ever looked like Henry, and so much the worse for it. He had a certain kind of slouchy, casual elegance, easy informal T-shirts paired with perfectly tailored jeans, and outlandishly expensive tennis shoes. Dark hair, thick eyebrows, and a slow, hard smile.

He looks at me wearily, then to his watch.

I wonder at the way Henry might hold on to someone, how he couldn't, not really, even if he was. There'd always be a distance there, a distance between him and forever, and a distance between him and me.

It wasn't even really that I was considering him; it was that I wondered if, in real life, he'd ever consider me.

"Henry," I say, and I reach out for him, grab on to the front of his T-shirt, balling it into my hand and tugging him over to me, until our faces are inches apart, where our foreheads could touch, another moment of intimacy. "Now would've been the time to say, 'Believe me, Jac.'"

"I don't play losing games." Henry's voice is low, charged.

"That's more my territory, isn't it," I say, waiting for Henry to go ahead of me and open the door.

Penultimate Episode of *the 1* Season 31

[Shailene is sitting with Marcus in a modern-styled living room on a couch.]

Shailene, near tears: I don't understand, Marcus. Why would you say that we slept together? And in front of [her voice drops] *everyone*.

Marcus: Don't do this to me. Don't you dare do this to me.

Shailene: How can I trust you? How can I trust you to keep intimate moments private? How can I trust you not to lie?

Marcus, with a sarcastic smile: So, now you're calling me an untrustworthy liar?

Shailene, fully sobbing now: What we had was private. It was important to me that it was private.

Marcus: You're being dishonest, Shailene. How can we ever move forward if we can't be transparent about our intimacy? You've always known who I was.

[Marcus speaks to someone offscreen.]

Marcus: My stuff is already packed.

Shailene: Wait. Please wait.

[Marcus gets up from the couch and goes out to the balcony, overlooking a winter wonderland in Scotland. Momentarily, Shailene is crying too hard to get up. After she has somewhat collected herself, she looks to the same person off camera.]

Shailene: Can he do that? Can he just leave?

[No answer.]

[Marcus is outside, his head bent, staring out over the landscape.]

Marcus: I can't believe this.

[He rubs his face, though no tears are on it. Shailene appears over his shoulder, slightly more collected, despite the mascara running down her face. She reaches for Marcus's hand and he tenses.]

Shailene: Marcus, please. Let's go back inside. Let's talk about this.

[Marcus pulls his hand away from Shailene and goes to sit in a chair nearby. Face still buried.]

Marcus, voice choked: I never wanted this.

[Shailene kneels on the floor next to him, touching him slightly. She's openly crying again.]

Shailene: Please. Please don't leave.

Marcus: I don't know if my dad is going to live through the next year, but he struggled through that to meet you. I left him, to be here, and all for what? For someone who can't even give me honesty? Who can't love me in a real way? In the way I need?

Shailene, sobbing: I can. I will. Please, let me try. Please stay. I'll do better.

[Marcus looks up, shaking his head resolutely.]

Marcus: I wasn't asking for that much.

Shailene: I'll do whatever you need. I'll figure it out, whatever you want. If this is really about physical intimacy . . .

Marcus, angry: It's not *about* that. It's about not even being allowed to have an open conversation about it.

Shailene: But we did. We did, didn't we? Off camera? I thought we understood.

   [Marcus gets up from the chair, going inside, leaving Shailene doubled over on the floor crying.]

15

The Patron Saint of Liars and Fakes

Rikki comes back well after three in the morning, and I almost cry. While she's in the bathroom, getting ready for bed, I set the binder outside of the room, leaning it against the door. The next morning, it's gone.

"We're going to go up to Kendall's room," Charlotte says when she comes to our door a little after ten. Rikki and I had ordered a big breakfast from room service, and the debris is scattered by our door. "Bring your book," Charlotte continues. Rikki goes to stand up from her bed. "Just Jac."

Suspicion aroused (*This has nothing to do with Henry,* I tell myself), I do as I'm told and follow Charlotte to Kendall's room. Instead of Kendall, Kady, Henry, crew, and a cameraman are the only other people in the room, all facing a sitting area with a plush red couch.

"What is this?" I ask.

"We want to give you two a chance to talk," Charlotte says. "About your problems."

Kady momentarily preens, flipping her hair over her shoulder. I sigh.

"Fine. If it'll squash the drama."

"Jac," Henry says, and I think the last time he said that, his body was pressed against mine. "Just sit here on the couch, read your book, and we'll have Kady tap you on the shoulder. Make it look more natural." He pats the couch where he wants me to sit, and I snort.

"Natural. Right."

But we do it, and it goes just like planned, the two of us like bad actors on a badly written TV show. *The cunt,* I think as I'm sitting there, feeling all their eyes on me. *I'll give them the cunt.* "Can we chat for a minute?" Kady asks me, really hamming it up for the camera.

"Pull up a seat," I say, indicating the empty space on the couch beside me as I fold over the corner of the page to hold my spot (*of course jac disrespects books,* some unhinged watcher posts online when it airs).

"I want to talk to you about what happened with Andi," Kady says once she's seated, her body turned to face me.

I narrow my eyes. "I wasn't even there when Andi went home."

"You know what I mean," Kady snaps, quickly escalating the argument. "You told Marcus to send her home."

"She told Marcus to send me home," I fire back, and then immediately hate the words coming out of my mouth. I sound like a middle schooler.

"We're just being honest with him about how you treat other people," Kady says. She's really been working on this speech for a long time, I can tell. "You're manipulating him, and now you're trying to manipulate me."

"That is," I say, "hilarious."

"You really don't give a shit about anyone but yourself, do you?"

I sigh, looking at Charlotte. "Do I have to do this?" I ask her.

"*Look* at me," Kady demands.

I stand up. "*No!*" I can't help it, my frustration spilling out. "I don't have to look at you. This is utterly ridiculous. Marcus is a grown man. You are supposedly an adult, too. Andi came after me for no reason, and actions have consequences."

Kady stands up, too. "It's because you're horrible! You won't even apologize."

"Grow up," I say, picking up my book and looking desperately at Charlotte, at the room we're trapped in. "I don't care about you. I treat you like you're beneath me because you act like a child. Let me leave," I say to Charlotte.

"That wasn't very productive," Charlotte tells me. Kady has stormed off to the restroom.

"Was it meant to be?" I ask. Henry is smirking at me beside her. *Asshole.*

"We're going to go grab some of the other girls for a chat. Stay here," Charlotte says, and I have no choice but to collapse back onto the couch to wait there.

"Stop looking at me," I say to Henry right before he leaves with Charlotte.

"Well," Henry says, sly, "keep that up and you will absolutely make the final two if that's your goal."

"It is," I answer petulantly, even though it isn't. The deeper this thing with Henry gets, the clearer it is I need to get out soon before everything blows up in my face.

It's another two hours before I finally get permission to go back to my room, which may seem like a prison, but is nothing compared to endless girl chats about Marcus.

I ask permission to go take a shower before afternoon filming (yes, really, like a prisoner of war). Henry walks me back to my room and closes the door behind himself, following me. "That was shit," I say, pulling my shirt over my head. His fingers immediately press into the bruise on my shoulder from the night before.

"You were fine," he says, taking off his own shirt as I slide off my heeled boots and start unbuttoning my pants.

"I forget how good I am at being a bitch," I tell him. I step out of my colored jeans, and my fingers slide to the button of his jeans, working on them as he kisses me, his hand twining my hair into a knot that he tugs on gently.

"But I like you this way," he whispers.

We run the shower as hot as we can stand, getting out after ten minutes because it's all we figure we can allow. I wrap my hair up in a towel as he pulls the blow dryer free of its place under the counter. "Should I leave?" I ask him with us both naked except for our towels, reflecting in the mirror.

He briefly kills the blow dryer. "What?"

"The show," I say. "Self-eliminate like Marcus did?"

"No," he says simply, then meets my eyes in the mirror. "Not yet at least. If you're going to self-eliminate, we need to do some damage control on your image first."

With the matter apparently settled, he blow-dries his hair, blows away all evidence of our shower. There's not time or silence to say more.

The elimination ceremony starts just after four in a room they've set aside for us off the second floor hotel bar. It seems unbelievable, but elimination ceremonies may actually be the dullest of all the dull things they make us do. Hours of sitting around, usually in uncomfortable clothes, to talk to Marcus for five minutes.

Priya is deep in conversation with Kady as I sit across from them, bored. I'm beyond annoyed at being made to further engage with Kady after the scene this morning, but I decide to be the bigger person and say, "I like your dress."

"Yeah," Kady says, "sure."

"It wasn't meant to be an aggressive statement, Kady."

She looks up, meets my eyes. "We see through you," she tells me, which is somehow a more effective way of getting under my skin than anything she said this morning. I feel the camera on me and instinctively know this will play out on television.

"What do you see?" I ask her, keeping my gaze on her steady.

"You think you're above the rules. You think you're special."

"I am special," I tell her, unable to stop myself. *The cunt.*

She shakes her head. "You're so fake." She goes to leave, but Priya grabs her by the shoulder and sits her back down on the couch across from me.

"You two need to work this out," she says calmly. I stare daggers over at her.

"Tell Jac what she has specifically done that has made you so upset," Priya continues.

When Kady doesn't say anything after a few moments, I venture, "Is it just that I exist and won't apologize for it?"

"You *want* us to hate you," Kady bursts out, and I think she may not be far off. Self-sabotage is a song I know well.

I don't say anything else, and eventually Marcus comes to get Kady.

A few minutes later, Henry collapses on the couch next to me.

"Look at you," he says, slinging an arm casually over me. The easiness gives me pause.

"Yeah," I say.

"Have you been thinking about what you're going to say to Marcus?" He takes a sip of my drink, something I don't think I've ever seen him do before.

"Do you like my dress?" I ask, a clear attempt to rattle him.

"It's not even in the top ten things I like about you," he says without pause. The ease of him handling me, I realize, is new; it's the way he treats the other girls. Before, there had always been a tension; a carefulness to how he approached me. Now, I could be any one of them that he's flirting with. "You okay with playing shuffleboard during your time? You're competitive so I figure that's the right vibe for you, right?"

One of my eyebrows goes up. "Yes?"

"Okay," he says, looking at me. He squints. "There's something weird going on with your hair."

I'm not surprised. I've run my fingers through it about ten times in the past minute, an unsettled reaction to the change in the air.

"Hang on," he says, reaching forward and putting both hands in it. I go completely stiff as he combs it out. "Like that, I think."

"Jac?" I turn around, and Marcus is at the side of the couch. I glance back behind and Henry has dived out of the shot, crouching down on the other side of the couch. I quickly look back to Marcus, who is frowning deeply. "Can I grab you?" he asks.

Then they make us film it again and ask us to try to "seem more realistic." He's wearing one of his many suits—this one is light blue and brings out the color of his eyes, his hair ruffled attractively.

He takes my hand, and I pull him over in the direction of the shuffleboard game, sinking back into my character with a flirtatious challenge. He accepts the game, twists my hand up to his mouth and kisses the backside of it. The tenderness of the gesture, the propriety of it. I get swept up in the act of it, in the magic of *the 1*.

"How's this week going?" Marcus asks me, running his fingers along the surface of the shuffleboard table as we walk to one of the ends together.

"Great," I lie. "I've always liked Chicago."

"It suits you," Marcus tells me. "What color do you want?"

"Red," I say, reaching for the first puck. We pile all the reds and all the blues on the table beside us.

"Ladies first," Marcus says.

Intently, I place my first puck onto the sanded table and use my hand to aim, then shove it across the surface of the board with all the subtlety of a raging bull. Predictably, it goes off the back and into the gutter.

"Easy, killer." I glance up, lock eyes with Henry, who has followed the two of us and is standing out of sight behind the camera.

"Don't know my own strength."

Marcus looks at Henry, too, his glare dark. The intense stare between the two of them raises my hackles. "Your turn," I say.

Marcus looks back at me, his expression light again. Smoothly, he pushes his puck across the table, too, and like mine, it ends up in the gutter.

"Tragic," I say, getting into it.

"How about a bet?" Marcus says. "I win, we find a way to spend extra time together."

"Really?" I ask. As far as I know, Marcus doesn't have that kind of power.

"What do you think, Foster?" Marcus asks, eyes still locked on mine.

"We'll see," Henry responds.

"I'll ask Janelle then," Marcus replies with a smile.

"Jac's not to be trusted," Henry answers.

"I'm a troublemaker," I agree, latching on to it, and Marcus and I both look at Henry, who says nothing. After a moment, I send the next puck across the table, and it lands in the number two tier.

"I know you're a troublemaker," Marcus says, tilting my chin up to his face to look down at me. "Good shot."

I stand up on my tiptoes and kiss him, a quick peck. "I think you should focus on me while you shoot. Otherwise, what will I think?"

"Oh," he says, maneuvering one arm around me while I face him with my backside pressed against the table. "War tactics."

He shoots the puck without his gaze leaving mine, and misses.

"It's not fair," he says, now pinning me against the table with his arms on either side.

"Well," I say, "all's fair in love and war."

"Yeah, guess so," Marcus says, leaning closer to me. "Think I read that in a book somewhere."

He kisses me harder, then grabs my hips and sets me up on the edge of the shuffleboard table. The camera gets closer to the two of us, and like monkeys, we perform. I forget and then I don't.

"All right, we're on a schedule," Henry calls. "Let's go."

Marcus pulls back and then kisses me again. I look at Henry over his shoulder, carefully neutral or maybe just really not caring at all.

Fuck him. Two can play this game.

Marcus helps me down from the table and I go back over to sit with the other girls.

Another three hours pass before the elimination ceremony finally begins. Marcus starts calling names and mine isn't called. I stand there, feeling stupid.

We get to the last name, and I actually feel nervous. Kady, Aaliyah, and I are left. Logically, it's me. Obviously, it's me.

My heart pounds. Marcus fiddles with the last invitation to stay, spinning it around in his fingers while Brendan makes some dire statement about how it's the last invite of the night.

"Jac," Marcus finally says. I go forward as he holds out the paper to me. "Will you accept this invitation to stay another week?"

"Guess so," I answer.

"Best for last?" he suggests, his lips barely moving, his body leaning toward mine.

"Fair enough," I agree as I go back to the group, Kady staring daggers at me.

"Ladies, I'm sorry, if you didn't receive an invite to stay another week, you are not the one," Becca says. All of the girls start hugging Aaliyah and Kady, and then they move forward to where Marcus is standing for their goodbyes.

Everything is quiet at first as Marcus whispers to Aaliyah, hugs her, and then turns to Kady, giving her a hug as well. But then, as Priya goes to walk Kady out, everything changes. "Are you kidding me?" Kady demands, stopping and shaking Priya's arm off of her. Vinnie, a sort of jack-of-all-trades guy who's always around set and could easily be mistaken for a bouncer based on his size and stature, subtly closes in on Kady, sneaking around a large potted plant.

"I don't want to go with you! I don't want to go anywhere with *any* of you. STOP FILMING ME!" She's worked herself into a lather and is now sobbing. The cameras are catching every moment. She turns back to Priya and makes what looks to be a running start before Vinnie grabs her. "You told me he was going to pick me!" Kady screams, flailing her arms. "You said he was talking about *proposing.*"

Janelle grabs Marcus's arm and leads him out of the room while several producers gather around Kady and start talking soothingly to her.

Charlotte appears as if by magic by my side. She gives Kady a look of distaste as she says, "Can I walk you back to your room?"

I nod.

Once we're on the elevator, she looks over at me. "Once that situation is settled, they're probably going to want you back for an ITM."

"People are obviously starting to develop a lot of feelings," I answer blandly.

"Yeah," Charlotte says, "that shit isn't going to cut it for the rest of the season. They'll interview you all day if you don't start giving them something to work with."

"I thought I already was," I say.

Charlotte shrugs. "Listen," she says, "I know I've been pushing you off on Henry a lot."

I don't say anything, staring over at her with a blank expression.

"I want to give him a chance on the next female-led season to produce the lead. I think he might be good at it."

"So why not let him produce the lead this season?" I ask.

"You know why," Charlotte says as the elevator door opens. She looks around, making sure that the coast is clear, before we continue on to Rikki's and my room.

I open my door, and Charlotte follows me inside. She closes the door behind her and turns to face me.

"I'm not really supposed to say this," she says, so I know she's about to start lying to me, "but have you thought about being the lead next season? *New York Times* bestselling author Jacqueline Matthis finally gets her own love story. It would sell itself."

I bite my lip, intrigued by the idea despite myself. The book sales alone would be reason enough. Not to mention, it means a clean exit from the show, actual money put into my actual bank account, and prolonged exposure. The biggest pitfall would be my continued exposure and infatuation with Henry Foster, but maybe I could work around that. Then reality hits me. "Aren't I your villain?" I ask. She knew; she left the binder in my room.

"Right now, yes," she says. "They're leaning toward giving you the villain edit, but edits can be changed, and I'll be there in the room to make them." *They.* Like she had nothing to do with it.

I brush my bare foot against the floor next to my heels. "Sounds vaguely like a threat."

Charlotte half laughs. "Everything is a threat on reality television."

"You don't think Marcus is going to pick me?" I ask innocently.

Charlotte shrugs. "He may, he may not; I'm just saying it's something worth thinking about. Besides"—her smile brightens—"he's not really your type, is he?"

I don't answer and she stares at me, straight through me, like she can see everything I'm not saying. Then she turns around and leaves without another word.

Rikki comes back with Priya after a while. Priya seems no worse for the wear following Kady's meltdown. I doubt it's the first she's caused.

An hour later, Henry appears at our door to take me to an ITM as promised. On our way to the interview room, I innocently ask, "Has Charlotte said anything to you about me being the lead next season with you producing?"

Henry glances over at me, his forehead crinkling. "No?"

"She says she thinks Marcus isn't my type. What's up with that? Isn't she supposed to be convincing me he's the love of my life?"

Henry stops, grabbing onto my arm to stop me, too. "What exactly did she say?" he asks me.

I tell him quickly, and he takes a deep sigh when I'm done.

"She's producing us," he says flatly.

"What?" I demand.

"Charlotte. She's producing the two of us."

"Why?" I ask. "Does she know?"

He shakes his head. "Maybe. I don't know. Maybe she just suspects but isn't sure how far it's gone. *Fuck*," he says. "Do not trust anything Charlotte tells you, Jac. From now on. I'm serious." He glances at his phone, grimaces. "We have to get to the interview room or someone is going to come looking for us." He starts to walk again, but I stay put.

"Wait," I say. "What can we do?"

Henry turns back to look at me, his expression grim. "Pray," he says, meeting my eyes, "that she goes into labor soon."

Jac's Voicemail after Episode 7 Airs

"Hey Jac, it's Charlotte. I know you probably don't want to talk to me right now, but several people have reached out to me and mentioned they haven't heard from you. You probably think I'm calling to give you a stern talking to about contractual obligations or whatever, but you're a smart girl, so I know you'll show up before you get sued. Mostly, I wanted to call because I miss talking to you, and I hope you're all right. Say what you want about me—and knowing you, you'll say a lot—but I did want you to fall in love. Maybe I went about it the wrong way, but I hope one day after this, we can be friends, even if it is completely outside of the context of *the 1*. Yeah, I do some fucked-up stuff sometimes, but who among us doesn't? We're a particular kind of people, Jac, you and me.

"Anyway, I don't call you on behalf of the show but on behalf of myself. And listen, *trust me*. I get it. All of it. Even if everyone else doesn't. Anyway, this is already too long and one of my children is crying, so I'll leave it at this: I hope you're okay, and I hope you feel good about the future. Whether that includes me or not."

Message deleted.

16

Everything Is Alright

The next morning, Charlotte is gone.

Good luck the rest of the way. I'll miss you xo, reads the note she left for me on our door.

"So, is it going to be better or worse with Henry?" Rikki asks me as I pluck the sticky note off the door and fold it up.

I squint my eyes at her. "What do you think?"

"You two are always making eyes at each other," Rikki says. She's doing what she always does, shoving everything back into her suitcase in a crumpled mess. It pains me every time I have to watch her do it.

"Eyes? What eyes?"

Rikki grins up at me, two pairs of lacy underwear and a slinky dress clinched into her fist. "Like you're in on a really good private joke you aren't telling anyone else."

"Well," I say, "we aren't." Maybe we are. Just not sure whose joke it is.

"He likes you better than the rest of us," she says.

"That's not true." My bags are packed and sitting by the door neatly, just like they always are.

"Just like Marcus," Rikki goes on. "We're all tired of losing to Jac at everything," she says, but she's laughing.

"Shut it, you," I say, tossing an empty water bottle at her that instead hits a side table and falls to the floor. A small part of me likes it, though, which is not the nicest part of myself to give in to. Henry liking me best, Marcus liking me best, feeling like I'm excelling at something. That's either deranged or completely normal.

"Do you ever wonder about Marcus?" she asks then. "Your feelings for him?"

It all sits on the edge of my tongue. Telling Rikki about me and Henry, confessing all my feelings, asking her what she thinks it means. Some part of me wonders if I broke the spell between Henry and me by giving in to it, as I so often did. Maybe, for him, it only existed in the forbidden fruit of it all, and now Henry was on to the next thing. That tracked, right? That tracked with who Henry should be.

I wasn't sure what it tracked for me.

"I don't know, Rik, I wonder about this whole thing. Who wouldn't?"

She is down on the floor, leaning all her weight on her bag, trying to get it to zip. Automatically, I get up and go to sit on top of her suitcase, legs crossed, so she can get it more fully closed. With great effort, she brings the zipper together and throws her hands up in triumph.

"At least there's one true love I've gotten out of this," Rikki says, reaching down and offering her hand to me to help me up from the floor.

"You're such a romantic," I tell her.

"Just promise to have me in the wedding."

"Let's not get ahead of ourselves."

She raises her eyebrows suggestively. "You didn't ask which one."

"Oh, ha, ha," I say, glancing down at my wristwatch. "There is nothing going on with Henry and me. Now, get your bag. He'll be here any minute."

HENRY AND I are crammed into a small airport bathroom and there definitely *is* something going on between us.

"Not exactly going to get us into the mile-high club," I mutter to Henry as he pulls back from me, both of us disheveled.

"What, the O'Hare bathroom not enough romance for you?" he asks me with a grin. I start to tuck my shirt back into my skirt—which, yes, I had worn strategically. When everyone else had gone for food at the airport, I'd lingered at the bookshop, and Henry had stayed with me. We'd missed out on eating, but we'd managed to escape.

"I feel like I'm a tenth grader," I say, combing out my hair with my fingers.

Henry's eyebrow quirks as he re-hooks his belt on his jeans. "Is this what you did in tenth grade?"

"No," I say. "This is what I wished I was doing in tenth grade. Look at me, I'm a neurotic mess. Do I *look* like I was cool in tenth grade?"

Henry laughs as he looks up, his gaze catching mine, and I imagine the way I reflect in his eyes.

"Hey," I say as he reaches out and loops an arm around me, pulling me closer to him, "what are we doing?"

Our chests are pressed together. I wish there was more time, the way we breathe in unison, the way I'm afraid he might disappear, might leave me.

"Something bad," he says, still playing the rogue.

"No," I say, pulling back again. "I mean, yes," I concede. "But to what end?"

"I don't know. The end where we aren't controlled by the arbitrary rules of *the 1*, I guess."

"It doesn't feel productive."

Both of Henry's eyebrows go up. "Would it be helpful if I graded you after each performance? Gave you homework? Nerd."

"God," I say, "you were cool in high school, weren't you?"

He grins. "Guilty." He looks at the clock on his phone. "We need to get to the gate. We've already been gone too long."

So, with nothing decided, nothing even discussed, we go.

We are almost to the gate when Henry casually says, "I talked to your mom yesterday."

I stop in my tracks. "What?"

He walks a few more steps forward before realizing I've stopped, and turns back, a hanging bag thrown indifferently over his shoulder. "Hometowns are week after next."

"Henry," I say, "Marcus can't meet my parents."

"Because?" he starts, like he's leading me somewhere.

"Because I'm fucking *you*. *Obviously*," I tell him, looking over at our gate. We are close enough to see but not to hear in the low voices we're speaking in.

"What?" he asks, like he's genuinely surprised at this. "I thought we agreed it wasn't the right time for you to leave the show yet?"

"Did we?" I ask, feeling like I'm having this conversation in another language. "You really think you can fix everything I've done here?"

"I think we have to try," he tells me. "To make sure you get something positive out of all this."

We're too close now. Too near getting on an airplane to Cancun to say the words I want to say, like *what is this* and *how do you feel* and *do you want me to leave* and *what happened* and *is it good or is it the worst thing that's ever happened to either of us.* The plane is boarding, and I don't know. I don't know anything.

"If I'm going to stay—" I start to say, and then I stop. "Do we keep doing this?"

"Henry! Jac!" That's Elodie, who has now popped her head back in from the loading dock and is calling us. "C'mon, they want to close up the gate."

Henry ignores her. "I just think, whatever this is between us, is separate. It's not the show."

My brain is going a mile a minute to imagine what he thinks *this* is. "I don't have any idea what is it you think we're doing."

"Listen," he says, and it's definitely *the 1* Henry I'm talking to now. "I promise we can figure out how to navigate this and get you off the show without putting a bigger target on your back. Now isn't the right time."

"Are you producing me or are we talking?" I ask him.

"Both. It's my job."

"Is it?" I ask him. "The lines are getting fairly blurry from my point of view."

Elodie's voice suddenly comes in over the loudspeaker; she is standing in front of the gate agent with the walkie-talkie to her mouth. "They are going to leave you," her voice booms over the speaker. Several of the attendants at nearby gates look around, confused.

"This isn't about me. *You* want something," I say, hitching my overnight bag up farther on my shoulder. "I'm not sure what it is, and I don't think you are either."

He pushes down his sunglasses. "We can't do this right now."

"Yet we could do that ten minutes ago."

"Enough," he says.

"No," I say. "I'll just stay here. Not enough."

He pushes his sunglasses back up, suddenly unsure where they go or stuck in a loop. "This isn't the time to have this discussion."

"When will be the time?"

"I don't know, okay?"

"No," I say. "Not okay." I glance over at the door, where Priya is now arguing with an attendant who is trying to close the gate door.

"They might actually fire me if you don't get on that plane," Henry says mechanically. The sudden robotic tone of his voice makes me wonder if he cares at all.

I move in closer to him, inappropriately close where someone might see the two of us. "We leave. Right now. The both of us, together. What do you say?" It's a challenge, one he reads immediately.

"Now who's playing games?" he asks.

I stare at him, silent.

"We'll figure it out," he says. "Please, Jac."

I look at the gate again. Priya is on her phone now and Elodie is smiling consolingly at the airline employees. I walk around him and make my way over to the gate without a backward glance.

Another One Podcast, Eighth Episode of Season 32

JULIA: Welcome back to *Another One*! We have a very exciting guest on today's episode. Please welcome Marissa Rayburn, lead of the twenty-third season of *the 1*!

MARISSA: It's awesome to be here in studio with you, Julia!

JULIA: Okay, Marissa, I want to spend some time catching up with you after we recap, but first off, we've got *so much* to dive into from this week's episode.

MARISSA: This season must be killing you, Julia! This show is back in fine form.

JULIA: Truly, probably the best season since yours! We've got it all. The villain, the love story, the girls you want to hang out with.

JULIA: For starters, with hometowns a week away, who do you see Marcus bringing through?

MARISSA: Let's be real, Julia. They can wrap this thing up right now. Jac is winning that ring.

JULIA: Ugh, I think you're right. But what about that meltdown they keep showing in the previews? I *really* feel like she might self-eliminate.

MARISSA: Beat Marcus at his own game?

JULIA: So you think he blew up the thing with Shailene last season on purpose?

MARISSA: He absolutely did, but I'd argue that's also why he and Jac are a perfect match. They're both in the self-destruction game and it makes them ravenous for each other.

JULIA: Interesting.

MARISSA: I've seen so many people say they're getting sick of the Jac show, but I gotta say, I find it to be a fascinating study in reality television. She's absolutely melting down before our eyes.

JULIA: Okay, let's dive into that a little bit. As someone who was both a contestant and lead on this show, what's that like? Why do you think it's affecting her so much?

MARISSA: Jac is neurotic, you can tell from looking at her. She thinks about everything too much, and when you have someone in your ear feeding that monster, things can really start blowing up around you.

MARISSA: And of course, she's responsible for her actions, but she's in a tailspin she clearly isn't emotionally equipped to pull her way out of.

JULIA: And why doesn't Marcus see that?

MARISSA: [Laughs.] That's the best part. Marcus *enjoys the ride.*

JULIA: I am loving these hot takes today!

MARISSA: I know people don't want to hear it, and aren't going to act differently, but y'all leave that girl alone online. She's already going through it.

JULIA: I can only imagine the kind of hate contestants get.

MARISSA: No need to imagine, happy to show you my inbox. All part of the fun of being the first Black lead.

JULIA: Disgusting behavior.

MARISSA: I'm used to it at this point.

MARISSA: But I can tell you from watching the episode previews for the next couple of weeks, it's all downhill from here.

CANCUN

17

Lying Is the Most Fun a Girl Can Have Without Taking Her Clothes Off

Cancun is so sunny, I wonder if it's going to make me sick. At least in cold, rainy Chicago, being locked away all the time hadn't felt so unnatural. Now, being stuffed inside a dark room to interview for hours and then trotted out like a prized pony felt even more dystopian.

We get there, and the remaining five of us are forced into our bathing suits, each pulled one by one to walk up and down the beach filming B-roll. As instructed, I stare out into the sun, the wind whipping my hair, then I stare into the camera, the hot sun on my exposed skin. This suit is green with an elaborate top of interwoven fabric across my breasts that is slightly too tight, a present in our gift bag from when we arrived. The beach is empty in the space production has cleared out, save for me and the crew. I can imagine how it might be peaceful in another life, but instead it is endless and exhausting.

"You don't really look wistful enough," Henry says, but he's laughing. With a straight face, I flip him off and turn away from him again, trying out a different angle for the camera. Several of the crew members cackle and whistle. But I don't give them what they want, what would make them feel better. I don't smile.

"You aren't making any friends," Elodie tells me when she comes to adjust my hair and re-tie my bikini string.

"Good," I answer.

"You're not here to make friends," she says, smiling at me.

"Please, don't try to cheer me up," I tell her. "I'm tired, I'm grumpy, I'm over it."

"This is the part of the season when everyone hits that point. You look really good, if it's any consolation?"

"Of course," I say. "I starved myself for three months, got 'tasteful' Botox, waxed all the hair off my body, cleared out every bad picture of me from social media ever, and now I get to look great in a bikini in a place where no one cares. This is thrilling."

"The important thing is that you have a good attitude," Elodie says without missing a beat. "Now smile," she says, giving me her own bright smile as she goes over to stand next to Henry. They immediately start whispering to each other, and for some reason, that only makes my despair grow.

We finish shooting the B-roll, and I get shuttled back to the house we're staying in, a shared villa a short walk from the ocean, still sleeping two to a room so that the remaining bedrooms can be transformed into ITM rooms and spots for girl chats. It's there that I start to feel the walls closing in on the tiny bedroom decorated with kitschy beach paintings. Time contracts and expands in on itself, and still, I don't know what I want. I don't have Henry and I don't really have Marcus. I open my books and stare at them blankly. I try to write in my head, all the things I can't admit out loud, but I keep losing the thread.

I'm putting on makeup because the day is not over. I've developed some sort of tremor in my hands, I think, but I'm not sure because I'm tired. I just keep styling my hair and applying eyeliner, and some stranger stares back at me in the mirror.

(I could've chosen right then to quit. They probably would've let me, and I should've let myself, but I chose to keep going. I was in a hole and I kept digging.)

After, we're sitting around playing cards when the first date card of Mexico arrives. Kendall begins reading it, and I'm shocked to hear my name called out.

"'Jac,'" Kendall says. "'Our relationship is climbing to new heights.'" She sets the date card down. "Again."

Immediately, I look to Rikki, who had been hoping to get her first one-on-one, but she's just smiling sadly over at me.

"I'm so sorry," I tell her.

She shrugs, the easy way she does. "It's not your fault," she tells me.

I look over at Henry, and of course, he's looking at me.

He averts his gaze and doesn't speak; Shae tells him something and he laughs, the fake way he does.

"Jac?" Rikki says, and I look over at her. She's watching me curiously.

I get up. "I guess I better go get ready."

MARCUS AND I take a Jeep through a mountainous area a few hours outside of Cancun. We drive across dirt roads, talking and laughing when we can over the noise of the road, Marcus touching my thigh every now and then in between shifting gears. Every time he does it, my brain practically short-circuits. I feel desperate for someone to be tender with me, someone to care for me in an uncomplicated way, and Marcus's touch still triggers that. Maybe this is what my life should be—living like other girls do with fake hair and buffed skin, malnourished, but looking beautiful and light and easy. Maybe Henry is just me falling back into my old, terrible ways, late-night pizza and too much bourbon and smart, unavailable men.

Neither really sounds like a winning scenario in my head, but I at least know what kind of destruction the latter wrought on my life.

At the end of the dirt road, we get out and head toward a hiking path. Janelle carefully outlines the route to us at the start of the trail. As she tucks the map back into her leggings, she says cheerfully, "The good news is, we haven't lost a lead yet."

"At least we know that if we go out, you're going with us," I say, and Janelle looks like she takes that as a threat. I wish it had been.

Marcus and I start up the path, and he immediately grabs my hand. It's a little hot for that, but I allow him to pull me along, admiring the muscles of his arms and calves in his hiking gear. I'm happy to be outside, in the air, doing something that feels like real, useful work. I'm moving my own body, sweating in a way that makes me feel real again, even surrounded by crew members.

I say so to Marcus.

"I know," Marcus says in return. "I hated how regulated my work-outs were as a contestant. 'You have forty minutes in the hotel gym.' Couldn't even get all my reps in on those schedules." He's right. We'd been free to do whatever we wanted at the mansion, out by the pool, but that had changed once we'd gone to Chicago.

"It's more than that, though, right?" I say lightly. Like I so often do, I sense Henry's eyes on me. He's around so much more than he was at the beginning of filming, with Charlotte gone, and it gets under my skin, always knowing he's there. Always feeling him observing me and wondering what that means, even though I know his job is to observe me. "Like, part of being a contestant is feeling like your personhood has been taken away. But out here, where we can breathe air and work our muscles to achieve a goal, it's beyond working out, right? It's feeling like yourself in your own body; it's autonomy. That's different. That's freedom."

Marcus laughs. "Sometimes, I worry you're too deep for me."

I almost recoil from the comment. *Can you stop, Jac? Do you have to overthink everything? Leave it, Jac.* Said to me by boyfriends and fuck buddies and men who always had enough of me, whether it took hours or days or weeks. It was always too much.

And as much as looking at Marcus still does something for me, what would we do together? Could we ever sit and talk about something outside of his workout routine? I'm not sure.

Marcus, realizing he perhaps said something he shouldn't have, pulls me closer, his fingers sliding over the thin fabric of my top to wrap around my hip. "I'm just glad to be out here with you," he tells me, recovering as quickly as possible. "It's always different than with the other girls. There's something else here."

"Yeah," I agree automatically.

"Speaking of the other girls," he continues, "how goes the house drama?"

"House drama?" I repeat. "We're still talking about that?"

He shrugs. "I care about how that's going for you."

"Do the other girls tell you about it?"

Nonchalantly, he answers, "Sometimes. It gets to some people more than others."

"Well," I say dismissively, "not me."

Nimbly, Marcus's fingers skim under my shirt, touching the bare skin of my lower back. I shiver. "That's my girl," he says.

Girl. Always *girl.*

The hike is hell for the cameraman, a guy named Jose, and we stop quite a few times for him to wipe off the copious sweat beading on his brow, and drink water.

"This was a bad idea," Henry observes, checking his watch.

"Well, you're full of those," Marcus says, his eyes glinting.

Henry ignores him. "Janelle, do you think we should scratch the drone shot? I think we're going to get off schedule."

"Oh, fuck no," Janelle says. "That was a huge pain in the ass to set up."

"He's such a snake," Marcus says as an aside to me, voice dripping with venom like it always does when he talks about Henry. Every time Marcus mentions him, it feels more personal.

"I don't know that he's a *snake*," I say, glancing over but not staring long enough to draw attention. "He's manipulative. They all are."

Marcus raises an eyebrow at me. "Henry's manipulation is different, though. He feeds off the girls loving him." Marcus's eyes are burning holes in mine, and I think he's going to say something more, but Janelle calls, "Okay! We're finishing this off. Shouldn't be more than fifteen minutes uphill, and we'll be in place for the drone shot."

Jose calls her a "bitch" under his breath and then we take back off.

There's not much time for us to enjoy the beautiful view when we get to the top of the trail, but I try to close my eyes and take it in for just a moment. Breathe in, breathe out, find myself in space and time. The sun isn't visible now, clouds gathered over it, but below us, a river cuts through the treetops as they sway in a gentle wind, an untouched quiet.

"It's beautiful," I say to Marcus.

"So are you" is the line that comes out, and then we're contractu-ally obligated to kiss or something, living in a flat love story.

It starts raining as if on cue, and then there's an even bigger scramble. PAs take our mics off to keep them from getting destroyed by the water. Janelle demands that we *still* get the drone shot, and everyone has to back away and give us space. For the first time ever, it's just Marcus and me, truly alone as the drone takes us in.

I look up at Marcus, his arms wrapped around me, and I feel something shift in him, a change in the temperature.

He leans forward, our faces inches from each other, the look in his eyes tender. "I know you're fucking Henry," he says.

It takes everything in me not to stumble back, away from him. "What—why do you say that?"

"The airport bathroom," he says. "Pretty bold, Jac."

His narrowed eyes surprise me then, the way they're so much sharper than I've ever seen them. I purse my lips, studying him as the cameras record this moment from a distance. "You've been holding back on me."

"At least you're fun," Marcus says. "Though of all the fucking people. Henry?"

"I should go home," I tell him.

"Oh, fuck no," Marcus says, keeping his face arranged to look perfectly pleasant to the surrounding crew.

"So, you're actually the asshole the internet said you were," I whisper back to him.

"Or the hero," Marcus answers. "Depends on your point of view." A chill runs down my spine, the realization settling in of just how much I have underestimated him. Each of his moves had been as calculated as Henry had told me, and now my fate is in his hands.

The buzz of the drone dies down. In a few seconds, we will be supervised again. "You don't even want me," I say, both a statement and a question.

"Unclear," he says. "I did really like the hot tub."

"Okay! That should be good!" Janelle calls. "Let's get the fuck out of here."

Marcus leans forward and kisses me again. I don't even think to flinch away.

A FULL MOON and starry sky are passing by outside the window, palm trees swaying lazily in the background. "Jac, are you even listening to me?"

Slowly, I turn my head to the side to look at Henry. We are in a black sedan together, seated side by side on the way to the main hotel of the resort hosting our villa, with one of the Mexican production assistants driving. I'm wearing an orange dress with a slit cut dangerously far up my leg that I'd picked up for two hundred dollars online.

"What?" I ask, sounding drunk to my own ears.

He turns his torso around so he's facing me fully. He isn't wearing a seat belt, a detail I can't help but fixate on.

"Are you okay?" he asks me. My brain runs a mile a minute as I search for anything I could say to him with my mic on.

"Yeah," I say, running up against the wall. "I'm fine."

"Is this about Chicago?" he asks, and I realize he means is this about him. I scoff.

"No," I answer icily, turning away from him. "This is not about Chicago."

The table for the dinner portion of my one-on-one with Marcus is set up on a balcony overlooking the lagoon below. The tables are polished wood, the chairs wicker, the whole thing projecting a laid-back vibe.

Marcus is laughing with Janelle when we get there. His eyes light up at the sight of us, and it's the first time I realize it's not some romantic notion guiding him. He's toying with me, and he can't wait for the fun he's about to have playing this game.

"What did you think of today?" he asks me once the cameras are rolling. He casually plucks an oyster off the table in front of him as if he's forgotten the rules. As if we can eat on camera. He loosens the meat and slurps it up greedily before washing it down with a long pull of white wine.

I sit so quietly as he does this that I almost feel like an animal avoiding a predator, but I snap to as he tosses the empty shell back onto the table.

"It was enlightening," I finally say.

He grabs up another oyster, face bright. "Wasn't it? I like when we're together. I like that you push my boundaries."

My brain circles the drain of this thought, inescapably caught up in its tide. The panic button is flashing in front of my eyes; no one is going to get me out of this but me. "There are things, though—" I start to say. My eyes flick to the cameras, the assistants, the producers watching us. There's always an escape plan; Marcus himself had an escape plan. "There are concerns. For me."

I swear I see the effort it takes him to hold back a smile, and I absolutely feel the way everyone watching leans in. "Concerns?" Marcus repeats, wiping his hands on a napkin.

I look around at the cameras again. "Them," I say. "Reality," I go on. "And what this is. Marriage in a few weeks seems daunting."

"I'm guessing marriage has always seemed daunting for you," Marcus replies easily. It's close to the truth, but maybe a dig as well.

"You too," I answer without a moment's hesitation.

"Guys," Janelle starts, her voice wary at where this is all headed, wanting to rein us in.

"Let it play out." That's Henry's voice, I know it. But I don't see him, not with the bright lights shining down on Marcus and me. "Keep going," he calls to the two of us.

"Sure," Marcus says, "maybe I panicked a little in the past. But that's because it was the wrong time. The wrong person."

"Tell me something true about me." I lean forward, elbows on the table, chin in my hands.

He licks his lips, like he's going to devour a juicy steak. "This feels like a test, Jac."

"It is," I say.

"Okay," Janelle calls again. "Perhaps a moment with your producers?"

My heart is pounding as Marcus drops his napkin into his chair and stands up, no longer interested in me.

Henry and Priya are whispering to each other, looking at me. I stand up, pushing my chair away, and subtly slide out of my heels. I take off walking quickly in the opposite direction before anyone can fully see what I'm doing. I feel someone following behind me with a camera at a cautious distance. I get to the barrier separating the dining area from the pool and grab my dress into my hand, put a leg over the barrier, and jump it. At that point, I start running.

"Jac?" someone finally calls. "Jac!" And then I feel them chasing me. It's a pointless escape but at least it gives me purpose. I glance backward, and a camera is following me. I can't yet decipher if that is good or not. "Leave me alone!" I call behind me, running past the pool and toward the beach farther on. Inevitably, there is nowhere to go, and Henry is sprinting after me in a considerably more casual outfit. He catches my arm, stares down at me. We haven't been this close since the airport in Chicago, where he let Marcus catch us.

I stop for a minute, trying to suck in air before I tell him, "I'm leaving."

He fights to catch his breath, too. "I see that."

"Let me go," I say. "I want to go." I pull my arm free and continue walking away from him, down the shoreline, even though there's nowhere to go. I can disappear.

Henry is following me, a few paces behind. "Why do you want to go?"

"This is fake," I call over my shoulder. "It's all fake."

"The way you're acting," Henry goes on, "seems like you're panicking because of something else."

I stop, turn to face him. He knew what those words would do to me, but still, he stays far enough out of the way to be out of shot; I don't miss it. "What is it then, Henry?" I ask him. It's amazing to me, the way I know he thinks it's about him.

"You don't think I should leave, or you don't want me to leave?"

They've got the light on me now. Bright.

He puts his hands in his pockets. "It's at least worth a conversation if you're going to go."

"Marcus has figured it out," I say. "The real me."

He flinches ever so slightly. He hears it, I think. He hears what I'm saying but he doesn't want to. "Who's the real you?"

"You already know," I answer, low. "A New York City bitch who wants all the wrong things. Marcus sees that. He saw it today and in Chicago and at the airport. I told you I want to go, and you know why. Marcus knows, too. *Let me leave.*"

Henry blinks, frowning deeply, and he understands. He takes a deep breath.

My heart is pounding. I see Henry see me, and it stupidly makes me miss him already, but anywhere but here has to be better than this.

His gaze drops from me, and he answers softly. "I'll try." He glances back up; his eyes meet mine, and I see a vision of him from across the table at a bar, dark eyebrows, joy and sorrow. "But it's not my choice, Jac."

"And what's going on down here!" someone calls, too bright by half. The disembodied voice takes shape: Becca in a matching two-piece with a palm tree design. "Can I talk to you for a sec, Jac?"

Henry meets my gaze for the last time and then we both look away. I rub at my eyes like I've been crying, which I definitely haven't, but I need to play into this act. It has to seem like a hard decision. People quit this show all the time; it's all in the performance.

I don't say anything to Becca.

"You mind if we go back up to the patio?" Becca asks me. I shake my head no.

"All right," she says, "then we'll just do it here!"

"Do what?" I ask.

"Jac," she says in her producer voice, "unlike everyone else, I know how hard this is. I've been here."

"I doubt it." A crew member has brought a lighting rig over to shine on us, and the two of us are now glowing like it's the middle of the day.

She smiles at me like I'm an old friend she knows well. "Marcus is up there crying, knowing you might leave." And I just bet he is, milking this for all it's worth. "He feels like he doesn't know where your hesitations came from."

"Marcus doesn't want this either," I tell her.

"You wouldn't say that if you'd seen him the way I did," Becca answers serenely.

"I want to go home."

"You think we wouldn't let you do that if we thought it was what you really wanted? But this is the first mention of it. You've been happy, Jac. It's okay to freak out. We *all* did it at one point or the other."

"I'm *not* freaking out," I return sharply, making the whole thing seem like a lie. "It's not possible to fall in love in a place like this. It's all an illusion."

"I've been married six years," Becca tells me. "And now Brendan and I are starting a family." She places her hand over her flat stomach. "That real enough for you?"

I look into her eyes to confirm what she's said. Christ. Becca just dropped a pregnancy announcement in the middle of my attempted escape. That's when I know they'll never let me out.

"Aren't you exhausted by it all?" I can't help but ask her.

Her mask drops, momentarily, and she does look tired. But she pastes a bright smile back on. "Would you be willing to go talk to Marcus?" she asks me, putting her character solidly back in place. "Before you leave."

I almost beg her not to make me, but I can't sink that low. I already feel the guillotine hanging over my head.

They walk me back up to the patio where Marcus is sitting slumped on the stairs, like he collapsed there. Everyone is staged around him for a conversation, so I take a seat on the stairs next to him. Without asking, he takes my hand.

"Becca said you wanted to talk," Marcus says, straight-faced. I'm almost amazed by him now. He's much better at this than I am. "You're thinking of leaving?"

I try for a diplomatic approach. "This is overwhelming, Marcus. You understand it better than anyone."

His hand tightens on mine. I fight the urge to pull it back. I can hear his voice in my head from earlier: *I know you're fucking Henry.*

"What happened?" Marcus urges me. I meet his eyes, eyes I now realize never quite match his expression. Is this his endgame? For me to confess on camera? To seal my fate as the villain?

"There's only a few weeks left," I say. True enough. "And today is the first time it seems like we're really seeing each other clearly."

I see it in him now. He likes it. He likes that it's all for show. He gets off on the performance.

"But isn't that—" He puts a hand on my cheek. Bold. "Isn't that the whole point of this? We're intense people, Jac. We test each other's limits. That's the kind of relationship I want. One where we're always discovering new facets of each other."

I release a breath. His hand is cold. Henry is here; I know he is. "Something burns too hot, maybe it leaves ashes in its wake," I whisper to him. The mic pack is like a noose. Solemnly, I say, "I think I should go, Marcus."

"But I don't want you to," he answers, his voice ringing out. The meaning is clear. "What could I say to convince you? That it wouldn't be fair to either of us if we don't see this relationship through to the end? That I couldn't stand to see you leave? I don't know what it would do to me. I don't know what I might do. Maybe I'd follow you. Maybe I'd be destroyed. Maybe you would, too."

He gives away his plan then, his eyes flicking over my shoulder. That's where Henry stands.

I don't think about the cameras at all, but they're also the only thing I can think about. Marcus is a breath away from giving this show its moment of the season—maybe even moment of the decade—at the expense of my reputation and livelihood.

I playact softening ever so slightly. "I'm scared," I admit. Marcus is exactly the type of guy who wants to hear that.

His index finger trails down my cheek, where his palm is still resting. "I know," he tells me. His face is dangerously close to mine, both of us leaning fully forward into each other. *"Stay."* It sounds like a threat.

I close the distance between us to kiss him, not wanting to give him the satisfaction, and he accepts it. It's my admission of defeat, so I launch my doomed last stand and sink my teeth into his bottom lip. He doesn't pull away; in fact, he is fully pulling me into his lap and we are kissing like the night in the hot tub until Janelle calls for him to stop. A part of me knows it should make me sick, but I've lost myself in it; in my hatred for him and myself, the violence of the kiss felt right. He pulls back at Janelle's command, though, pulling away from me, our eyes locked.

"That was really good, Jac," he whispers to me. "Almost worked."

"You're welcome," I answer, neutral.

"Holy shit, y'all," Janelle says. "That was electric. You two make *great* television. Give them a round of applause." And then they actually do. I'll be in ITMs all night explaining that show. My attempt at a getaway had backfired big time—Marcus had seen to that.

Great television. That's all I existed for to them. I knew what creating a moment was; I knew before I got here. I wrote them all the time, and I'd never fully considered what it meant to live in one. (I considered it a lot over the next few months as I watched this play back. The pain of giving in to your worst impulses and seeing it replayed as good television. Seeing the way the world reacted to you, the way they hated you.)

"I need to talk to you," I mutter to Henry as we walk back into the villa for filming. "Privately."

"I'll try," he says. "This is going to take some cleaning up."

"Marcus—" I start to say. *Marcus knows.*

"I know" is all Henry says, averting his gaze.

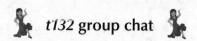 *t132* group chat

Aaliyah: Jesus, that episode was brutal

Hannah: bitch jac strikes again

Rikki: Jac and I had a girl chat about our families for, like, 3 hours while we were filming that one and of course they didn't include any of it

Eunice: What was THAT about, Rikki? Did she tell you she wanted to leave?

Rikki: honestly, I didn't know that happened

Andi: w t f

Andi: so desperate for attention

Eunice: I know no one wants to say it but I'm starting to feel bad for her. It's really nasty online.

Andi: she deserves it as far as I'm concerned

Aliana: Rikki, have you heard from her?

Rikki: I know she's alive

Rikki: that's about it

18

Hard Times

Jac, when is the last time you slept?" Kendall's voice. Without asking, her cool fingertips are on my face as she tilts it from side to side to survey.

"Chicago," I say, unsure whether or not that's a lie.

"What's up with you?" she asks me. I'm having a breakfast of a single boiled egg in the white marble counter–topped kitchen of our villa that morning. There aren't even cameras in the immediate vicinity. She's just asking.

"I've stopped sleeping," I say, concentrating all my effort on peeling my egg instead of looking up at her. I keep replaying the date with Marcus. What I could've done differently to free myself.

"Haven't we all?" she says tragically. "I feel like my essence has been drained."

"Sounds dirty," I respond, popping off the last piece of shell and biting off the top of my egg, finally looking up at her.

"I miss Charlotte," Kendall says, in a way that makes me wonder if she's prompting me. Maybe Henry put her up to it. "She always gave me a heads-up when we were going to get disgustingly early wake-up calls."

"Yeah," I agree. Kendall has her repeat one-on-one this week. It's clear to everyone that both of us are going through to home-towns. "We signed our whole lives away and barely even thought about it."

"We sold our lives away for the clout," Kendall corrects me. "If you don't know what you're going to get in this day and age on this show, then you're an idiot. And you, Jacqueline Matthis"—she points at me—"are no idiot."

"Stop or I might think you like me," I answer.

She shrugs.

"You think there's a way to outsmart the producers?" I ask Kendall.

"You can try, but you'll pay for it. Who was that girl a couple of years ago who met up with her winner off-camera? Tamara? They wouldn't even let her do hometowns after that. You willing to suffer?"

I tap into some of my old animosity, smile. "When am I not?"

"Always go for the rookie then," Kendall tells me. "That's who's going to fuck up."

I don't answer, just get up to throw my meager breakfast leftovers in the trash can.

THAT NIGHT, RIKKI, the absolute hero, talks Priya into ordering us pizza. Kendall is gone on her date, so it's just four of us left, Rikki, Shae, Eunice, and me, sitting around in a circle with the producers going to town. I eat four pieces, greedily sucking down the grease.

"Where's Henry?" Rikki asks. He's been around conspicuously less the last few days, and I have done my best not to care.

"He's trying to finalize things for hometowns," Priya explains, sipping a Diet Coke.

"It's weird this is almost over," Rikki says.

"Over?" Priya says with a laugh. "We still have over a month of filming. Speak for yourself."

"I guess, just like, this part of it. Of us being together. I don't know." She shrugs. "I'll miss you all. I'll miss my friends. It's the first time in a while I've really felt, like, I could think about anything that wasn't my sister."

I reach out and take Rikki's hand. Elodie smiles knowingly.

"We want another round?" I ask, holding up my empty whiskey glass. Everyone agrees and I head to the kitchen to make a fresh round of drinks. I pour generously.

Two hours later, everyone is drunk. Priya is drunk, Rikki is drunk,

Elodie is drunk, Shae is drunk. Eunice was drunk, but she claimed she was going to the bathroom half an hour ago and never returned.

"God," I say, "I'm so drunk."

"I'm so drunk," Shae says, standing up. "I'm going to bed."

"Me too," Priya says, looking around at all of us like a mother hen. "Girls, we have an early day tomorrow."

"Rikki," I say, reaching out sloppily and grabbing onto her forearm. "Come outside to the beach with me and keep drinking. I have something I want to tell you."

Priya eyes us, and I don't miss the way her eyes meet Elodie's. *Jackpot*, they say.

"I'll have another," Elodie says.

"That's the spirit!" I answer, about two octaves higher than my normal speaking voice. I take a bottle of vodka with me and head out onto the porch, Elodie, Rikki, and a camera following us.

"Here's to the real fun," I say, splashing straight vodka in everyone's cups and knocking it back.

Elodie's cheeks have gone red. She's got to be close to Rikki's age, maybe twenty-five, but she has a baby face. She's a cute girl, not pretty enough for *the 1*, but pretty enough for real life.

"What do you do in the real world, Elodie?" I ask her. I pour her another vodka.

She grins at me, leaning back. "I'm from Virginia, originally. Cavalier."

"Boo," I say with a smile.

"I like hiking, I miss winter, but I'm a fair surfer."

"Badass," Rikki says. She leans into Elodie, curling against her like a cat. "Elodie is going to start coming to my classes when we're back home, aren't you?"

"Is Jac coming, too?" Elodie asks.

I shrug. "We'll see. Maybe I'll never set foot in California again once this show is over."

"That's hurtful," Rikki says.

I kiss her on the cheek.

"It's good to see you smiling, Jac," Elodie says, her words starting to slur. I almost feel bad as I tip more vodka into her cup. "I've been worried about you."

"Me?" I ask, innocently. "I'm not the kind of person you worry about, am I?"

Elodie frowns. "Of course."

The shots are poured and poured and poured. Mine are dumped and dumped and dumped, but still I slur and still I pretend I'm right on the verge of saying something good.

"If I were Marcus," Rikki says later, much later, "I would marry Jac."

"You're so stupid," I say, laughing. "I'd marry you."

"Maybe we should just get married," Rikki says.

I look over at Elodie. "C'mon, Elodie, tell us the truth," I say, a test. "Who is Marcus into? Really?"

My eyes travel to the cameraman, but he doesn't do anything. He's just there to let the producers guide him.

"Wellll," Elodie says, and then she points at me. She winks. "Good try."

"What about Kendall?" I say, undeterred.

"God, Kendall. Her hometown is going to be a shit show."

"Mm," I say, not pushing my luck.

"Why?" Rikki asks, doing the work for me. When Elodie is distracted looking at her, I refill her cup.

"Her dad died when she was five. She's estranged from her mom, and we're putting them all together, along with her stepdad who she *fucking hates*," Elodie says. "God." She tilts her head back.

I do take a shot after that.

"Good times," I mutter under my breath.

"Poor Kendall," Rikki says, soberly.

"Right?" Elodie says, and then she giggles. "God, I'm *drunk*. I wasn't supposed to get drunk."

The night is quiet, the production almost dead. Kendall isn't back from her date, or she is, I don't know. Everyone is in bed who can be in bed, but we're still here, somewhere past time and space.

I glance over at Rikki, and she has fallen asleep in her chair. I turn my attention fully to Elodie, my feet pulled up into my Adirondack chair, curled in on myself.

"You were in Scotland last year," I say. "Weren't you?"

"Scotland?" Elodie says.

"Marcus and Shailene," I say simply.

She thinks about it a moment. "Oh. Yeah. I was there when they broke up."

I shift uncomfortably in the chair I'm sitting in, setting my chin on a knee and staring over at her. As I'd hoped, she starts talking. "Henry was with Marcus always. *Always.* Charlotte thought it was over-producing, but Marcus just shut off if Henry wasn't around; he could barely hold a conversation. It seemed like he was bored or something."

"Why?" I ask.

Elodie shrugs. "Shailene was ready to marry him, I'm pretty sure."

"Marcus?"

She nods. "Yeah, I think it was a done deal." I keep watching her, wondering how I could be wrong; how I could've read everything so wrong.

"Anyway," she continues, "everyone knew that Marcus was more interested in being the lead than Shailene. Priya and Charlotte cut a deal with him behind Henry's back to say he and Shailene had sex. It was bad. Henry went ballistic because Shailene was his favorite, and he almost got fired."

Slowly, I nod my head.

"Then she tried to kill herself last summer because the online harassment was so bad." Elodie leans her elbow into the side of her chair, almost falling over. I make no move to help her, simply process and keep going.

"Shailene tried to kill herself?" I ask, shocked.

"John cleaned it all up, and she came back, so . . ." Elodie sighs and shrugs.

"Why am I the villain?" I ask her quietly. "When this all exists?"

Elodie surveys me, knocking back another sip of her drink. I imagine her in Santa Monica, at a club with her friends, too drunk and spilling a secret. That's where we are right now. "You're not very nice, Jac," she says.

"That's true." I press my cheek into my leg, my skin still sticky with humidity in the middle of the night. "Do you like me?" I ask.

"Yes," she says.

"Is it just because you're drunk?"

"You're successful and beautiful and too sad to enjoy it. America hates that." She hiccups. "I'm sorry."

"I think America loves it. We love our own misery, we just hate when someone else does."

"It's not that deep," she says, her eyelids fluttering. The color all around us is gray and coming alive. "What were you going to tell Rikki anyway?"

I watch her a long time, pale and young and too drunk to even know what she's saying. "It sucks, doesn't it?" I say at last. "To be the one made a fool."

"What?" she asks, and looks up, just as the glass door slides open behind her.

"Jac," Henry says. He looks furious, just as Elodie leans forward and vomits all over her feet.

"Good morning," I say.

I GET THE last invitation to stay. Again. It's tiring, but I guess they expect the audience to be so desperate for me to go home by this point, that they want them dreaming of it at every elimination ceremony (spoiler: they are). I've been pitted against the beloved Rikki, her hand squeezing mine as my name is called.

I go to take the invitation held out to me, and Marcus winks at me for good measure. "I can't wait to meet your family, Jac," he says. "I hope you won't miss your friend too much." Then he tells Rikki that, unfortunately, she is not the one.

Brendan grins at the two of us in his wacky pink suit like we're having fun, when in reality, Marcus has just knocked another piece off the board for me.

I turn back around and go to Rikki. I grab her into my arms and hug her tight. "I love you," I say.

She smiles sadly. "Just not enough to not use me, right?" she whispers, but she is whisked away before I can respond. I stare after her, blank-faced.

"Congratulations, Jac," Kendall says to me.

"Gird your loins," I tell her. "They're throwing your stepdad at you."

Kendall frowns, but everything is too loud and happening too fast for her to respond.

"Let's get everyone for a champagne toast," Priya says, calling Kendall and Shae and Eunice over, handing us all glasses. Elodie has been gone since yesterday.

"Here's to the final four," Marcus says, and we clink glasses. "Here's to love." The other girls echo him.

"Jac." Priya is at my side again before I can even get a sip of champagne down. "Someone wants to speak with you. We're going to drive you over to a hotel where the crew is staying, and then you'll fly out for hometowns. You ready to go?"

Mystified, I agree. All of our bags are already packed, so I just follow Priya out to a van. She puts me in it, and Henry hops in next to me, seemingly appearing out of nowhere.

"What's going on?" I ask him, after the door is slammed and the car is driving. "Am I in trouble?"

He glances over at me, his eyebrow raised. "What do you think?"

"God, this is dull," I say, leaning my head back against the headrest. Henry neither assents nor dissents, so we are quiet on the ride to the hotel. He helps me out of the van once we get to the resort, still in my evening wear from the elimination ceremony—actually, shit, it's Rikki's gown and I need to give it back to her—and I follow him as he leads me to the elevator and punches the button for the fourth floor.

"Just," he says, as the elevator door slides back open, "don't say anything," he finishes cryptically.

"Oh, because I'm so good at that."

He turns down a hall carpeted in beige with royal blue coconut wallpaper and stops in front of one of the doors. He knocks.

After a few seconds, the door opens to a partially deconstructed production room, full of televisions and chairs and assistants dismantling them. In the corner, not doing anything except scrolling through his phone, sits a white middle-aged man, broad, but not quite overweight. His eyes flick up as Henry comes in with me.

"Give us a minute. Uno minuto," he says to the crew, and a dark-haired woman wearing a black hat gestures for everyone to follow her out of the room, closing the door behind her.

"Miss Matthis," the man says, putting his phone away and standing up. "Our little star. Is it okay if I call you Jacqueline?"

"Miss Matthis is fine," I say.

He barks out a laugh, and I feel Henry shift beside me. Is this it? The firing squad?

"Jac, this is John Apperson. He's the creator and executive producer of *the 1*," Henry tells me. The second part isn't needed; I remember our conversation weeks ago at the mansion in LA.

"I'd say it was a pleasure, but—" I shrug.

"You're fun," John says with a smile. He's got that slick look of Hollywood about him—late forties, unmistakable hair plugs giving him wavy light brown hair. He wears dark-rimmed designer glasses over a face bloated from too much alcohol.

"Henry did tell me you liked hot, mean women."

"Henry and I have that in common," John says, and when I look at Henry, his cheeks are red. "But you've crossed a line here."

"Can't wait to hear which one that is," I say.

Henry glances over at me. I feel him sweating, begging me to shut the fuck up. "He's talking about Elodie," Henry says.

"What else would he be talking about?" I answer lightly, my gaze not leaving John's.

"Stop fucking around," John tells me, cutting to the chase. He isn't angry; more like a dad of teenage kids sick of our shit. "We can still make things good for you. You're an author—there's no contestant we had on this year who can benefit from what we're doing here more than you. God knows the fucking failing publishing industry could never drum up publicity this good. *Let me help you.*"

I pause, like I'm considering the offer. "I've had enough of your team's help to last me a lifetime. I think I'll just play by my rules now."

John frowns. "We're going to have to fire Elodie. You realize that, right?"

I touch one of the devices on the desk next to me, fingering the speaker. This must be where they feed info into the producers' ear-pieces from. Someone wasn't paying enough attention to Elodie the other night.

"She had a lot to say. A lot of interesting things about Marcus and Shailene that I think the public would want to hear."

"You're under an NDA," John snaps.

"I don't believe you're going to fire her," I say, ignoring him. "Then again"—I meet his gaze squarely—"it would be nothing for you to throw a woman under the bus for this television show, would it?"

"Jac," Henry hisses.

"Aw, babe." I look over at him, grab his arm. "Is Daddy mad?"

"Enough," Henry says, shame written all over him, as he pulls my arm away.

John doesn't look so amused now. "Are you going to be able to control her for another month, Henry?" he asks, like I'm not even there.

"Jac's not stupid," Henry tells John. "She'll finish out the season and keep quiet."

"You're damn right," John says, looking back at me. "If she doesn't want to be sued into next century for violating her contract."

"It doesn't have to be like this between us," I say. "You could eliminate me. I could keep what I know about Shailene a secret."

"Let me get something straight with you, sweetheart," John says. "You have no power here. You go home when we say you go home. You keep your mouth shut and make good TV, or we'll make this ten times worse for you. Because we are headed down a very dark path right now, and you do not make the rules."

I stare at him, my eyes burning with unshed tears. I have all that ammo, and still I know he's right. I signed my life away. Instead, I say, "Do your worst."

"We could've helped each other," John replies, clearly disappointed in me.

I don't answer.

"Go," he says, pointing at the door. "And God help Marcus Bel-lamy if he chooses you. Henry, you stay."

"Wait for me," Henry says, grabbing my forearm before I can stomp off. "I'll just be a minute." His voice is soft, but it's not like John can't hear us, can't *see* him touching me.

I leave the room and slump back against the wall next to the door. John's voice is rising through the wall, but I can't make out anything he's saying.

After about ten minutes, Henry exits, adjusting the jacket he's wearing over his T-shirt. He's staring down at his expensive sneakers, almost collecting himself for a moment, before he looks back up at me. "Well," he says, "you really fucked that."

"Yeah," I agree. "What now?"

He drops his voice. "Why didn't you tell me in Cancun as soon as Marcus told you he knew?"

"Because I don't trust you," I say without a moment's hesitation. Only partially true but I'm not willing to admit that.

His expression doesn't change. "I could've gotten you out then, if I'd known. If you'd talked to me first. Production doesn't like to be blindsided."

"And if I'd left? Would that have been easier for you?"

"Of course it would've, Jac. Don't ask stupid questions. The way you went about things opened us up to a hundred more problems. Marcus knows and is out for blood, and John is threatening lawsuits over the NDA. You didn't trust me and now you're here."

"I asked you to leave!" I yell. We both go silent, stewing in our own anger.

Finally, in an even voice, he says, "You asking me to leave wasn't real. It was just a test that you knew I would fail."

Then I say what has been eating me up for days: "Why do you care?"

Henry swallows, and it sits there between us like the seismic shift it is. "I swore I wouldn't get this involved with a contestant again, not after I fucked up so badly with Marcus, and look at the damage I'm doing."

It feels like his apology, and maybe it is. We're quiet for a moment before I say, "I know why you didn't recognize me at the bar in Santa Monica."

Unperturbed, as if this is the conversation we were having all along, he answers, "Face blindness?"

"It's because you've never seen any of us as real people. You can't here. That's the only thing that makes this job doable for you."

He doesn't argue with me; rather, he looks slightly dazed.

"So, what are we going to do now?" I ask when it's clear he has no response.

He takes a deep breath. "I'm going to do everything I can to get you out of this without you getting hurt any worse."

I lean back against the wall, close my eyes, and absorb it. Nothing more is said.

It was the moment, and now it's over.

It was the moment, and we both let it pass us by.

1 in the Sun Trailer

Rikki, sitting in a bikini and drinking from a coconut: Things are about to get *hot!*

[In its trademark kitsch style, a cheesy '70s love song starts playing while castoffs from the 1 meet and drink together. Andi meets with John Michael Reston, the bro-y eighth place finisher from Shailene's season.]

Andi: Something about John Michael just does it for me.

[Cat Butler from Amar's season walks onto the beach.]

Cat, smiling: The bitch is back!

Voiceover: Things are going to get wilder than ever before!

[Footage of Rikki making out with three different men: one under a waterfall, one at a beachside picnic, one on a bed on the beach. Finally, she is crying at the famous 1 in the sun bar.]

Rikki, sobbing: I really think I love him.

Aaliyah: Bless that girl's heart, but she falls in love with every man she meets.

John Michael: I'd do anything for her.

[Andi sobbing.]

[Henrik from Shailene's season stomps across the beach and gets into an unseen contestant's face.]

Henrik: You wanna go, bro?

Voiceover: Don't miss any of the drama on season 8 of *1 in the sun*, premiering Tuesday night after *the 1* finale.

THE CAROLINAS

19

A Decade Under the Influence

Home.

It's a loaded word for me.

Home was always a place I was leaving. Somewhere to avoid. A funny story on a cold New York night about Civil War reenactments (no one I know has ever actually seen one) and terrifying rednecks (really just tobacco-spitting frat boys in camo). But home now was *home*, the place that had come to define me.

Home ended up being the place I returned to.

My hometown, the farthest from Los Angeles of any of the girls, is the first one filming.

I was disappointed but not surprised to learn how little I would actually be seeing my family on this hometown date. Priya and I fly into Charlotte, drive the three hours down to Charleston, stay in a hotel there for the night. I meet up with Marcus, see my family for a few hours that night, and then we drive back to Charlotte. We never go to my actual two-bedroom farmhouse in a small town outside of Charleston, but to the fake house on Folly Beach production has rented out for us.

I miss my family. My mom, somehow optimistic and surprisingly to-the-point; my dad, both easy and stern; my brother, quick with a joke and a drink; and even his fiancée, Eileen, friendlier than me but quiet with a solid smile. I haven't spoken to them since I left for filming. All of them took this as another lark of mine—the adventurous black sheep of a born-and-bred Southern family, always doing something unexpected and off-kilter. Still, I don't see how my family, the people who belong to me, can exist in a world where Marcus and Henry do. I don't see how I can balance everything rolling around inside me with real people, who know the real me.

The day of my hometown date, I'm wearing jeans and a crop top, almost feeling like myself now that everyone's talking in accents and wearing sundresses.

I'm meeting Marcus at the beach, I've been told. We'll take a walk, eat at a restaurant, and apparently that will be an authentic representation of what my life is. I had mentioned to Henry once I enjoyed going to walk on the beach and eating dinner alone because I found a certain peace in it, in enjoying your own company. Apparently, he wants to ruin that for me, too.

Priya is staring at her phone as we walk toward the filming location. "Can you do a huju with Marcus when we get there?"

I look over at her. "What in the sweet fuck is a huju?"

Priya sighs deeply, anciently, before finally looking up at me. Brendan is with us to film the show opener for the hometown episode and his too-smooth face is shiny in the bright Carolina sun as we walk down one of the side streets leading to the beach, cars parked up on the grass outside of houses. "Come on, you've seen one, Jac!" Brendan says enthusiastically. "It's a running hug jump. You run into Marcus's arms, he sweeps you off your feet, you wrap your legs around him? Huju? Looks great on camera."

"No," I say. "I don't think so." Priya sighs again while Brendan's face goes blank.

Marcus's smile when he sees me standing alone on the beach is so radiant, I almost forget the vitriol now between us, imagine it was all a dream. It's good because that's the only thing that gives me the power to smile back, to accept the kiss he gives me as he literally scoops me up into his arms with the waves crashing behind us. Still, no huju is achieved.

"Jac," he says. "Jac, Jac, Jac, Jac," like a mantra, like a thing he can't believe he's lucky enough to say.

It surprises me how much that hurts.

I give him the spiel, on the beach, on the city ("As beautiful as you," he says—fuck, I'm so tired of that line). We clasp hands and we walk. I feel a barrier, between the real me and *the 1* me walking down the beach, saying things, playing along with the game. A barrier between the man holding my hand, and the one who so casually threatened to ruin me on a mountainside in Mexico.

At the restaurant, I sip a beer and ignore a burger.

"So, who am I going to be meeting today?" Marcus asks me.

No one, I want to say. *They're mine.* "My mom, Carol, and my dad, Kevin. My brother, Austin, and his fiancée, Eileen."

"Anything I should know about?" Marcus asks.

"Just don't indicate any positive feelings toward Gamecock football, and you should be fine," I say with a shrug, and immediately know it will air this way. Me, the cool girl, looking hot but casual in jeans, drinking beer, talking football, and Marcus, laughing, mesmerized. Eat your heart out, Gillian Flynn.

We meet up an hour later at a huge house my family certainly does not live in. It's on the beach, keeping up the theme of me as some casual, laid-back beach girl. Marcus has brought flowers for both my mother and Eileen and professes to be nervous.

"Mm," I respond halfheartedly, and note the way his eyes flash.

My mom and a camera open the door, and she immediately pulls me into a hug. I start crying, like the unhinged bitch the show has made me out to be.

"Oh, honey," she says, rubbing my back. "I've missed you, too. Marcus!" she then says, spotting him behind me. "Oh, my goodness, there you are! Please come in."

She scoots me inside, and I push my stupid tears away. Mom hugs Marcus, thrilled; she's wearing a very pretty blue dress with a floral pattern. She must think I'm winning this game. Her desperation for me to no longer be single bleeds through all rational thought.

When I'd officially been offered a spot on the show, I'd waited as long as possible to tell my mother. I'd asked her to dinner and dropped it to her over her second cordial.

"You're going on what?" she asked me.

"You know"—I felt my face heating up like I was a teenager confessing to needing birth control—"the big reality dating show."

She fully set down her drink. Then she laughed. *"You?"*

I grimaced.

"Don't get me wrong," Mom quickly said. "It's—well, it's something. I didn't know how much you were prioritizing finding a partner." *Partner.* That was one she'd just learned at her monthly book club—"much more polite, just in case," she'd explained to me.

"Mama, no," I said. "It's not like that. It's good exposure. For my book, for my career. I can't write so I need to do *something.*"

"Oh. So, this is about . . . publishing." She took a long look at her drink and then had another sip. "Well, it's a bit out of the box, honey," she finally said.

"It'll just be twelve weeks," I told her. "At most."

"You'll give it a chance, won't you?" she asked then, something hopeful in her eyes. "Love?"

I swallowed. "It's not about that," I told her. She surveyed me with her gimlet eye, looking poised to say more. My mom and I had butted heads often when I was younger, what with our different priorities, but she'd been doing her best to adopt a more modern way of thinking. Still, I knew sometimes she just wished for me to be the good Southern girl she had been.

"Well, all right then," she finally said, and then turned the conversation to my brother's upcoming wedding.

The last thing she'd told me before I left for California was to not embarrass the family.

"Where is everyone?" I ask there, in the midst of embarrassing my family, in the massive, nautical-themed foyer.

"Oh, they're all in the den," she says. "Your father has—well, he's made quite an interesting situation for us."

I raise an eyebrow, following my mom and the crew into the brightly lit den. It is huge; wide and spacious, with colorful décor and white accents, a balcony overlooking from the second floor. Dad, Austin, and Eileen are all sitting around the television, Dad and Austin with glasses of bourbon, Eileen with rosé. Henry told me they'd even tried to convince Sarah, Josh, and the baby to fly in for the meeting, but Sarah had scoffed at the idea of being on camera.

"Sweet baby Jac!" my dad calls, getting up from the couch and wrapping me into a hug. I manage to keep my composure this time, quickly making the introductions to Marcus, who seems to have no problem charming my family with his easy smiles and quick words. I start thinking about what Henry said, about him mimicking people, and I see little moments of it. Pivoting from decoration talk with my mom to college football with my brother to rosé and outdoor concerts with Eileen but always sounding genuine. Last season, I'd felt compelled by the way he spoke to Shailene, his emotions present, but always held slightly at a distance, his openness about his struggles.

I didn't want to think about that too hard, though. Not anymore. Not now that I knew who Marcus really was.

"Game just finished up," Dad says. "Told them they'd have to push back filming if it went into overtime."

"Brendan said we won," I say.

"You're damn right," Dad agrees. "Told 'em they could set up whatever they needed in the house, but I was watching the game. Got them invested eventually." He points at the person behind me, and I turn to find Henry.

"Clemson fan now?" I ask him.

"The biggest," he agrees. But I notice as he says it, he slurs his words slightly. "Your dad's the greatest, Jac."

Dad enthusiastically claps him on the shoulder. "For a Hollywood guy, Henry isn't half bad," he says in his thick Lowcountry accent.

I tilt my head to the side, watching him. "Henry . . . are you drunk?"

He smiles, slowly. "It was a good game. And good bourbon." And then, as if it's a defense: "Most of the crew is drunk, too."

"That is . . . accurate," Dad agrees, scratching his chin, like he doesn't know how they got that way. I glance at Austin, sitting behind him, and he meets my eyes and nods, Eileen laughing at his shoulder.

"Well," my mom says, drawing her words out just as slowly as my father, "I was just making some appetizers . . . or as we call 'em around here, Marcus, tailgate foods." She is *really* hamming it up.

Marcus smiles gamely. "Ma'am, I come from Big Ten country— you won't be able to keep me away from the tailgate food."

Mom fawns, and I know why. Marcus is charming; he's handsome, square-jawed, and almost absurdly broad and tall. My life has been a shit show for the past two years, and now I have *this*. She can never admit it's what she wants for me, but it's exactly what she wants for me.

Eventually, the six of us, Brendan, Henry, the cameras, and everyone else head into the kitchen, standing around the island and pretending to eat jalapeño poppers.

"Where all have the two of you been?" Mom is asking us, soaking up every moment of camera time.

"Let's see," I say. "The mansion in LA . . . we went down to Malibu, too, Cancun . . ."

"Chicago," Marcus supplies helpfully, and our eyes meet, and I nod.

"Chicago, that's right."

"Maybe while Henry is having so much fun, he'll share where you're off to next," Eileen says with a conspiratorial smile. Eileen is a dedicated watcher of *the 1* and knows enough to know what Henry's job truly is on the show, unlike either of my parents or my brother.

"You ask of me the one thing I cannot give you, alas," he says.

"Do you become Shakespeare when you're drunk?" I can't help but rib him.

He's moving a little slow as he says, "Look, we have all bonded while you were on your date, Jacqueline," and the way my family all look at him, I can tell it's true. Marcus looks slightly miffed as Priya takes over the situation.

"Okay, we're going to do a couple of one-on-ones in groups. Jac, why don't you and your mom start? Carol, if you don't mind, just ask Jac on camera if the two of you can go chat."

Mom lights up. "Jac, honey, why don't we go outside and have a little chat?" She picks up her drink and I grab mine as well, smiling at Marcus over my shoulder. As we walk out, Henry calls, "Absolutely nailed that, Carol. You're a natural."

"He's so charming," Mom says, swatting my hand as we go. I bristle but don't say anything. The two of us sit out on the deck of the house, lit up with a thousand watts, in a little swing that I'm fairly sure production brought in themselves based on its strange placement on the deck.

"You look so good, sweetie," she says, which is a lie. I look tired and too skinny, and I know that because I've stared at myself in front of every mirror for longer than I should have.

"I'm just happy to see you," I say, feeling near tears again.

"Oh, hon, I know you are," Mom says, giving me a hug then. "Tell me about Marcus."

I search for the words because there's nothing I want to say, except to beg her to not make me talk about Marcus. "He's really . . . Marcus has something about him. There . . . there's been something magnetic between the two of us since the start."

Her face wrinkles up in confusion at my lack of enthusiasm. "And what kind of person are you with him?" she asks.

"With him?" I repeat, scrambling for anything to hold on to in this conversation. It's just like my mama to do that, to strike right to the heart of something. "I guess it goes without saying that in a situation this strange, things have been complicated. Messy, even." I realize in that moment that this will be easier if I just talk about Henry. If I forget Marcus altogether. I stare down at the space between the two of us, the swing, seeing him so clearly in the back of my mind. "But I guess being anywhere with him makes me feel okay being me, not constantly questioning how I convince him to love me. This show makes it so hard to say things that are real because everything is always a fairy tale. With him, it goes beyond that. I think . . . we really understand each other." I glance at the camera as I say it, and Priya, looking fascinated, silently redirects my attention to my mother.

"Do you love him?" Mom asks me. I immediately look her in the eyes, taken aback by the question. It was planted by a producer—Priya, if I had to guess—but when I meet her eyes, I know Mom wants to know, too. She's my mother and she loves me; she wants to know if I did what she asked. If I truly gave finding love a shot.

I bite into my lip. I don't think about what I'm really saying when I automatically reply, "Of course I love him."

My mom, who I know desperately wants this to be true, looks cautiously surprised. "You love him?" she asks, not unkindly. "That doesn't sound like you."

"I know this seemed like an insane lark to all of you at first," I tell her. *And you were right*, my eyes say. "But, it's given me clarity. On myself. The clarity I think I was missing."

Mom folds one of my hands up into both of her own, her eyes shining. "As long as this is right for you, Jackie." She kisses my hand. "I love you so much, sweetheart."

I bow my head, blink away a tear.

After a couple of requested reshoots, Priya sends Mom back inside with one of the assistants. Priya gives me this look, like perhaps we are friends or perhaps she is a mother figure to me.

"Jac, that was a really beautiful conversation with your mother," Priya says.

"Yes, I know," I answer, dead-eyed.

Priya shifts uncomfortably, sensing her overreach. "You know what I'm going to say then," she says anyway. When I don't answer, she goes on, "You should tell Marcus you love him. He's still worried that your walls aren't all the way down. It's a really beautiful moment, seeing you finally able to open up with your mother in a way you can't with everyone else. It will make the audience understand you better. It's humanizing."

"Too bad I'm not a human, right?" I ask. I pick up my drink and walk back into the brightly lit house.

It goes like that, next with my dad and then Austin and Eileen. I stew in what I've done, in the mess I've made as I sleepwalk through the conversations, and then it's Marcus's turn to be individually grilled by my family.

Henry creeps to my side when Austin and Eileen go out onto the deck with Marcus. "What?" I say, feeling him there like a ghost.

He's barely moving his mouth, whispering to me. "Did you tell your mother you were in love with Marcus?"

I look at him over my shoulder. "Can we talk about this later?"

"Priya is going to lose her shit on me if you don't say it to Marcus by the end of the night," Henry says. There's a layer missing—a layer of manipulation or charm or something. Just the unvarnished truth: Henry and his job.

"Sounds like a personal problem," I say. "You didn't bring my dog and you promised you would." (Shae's dog was in her hometown. I guess they figured they'd save the moment for the more likable contestant.)

"I *tried* to talk John into it," he answers. "But after the incident with Elodie—"

"Fine." I don't meet his eye, staring off in the distance.

He lets out a breath, the smell of booze, and leaves the room, leaving me alone. I lean into the cool marble counter, close my eyes, and breathe. I feel someone watching me and open my eyes to see my brother in front of the open back door. Austin is staring down at me, his brow furrowed. He closes the door behind him quietly and comes to stand at the island opposite me. "You don't seem like yourself, Jac," he says after a minute. I look away from him, my cheeks coloring. "Are you happy with all this?" he asks.

I swallow down every real thing I want to say. Because I'm miked up, because they're all here, because I'm always miked up. "I think I could be happy," I say. "This is my way back from New York."

"I'm not sure a television show can change you that easily," he says. "You never give yourself a break. So, you don't write for a while. That's fine. You didn't do anything wrong moving back home."

"What did you tell Marcus? About me?"

Austin sinks down farther against the counter, a small smile playing at his face. "I told him about when Eileen was studying abroad and Mom and Dad were on vacation and my appendix burst. How you slept next to my bed all night in the hospital. I told him that's the kind of person you are."

I feel myself wanting to cry and hold back. This isn't staged; we aren't faking it for the cameras but we're not alone. "What did Marcus say?"

Austin squints, a poor imitation of the way Marcus looks when he is pretending to be genuine. "He loves that about you."

I laugh. "Shut up," I say to his unspoken but clear mocking. "I've actually done a lot of self-examination on the show." That part is true at least. "It's like having all my flaws magnified and spelled out for me by thirty other people or so."

"That sounds awful," Austin says.

I glance over at him. "It was."

"Is this really it?" he asks. "Marcus."

I close my eyes, take another deep breath. "Maybe."

Just another thing for me to get absolutely brutalized for when the show airs.

An hour later, we are finally, blessedly wrapping up this charade. My family is gathered back in the den, and I feel the time slipping away, myself disappearing.

Eileen is looser than she was when the filming first started, learning a lesson about alcohol and *the 1* that I have learned many times over. Lightly, she says, "So, Marcus, you gotta tell us, what do you like best about Jac?"

The words clearly take him aback. He looks at me as the seconds tick by, and we all see the gears turning in his head. "She's just"—he grasps, that blank smile still on his face—"she's laid-back, kind of a guy's girl. And she's so beautiful."

Henry scoffs, and we all look over at him in surprise, my eyes going wide. "That's it?" he asks. "Not that she's incredibly intelligent? Her acerbic sense of humor? The fact that she's by far the most interesting person here?"

Marcus laughs, looking thrilled. "You trying to get on camera now, too?" he asks Henry pleasantly. "You want to ask her on a date?" Eileen's eyebrows are practically in her hairline as she watches the two of them. Mom and Dad are both looking from Henry to Marcus to me. *Fuck.*

Henry holds on to Marcus's bemused gaze for a moment before he says, "That's fine. I think we have enough here. Sorry, I need to use the restroom."

As the crew members start resetting us, as casually as I can, I get up myself and follow him. It seems impossible to be subtle after that showing. Henry's in a dark hallway, his forehead pressed into the wall.

"'Don't drink with my dad' is the number one rule of fight club," I say. "You still drunk?"

He twists his head to look at me, his cheek then pressed into the wall. "Sobering up. Painfully," he answers, his pretty face smushed up against the wallpaper. "Need to learn when to shut the fuck up."

"Don't we all."

"I hate this, Jac," he says.

"What?" I ask, and he glances at my mic, then back at my eyes. He pushes himself off the wall.

"Nothing," he tells me then. "Let's just finish this godforsaken night so we can drive back to Charlotte and go to sleep."

"Fair enough," I agree. "Just promise me I don't have to say it."

Almost imperceptibly, he sinks down the wall slightly. He's still leaning against it, staring at me in a way that makes me one hundred percent sure he wants to push me against the wall, relive that night in Chicago all over again.

He shakes his head. "Don't," he mouths to me.

I hold my hand out, and he takes it, barely, and then lets it slide between his fingers. At the same time, we go our separate ways.

Before I leave, I hug them all. Eileen and Austin and Mom and Dad.

My mom hangs on to me the longest, both hands on the side of my face as she pulls away.

"Don't let anyone decide who you are for you, Jac," she says, leaning her forehead into mine.

I breathe in her scent for a moment, her perfume and detergent.

"I love you," I say, and that still means something. I saved it for them. "I love you all."

Marcus walks with me to the car I have to drive away in on camera, his fingers loose against mine. "Your family's nicer than you," he says with a smile.

"Heard that one before."

"It's cruel," he says, "to part from you, isn't it?"

We stare at each other, a certain heat still between us, a different kind of challenge, and for the first time since Mexico, when he kisses me, I don't want to recoil.

I get into the car, in a seat next to Henry. To my surprise, Priya is in the car, sitting in a seat opposite us. This can't be a good sign. "Please tell me we're done," I say, more to Priya than Henry.

Priya doesn't say anything for a moment, her eyes on me, somewhere near homicidal. "We're done," she says. "You two are done."

I look at Henry, an eyebrow raised, but he doesn't return my gaze. However, my gesture redirects Priya's ire toward Henry. "You," she begins, her voice accusatory, "have always thought you were above the rules, but you've never been *stupid* before. Jesus, you're practically drooling over her in front of her family."

Henry's eyes are on his lap. He doesn't respond.

"You tired of playing for the patriarchy yet, Priya?" I ask.

"You clearly actively want us to hate you," Priya says, turning on me just as fast. "I don't spend months a year away from my family to deal with assholes like you. Self-sabotage on your own time because I'm fucking sick of it. I'm *sick* of both of you! Not everything is about you. We have a show to run, and you are not the main characters. Cut—it—out."

"Are you—are we . . . not together anymore?" I finally manage to say. Henry still isn't responding.

"The team isn't stupid," Priya says. "We all know Henry is the only reason we're getting *anything* out of you. It's two and a half more weeks, and if you two don't get your shit together, I will take great joy in personally delivering the lawsuits brewing for both of you. Seriously, Henry, this message is from God above, do you hear me?"

Henry finally looks up, his face clear. "Got it," he says.

"And my favorite delightful contestant? You willing to go toe-to-toe with that contract you signed?"

I sigh deeply. Mostly, I just want to go to sleep. "Fine," I say. "Whatever. We're already on the threshold of hell. What's the worst that could happen?"

No one says anything.

Jac's DMs

Monday, 8:33 p.m.

You are a whore.

Monday, 9:02 p.m.

Imagine being such a terrible role model for children everywhere. I hope you die.

Monday, 9:04 p.m.

I'm surprised no one has come to your house to rape and murder you yet.

Monday, 10:02 p.m.

Die.

Monday, 10:45 p.m.

Die.

Monday, 11:17 p.m.

Die.

Tuesday, 5:40 a.m.

Die.

20

Hands Down

Henry and I get back to Charlotte at four in the morning, no words exchanged between the two of us on the entire trip back. Five hours and some mediocre sleep later, there's a knock on my door. After a lengthy debate with myself over answering, I finally give in, and, as I suspected, it's him.

"What do you want?" I demand. "We aren't flying out until tomorrow, are we?"

"We're getting the fuck out of here," he says. "Get dressed. Bathing suit, something sporty."

"Is this a setup?" I ask, suspicious. After Priya's speech yesterday, I don't know what to expect.

"It's your day off," Henry says. "The crew is long gone to another hometown."

"Did John approve this?" I can't help but ask.

"Fuck John," Henry answers. "I've done more than enough for him over the years. I already planned this and Charlotte approved it weeks ago. Let's go."

I continue to stare at him, every betrayal fresh on my mind. He reads my hesitation.

"This isn't a trick, Jac," he finally says. "Do you want to spend the day in your hotel room or do you want to spend it somewhere a little less claustrophobic? This can't be what it's come to between us."

"Well," I say at last. "It is. Give me fifteen minutes. And don't fuck with me."

He nods, and I close the door in his face, getting dressed. I wish

I had something sloppy to wear, something to make me feel as separated as I can from the girl I've been these past few weeks, but no dice on packing anything even slightly not flattering in the small amount of luggage I was allotted. I opt for no makeup, hair in a boring ponytail with a hat on top, and a pair of sunglasses that came in our sponsor-provided gift bags at the start of the show.

Henry is waiting in the lobby when I walk down, and he doesn't say anything to me, just gets out his phone and calls a Lyft. I remember him last night, his fingers falling through mine, the promise of something and then nothing. His gaze down in his lap as Priya read him the riot act. I don't know what I want from him—to not be such a coward? To maintain his icy façade?

It doesn't matter. This is one day of my life and one day without *the 1*. I'll take what I can get.

THE NATIONAL WHITEWATER Center is twenty minutes from our hotel, out hidden away in a copse of trees just off the interstate. Even this early on a weekday, the parking lot is filling up.

Henry buys us tickets with what is presumably a *the 1* credit card. As he hands my wristband over, he says, "What do you want to do first?"

I look at this list of options. Zip-lining, whitewater rafting, ropes courses, kayaking. Finally, I point toward a description on the brochure I grabbed at the register.

"Climbing," I say. "The freefall climb over the pool."

"Aggressive," he states neutrally, and I can't help the small smile that curls at the edge of my mouth.

Henry had briefly mentioned to me on the way over that typically, the contestants got a day to relax before their hometowns, but since mine had come first, I got the day after. Last season, he said, he and Marcus had gone to a Cubs game together.

"That must have been quite a day," I said.

In the back of the Lyft, Henry shrugged. "Marcus and I did have things in common. I don't know. It was complicated."

I leaned my head against the window. "Yeah."

It's hard to resist the happiness I feel bubbling inside of me. Me, an anonymous stranger in the crowd, outside, the smell of flowers and chlorine and life in the air. I could be anyone, I could be Jac Matthis, and I remember her, keep her close to my heart.

The climbing wall juts out at an angle over the pool, getting progressively more angled as you climb. I feel weak when I start on the first wall, the third easiest one, my body not quite functioning the way I remember it, arms and legs clumsy.

I make it about two thirds of the way up, and then drop, submerged in the pool below, before swimming back to the ladder to climb out. I get back in line to go again, a glutton for punishment. I focus myself, my whole body, whole purpose on climbing this third easiest wall, push myself.

I make it to the top and progress to the next wall. I conquer that one and on to the next. I end up behind Henry on the seventh wall.

"You want to go first?" he asks me. I shake my head, concentrating on the wall, building a plan out in my mind, in the grip that will get me to the next grip, into where my feet will go, where I will need to swap them out.

Henry takes to the wall, bare feet curled on oddly shaped footfalls, his bare back flexing with the effort of going against the wall. I hardly think about him at all, but rather, his body, the way it moves, the way he plans. Where I had planned to use my body weight to push up to a higher left handhold on the wall, he crosses over and grabs a handhold to his right, and I admire the way he does it, changing my own strategy. He gets stuck at a foot switch, loses his grip, and falls into the water below, his body going as straight as possible as he falls, just like the instructor taught us. He swims to the ladder and pulls himself up.

I climb onto the wall, securing my feet, holding my body as close to the wall as possible. For a few weeks two summers ago, I'd briefly dated a travel writer with a passion for climbing. He'd taken me to the gym with him, showed me how to shift my hips just right to get momentum, to find the top of the wall. I'd started going when I knew he wasn't there, practicing, so I could impress him the next time I saw him. Not much impressed him, I soon realized, as I quickly graduated from V0 to V1 to V2 routes, but I found it didn't matter that much to me. I'd tried to grow used to a world in which practicing and succeeding didn't elicit applause from an eager audience, but with climbing, it was a bit easier. The wall itself congratulated me, each time my two hands landed on the piece of tape telling me I had completed a route. *You're good, Jac,* it seemed to say. *You did it.*

I think of him, just briefly, on that wall as I climb. I stopped going to the gym once we ended things; it was too expensive and too likely I'd run into him. But I remember that satisfaction as I climb. I remember working out the puzzle of a wall, outsmarting it, beating it, and it being happy for me.

Gravity pushes against me as I get farther up the wall, my mind clear, focused only on the task at hand. At the spot where Henry struggled, I move to swap feet just as he had, not fully getting a grip on the first try as he had, but hanging on, both of my arms straining to keep my fingers tightly wrapped around the handholds. Swinging myself for momentum, I get my foot planted against the foothold—just barely—and manage to push myself up enough to get hold of the next highest handhold, hugging my body to the wall and shifting my right foot up, allowing me to finally, easily, push myself up the wall. The rest is fairly simple after that, and I touch the top, a feeling of satisfaction deep inside me. *This* is who I am. This is who I can be.

I let go and fall into the pool below, cold water replacing sticky sweat as my momentum pushes me deep under the water. I tread water underneath for a moment, feeling every ache in my muscle, every pull against my shoulder, before I have to go up for air. I swim over to the side and climb out, going back around to the fence and exiting. Henry is standing there with a stupid look on his face, a closemouthed smile. I stand there, dripping wet and staring at him.

"What?" I finally say, and the word unlocks something inside of me. I'm smiling, too, unable to stop myself.

I don't think he's sure what he's going to say for a minute, but finally, he looks away from me, shaking his head. "You kicked my ass," he says.

"You deserved it," I tell him.

"Sure," he agrees, looking at me again, nodding.

"That was fun," I say, and it seems to please him, this change in my demeanor. I don't want to ignore him anymore. I want to pretend the past few weeks haven't happened. I want to pretend *the 1* hasn't happened, and we could be any two people out here at the water park. We are that.

"How about," I say, "you buy me a bottle of water and we go paddleboarding?"

"Sounds like a plan," he agrees.

HENRY AND I head down a winding path off the other side of the whitewater center and come upon a river shore, where we rent stand-up paddleboards. Most people have paddled out a bit from the shore and stopped, but there's a wide-open river in front of us ("Just don't go past the bridge," our guide said), and I push through the water past the crowd.

We paddle, hard, almost all the way to the bridge, and I take in a deep breath of clean air. I stop and get onto my knees, then lean back, lying down with my knees bent and my shoulder sticky against the board. Henry sinks down onto his board next to me, sitting up straight with his feet dangling off his board in the water. I stare up at the sky, so blue and endless.

"I had forgotten," Henry says after a minute.

"Hmm?" I respond.

"What you're actually like. It's been a while. Chicago, maybe?"

"Yeah," I answer icily. "And whose fault is that?"

"Mine, clearly," he answers without conviction.

It sits there between us, his bullshit and my distance, until I can't take it. "What's wrong with you?" I ask, my voice neutral.

"Can you be more specific?"

"You tell me in Chicago that you desperately want to burn this show down to be with me, and then what? You panic? You get a slap on the wrist and fall in line?"

"I've been working here for twelve years. My relationship with *the 1* is the longest of my life." He floats there a moment more before he says, "It's hot. I'm getting in."

He slides off his board, the water covering him up to his chest.

We both have on life jackets, so he floats to the top, putting his elbows up on his board.

"So, what were you like before the show?" I ask.

"I feel like you're interviewing me."

"Then impress me."

"I don't know." He splashes me lightly, and I splash him back. "You know what I'm like."

"Manipulative, withholding, and kind of a dick?"

Henry laughs. "Sure." He tilts his head back, his black hair getting wet and sticking to his forehead. "I transferred after my first year in school, out to the East Coast. Thought the change of scenery would do me some good."

I glance at him over my shoulder. "You don't really strike me as the East Coast type."

He sighs, almost says something, and stops. "I went back home eventually," he says. "Obviously. Everything after that was kind of an accident. I wasn't trying for any of it. It just happened to me."

"And you let it," I continue. Sweat is rolling down my back, and I work so hard to keep myself focused. There's something that feels dangerous about falling too deep into Henry's words. That's where I keep getting lost. I love hearing him talk to me, and I love hearing myself talk back to him.

"I let it. I didn't—or at least, not on purpose. I kind of stopped trying to steer the car anymore."

"And you wound up here," I finish for him.

He flattens his forearms and sets his chin on them, watching me. "Guess so."

With the heat and the intensity of his gaze, I find myself wanting to escape. I clumsily fall into the water myself, releasing the straps of my lifejacket and diving under, coming back up quickly and pushing my hair out of my face.

"Why'd you pick this place anyway?" I ask, paddling back over to my board.

"Because of what you said on that date with Marcus," he says as if it's the most obvious thing in the world. "You said being outside and hiking made you feel like a person again."

It shocks me, the effect the words have on me. The memory of it, the idea, in that moment, that I *exist*, that I am not a character on a show, but a real, alive person who thinks and feels and hurts, almost takes my breath away. I exist. I exist. My stupid heart almost bursts open in that moment, and entirely without my permission, a gasp escapes me as if the last few weeks are spilling out, me barely holding back a flood of tears. I put my hand to my chest and push the rest back in. Henry stares out over the bridge behind us, leaving me in a moment of privacy. It's too intimate.

I swallow the lump in my throat, wait until I'm sure I can speak rationally again. "You have to quit the show."

He absorbs the words. "I don't think you get it," he says. The simplicity of this scene feels wrong, two people floating out on SUP boards in the shadow of an overpass in the quiet of a Carolina fall, the opposite of *the 1* with its extravagant settings and inane platitudes. "I wish I *could* quit the show for you. Make a big grand gesture."

"Oh, fuck off," I say. "I don't even mean to do it for me. Do that shit for yourself."

His eyes pierce mine. "And then what?"

"You figure out how to be happy," I say, pulling myself up on the board and pulling my knees into my chest, drying myself in the sun. He doesn't say anything.

We sit there like that, in silence. After a while, I stand back up on my board and paddle over to a secluded beach cove, lying back in the sun, life jacket off, waiting to dry. Henry follows me, sits next to me, the sun shining off his skin, sunglasses over his face, just slightly behind me. I think about him like that so often, a hidden smile playing at his lips.

"Can I ask you a question?" Henry asks. I don't answer, so he says, "What's going on here?"

"I don't know," I say. I train my gaze on a cloud covering the sun, squinting up at it, thinking if there's some easy summary of *this*. "I've always been a little too much for most well-adjusted people. I really fucking want to succeed, but more than that, I want to be *seen* as successful, and that's what drove me. And when I'm not, I turn to men and alcohol, and sometimes, it all feels like a vicious cycle."

"And I'm what?" he asks. "The alcohol? The men? Or the cycle?"

"I think I'm in love with you," I tell him. I glance over at him. "Or something like that? I think you're in love with me, too, only maybe you're not? I don't know, you turn it off and on like a light switch."

"Yeah, well, we're all fucked now anyway." He leans his head forward against my shoulder, and I exhale. I knew he couldn't say it. "I don't want to do this anymore." Faintly, he presses his lips into the skin there, waiting to see my reaction.

"Yeah?" I reach up, push my fingers into his hair, the barrier officially crossed.

"Yeah."

"I would've left with you," I say. "After Chicago. It wasn't real, but it was."

"I think I knew that," he admits. "And I couldn't let it go."

I sit with that. "But you could've let me go?"

"I don't know," he admits. "I've been trying, haven't I?"

"Why Marcus?" I ask him, the question that's been eating at me since Mexico. "Why is he the one that broke this open for you? After everything you've done on this show?"

"Marcus?" He sighs, running his hands through his hair before he begins, taking his sunglasses off as he does so, letting me see his eyes. "When we started filming the season last year, everyone who talked to Marcus loved him, but he wasn't translating onscreen at all. It took me about a week, but I finally realized it was because he mimicked whoever he spoke to. He could mirror another person perfectly, and that's why people liked him. He knew what they wanted to hear because he could essentially become them; he was a hell of a salesman. So, I did what made the most sense—I told him to be me. And eventually, toward the end of the season, it got to the point that I couldn't just tell him to tell Shailene how he felt, I had to instruct him on *how* he felt, but he was so good at it. At saying my words and making them feel true. Hell, most of what he said sounded truer than anything I ever did. And that *really* fucked me up. That I could give him my thoughts and he'd be better at being a person with them than I was."

"That's not true," I say.

"Sure it is. He was easier for you, too, at first, wasn't he? And I couldn't stand it. I couldn't stand you with him. Then I couldn't stand me obsessing over it. He took what I gave him and hurt Shailene, and then he was using it on you. It made me sick."

We look at each other, and I can tell both of us are wondering what the other is thinking, always wondering. Finally, I say, "Why couldn't you have told me that before?"

"My mom died," he answers. Something about the way he says it is strangled and it takes longer than it should have before he continues. "You want to know how I ended up with this life? My mom died and I took all my grief and started working on *the 1*."

"*That's* your big tragic backstory?" I know I sound callous as I say it, but how many contestants has he produced on *the 1* with the exact same story?

"You think I don't know it's weak? You think there's a reason I don't talk about me? The first thing I learned working on *the 1*," he says, "is you give anyone a piece of you, they'll use it against you, so no, I don't talk about my dead mother." He takes a deep breath, collecting himself. "Cancer, since you're wondering. Pancreatic."

"I'm sorry," I say, uselessly, too late.

"Me too." There's a tic in his jaw as he stares straight ahead. "This woman—this strong, smart, vibrant woman who raised me—wasted away to nothing. I had to lie to her constantly, tell her she looked like she was getting better, and it made me think that maybe lying hurt the person doing it more than the person who was being lied to.

"I couldn't talk about that, could I? All I could do was be on the set of *the 1* and consume other people's feelings and alcohol until I felt like I was on the edge of real humanity. When I was off set, that was where I had to act, right? But on the show, it was nothing but emotions and projection and—" He shakes his head. "Somewhere along the way, there was nothing else."

I almost laugh. "Fucking irony," I say. "You get off on the pain because it's the only place you let yourself feel it."

"It's asinine. To pinpoint my mother's death as the turning point in my life. The worst part is it wasn't even the dying, in the end, that really broke me. It was the waiting. I was a kid in school on the other side of the country and drunk and stoned and honestly, sleeping with more girls than I'd ever thought I could sleep with, and then she was sick and I was suddenly back in this godforsaken sun-bathed place. She was always dying. She used to cry every night, saying she wanted to go home, back to Malaysia, and she'd stopped speaking English, so I couldn't understand her, which is a fun mix of pain and shame. Her hair fell out and I had to give her baths and I became numb to seeing her naked or shitting herself or to my dad drinking himself to death instead of helping. I even taught myself to cook pan mee, like she loved before, and she'd get a couple of bites down, smiling at me, telling me what a good son I was, and then throw them back up. She knew she was dying and I knew she was dying and she was ready to go but she couldn't. She stopped eating—that was two fucking weeks before the end. Stopped drinking. Stopped speaking. She was still alive, but there was nothing left, and that was somehow worse. Because what if that was all that was left of her when she went to the next life? That isn't fair."

He rubs his free hand against his face, almost clawing at it, leaving dark red marks behind on his skin. I see him doing that in my mind's eye, twelve years ago, on another sunny beach, all alone. I grab his hand before he draws blood, and it flexes around mine. "It's easy," he says, "to give them what you're feeling. It's easy to tell them, 'Hey, remember when your grandpa killed himself? Did you ever stare at your skin so long, you considered carving it open to see if there was still anyone inside?' And then pretend that thought has nothing to do with me, was always theirs."

The silence lives and breathes between us in a way it feels it must. I feel my pulse, quick against his where our hands are touching, where he's holding on like he's afraid I'll let go.

I take a deep breath. "It was you," I say, the realization sinking in. "Marcus's speech about his dying dad. *You* fed it to him."

He shrugs one shoulder, embarrassed. "I saw him, and he talked to me about his dad's cancer until I almost couldn't breathe because I was right back there again, reliving my mom's death. I was so sure I could make things better for him than they had been for me."

"Why didn't you tell me?" I ask him. I grasp his hand, digging into it as he digs back into mine. He meets my eyes. "You knew what that made me feel about Marcus, and you just let me believe it was all him? After everything?"

"Would you have believed me?" he asks. "There's no big answer I'm going to give you that's going to make you okay with who I am."

"That wasn't the right thing to say," I say.

"No," he returns. "I didn't think it was."

"Okay," I answer.

"You're right, you know," he says. "About me. I turn it on and off. Love? I guess. I don't know." He doesn't look at me; he wants me to say it for him, and I can't.

I move on the sand, in front of him, straddling his legs, on my knees. His fingers slide into my hair, pushing it back from my face.

"Why?" he asks me.

"Because—" I swallow. "Because my heart aches whenever I see you."

His mouth captures mine without further hesitation, his hand sliding up under the back strap of my bikini. I push myself against him, hovering over him. There's something different in it, something open, a nexus crossed. His fingernails skim across my back, not enough to break the skin, but reminding me of when he sank his teeth into me in Chicago.

He climbs up to meet me, his pulse racing under my fingertips, his other hand sliding into my bikini bottoms. His fingers instantly finding the most sensitive spot, expertly, easily bringing me to him, distracting me from his mouth, working in and out until I'm gasping.

"Don't come yet," he whispers in my ear.

"Don't tell me what to do," I manage to return, but still, I let him change the playing field, my back against the sand as he presses me down, his tongue trailing from my belly button to just above my bottoms before he slides them off, licking the water off my skin. His shoulders press into my thighs as his tongue flicks into me, more heat, more humidity. I press my hands into his bare bronzed shoulders, curling them, digging fingernails in until I draw blood and come, my body shuddering against him.

He lays his face against my stomach as I pant, recovering. I get in a couple of breaths and can't imagine stopping, can't imagine ever stopping, tugging at his hair, commanding him to climb me, and then, flipping over, taking him back into my control, sliding his swim trunks down past his hips all the way off, exposing his erection to me. I touch him first with my hands, all of him, and then take him into my mouth, licking the full length of him before I wrap my mouth around him, his body tensing all around me. "Don't come yet," I say, grinning up at him when he starts squirming.

He closes his eyes, head against the sand. "Come on," he breathes out.

He comes up to me, chest-to-chest, greedily tugging my bathing suit off. "This is a public place, Jacqueline," he whispers to me.

With a smile, I pull away from him, dive back into the water, knowing he'll follow. He does. Hip-deep in the water, he slides into me, eliciting a small gasp. Over his shoulder, I watch the blood drying on his skin as he slides in and out, not giving himself over to it, not letting me give myself over to it, until we can't take it anymore. We are fucking like two broken, brokenhearted people who can't quite give in and can't quite let go.

And when it's over, I collapse against him, sticky skin, panting, sand on our hair and faces and upper bodies. I go completely under the water, my hair falling flat and soaked again. Henry swims after me, grabbing me from behind, his naked body pressing into mine.

"Hey," I whisper to him. "What's wrong?"

He presses his cheek into the warm skin of my shoulder and laughs.

"I'm sorry," he says, but never why.

Women Tell All

[Cut back from commercial with Becca and Brendan smiling at the camera, sitting on a dais in two armchairs side by side, directly facing the contestants with stiff, Botoxed smiles on their faces.]

Becca: Welcome back to *the 1* season 32 Women Tell All. We're once again joined by the beautiful women of season 32.

[The camera sweeps over to show all of the women sitting in two rows of chairs on the stage in beautiful dresses, in order of when they were eliminated, with Rikki on the last chair in the bottom row, having been the last eliminated prior to Women Tell All airing. The audience claps appreciatively.]

Brendan: Now, we think it's time to discuss the elephant in the room.

[Aaliyah covers her face, already laughing.]

Becca: That's right. Let's talk about the girl most of you love to hate. Jac Matthis.

[The audience boos. A montage begins, showing Jac getting out of the limo, calling hello to Marcus.]

Hannah, voiceover: She's *so calculating.*

Jac, sitting in an interview room: The other girls? I don't think about them at all.

[In quick succession, the clip shows Jac confronting Stasia on the first date, Jac telling Hannah she will never compare to her, and Jac dismissing Kady during her final cocktail party.]

Jac, at the mansion by the pool at night: You have to tell me that so I'll be invested in this stupid show.

Kendall, crying in an interview room: She's awful.

Jac, back at the pool: I might be a bad person.

   [Cut to Jac sitting in an interview room in Cancun crying.]

Jac: I guess I just really want to be loved.

   [Marcus, being interviewed at Jac's hometown.]

Marcus: Two of the other girls have told me they're in love with me. Jac hasn't. [smiling self-consciously] I guess she's just making me sweat it like she always does.

   [Shae is sitting around a pool with other girls.]

Shae: How far do you think she'd go to win?

   [Cut to video of a closed door, splashing sounds, and then a whisper, captioned on the screen.]

Jac, whispering, voiceover: Send Andi home. Tonight.

   [The screen cuts to black, then opens back on the girls onstage, some with smirks on their faces, others with eyebrows raised. Hannah mouths "wow."]

Becca: Andi, do you want to start?

   [Andi swallows, once, as if to start, but then stops herself, hand on her chest. Kady rubs her arm tenderly.]

Andi: It was so hard to watch my breakup with Marcus back because I could see how dumbfounded I felt at the time. It was so out of nowhere and then to find out there were such negative intentions behind it? It's just really, really hard.

Brendan: And what would you say to Jac, if she were here tonight?

Andi: Your actions have consequences. We weren't all here as game pieces for you to clear out of your way.

Hannah: Jac was never willing to see any of the rest of us as people, and now she wants sympathy for how the show is portraying her? It *kills* me. We were all there.

Rikki, turning her head, looking at Hannah sitting in the row behind her: I don't think Jac has ever asked for sympathy. As far as I can tell, she hasn't said anything since the show started airing.

Kady: Because she's too big a coward to face up to what she did.

Rikki: Maybe because, unlike all of you have been claiming, she isn't in this for Instagram followers?

Aaliyah: Oh, please, Rikki. Jac doesn't need you to be her attack dog.

Grace-Ann: We all heard what you said to her when you left. She said she loved you [Bonnie scoffs] and you said, 'Just not enough to not use me.' What was that even *about*? What did she make you do?

[Rikki swings back around to the front, crossing her arms.]

Rikki: Didn't you go home in episode 4?

[The crowd cheers in appreciation.]

Brendan: That's a good point, though, Grace-Ann. Rikki, would you like to clear the air about what happened between Jac and you? Do you have anything else you want to say in defense of your friend?

[Rikki purses her lips, thinking it through.]

Rikki: This show is hard for people to get through, and I knew when push came to shove that Jac always had my back. Jac always goes to bat for the people she cares about, but it takes her a long time to trust another person.

Rikki: I'll leave it for her to speak for herself about everything else.

[With some light applause, the camera pans back to Becca, radiantly pregnant in an orange patterned caftan, nodding.]

Becca: Well said, Rikki.

[Becca and Brendan move on to the bloopers segment.]

21

The Space Between

I wake up in Henry's room the next morning, skin touching skin, neither of us wearing anything. Instinctively, I slither onto him, my legs crossing his, my arms across his stomach.

"Good morning," he mumbles without opening his eyes. I press my lips into his chest, leaning my head there. "I don't think this is how I remember us waking up together last time."

"Stockholm syndrome," I mutter, and he laughs, his hands going into my hair. "I've got to get back to my room and shower before our flight."

"Not yet." He pulls me closer even though I've made no move to leave.

"Okay," I say, "but if you want to kiss, I'm going to brush my teeth first."

"Hold that thought," he says, lifting up his vibrating phone. We both see the name on the screen. *Charlotte*. He unnecessarily gestures for me to be quiet as he picks up the call.

"Henry." Her familiar voice is like an old friend. Stockholm syndrome for sure.

"Good morning," Henry answers cheerfully. "Aren't you in labor by now?"

"Don't be dramatic," she says irritably. "Let me talk to Jac."

His eyes meet mine, and we both stare at each other. *We are fucked.* The silence sits there, between him and me and him and Charlotte.

"It's not—" Henry starts, sounding like a worse liar than he actually is.

"Jesus, just let me talk to her," Charlotte finally cuts in. "I don't care, okay? Hand her the phone."

Wordlessly, he does.

"Well," I say into the phone after a moment of silence.

I hear the smile in her voice. "Knew it. I fucking knew it when I called your room and you didn't answer."

I sigh. "Well, I guess that's a small comfort. I thought you knew in Chicago."

"Yeah, I suspected in Chicago. I suspected from the moment you started spilling your guts to him on the fifth day. This is what I get paid to do. If I hadn't known, I would be shit at my job."

"So, what now?" I ask her. Henry puts his finger on my thigh, running his nail up and down it lightly, and I shiver. I wonder if this is good for him, now that the game is up. If this is when we both breathe again.

"Well," Charlotte says, "if I was there, I'd make you two the main storyline of the season, but I'm not, and trying to explain to John how to do it would be a fucking mess. Besides, you two are so obvious that he already suspects something, but he doesn't know for sure. Not like I do. I would just seriously consider what you want out of this. You will get *destroyed* if this gets out."

I glance at Henry, who is diligently pretending he isn't listening. "I know," I say, the noose suddenly tightening around my neck again. It'll be back to Marcus soon, back to *the 1*.

"You still don't believe I'm on your side?" she asks.

I swallow. "I'm not sure," I admit.

"Well, that's progress. You should watch out for Priya, though. She's looking to make a name and this would do it. The promotion is in her sights."

"We've been careless," I say. Henry's fingers stop moving.

"Yes," Charlotte says, "obviously. But just finish out the season. *Don't* let them catch you on camera for the love of everything. After that, the two of you can do whatever you want. This is hardly the worst thing to ever happen on this godforsaken show."

"Marcus knows," I tell her.

"Well," she says, taking a deep breath, "shit."

"But he doesn't want me to leave."

Charlotte sighs deeply. "Marcus doesn't know what he wants, aside from attention. Ride the wave if he's letting you."

I clench the phone tightly. "You want to talk to Henry again?" I ask.

"No, I can talk to Henry whenever I want. You need to get back to your room."

"Fine," I say, feeling like a child being scolded by my mother.

"I'll see you at After the One," Charlotte tells me.

"I can't wait," I mutter.

"Are you going to ask?" she says.

"Ask what?"

"Fine," Charlotte says. "I had a girl."

THE NIGHT OF the next elimination ceremony is the coldest I can remember. None of the other girls say much about their dates, at least not to me. And we sit up there in front of the cameras and Marcus and shiver, awaiting our fate. I have on a slinky cobalt dress with spaghetti straps and a slit up to my thigh. It's one I'd been saving for later in the season, but when I'd stared at myself in the mirror earlier, seen how striking I looked, it felt hollow. We put on coats between takes, but it's not enough, the cold sinking into our bones. I stare across the distance to Marcus, wishing nothing but pain upon him, wishing I could run screaming away from all of this.

I had been so close to escaping. Out on the water, with Henry, twenty-five hundred miles away from this, I had been so close.

Now, I feel as far away from that girl I found for a day as I ever have.

"Jac," Marcus calls, brandishing his first invite to stay, and like a traitor to myself, I smile. I win. I lose myself, but I keep winning this game.

I go back to my position and my eyes flick to Henry, who is studiously not watching me.

"Kendall," Marcus says, and she lets out a breath, her small frame squeezed inside of a black and white blocked dress that looks stunning on her. I have this stupid thought that, if we were friends, I'd ask her to borrow it.

Becca and Brendan come out in matching orange outfits and somberly announce to us that one of the remaining contestants is not the one. Then Marcus calls Shae, and Eunice crumples. I don't know her, won't grieve for her the way I would Rikki, but it's one step closer to the end.

I wear that dread like a second skin as we toast the final three with champagne.

"Are you okay?" Shae asks me quietly. Marcus and Kendall are talking to a group of producers.

"Just—a little under the weather," I lie.

"I know what you mean," she says. "This is exhausting, isn't it?"

I don't answer. It's too late to make friends now to help me get through this.

"What now?" I ask Priya as she passes by me.

"Now?" she says. "Paris."

Weekly Reprint Memo

HOT TITLE RUSH REPRINT: 50,000 copies of END OF THE LINE by Jacqueline Matthis to cover incoming Readerlink and Amazon orders plus 20,000 additional jackets to hold against future printings.

Warehouse to drop-ship to accounts no later than EOD Friday.

NOTE PRICE INCREASE: was $15.99 now $18.99

FRANCE

22

In Too Deep

We take a brutal overnight flight from LAX to ATL to CDG in Paris, sitting with the producers. They did at least spring for the extended leg room. I read all of *Persuasion*, a comforting blanket of a book amid everything else. Shae, Kendall, and I ride in a van along with Priya and Henry to our lodgings, just outside of the Paris municipality. We each have our own room, stocked with a fridge and shower, a shared sink between the two of them. There's a separate room for our usual girl chats, where Shae, Kendall, and I can talk or film B-roll, but even that is regulated to when the producers deem it necessary. I sit and talk with Kendall when Shae goes on her overnight date, and then with Shae when Kendall goes for hers two days after. We don't see Paris—don't walk the streets, don't day-trip to Versailles despite the fact Henry promised he'd *try* to get permission to take us on one of the off days.

My life shrinks. To a mid-range hotel room, to producers and cameramen, to Henry and two beautiful girls disappearing and me disappearing in between.

I'd had this idea—this moronic idea—when I signed up for the show that it would at least be a chance to travel, to escape the smallness I'd started to feel in my life. But, instead, I am trapped in this tiny room, the ultimate cruel joke.

Henry did briefly take me on a walk yesterday, with another crew member who had the day off trailing behind us. I was so focused on how the two of us looked together that I couldn't think of anything else. Today—the last before my overnight date with Marcus—

Henry brings me a new book to read, just as he has every other day this week. A small consolation prize.

"It's you," I say when he comes in with a bag and closes the door behind him.

"It's always me." He lays the book out in front of me along with the bottle of red he's brought me from one of the markets. It's a Curtis Sittenfeld novel, one I've already read, but at least he knows my taste.

"Where's my fromage?" I ask.

"Cute, but I know you're barely eating. You've got two fromages in the fridge and your baguette from yesterday is going stale. You want me to get those out and we'll eat?"

I lean back into the couch, crossing my arms over my chest defensively. "Who can eat under these circumstances?"

He doesn't respond, only sighs and goes to the fridge to put in a couple bottles of water.

"What have you been doing today?" I hear Henry ask, but I'm completely focused on my hands, my arms, how pathetically small and weak my body looks and feels. I try to take a deep breath and I miss it. Tears well in my eyes and my hand goes to my mouth as I struggle to get anything in or out. I *really* can't breathe now, my body physically acting out the thought, like it has more control than I do.

"Hey," he says, crouching down in front of me, his hands encircling my wrists I'm still staring at. "Jac."

Instinctively, I pull away. Henry releases me, crouching down in front of me. "Jac, listen to me," he says, his hands on my thighs. I choke on my breath, keeping my head down.

"Breathe," he says, digging his fingers in ever so slightly, a source of pain to concentrate on as I choke out breaths, willing myself not to cry in front of him. "You're okay."

"I'm—" I start, but I can't. I take another shallow breath. "I'm not." I clutch at my chest and then release my hands.

"Okay," he agrees. "You're not."

I look up at him, his dark eyes and calm features. He's seen it a thousand times, I think. A thousand contestants.

That night, in his room in Charlotte, he'd stared at me like that. Openly, unafraid of being caught. Something raw in his face as his fingers tangled in my hair. We'd had sex and then drank red wine, tangled up in his sheets.

"So," he said to me, "my dad fucked off to Vietnam literally six months after Mom died, and got married a month later to a woman my age." He removed his free hand from my bare back and made a jazz hand. "Anyway, my makcik—Mom's sister—called me having an absolute meltdown when she heard about it."

I propped up on my elbows with a pillow under my chest, looking over at him. "Why'd you stay in LA then?"

He shrugged, his broad shoulders going up and down. "I don't know. I guess it was nice to be in a place that reminded me of my mom. It was complicated, but I needed it those first couple of years. Plus, the job. It was easier. I got caught up in it."

"I know what you mean," I said, reaching forward to the end table and grabbing up my own glass.

"Remember that family emergency on the day I was supposed to meet you? I had to fly out to Vietnam because my dad got drunk in a bar, got in a fight, and then told his wife he was going to throw himself into the South China Sea. So, you know, really functional shit."

"Oh," I said. "I'm sorry."

"Me too," he answered bitterly. "So, now, tell me about your sob story. New York."

"My downfall," I answered.

He raises an eyebrow. "New York was your promised land, though."

"Sure," I said, pulling my glass from my lips, nodding. "At first. And a published novel was my pot of gold at the end of a rainbow. Not to mix metaphors."

"Never." He smirked, and I removed the pillow from under me and hit him with it. "Hey!" he answered, fighting back, rolling over on top of me, play fighting, and then, sliding his fingers up my jawline, leaning in and kissing. "So, New York?" he asked again.

"How can you think about New York at a time like this?" I whispered back, pushing a piece of his black hair back from his forehead.

"Tell me," he said. "Tell me off camera."

That meant something to me. Those words. "New York was like

a wonderland. A different rabbit hole down every corner, and I thought I'd follow them all. I'd be a million different people and write a million different stories. I wouldn't be like everyone else."

"And?"

"And—" I laughed. "I was. It was exhausting. I was just like every other single girl in New York who'd spent their whole life being told how different they were from every girl around them, how special."

He scooted in closer to me, one arm sliding farther under me as he sank onto his elbow, hovering over me. "What's so great about being special anyway?" he asked.

"Well." A small smile played on my lips. "I've seen this show. Isn't that how you get the girl?"

He'd laughed and kissed me again.

That hotel room feels like a pocket in time, one that can only be accessed via some magic wormhole I will likely never re-create. That's what I'm thinking trapped here in this tiny French hotel room.

"What if I just do it?" I say after my heart rate has slowed down. "Confess, before Marcus can tell on me?" I take a shaky breath.

It's hard to miss the way he recoils. "You want to play it out?"

"I don't know," I say. He pops up from in front of me and goes to the fridge. Coming right back, he hands me a water, and I take it, take a deep drink, before I look at him again. "Do I?"

"You say that you and I are . . ." He glances around almost like he's expecting someone to jump out from behind a piece of furniture.

"Are . . ." I say.

"Yeah," he says. "That we are. Then what do you get out of that?"

The question stops me. It's been so long since I've considered getting anything out of this mess than pain and embarrassment. "I don't know," I admit. "I'm free from this shit show."

"And in a brand-new one," Henry quickly responds. "I just—I think that's worse for you than this, Jac. You'll forever be known as the girl who fucked the producer on *the 1*. That's not who you are. You're an author. You're a woman other women wish they could be."

"Says the producer I fucked," I answer.

Henry stares at me, swallows slowly. "Call his bluff. Ride it out. He isn't going to propose to you just to spite me."

"You really don't think so?" I ask. "Seems to me he's already done plenty just to spite you."

"Marcus cares too much about his image to do that. He wants to keep this publicity going as long as possible, and that only works with a girl who's madly in love with him. Anyone can see that's not who you are. You keep going, you get dumped, you *win*. The book sales, the sympathy, all without doing the last thing I know you want to do. Drag your shit out for everyone to see."

I feel myself relenting, giving in to the idea, to the idea of getting to have a *me* again, Jacqueline Matthis, *New York Times* bestselling author.

She never really existed, but God, do I want her to.

"Okay," I say. "You're right. It was a bad idea. I know they're never going to make me the next lead, but maybe I can salvage something out of this mess before I never have to think about this franchise again."

I hold the empty water bottle out to him, and he takes it.

"I think you need to do one more thing," Henry tells me.

"Go on," I say.

He swallows, almost steeling himself. "You have to tell Marcus you're in love with him," he says.

The suggestion takes me back so much, I recoil from him. "Did we or did we not just have a conversation about me leaving the show?"

He nods; he anticipated the reaction. "And if I recall correctly, we both agreed that staying is what's best for you. In fact, I think this could be the right thing for other reasons—when is a better time to get rid of you than right after you confess your love? Narratively, it works. It's good TV and it gets the rest of production off our backs."

I get up myself, go to the fridge, and get myself a beer, leaning against the counter, considering. I hold it against my neck for a minute, the chill like clarity, focusing me. "It's a good end to a villain, isn't it? After she's fallen in love, give her comeuppance."

"See," Henry answers. "We're all still telling the same story."

I stare at our hands next to each other on the counter in the kitchenette, our skin almost touching. "And then what?" I ask.

"We just need to make it through the next two weeks. Then we figure out how to spin the rest of this. We escape without getting exposed to the whole fucking world, without the full fury of *the 1* establishment raining down upon us, and that's going to be a hell of a lot worse for you than this is. You know that."

I bite my lip, training my eyes on the peeling wallpaper on the wall opposite him.

"This part of the show is always hard enough as it is without this extra thing. Without *us*. What you're feeling is normal, but this shit with Marcus and me is obviously not."

I watch him, staring at me, calculating what I'll do. I'm calculating what he'll do.

I set my beer back on the counter with a clank, empty.

"Fine," I say. "You're right; I'll do it. But don't fuck me over, Henry."

"It'd be nice if you believe I'm on your side."

I flick the beer bottle over and it rolls on the counter, landing in the sink.

Writers' Room Private Slack Channel

C. Duncan
Catch My Love out now!
ok live watch of the overnight week of t1 commencing now

Anika K. Wright
Bestselling author *of In Your Arms* series
Wine is poured. Popcorn is popped.

Brynn Riley
I write books and shit
marcus and jac are def gonna bang right?

Anika K. Wright
What do you mean "gonna"? THEY ALREADY HAVE!

C. Duncan
Jac had that platinum vagine

Annie Kate
Texas Stars at Night, Rhode Island Lights, Last Stop in Carolina, Lost in Louisiana
Shoot, I just turned it on. I'm behind.

C. Duncan
Dude, check out the cut of that suit. if I were into men, Marcus would totally be my type

Brynn Riley
he gives me serial killer vibes. why is he always smiling like that?

Anika K. Wright
Oh! There's our girl

Annie Kate
CD

I really like Kendall and Shae. I still don't get what Marcus sees in Jac.

C. Duncan
CD

lmao don't talk about Anika's girl that way!

Anika K. Wright
AK

LISTEN now that her book is selling, people found a list she did a few years ago recommending my book. Us authors got to stick together.

Brynn Riley
BR

jac is always dressed like an evil bitch I love her commitment to aesthetic

C. Duncan
CD

Her book was actually really smart

I read it, so sue me

I maintain not a romance, but romance adjacent. It actually broke my heart that they didn't end up together, but it also felt really poignant? And the second one followed through on the idea that it was a different choice for every woman or whatever

Brynn Riley
BR

homegirl's going to be fine after all this. whoever said all publicity was good publicity was probably jac matthis's publicist

Annie Kate
AK

Shit, sorry, a bunch of messages just loaded!

Is it just me or does Jac seem drunk?

23

Sweet Talk 101

My overnight date with Marcus starts out as a walk-through of Paris that involves quite a bit of ferrying by car. We stop at the Arc de Triomphe, Marcus's hands placed firmly and warmly on my hips as we look at it together. As soon we've had time to aww appropriately, we are taken to the Louvre (but not into the museum itself; Priya said we should get the "vibes" from the *Mona Lisa* just from walking around outside. None of that footage ever airs anyway). Then we stop over for some wine at an outdoor café (a conveniently placed couple who looks well over seventy drops in for a quick conversation on the secrets on a long-lasting relationship). Even with everything else, the café is the first time I get to imagine what Paris might be like in my real life. Sitting with a coffee, watching mopeds go back and forth, small cars taking the loops of roads with stunning architecture. The Parisians at the café all chain-smoking, drinking wine, and watching us with derision. I try to imagine myself with Henry instead, but seeing him there, just off-camera, watching us in his ratty T-shirt, makes it feel impossible. I've noticed throughout the day how much Henry tries not to look at me, knowing what it will do to Marcus's ego. I hate watching him work.

But then when we're sitting in the car together, going back to the production hotel so I can change before dinner, I feel Henry's fingers brush over my exposed back like reassurance.

The dress I have on for dinner is one Rikki left for me, and it feels like both solidarity and betrayal to wear it on the date. It's midnight blue with a high neck and the back completely cut out ("Business in the front, party in the back," she'd said with a laugh).

Henry and I arrive together at the Eiffel Tower.

"A bit cliché at this point, isn't it?" I ask, but it's not what I'm thinking. What I'm thinking is that I'd feared the Eiffel Tower would be overrated, but it's not. It's breathtaking, lit against the night. I wish I knew how to say that, to let that part of myself go, but I can't. Not here, not now.

Thus unmoved, Henry says, "You know the drill," as I go to get out of the car. "Just act like you're amazed Marcus set this date up." He says it like he's tired of it. I sure as shit am.

The crew gets the two of us in position in front of the tower and then cues us. "You look beautiful, Jac" is the first thing Marcus says to me when the camera turns on.

"*You* look beautiful," I answer with my plastered-on smile. He kisses me, and I'm getting better at pretending there's nothing wrong here. I'm used to writing stories, but I am the story now.

We ride up the elevator to the restaurant, me thanking Marcus profusely for making this happen for me. (When I watch later, I think how stupid I sound, how absurd. I know Marcus didn't plan this, the audience knows he didn't plan this, but still I'm playing along.)

I sit down at the meal with Marcus like I always do, and we pretend it doesn't exist like we always do. It looks appetizing—steamed mussels in white wine and small steaks with fries, but we are always forced to focus on our conversation at dinner, and that does not allow for eating. Not like I have an appetite anyway.

"There's something I want to talk to you about." Marcus launches into the conversation in a way that makes it clear that anything he is about to say will be words directly from Janelle's mouth.

"Okay," I answer.

"I know how deeply I care for you, Jac—maybe even more than anyone I've been with before." My heart pounds against my chest like this is real. "But I feel like there's still something between us. A wall. I thought meeting your family would make things clearer to me, but I feel more confused than ever."

I can't say why I say it—if it's because I am so broken or so tired. "It doesn't make any sense, right?" I look down at my food, picking up a fork, pushing it around, and he waits patiently until I go on. "There's nothing wrong with my life, but there's something wrong with me."

He takes both my hands, firmly pulling me from my reverie, and for that briefest moment, I remember what I liked so much about Marcus—that quick action, decisiveness. There weren't always layers upon layers of meaning when he spoke, when he acted.

Except there totally are. But on the surface, you don't have to wonder what he wants when he wants it. You don't have to worry who he'll be today or tomorrow or the next day because it's consistent. It's right there. "That's not what I meant," Marcus says.

"It isn't," I say, "but it's what I heard. I want to believe in love, but I don't. I don't believe I'm worthy of it."

I blink, a tear rolling down my cheek. He wipes it away with the pad of his thumb and kisses me softly.

"I always," I say, my voice breaking up, "leave before I get left. It's the only thing that's made me feel good for a long time."

"I'm not going anywhere," Marcus says to me, cradling my face in both of his hands. "Believe that."

It had started somewhere that scared me, but now, now I've found it. I talked my way into the right thing to say. I'm so good at this.

My whole body betrays me and I look at Henry. His face is stone cold, and I don't know what that means, so I do it.

"Marcus," I say, closing my eyes, taking a deep breath, "I'm in love with you." I fear opening my eyes because of what I might find, convinced my skin is sloughing off my body.

"Hey, look at me." I do. He's smiling. "I love you, Jacqueline Matthis." He kisses me, his lips warm on mine, and I imagine being someone else.

THE OVERNIGHT INVITATION comes as we all knew it would, and production takes us back to the hotel suite they have reserved for us. Marcus pours us both glasses of red wine.

"I've been looking forward to this for a long time." He eyes me, clinking our glasses together. The act is over now; we revert to ourselves.

"Finally," I say, "it will be just the two of us."

He smiles. "We'll really get to know each other at last."

We joylessly make out on a bed for the camera in a way that makes my sexual appetite shrivel up and die the way my actual appetite already has, and then, finally, Janelle says they have everything they need. She orders a pizza, and all of us—Marcus, me, the rest of production, and the crew—all sit around eating it, drinking wine and beer and shooting the shit.

I'm talking with some of the crew members when Henry subtly joins our conversation. The other two guys leave, and Henry takes a long look at me. "Clothes are so wasted on you."

"Do you ever think with any other parts of your body?" I whisper back to him.

"More often than I wish I did," he answers, taking a drink.

"Why are you flirting with me?" I glance around, feeling us right on the edge of danger.

"Because I know I'm about to leave you with him, and I feel like shit," he answers.

"Did you like what I did?" I say then.

"No," he returns, sensing my thorniness. "Of course I didn't like it."

"Didn't me spilling my guts give John his editing boner?" I don't know why I'm giving him a hard time; I agreed to it. But it's a funny thing, how often I find myself agreeing to things I wish I hadn't.

"Jac," Henry says, his head going down to mine. Before he can say more, though, Marcus appears at his side, wrapping an arm around me.

"Ah," Marcus says, "my girl and her producer."

"You having fun?" Henry asks him, putting his hands in his pockets.

"About to be having a lot more," Marcus answers, his arm tightening around me. "I asked Janelle if everyone's about ready to wrap up here."

Henry glances at his watch and nods. "Yeah. Damn, it's getting late."

"I'm in Paris," Marcus says. "We don't plan to sleep, right, Jac?"

I squint at him. "Don't go quite that hard, Marcus. It's not a good look on you."

He laughs.

The crew starts to clean up their mess and go. Henry and I watch each other more openly than we should.

Then Henry leaves. Everyone leaves. The door closes, and it's just the two of us and this suite.

"Finally alone," Marcus says, leaning casually back against the door he's just closed, looking over at me. "What do you want to do first?"

My heart is pounding. I've waited for this for so long. To finally, *finally* be alone with Marcus.

"What in the ever-loving fuck is your game here?" I ask him.

He pushes off the door, shrugging casually. "I'm not much of a planner." He puts his hands in his pockets. "You're still doing it, aren't you? With Henry?"

I turn red. "What do you care?"

"C'mon, Jac," he says, approaching me, his hand pushing my hair from my face. I don't think to flinch away; the intimacy all day feels like a given. "You used to like me, remember?"

"I liked someone like you, didn't I?"

"Sure." He pulls his hand away without my prompting. "We all do. Someone like someone we could love. That's *the 1*."

"Shailene was never really your type."

He shrugs. "Am I supposed to know?" He narrows his eyes at me. "Are we going to have sex?"

"No," I say. "You already knew that, though, right?"

"I liked it the first time," he says. "*You* certainly seemed to like it."

"Right," I say. "We had a good time." I hedge my bets; the conversation seems to be going well. "And we're no longer having a good time. Send me home, Marcus."

"Henry," he says. "It had to be fucking Henry. Why couldn't it have been Brendan, or, like, a lighting technician? I'm not picky about who you fuck, Jac."

"So this is personal? Because it's Henry?"

He frowns. "It is. You're just caught in the middle, and I'm having fun." He thinks about it for a minute. "You could just confess on camera and get out of all of this. They'd love that."

As he says my own idea to me, I realize exactly how bad it sounds. "*You'd* love that. Your ratings would be through the roof and people would feel bad for you."

"You've just made a very compelling case for exposing you."

I sigh. "Just do it. Whatever you're going to do, do it and put us both out of our misery." I know he won't; I picked someone over him, and Marcus would never want the world to know that.

He sits down on the bed, starts taking off his shoes. "I haven't decided exactly what I'm going to do."

"You've got two girls who want to be with you and you've got me. What's the decision?"

He leans back on the bed, folding his arms behind his head, elbows pointed out to the side. "I've got Kendall who is here only to win and honestly doesn't do much for me, and Shae—let's just say, I was very nicely asked to keep her around so she'd be in line for the next lead. Gotta get those brownie points. You're easily the most interesting person left."

"So, what makes the story more satisfying? If I get my heart broken or . . ." I trail off, avoiding saying it and allowing it to become real.

"Or the two renegades ride off into the sunset together," he finishes for me. "I know you say you don't like me anymore, Jac, but we think a lot alike."

"Henry has enough self-loathing to power a small country. You don't really need to go to such extremes to get back at him."

"Don't need to do anything," Marcus says casually. "Don't need to do any of this. Nor do you. Look at us. We're both good-looking. We're not having trouble finding romantic partners, so why are we doing it?"

"Desperation," I say flatly.

"Money," he answers. "I can't believe Henry's got you fooled into thinking he hates himself. It's all of us he despises. He's spent like fifteen years thinking about how much smarter he is than the rest of us, and then we leave and make more money, get more attention than he does. That's why they want to keep bringing us back for more shows, to see if they can actually ruin our lives for good the next time. Fuck him. If you had half a brain, you'd be on my side."

"Yeah, that condescension is really winning me over," I say, but the words get under my skin. Marcus is wrong, but he's not *wrong*.

"What happened with you and Henry anyway?" I can't help but ask. I want to hear it from Marcus.

"Come on, surely he's told you," Marcus answers, but he smiles to himself after a moment. "No, I guess not. Not his style. He still blames me for everything with Shailene, right?"

"That pretty much sums it up, yeah."

"Shailene can keep running her mouth however she wants; we both know what happened. But Charlotte and Priya promised me the lead if I said we had sex on camera, and I had no interest in becoming some small-town Midwestern husband. I don't know why Henry is still so mad about it. I mean, I *do*, but it's because he thinks he gets to do whatever he wants, but the second I become an active participant in the game, things suddenly aren't fair."

When I don't answer, he keeps talking. "Don't think for a minute this is real," he says. "Henry. You might see me as the enemy right now, but it's us against him. I guarantee you know more about who I really am than you know about him."

"Mm" is all I mumble as I move away from him, tugging my sweater over my head to expose my black bra. Marcus raises an eyebrow at me.

"You know his playbook, right? He'll tell you his dad is an alcoholic and kind of a hard-ass. We bonded over that. He'll bring bourbon outside to drink with you at the mansion at the pool, so just the two of you can have a conversation. He'll tell you about his band and convince you you're friends."

I swallow. My blood is running hot as I turn away from Marcus, try not to let him see me unwind it all.

"I don't know what you're talking about," I lie. He hears the lie.

"You and I would be a good couple," he says, pushing himself up from the bed behind me, standing at my shoulder. "We look good together. It'd be worth it for the social media followers alone. If we were engaged for two years, you get to keep the ring, too. You'd sell it and we'd split the cash."

"You have a talent for casual cruelty that makes me think you won't be an ideal partner," I say, still hiding my face as I pull a T-shirt on. "Because nothing makes what you did to Shailene seem okay."

"Shailene didn't understand me. She had a lot of shitty notions about relationships and now she's suffering the consequences of her choices. We'd understand each other, Jac."

I don't say anything for a moment, just letting the quiet of the room weigh on me. "I want to sleep," I finally answer, crawling into bed, still avoiding looking at him, but letting him crawl in beside me, feeling his weight there. The camera crew will be back in three hours to film our morning after; maybe if I close my eyes, I can wake up and this nightmare will be over.

I can't help but wonder if he's right. If maybe this ends, and I make the wrong choice. If I thought I saw it all clearly, but Henry was always right there, amorphous.

And then I end up as hollow as Marcus.

SHAE IS VERY composed when she gets eliminated.

The elimination ceremony is outside of Paris because Henry said they'd been given very few days to film in the city. It's not cold, but cold enough that I'm freezing in my pleated long-sleeve pink gown with its plunging neckline, goose bumps on my exposed skin.

Marcus walks Shae to the car, and then, after another godforsaken staged toast to the final two, assistants take Kendall and me to our own cars. I don't think we're going to speak at all until she says, "What do they like about you anyway?"

I sigh, bored. "Who?"

She stares over at me, lips pursed. "Marcus," she says. "Rikki. Henry."

I whip my head toward her so fast, I almost pull a muscle in my neck. But her expression is flat; she's not prying for details about Henry. She doesn't know anything about it. So, I answer, "Probably that I say what I mean instead of playing fucking games."

"You take everything so personally," Kendall says, flicking her nails. "You're so abrasive and angry all the time, and you do all that while hating anyone who doesn't fit into the Jac Matthis box of exactly what a person should be."

"And what is that?" It's just the two of us waiting for the cars, and I'm wrung out. We both watch each other, waiting for the other to change or apologize or do anything, and we stay the same people in the same ridiculous situation. "Who do you think he's going to choose?" I ask.

She smiles slightly, closed lipped, and looks over at me again. "What do you care?" she asks. "You're just here to sell books."

Goodreads reviews for *End of the Line*
by Jacqueline Matthis

Jane Austen lover4

★ ★ ★ ★ ★

Not reading this on principal. Jac Matthis is a huge bitch on the 1

Skelly

★ ★ ★ ★ ★

jac hawking her shitty canceled books on t1

[gif of cartoon fox dressed as a beggar, shaking an empty tin cup]

stealth cow

★ ★ ★ ★ ★

I was so sick of reading the main character of this book make bad decision after bad decision. She didn't even have a hard life. The male main character was okay, I guess, and there were a couple of steamy scenes but I don't waste my hard-earned money to read about petty bitches with ennui issues!!!!! That ending was NOT worth the journey.

24

Almost

"Marcus is proposing to you," Henry says to me as I'm sitting in my cottage in the shadows of the Cévennes. It's an absurd thing to say in an absurd place, blue skies and snow-topped mountains on a wall of windows in front of us. He's just walked in, and his voice is dark with a hint of anger behind it. He stands behind me and I glance up, tilting my neck at an awkward angle to look at his concerned expression.

I don't say anything. Yesterday, production had taken me to a hotel in Chantilly, where they had staged a room for me to meet Marcus's parents—his dad, in remission from cancer, and his mom. They were seemingly wonderful people, and the whole thing made me vaguely sick. We'd had our last date, a hot air balloon ride with breathtaking views and a picnic in one of the most beautiful places I'd ever seen, and I'd hated every second of it.

I'd been preparing myself for Marcus's inevitable decision to propose since our conversation in Paris. "I guess he's calling our bluff," I finally say, picking up a magazine to flick through. It's in French, so I am, in fact, just being a bitch.

Henry's made his way around my chair to stand in front of me. "I don't think you fully understand what I'm saying to you. This is how the show is going to end. He's going to propose. If you say no, he's gonna go rogue. He'd absolutely air out all the dirty laundry. If you say yes, then you're going to be a celebrity couple. It'll be a fucking madhouse."

"Maybe it's for the best," I say, flipping a page. "Probably the best thing for my career, right?"

"Where is this coming from?" Henry asks. I can feel his eyes boring into my skin even as I continue not to look up. He puts his hand on the magazine to stop me. "Do you want Marcus to propose to you?"

I close the magazine and toss it on the coffee table, looking up at him. "Since when do you care what I want?"

He stares at me, confused.

"You're a producer," I say. "Produce Marcus into choosing Kendall."

"You cannot be serious. Marcus is only choosing you because of us."

"So, what do you want me to do?" I ask, crossing my arms over my chest defensively. "Why do you care all of the sudden?"

"*What* are you talking about?"

"I'm talking about last week. I'm talking about every time I begged you to get me off this show. Now it's real, now you're really losing me, and you suddenly care."

His expression changes, the anger momentarily falling away. "I *always* cared," he tells me.

"But not enough. Never enough to give up the one thing you truly love. This show."

"That's bullshit and you know it," he says. He turns away from me, goes to sit on a bench seat in front of one of the huge portrait windows, picturesque as he thinks, his head in his hands. Seeing him that way—unguarded, if only for a moment—almost softens me.

"I don't know why I wanted you to stay," he finally admits, looking back up at me.

"Because you knew it was good TV if I did."

He releases a breath.

I get up from my chair and go to him, sitting with my body facing his, one leg propped up and the other hanging off. We're close again. "Look at me," I say, tilting his chin up with my hand. He swallows, turning his face to me, his Adam's apple pulsing against my fingers.

"Admit to me that you don't want me to get engaged," I say, leaning forward ever so slightly. "Tell me to turn him down. He'll probably out us, but isn't it better than the alternative?"

"What is this?" Henry asks wearily, his eyebrows knitting together. "Some sort of ultimatum?"

I keep my expression neutral. "No, Henry. It's a simple request. Tell me you don't want me to get engaged."

He averts his gaze, pulling away. "Why are you doing this?"

"Why can't you say this simple thing?" I ask him.

"Because this isn't about me!" He's not quite yelling, but his voice is loud enough that I flinch, standing up from my spot.

"Of *course* this is about you!" I yell, further escalating in a way that gives me satisfaction. "*Christ*, Henry, all I asked was for you to say, 'I don't want you to get engaged to him, Jac,' after all this and you *can't*."

"I can," he insists.

"You just won't."

"I don't see the point. I don't see where this ends."

I shake my head. "You're such a coward. You won't do anything unless there's three escape hatches."

"You're not understanding me," he says, his tone changing, going quieter, softer. "I just need a beat to think. This isn't going the way I thought it would go."

"Because you can't *control* us anymore!" I shout back at him, not calmed at all. "You always need a beat to put us all on the tracks you planned, but now I'm a real person making my own decisions and so is Marcus, and that doesn't work for you."

I make my way back to the chair I was sitting on when he arrived, curling my legs up into my chest, folding in on myself. "Maybe Marcus and I belong together because we both finally saw through your shit."

"Jac," he says, but even I can tell he doesn't mean it.

"*Get. Out.*" I pick the magazine back up, waiting for him to protest his dismissal.

He doesn't. He waits, probably a producer-timed two minutes

to see if I'll change my mind, say something else. When I don't, he leaves, and I hear the door close behind him.

I'm alone.

THE DAY I'M going to get engaged starts like any other.

The sun rises to the east of a cabin in the French countryside, and I never slept anyway. I drink my coffee wrapped in a blanket, staring out the window, watching. Henry and John both show up while I'm there, like that, along with a hair and makeup team, the first since that first night in the mansion.

"You made it, Jac," John says to me.

"Much to your consternation," I answer without much venom.

John doesn't disagree. "Love is a chaos agent," he says. "I'm happy for you. Certainly makes my life easier. I love a happy ending."

I take a long sip of coffee.

I wonder what it's like for the other women who found themselves in this situation. Maybe the not knowing would be worse. Believing you will get proposed to and then getting dumped—or maybe realizing after the engagement that you've agreed to marry a stranger, so caught up in the moment that you don't see it for what it is.

I know exactly what this is.

Then I think of Kendall, right now, likely in a château just like mine, maybe with Priya and one of the other exec producers. She'll go first because the loser always does, so she probably started earlier than me. She'll have watched the sun rise with a cucumber water after eight hours of sleep. She'll be confident, one of the things I like most about Kendall, who I don't really like at all.

I wanted to wear my red dress from the first night, something symbolic about it, but that had been shot down from the get-go.

"This isn't a romance novel," John says with an air of derision. Henry, much like he has all morning, doesn't say anything.

So the dress is white, a deep V-neck down to just above my belly button, woman in red in white, even to the end.

I'm standing at the door, fully dressed and made up. I'd never look like this in real life; I'd never even wanted to. Henry is next to me, and for the first time this morning, we're alone. His eyes are on me, and I take a deep breath, self-conscious.

"Look," I start.

"I don't want you to get engaged," he says.

Something happens then. Something so subtle, I'm not sure I would've noticed it had we not spent so much of the last two months together, had I not constantly been on the lookout for something real. There is a raw, genuine pain on his face, the kind I only saw that day in Charlotte. The kind that says he feels something again, finally.

"It's too late," I say, not bothering to keep my voice low, "but you knew that."

He shakes his head, pushes his hair back. "It's not. It's really not. I'm sorry."

I wrap up the small train of my dress in my hand, ready to step outside, where Becca and the car are waiting for me. I've only taken two steps when he says something else. "Don't do this."

I look at him over my shoulder, give a half shrug, and go.

The car takes us to a helicopter that takes us to the trail leading up to the mountaintop where the proposal will take place. I realize how numb I've become to things like this, to a helicopter and a château in the French countryside, and mentally try to talk myself into enjoying it. Into enjoying this too tight white dress that John forced me to wear. I lost feeling in my toes over a month ago thanks to all the high heels I've been wearing. But still, I feel pain.

I'm nothing anymore except an open wound, and maybe that was the only logical way this could end.

When we land, Henry offers me his hand as I step off the helicopter, and I don't mean to, thought I'd already had my moment, but I meet his eyes again. They betray nothing, the way they must have at a dozen other proposals.

"ITM?" he asks.

"Can't my last fuck-you be that I don't give one?"

"It's the last day of filming and you're still hostile."

"It's not like anyone's going to start liking me now, anyway."

"I like you." That's Rene, our French cameraman.

I smile at him, tilting my head sideways. "None of the other cameramen ever talked, Rene," I tell him.

He shrugs. "I'm French," he says simply.

"Over here," Henry says, pointing to a spot that has already been set up for filming, overlooking the beautiful blue sky, the mountains rising in the distance behind it. "It'll be a quick one."

"That's so like you," I say without emotion, and even that doesn't make a dent in the exterior. I shouldn't feel disappointed.

"How are you feeling?" Henry asks, once we're set.

We're both drained, so drained. But I want to put on a show. I should make my last stand something good. "I feel like I've been waiting my entire life for someone like Marcus," I say. "I really believe this is actually the beginning of a journey, one we started twelve weeks ago, and I still see so clearly the first time I saw him. I think I knew then."

"Knew what?" Henry asks.

"I knew he and I were the same type of person. It took a while for that to sink in, for my feelings to catch up to everything else, but there's no doubt anymore." I stare straight at the camera. "This is what I deserve," I say.

"You can just say no." Henry's mask is gone; it's bordering on desperation.

"And then what?" I ask.

"Should I still be filming?" Rene asks.

Priya is hurrying back over to me, and we are back in motion all over again.

After the interview, I wind up the train of my dress in my hand and wind my way up a hill with everyone else. I spot Marcus when we're about fifty yards away, standing there with his crew surrounding him. A slate gray suit, jacket open, white button-up with no tie underneath. Trim, tall, standing there like a storybook prince. He's, inexplicably, smiling.

I almost let the stupid fairy-tale moment suck me back in.

I remember when I arrived at the mansion that first night, saw him, and almost fell for the trick. Now, everyone else is seeing this moment, and they're believing it, too.

I play my part.

Deux Moi Blind Item

Friday, 3:22 p.m.

Anon please. You won't believe this, but a friend of a friend works on *the 1* and I've heard a certain contestant got close—very close—with a producer this season. Yep, that's right, the villain you all love to hate herself carried on a relationship with a producer on set. Like this season could get any juicier.

AFTER THE ONE—
FIVE MONTHS LATER

25

Ain't It Fun

I saw it. I saw all of it.

Every Instagram message, every Reddit post, every article, every motherfucking TikTok.

I've taken up watching survival shows.

Not the kind where a bunch of people sit around talking and eating their eighth coconut of the day while planning each other's ouster, but the ones where they drop someone off in the middle of a forest and tell them they'll give them a million dollars if they survive for a year. Really sick stuff, but in, like, the most transparently honest way.

I think I relate to them.

I'm in my apartment in Charleston, the one I rented out before I left for the show. My living room is dark. I'm curled up under a blanket with my dog, watching a guy build a shelter in below freezing temperatures while nursing a broken finger, when someone rings my doorbell. I almost jump out of my skin, and Yank starts barking like it's the end of the world. Heart pounding, convinced that some *the 1* superfan bent on my destruction would show up to my door unannounced in the middle of a weekday, I look through the peephole.

It's Rikki.

I open the door.

"Are you good?" she asks when she sees me, an eyebrow raised. Her hair is freshly dyed, but shorter than the last time I saw her. She's tan and made up, and I'm in a fifteen-year-old holey T-shirt with a Clemson blanket wrapped over my shoulders.

"Am I . . . good?" I repeat, not even giving in to the shock of seeing her at my door.

"Fair enough," she says with no preamble, and slides a rolling suitcase past me and into my foyer, closing the door behind her. She keeps walking through the hall and past the half wall that leads into the den. Her gaze goes to the TV screen. "Why is that dirty man crying?"

I follow behind her, looking over her shoulder. Yank circles her feet merrily as she bends down to pet him.

"He could die if he doesn't get a warm place to sleep soon? Aw, I don't think he's going to make it even the first month," I say as the man onscreen curls up on the ground, adjusting his camera to film himself.

Rikki is giving me a pitying look. She reaches out and puts a hand on my arm. "Why don't you take a shower and I'll order pizza?" she asks. "And maybe we don't watch TV?"

I shrug.

An hour later, we're at my kitchen table, both eating pizza from my place down the street. Rikki remembered I like an obscene amount of red pepper on my pizza and had asked them to send extra packets.

"How's LA?" I ask.

"Fine. Spin classes are fine, absolutely raking in the spon-con deals right now, to be honest." She frowns at the look on my face. "Hey, a girl has to make a living. Also, I'm dating someone at my spin studio."

"Oh?"

"She's quite sporty. You'd like her."

"Oh." I half laugh. "We lived together so long, I just assumed I knew everything about you. Is this . . . a new thing? You're bi?"

"Bi?" Rikki laughs. "God, you're such a millennial."

"Yeah," I agree, laughing myself. "Factual."

As we quiet down, I catch Rikki surveying the scene, the dirty dishes in the sink and the dead plants all over the kitchen. "Are you leaving the house much?" she asks like she already knows the answer.

"What, and end up all over Instagram?" I answer, setting my

pizza slice down. "I think not." One of my neighbors had spotted me out in my sweats walking Yank and snapped a picture, which had ended up on TMZ. Even setting aside being photographed looking so ragged, it had unsettled me to see a picture of myself so close to where I live.

Rikki shrugs, tilting her head to the side, as if conceding the point. "So, how's the writing going?"

"What's the point?" I ask. "Who would want to read a book by me?"

"Come on, Jac!" she says, exasperated. "You can't lock yourself away in your house forever. Sarah literally called me and begged me to come out here because you were only answering every tenth text she sent." Sarah had texted me that she connected to Rikki over DM on Instagram, but I didn't expect her to send a search party.

"You didn't have to get involved in my personal life," I say, taking a swig of an old, flat Sprite I had poured from my fridge. "Didn't sound like you were interested in that the last time I saw you anyway."

"Don't play dumb," Rikki says, her voice solid in a way that belies her refusal to argue with me. "You got Elodie fired, and I *liked* Elodie. She liked you. I never would've agreed to help you humiliate her."

"Elodie would've done the same to any of us without a moment's hesitation," I answer. She'd texted me last week. I'd blocked her number.

"Maybe she would have," Rikki says, "but it seems worth a conversation."

"Production sent you, didn't they? I already told them I'd come to the fucking aftershow. I'm not trying to get sued."

"Charlotte isn't so sure you're going to show up," Rikki concedes. "But that's not why I'm here. I'm here because I *care* about you. You're my friend, in case you've forgotten."

"And you still believe *they're* your friends?" I ask her, incredulous. I push my food away. "I'm not hungry."

"Eat," she says.

"I can't."

"I like to think of my relationship with the producers as mutually beneficial," Rikki tells me. "They like me, I get good edits. I get good edits, I make more money. I'm a popular contestant; they want me back on the shows."

"For now," I mutter.

"Well, that's on my own head."

I snort, picking at the pepperoni on my pizza.

"I know it's not the same volume, but I know how they are online. I cried for like an hour the first time someone sent an actual racial slur to my Instagram."

"Oh, Rik," I say, living outside of my own misery for a moment, grabbing her hand. "Of course you do. I'm sorry."

"It's okay. I'll be there with you," she says then, tilting her face down toward me, squeezing my hand in hers. "I'll go with you to After the One so you don't have to go by yourself. And yes, the producers asked me to, but I *wanted* to so you wouldn't be by yourself."

I sigh deeply, my fingers tightening around hers. "This is humiliating," I say.

"It's all in the service of good TV. It's not real. Anyone who has half a brain knows that." She finishes the sentiment, releasing my hand and taking an aggressive bite into her pizza.

"It feels pretty real to me," I tell her. We both take a beat, sitting in the quiet of my house, Yank's paws clicking on the kitchen tile as he paces back and forth between the two of us. "Was he in Mexico?" I finally ask. Rikki had been filming *1 in the Sun* there during the winter.

Rikki grabs up a napkin, all the while looking at me, confused. "Henry?" I nod. "No. Elodie said he flew back from France the day you wrapped filming and put in his notice. He didn't even help with editing the season."

I slump back in my chair, momentarily speechless, my heart pounding. It sits between us, tilts the world.

Twenty-five hundred miles away, I still imagine him alone out on that beach.

"Have you talked to him?" I ask her.

"No," she says. "Well, yes. At Elodie's birthday party. He was only there for a bit. He said he'd been spending some time getting to know himself; you know how he is, all cryptic and smirking and hot." I do. "He asked about you," Rikki says, a slight smile on her face.

The words are like a punch to the gut, and I almost whisper as I ask: "He did?" I haven't spoken to him, of course. I can't. It's too painful, and judging by his lack of contact, I figure he's moved on. Another season, a new story.

"Jac," Rikki says, finally pushing the pizza box away from her, folding up her napkin, and throwing it on her plate. "Come on, you think I didn't notice all the eye-fucking you two were doing? Or you sneaking out of the room in Chicago? What happened?"

I sigh. "What do you think? He loved *the 1* more than he loved me."

She sits with that, nodding. And then: "Is there anything I can do to help you? Seriously? Like, what's even going on with you and Marcus?"

"Marcus and I are going to push through the media storm and quietly break up," I tell her. That endgame is all I've been thinking about for months.

Rikki nods, her face passive. "So, what's next?" she asks.

I think about it for a minute, back through the months, back through all of the plane rides and fights and unending elimination ceremonies, back to the last time I really felt happy.

"I don't know," I admit.

It's FINALLY THE end—gratifying and terrifying. I'm here, back in my stage makeup and perhaps the most unforgiving white dress yet ("C'mon, you're engaged," Charlotte had said). Backstage, live, while they play the last episode of *the 1*.

Contractual obligation, to go out and face a crowd that hates me. You'd think I'd be used to the hatred by now, absorbed enough of it via social media, but I'm still not.

"You look great," Charlotte lies to me, touching my arm almost affectionately. "You're going to do great."

I take little comfort in that. "Is this going to be even worse than the Women Tell All?" I ask.

Charlotte scoffs. "Of course not. You're in love, you're getting married, and, more importantly, you're here to defend yourself. This is going to be a celebration. I'm sure you'll have a chance to explain yourself, but that will be all."

I stare straight ahead. "I'm not going to explain myself."

"Sure you won't," Charlotte says, the touch of irritation in her voice unmistakable. "That would be too helpful. Might get the audience on your side, and we wouldn't want that, would we?"

Both of us watch the backstage television as Kendall's face comes onscreen, bright, beautiful, and moisturized in the French countryside. "I don't know," she says, her eyes shining so much, I almost believe her. "After our date, I really feel like this is it—Marcus is my person."

Marcus's parents had already run the hard sell on Kendall in this episode. They found me difficult to connect with, surprise. I had sweated through those conversations, wishing to be anywhere else. I was constantly reminded how seriously his family took this, when to him and me, it was nothing more than our own sick little game.

And now, onscreen Kendall is walking up the same mountain where Marcus and I got engaged. Like a tic, I automatically stare down at the ring on my finger, the one production had been holding for me until this moment. I tilt it this way and that, watching it shine. It is honestly beautiful—vintage and elegant, per the jeweler employed by *the 1*, a 3.25-carat emerald-cut stone, surrounded by twenty-seven round diamonds, with the platinum band sporting another sixty-seven round diamonds. I suspected one of the producers had pushed Marcus strongly toward a classic look for me.

Watching Kendall almost makes me sick. She'll go onstage before me, and then they'll show our engagement afterward, but once the footage is aired, everyone will know that the spoilers were true, as they've suspected for weeks. The Wicked Witch of the South got the ring. There will be media appearances upon media appearances where I'll have to play the love interest again.

"Listen," Charlotte says, eyes trained on me. "They're probably going to ask you about the tabloids. There's nothing I can do about it."

"Nothing you can do as an incredibly powerful producer on the show?" I retort, venom in my words.

"Listen, Jac, not to be cute, but sometimes, when you've made your bed, you do have to lie in it." Then she stalks off.

"I was surprised," Kendall says onstage. "After everything with

Jac, I guess she was the one for him. You can't always predict people, you know?" She smiles winningly as the crowd boos me. "Hey, I'm going to be fine, and I truly do wish both Jac and Marcus all the best moving forward, whatever else happens in the finale. It's as much a mystery to me as all of you." Complete bullshit. She knows good and well that we're engaged.

"There's some other exciting news, right, Kendall?" Becca prods her.

"Wellllll," Kendall begins, dragging the word out. "I guess it's time to let the cat out of the bag."

"Or better yet," Brendan jumps in, "let's roll the promo."

Then Kendall appears onscreen in a taped promo, wearing an emerald green dress in front of a white background, smiling wryly as petals fall around her. "This time"—she kicks up the petals—"it's my turn."

I watch, with my soul floating somewhere above my body, as the thirty-second promo plays, introducing us to Kendall's season of *the 1*. The camera cuts back to Kendall, looking radiant, as the audience applauds furiously. Just like she always wanted.

She'd do this, again, I think. Even with the good edit she received, even with everything, she'd really do *this* again?

Priya is sitting in a chair near me, scrolling through her phone. "I thought it was supposed to be Shae?" I ask her.

She smirks up at me. "The network vetoed her. Wanted someone more relatable. Shae read as more of a *1 in the sun* type to them." *The 1* had seen three Black female leads and one Black male lead, as well as one Hispanic female and male lead apiece, and one Asian female lead, and, count them, zero male Asian leads. Brianna Smith, a veterinarian from Georgia, had been their last Black lead, three seasons ago; I guess the powers that be decided it was too soon to go down that path again.

"Fuck this show," I say, looking back at myself in the mirror, the face of this show.

Watching Marcus propose to me onscreen is bizarre. I fool even myself when I accept the proposal, crying, holding Marcus's face between my hands, kissing him, drinking champagne. But the audience will still think it's as fake as everything else I've done all season and will hate it equally as much. And best of all, they're absolutely right.

"I got the ring after all," I brag to the camera in the closing moments. I was really drunk for that. "I finally got the guy." That's when it slips, and the camera shows how I go dead behind the eyes.

"Okay, it's show time," Priya says, getting up from her chair and lending me a hand to help me out of mine. She walks me to the edge of the stage, and we wait for the line producer to cue me to walk out. I'm standing there when Marcus hurries up behind me and grabs my hand. He squeezes, some sort of gesture of solidarity.

We'd spent four nights together in our château once filming wrapped, quality time given to the final couple to finally be alone together.

I'd gotten stupid drunk on our first night together, after I'd gotten my phone back and been obligated to call my family and tell them I was engaged. "I'm happy for you," my brother said, and he really sounded it.

"We're so excited to have Marcus join the family," Mom echoed.

The producers and crew stayed up, drinking wine with us that first night, celebrating the end of another successful season, and neither of us tried to dissuade them. I suspect Marcus didn't want to face the consequences of his actions, just as much as I didn't. Henry had, of course, been absent; Priya told me he decided to fly back early.

When everyone finally left well after 2 a.m., I'd started kissing Marcus, crawled into his lap like I might be absorbed into him. I was drunk, of course, wondering if I could re-create who I'd been at the start of this experience. Want him the way I did before. Get something enjoyable out of this.

He'd let me for a while, and then he'd backed away when I'd reached for his belt.

"You don't need to do that," he said.

I was slurring my words at that point. "Why not?"

"I don't want to fuck you while you're thinking about *him*," he said darkly.

He'd left me there, in a puddle on the couch, crying. I'd eventually fallen asleep there and woken around midday the next day, violently ill.

"Let's just get through the press cycle," he told me that night, sitting next to me, where I was still curled up on the same spot of the couch. "And then we'll figure out what's most advantageous for both of us."

Practical to the end, the rest of that week and our two subsequent planned "happy couple" weekends had passed an amicable enough truce, with the two of us bingeing Netflix and ordering takeout.

In the meantime, he'd engaged heavily on social media, eagerly commentating throughout the season and acting as if he was as shocked at the antics of Jac the Villain as anyone else. I, on the other hand, had posted my contractually obligated two Instagram posts, turned off the comments, and still kept a running tab on the nastiest hashtags (#jacthebitch, #matthismonster, #jaciskindofugly). At the same time, sales on my backlist book had steadily increased, and I'd felt no satisfaction in any of it. I'd been dumped by my agent a couple of months before the show, and I'd even had two or three agents send me kind emails. I hadn't responded to any of them.

Marcus and I had been together the weekend the Andi elimination episode aired, and he'd been glued to his phone.

"You're starting to really hurt my likability."

I was shoveling Pad Thai into my mouth. "Maybe you made the wrong choice."

"I really had been planning to keep Andi before what happened in the hot tub, but I wanted you a lot more, Jac," he said. "That's why I did what you asked."

"You got me," I answered, and he frowned.

"I'm going to post about what editing can do, I guess," he said with a sigh.

"You do that," I muttered, refilling my wineglass and checking the time again.

Here, tonight, he's back in his perfectly tailored suit with his perfectly tailored smile, an All-American boy to the end.

"Let's give 'em a good show," he says to me with a smile. He's still fine with this. He's fine with all of it.

In the studio, the producers throw to Becca and Brendan, and they both put on their best, happiest faces. "Welcome to After the

One! Please join us in welcoming your newly engaged couple to the hot seat—Marcus and Jac!"

Hand-in-hand, Marcus and I take the stage, head toward the couch across from Becca and Brendan, the sound of applause echoing all around us. I feel warm for a few moments, safe. This must be what it feels like to be one of the chosen ones.

I straighten my white dress as I sit next to Brendan and Becca and stare into both of their too-Botoxed faces. Becca is glowing in her third trimester, in a black jumpsuit that fits her like a glove. I can tell they are genuinely happy for us, and I almost feel guilt for letting down these two ridiculous people.

"Well, first of all," Becca says enthusiastically, "congrats, you two!"

"Thanks, Becca. Can't tell you how excited we are," Marcus answers while I smile blandly at his side.

"First things first." Brendan hops right to it. "This season must have been tough to watch back."

"Sometimes," Marcus admits, "but it's also such a gift to watch our love story unfold again. Something we can share with our children one day." He squeezes my hand and our eyes meet. I smile, making eye contact only briefly, before glancing back down at my lap. Priya is just behind the camera, ready to feed Becca and Brendan all the lines they need.

"What about for you, Jac?" Becca asks. "Some of that can't have been easy to see."

I swallow, put on my most contrite face. "I couldn't watch it all, to be honest," I say. "It got hard."

"Do you feel like you were fairly portrayed this season?" Brendan asks, really digging into it. They have to give the people what they want.

I pause, let the people at home think I'm really taking a moment to digest the question before I answer. "I said all the things I said at some point or the other," I concede. "Sometimes, I didn't mean them, or sometimes, context was removed, but that's the job of the show. To tell a story. You just don't realize at the time that you're the villain in the story they're telling."

The audience is quiet, hanging on my every word. I hadn't planned this, not exactly, but I didn't come unprepared. I knew an angry mob awaited me.

"What do you mean by that?" Brendan asks.

I take a deep breath, ready to do the whole monologue I knew they wanted, the grand apology, staring out at the audience. "I—" And then I see him. Right there, in the second row, in a button-up shirt and tan blazer, hair slicked, staring right at me.

Henry fucking Foster.

"Jac," Becca prompts me. "You were saying?"

I turn back to her, shaking my head as if shaking out of a reverie, knowing he's there, knowing he's watching me. "Becca," I begin again, releasing Marcus's hand, "what are we all doing here?"

"Sorry?" she says.

"Like," I say, "why? Literally all of this, why?"

"We're here to celebrate your relationship with Marcus," Brendan says, his eyes going to one of the producers. But they don't cut to commercial—of course not. This is great television. They have to see where it's all going.

"But not really, right?" I ask them, my heart pounding. "What we're really here to do is to remind everyone how much they hate me and how unfair it is that I get to be happy when Kendall was heartbroken. But Kendall isn't heartbroken either, is she? Kendall just got the score of her life."

"Jac," Marcus says warningly.

"You're here to ask me about all the rumors online. You're here to burn me at the stake. And I'm here because y'all said you'd sue me if I didn't come."

"I think we better cut to commercial," Becca says, cheerfully. "When we're back, we'll find out what Jac and Marcus plan to do next."

I stand up. In the audience, Henry does, too, buttoning up one button on his jacket. He looks like a dream, or maybe a nightmare. I can feel the crowd murmuring, watching the two of us. But fuck them. I'm happy to be their villain at this point.

"Still!" I say, my voice rising precipitously as I stare him down. "You're *still* here!"

"Jac, calm down." Charlotte's there now, hurried onstage, hands on me.

"Is he back on the fucking show now?" I demand, gesturing at Henry, who is making his way through the audience, everyone staring up intently at him. "Are you going to put him on camera?"

Henry is in front of me now, alive and in the flesh. I'd been so sure he was gone forever.

"You're still here," I whisper.

"Let me talk to her," Henry says.

I take a step away from him, turning my gaze to the person at his right. "Charlotte, come on! You got me again." She doesn't meet my eyes as I laugh darkly. "Trust you, right? You were just waiting for the opportune moment."

"We're both getting what we want," Charlotte answers, not bothering to keep her voice down.

"Fuck off, Charlotte," Henry shoots back at her.

"I want out of here," I demand.

Priya looks pissed, but at the unfazed look on Marcus's face, she shrugs. "You take it, Marcus. We'll bring her back out when she's calmed down."

"Fuck you, Priya."

Henry, clearly having given up on maintaining this charade as much as I have, grabs on to my arm and drags me off set, out through the backstage, into a utility closet of some sort, closes and locks a door behind him.

"You're on live television, Jacqueline."

I can't help but let my gaze devour him, something I never thought I'd do again. Henry's face is Henry's face the way it always is, carefully controlled, both distinct and wanting. I could never see another face for the rest of my life and maybe that would be fine. Maybe I could die now and it'd be over, and I'd remember his face forever.

One last happy memory. One last betrayal.

"You look terrible," I say.

"So do you," he answers in a way that lets me know he couldn't resist.

"One final con," I say. "You here, waiting to break me down one last time. When do you think it'll be enough?" I grip my hands tight, into balls, nails digging into my palms. I feel myself near tears, near feeling, near giving in.

"I'm contractually obligated to be here, too," Henry says. "This was the deal when I left France. I was out once they considered the season over. Surprise, they didn't need me for edits, but they needed me sitting in the audience for the season finale."

"Being a pawn in the game feels pretty shit, huh?" I can't help but say.

He swallows, putting his hands in his pockets. "You won't believe me, but I actually didn't want to hurt you again."

I bark out a laugh. "You can't resist editorializing even this, can you?"

"Fine," Henry answers sharply. "I didn't fight it because I wanted to see you. Because some part of me feared you really had decided to go through with this suicide mission with Marcus to prove a point to me, and I didn't want you to do that. So, here I am."

"It's not *your choice*!" I yell back at him. "I have to get *something* out of all this misery."

"So, do it on your own terms, not on this show's."

"The show always wins," I say, my voice ragged. "You know that."

"I—" he starts like he's headed somewhere, toward a fight, but then he stops, slumping back against the wire shelves behind him. "Not this time," he says, pushing his hair out of his face.

"Did you find what you were looking for, Henry?" I ask him.

"What do you think?" he answers, his voice low.

"How about this time," I answer, my voice dropping to meet his, "you don't make me say your feelings for you?"

He takes a deep breath, nods, and says, "This is what I want. *You're* what I want. More than this show. More than whatever this show gave me."

I swallow.

"Is it still too late?" he asks, taking a step back, giving us room to breathe. I reach out for the doorknob behind me, press my palm into the cool brass until it hurts.

"Right now?" I ask, my voice coming out hoarse. "Yeah," I say. "Yeah, this isn't exactly ideal timing."

He watches me.

I wait a minute, two, before I quietly pull the door open and walk back toward the stage, right past Priya, who hurries along beside me, trying to stop me. Marcus is still talking when I barge back onto the live set. Someone in the audience actually gasps.

"Jac!" Becca says, flustered. "Are you okay?"

"I can't do this," I say. "I'm sorry. I don't want this." I twist the ring off my finger, place it on the table in front of Marcus, look straight at the camera. "You got your wish, America. Or maybe not, because little did you know, I hated myself long before you all ever started." I look straight into Marcus's eyes. "Good luck, Marcus. You make amazing television." The audience sits in stunned silence, but somewhere, I imagine John Apperson is laughing. *Great television.*

As I pass by Charlotte on my way offstage, I simply say, "You're welcome." She smiles knowingly. Almost instantly, Rikki appears backstage with Sarah; they had come for moral support.

"Holy shit," Rikki says.

"Are you okay?" Sarah asks.

I laugh, kicking off my heels and unzipping my dress simultaneously. "Let's go get a drink."

Page Six: *"the 1* lead Marcus Bellamy heartbroken following live breakup"

Following Jacqueline Matthis's dramatic onstage breakup with Marcus Bellamy during last month's After the One live show, our sources tell us that Marcus has been focusing on himself, spending time with close friends, and working out. Rumor has it he may have a place on the next season of *Dancing with the Stars*, and insiders have gone as far as to suggest that we may be in for a second season of Marcus on *the 1*—America is praying you'll make the right choice next time, Marcus.

Meanwhile, Jac Matthis has kept a quiet profile, with no more follow-up on the rumors that she carried on a relationship during filming of *the 1* with producer Henry Foster. Sources also tell us that Foster appears to have left the show following the dramatic After the One showing. Audience members at the live taping say he pulled Jacqueline Matthis off the stage following an outburst, leading to the subsequent live breakup.

Meanwhile, we prepare for Kendall Dyer's season of *the 1*. While Marcus's finale drove the highest *the 1* ratings of the season, overall numbers continue to fall for the once-network hit, and sources say the show could be eyeing a shift to streaming soon.

26

I'm with You–
One Year Later

The production studio is in Burbank. An eager assistant in a button-up and pencil skirt offers me water, coffee, soda, and almost desperately as I refuse them all, booze.

"It's a 4 p.m. meeting after all," she says, as if she is forgiving me for a sin I have not yet committed. I know she's seen the show, and she knows it all.

"If I haven't started drinking by 10 a.m., what's the point, you know?"

She laughs as if I am perhaps the funniest person she's ever met, leaving me alone in the glass conference room, her laughter echoing behind her. I glance down at my phone, think of sending a text, and stop myself.

I sit down in the chair facing the window, a speck in the huge conference room, alone in the middle of five chairs. The glass door to my back opens and Charlotte and Priya step into the room. I get up and hug them both, which they are conditioned to receive. No hard feelings. It's just show biz.

"Jac, look at you!" Charlotte says, pulling me back and holding me at a distance. "You look good! I'm so thrilled you could come in."

I smile. "Yeah, Rikki had the big opening for her new studio, so I didn't want to miss it."

"I saw your first book hit the bestseller list," Priya says, going to the opposite side of the table and smiling at me as she seats herself in one of the chairs there. The shiny promotion had come through, just like she'd wanted. *"End of the Line."*

"Yeah," I say, like it's not a big deal, sitting down again as Charlotte makes her way over to the other side. "It's nice to see some positive momentum. Even starting to leave my house again."

"There's our girl," Charlotte says, thrilling to it. "I was worried you might be up to something, coming in and making all nice, but I can see that you're recovering."

I lean back in my seat, watching Charlotte watching me. Put my hands on the table in front of me to show I have nothing to hide. "So, y'all know why I'm here. I know everyone else from our season has gotten assurances they're free of their NDA. I've been a good girl and followed the rules. I want out." Our contracts had stipulated a one-year NDA that could be extended at the producers' discretion.

"Jac," Priya starts, exactly the way she always talked to me on set, as if I were a demon child who must be placated, "you can understand why this is a bit sensitive to us, what with the Marcus and Henry situation."

I blink, expressionless.

"Don't patronize her," Charlotte says, forever the good cop. "Jac, there's no need to drag this out. We're extending your NDA another year at least. I'm sure you understand."

My smile falters ever so slightly as my eyes go between the two of them. Even if it was what I expected, the idea of a never-expiring moratorium on discussing the show makes me feel vaguely sick. "That wasn't the answer I wanted," I say. "Feels a bit punitive, doesn't it? Especially considering none of what happened with Marcus and Henry was really in my control."

Charlotte's mouth is a straight line. "That's not how I remember it," she says.

I bite my lip, staring down at my pink fingernails against the desk. Then I look up. "Hey," I say, visibly brightening back up, "y'all got any of those yogurt-covered raisins you had last time I was here?"

I remembered the little bowls they brought out from the kitchen and set in front of me as I interviewed. I had one-two-three and then stopped myself from more, opening night red dress lodged in my mind.

"Yeah," Priya answers, a bit mystified. "You want some?"

"A big bowl if you don't mind." I lean back in my seat as Priya gets up to leave the room.

"What's your game, Jac?" Charlotte asks me, a small smile playing at her lips once she's gone.

"Maybe I just miss you," I say teasingly, crossing one of my jeaned legs over the other, bright red heels on my feet.

Charlotte glances down at my shoes. "Are you watching the new season?" It was some guy Kendall had rejected on her season. I obviously wasn't.

"Wouldn't miss it for the world," I answer airily as Priya comes back with my bowl of yogurt-covered raisins. She sits it in front of me, and I greedily scoop up three at once and eat them as she retakes her seat.

"I've spent a lot of time thinking about our season of the show recently," I say to both of them as they watch me nibbling on raisins. "It seemed really dire at the time, didn't it?"

"We did provide counseling," Priya says, a note of warning in her voice. Yes, *the 1* counseling with a therapist they had picked. Hush money. A concession. Even, perhaps, an acknowledgment of what they'd done to me. An assurance that I wouldn't do what Shailene had done.

"Right," I say. "Good of you. And it helped. It gave me the right amount of distance. Charlotte kept promising me I would get there eventually, and I guess I finally have."

"The book sales helped, too," Charlotte chimes in helpfully.

"Exactly," I agree. Eat another raisin.

"So, what?" Priya asks.

I start to say something. Hesitate. Stop.

"You've been thinking about our offer?" Priya asks, too eagerly.

It had come from Priya two months ago. A sizable amount of money to return for the new season of *the 1*. As the lead. Audiences were salivating for my return now that I was single, and the current crop of girls were not going to bring in the ratings, from the sound of things.

Every season needs a proper bitch.

Appropriately suspicious, Charlotte doesn't even give me a chance to answer. "Why would you do that after everything you've said to me post-show? I think you've blocked me from at least two different numbers."

I take a deep breath, working it through in my head. "Well," I start. "You're obviously going to be increasing my salary $50K over the first proposal you sent me before I sign shit. I'd also want a contractual obligation about the number of times my most recent book is mentioned by name. And I want out of my NDA." I let that hang there. "But I'll happily sign a new one."

Priya smiles at this news, but Charlotte doesn't. She sits back in her chair, watching me.

"You're willing to do it again?" she asks.

"Sure," I say. "For those terms, I'll do whatever you want me to." I lace my fingers together, elbows on the table between us, resting my head on my hands and meeting eyes with both of them. "You kept telling me it would pay off, Charlotte, and it finally did. I've only got one other thing I really want."

At that moment, John Apperson pops his head into the room. He's energized—maybe high—with sunglasses perched on top of his head, a ridiculous raccoon tan, and wearing shorts.

"Heard Jac Matthis was in the office," he says in a booming voice.

"John." I smile.

"You going to do it?" he asks, stepping fully in. I hadn't seen him since our one encounter during the show, and here he was, acting like we are best friends.

"Jac was just telling us her final stipulation," Priya says, eager.

"I want," I say, "Kendall to come advise me." I lean back, smiling with all my teeth. "I want her to be there to see me thriving." Kendall's relationship after her season hadn't even lasted until the finale; they'd shown the tearful breakup on camera, when it turned out her final pick had a girlfriend before he left for the show.

John looks thrilled. "Of course. You need to one-up Kendall one last time. I know she'll do it."

"Well then—" I shrug nonchalantly, playing my character to perfection this time. It's the part I was always meant to play. "Sounds like we have a deal."

John and Priya couldn't look happier, but Charlotte hesitates. Finally, she looks me over one last time before she makes the decision. She sees it in my eyes.

"I'll go get the paperwork," she tells me.

I WALK INTO the house, tossing my keys onto the glass side table. The day is already cooling outside, teasing me to put on my favorite USC crewneck sweatshirt and curl up in a chair on the deck with a good book.

I've always had a soft spot for Venice Beach.

Yank bounds up to me, a stuffed giraffe in his mouth, and I scratch behind his ears. "Is that you?" a voice calls to me as I slide off my red heels. I follow the sound into the kitchen, leaning against the door frame, watching him as he stands there, gloriously tall and elegant, the picture of simplicity in his athletic shorts and ratty T-shirt, chopping onions at the marble island in the kitchen.

"It's me," I say.

Henry smiles, his eyes going to me.

"Well?" he asks.

I laugh. "Hook, line, and sinker."

"I *knew* it!" He drops the knife, walks over to me, and leans down, his mouth against mine, pushing me against the door frame, his hands casually resting on my hips. I start laughing again and he does, too, pulling back and staring down at me.

"I did have to bring up Kendall. They're like moths to the flame of misogyny. Brought me the contract to release me from the NDA right then. Their lawyers are drawing up the paperwork for me as the lead."

"Good thing you've been writing so much," he says, his hand cupping my face.

"You really are a hell of a producer," I whisper to him.

"Don't say that," he tells me. "Or I'll have to spend an entire therapy session unpacking it."

"I'm just going to go send an email," I tell him. "And then I'll come help you cook."

"Don't worry about it," he says. "Open a bottle of champagne. I'll finish dinner and then we'll celebrate."

Unable to stop smiling, I walk out through the kitchen and into the living room, scooping up my laptop as I go, flopping down onto the couch and getting comfortable with an armrest behind my neck and my feet propped out in front of me.

I open up my computer and start typing out an email to my new agent.

Released from my NDA. Book draft will be in your inbox shortly.

I hit send, close my computer, and sit in the quiet. The sound of Henry cooking in the next room, of Yank's toes tap-tap-tapping on the tile. The quiet of a life.

I breathe.

Publishers Weekly: *Not the One* by Jacqueline Matthis

Jacqueline Matthis is pissed. She also may finally be at peace.

The controversial contestant from season 32 of popular reality dating show *the 1* has penned a memoir about her life and time on the show, exposing the manipulations and humiliation tactics many have long suspected are used on contestants while filming reality shows. Even juicier, she has exposed her own romance with a producer on the show (no actual names are used to protect the privacy of those involved, but it has long been rumored that the subject of her romance was longtime *the 1* producer Henry Foster, who left the show following Marcus Bellamy's season, on which Matthis was a contestant) as well as machinations by the male lead of *the 1* itself.

What truly makes *Not the One* stand out is Matthis's insistence on being seen as more than a villain while still embracing her own flaws. She is certainly not unapologetic, but, wielding her words like a scalpel, she paints the picture of the misogynistic culture of reality television dating shows that often leave the contestants with long-term trauma. She does all of this while also coming to peace with herself, even if that means embracing being cast as the villain.

You'll be happy to see Matthis get her happy ending after all.

(First printing: 250,000)

Email from Charlotte Summers

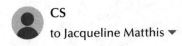

CS
to Jacqueline Matthis ▼

Hi! Sending this via self-destructing email and if you ever tell anyone I messaged you, I will deny it until I am in the grave.

I read your book, and it was pretty great. I was my favorite character, and I'm thrilled you wanted to be my friend. From the bottom of my heart and even knowing you probably wouldn't accept it, I would be your friend, too. I only get a Jac Matthis every couple of seasons. I'm sorry you're such a good bitch! I would be one, too, though, if I was on the show! That's why you're my favorite.

Mainly I'm writing to say congrats on the success. I saw them talking about you on *Good Morning America* this morning and saying you were a bestseller in like twelve countries, and that's what I always wanted for you! #1 on the *NYT*! Five weeks in a row!! Marcus Bellamy wishes (related: I heard after he lost out of *Dancing with the Stars* in the second round, he moved to LA to continue his "influencing" career and his only current sponsor is mobile card games—ick!). And okay, I wish you wouldn't have played us to get out of the NDA, but, as the kids say, game respects game.

Anyway! I've got a crying kid. Your breach of contract is still sort of gnarly, but I'm sure you cleared it all with your publishing team and hopefully, we just keep on churning along. It's good publicity for the show, ya know? That's what I've been selling John on.

Much love and see you in court etc. xo Charlotte

Instagram Post from Jac Matthis

Time stamp: Thirteen months after the finale of *the 1*

[Photo of a Polaroid of two people in a dive bar, sticky bar top and shitty, barely stuffed seats. Henry Foster, in profile, with his arm wrapped around Jac Matthis's neck as he kisses her cheek while Jac Matthis looks defiantly at the camera, flipping it off.]

No caption.

Acknowledgments

Well, another book down, and it almost goes without saying, I have SO many roses to hand out.

My sincerest thanks go to my agent, Sarah Landis, whose belief in this book sometimes outweighed even my own.

Rachel Kahan lent a keen editorial eye, helping strengthen all the parts of this story I love the most. I can't thank her enough for her advocacy and passion.

Every show needs a strong crew behind the scenes and publishing a book is no different. Diahann Sturge crafted the fantastic interior design and tweaked for me right down to the emojis. Ariana Sinclair kept the whole process on track. I'm also so grateful for the support of Erika Tsang, Brittani DiMare, Jennifer Hart, and Clifford Haley.

Thanks to Amy Lukavics, Courtney Summers, and Kaitlin Ward for reads on early drafts of this book—what I couldn't include in the text lives on in emails forever. I am so appreciative to Maurene Goo for invaluable feedback. Love to my petite sorciere, Diya Mishra— we'll always have France. And of course, to the other writers who keep me sane amid the turmoil of the publishing industry: Somaiya Daud, Kate Hart, Michelle Krys, Veronica Roth, and Kara Thomas.

Many nights of *Bachelor* research were conducted with Jaime, Kayla, and Sarah B. Thanks for the wine, cheese, and the memes. In addition, much love to Sarah S., Sarah W., and Erin, just for being pals.

Hearts always to my wonderful parents, Bob and Pam Devore, and my sibs, Drew and Chambe Devore.

Lastly, let's talk about the elephant in the room, the show we keep tuning in for and are never quite sure why, *The Bachelor*. It's true, I know more about it than any single person should. And for that, I must give shout-outs to a LOT of research material. First and foremost, *I Didn't Come Here to Make Friends: Confessions of a Reality Show Villain* by Courtney Robertson. It is widely considered the best *Bachelor* memoir; I wholeheartedly agree. Also helpful on my journey were *Bachelor Nation: Inside the World of America's Favorite Guilty Pleasure* by Amy Kaufman and *The First Time: Finding Myself and Looking for Love on Reality TV* by Colton Underwood, along with excerpts from *It's Not Okay: Turning Heartbreak into Happily Ever After* by Andi Dorfman and *God Bless This Mess: Learning to Live and Love Through Life's Best (and Worst) Moments* by Hannah Brown. Equally as helpful were the plethora of Bachelor Nation podcasts, including *Dear Shandy* (as well as Sharleen Joynt's fantastic *All the Pretty Pandas* blog), *Game of Roses*, *Bachelor Party*, and the gone but not forgotten *Mouthing Off with Olivia Caridi*. Even more interviews and tidbits were consumed along the way, but this list should at least help you to get started. To all former and future dating show contestants who provided me with fodder along the way: God bless and good luck.

For non-dating book research, I was so fortunate to read Michelle Zauner's *Crying in H Mart*, a book that cracked my heart open, exactly when I needed it. And, of course, I wouldn't be who I am without the many pop punk bands of the 2000s, who made a girl in upstate South Carolina imagine she was driving down the Malibu coast.

Lastly, thanks so much to YOU, my wonderful readers, who make this all possible. Will you accept this rose? 🌹

About the Author

Laurie Devore is the author of four novels. She is a graduate of Clemson University and can be found, from time to time, yelling helpful advice at Clemson sporting events. In her spare time, she enjoys reading at the beach, watching too much TV, and spending time with her dog, Wrigley, in their home of Charleston, South Carolina. *The Villain Edit* is her first novel for adults.